PRA

THE SHARK
"This romantic thriller is tense, sexy, and pleasingly complex."
—*Publishers Weekly*

"Precise storytelling complete with strong conflict and heightened tension are the highlights of Burton's latest. With a tough, vulnerable heroine in Riley at the story's center, Burton's novel is a well-crafted, suspenseful mystery with a ruthless villain who would put any reader on edge. A thrilling read."
—*RT Book Reviews*, four stars

BEFORE SHE DIES
"Will keep readers sleeping with the lights on."
—*Publishers Weekly* (starred review)

MERCILESS
"Burton keeps getting better!"
—*RT Book Reviews*

YOU'RE NOT SAFE
"Burton once again demonstrates her romantic suspense chops with this taut novel. Burton plays cat and mouse with the reader through a tight plot, credible suspects, and romantic spice keeping it real."
—*Publishers Weekly*

BE AFRAID
"Mary Burton [is] the modern-day queen of romantic suspense."
—Bookreporter.com

HIDE
AND
SEEK

ALSO BY MARY BURTON

Cut and Run
The Last Move
Her Last Word

The Forgotten Files

The Shark
The Dollmaker
The Hangman

Morgans of Nashville

Cover Your Eyes
Be Afraid
I'll Never Let You Go
Vulnerable

Texas Rangers

The Seventh Victim
No Escape
You're Not Safe

Alexandria Series

Senseless
Merciless
Before She Dies

Richmond Series

I'm Watching You
Dead Ringer
Dying Scream

HIDE
AND
SEEK

MARY
BURTON

Published by Montlake Romance, Seattle

www.apub.com

Amazon, the Amazon logo, and Montlake Romance are trademarks of Amazon.com, Inc., or its affiliates.

ISBN-13: 9781503905269
ISBN-10: 1503905268

Cover design by Caroline T. Johnson

Printed in the United States of America

The Japanese say we have three faces.

The first face, you show to the world.

The second face, you show to your close friends and family.

The third face, you never show anyone. It is the truest reflection of who you are.

—Unknown

PROLOGUE

Thursday, June 15, 2006
Deep Run, Virginia, in the Shenandoah Valley

Rhonda Burns was a small woman with dark hair and a laugh that could cut through the hum of conversation at the Cut & Curl Salon. She was popular with the customers because she was easygoing and could copy any hairstyle found in a magazine. Though she was only nineteen, she was ambitious and had her sights set on the manager job. She was ready and willing to work harder than anyone, anytime.

As he had tracked her, he had noticed the long hours took a toll. She flexed her hands as if they cramped, arched her back when she'd been on her feet too long, and bought more moonshine from the guy in the trailer down the street. He'd been watching Rhonda for weeks and now knew more about her than she did herself.

When she arrived home on Thursday night, clouds obscured the stars and moon, bathing everything in black. It had already been a fifty-hour workweek, and she was clearly dead tired. He'd bet good money she'd head straight to her refrigerator, grab the cold pizza and soda she'd stashed in there last night.

As she approached her mobile home, she paused when she came upon her overturned trash can. He watched as she grumbled about raccoons and scooped up the empty beer bottles, chicken bones, and paper plates strewed all over her front yard. As she bent over, he stared at her ass and imagined what it would be like to strip those tight pants off her.

He wondered if she'd connected the scattered trash to last week's puncture in her tire or to the confusion she felt when she couldn't find a favorite shoe or earring.

Rhonda might have chalked it up to a scattered mind and bad luck, and likely never imagined a dark shadow lingered close enough to consume her.

She picked up the debris, tossing it into the bin and cussing under her breath. A cat in the nearby woods hissed and spat as if it were under attack. She glanced toward the thick stand of trees as she scooped up the remnants of a fast-food wrapper. A breeze rustled through the leaves, and she shivered.

"Rhonda, you're turning into a damn scaredy-cat," she muttered.

He had been inside her trailer three times now. The first time, he'd been scared and nervous, terrified he'd be caught. The second time, he'd left a coil of red rope under her bed, knowing the restraint would be there for him when he wanted it. Last week, he'd sneaked in her house and lain on her bed. As he'd masturbated, he'd pictured binding her arms to the posts and then wrapping his hands around her neck. He'd come into a pair of her panties, which he'd pocketed.

The trash finally collected, Rhonda searched around, moving toward his hiding spot in the woods. He tensed, realizing she might have seen him. If she saw him, he'd have to go in for the kill quickly before she screamed.

She stepped closer to him and then stopped at the edge of the shadows. She hesitated only a moment or two before bending down and retrieving a large rock. She headed back toward her trash can and smacked the rock down hard on the metal lid with a loud clang. While making her way to her front door, she suddenly stopped and stared back at the woods. A little more light and a little less foliage, and she'd have seen him standing less than fifteen feet away.

She unlocked her front door and dropped her purse on a chair just inside before she closed the door again. He knew the lock was flimsy and could easily be popped with a switchblade.

He moved out of the shadows toward the trailer and walked around the back to the window that looked into her bedroom. He could see through the screened window that she had moved into the bathroom and stripped. He grew hard as she ran her hands over her round hips and stepped into the hot spray. She showered and dressed in her favorite sweats and T-shirt. She placed a few slices of the cold pizza into the microwave. When the timer dinged, she grabbed the pizza and a soda and climbed into bed. As the scent of pizza drifted out her open bedroom window, he stepped back toward the shadows as he watched her.

Rhonda clicked on the TV with the remote. It must have felt good to sit. She'd been on her feet for days. She had the next day off, though. It meant no one would even miss her until Saturday morning.

Popping the last bit of pizza into her mouth, she settled back onto propped pillows to watch television. It wasn't long before she relaxed back against the pillows and closed her eyes.

He waited a full twenty minutes before he walked around to the front door and, using a switchblade, jimmied the front lock. He stepped inside her house, his erection pulsing as he pictured her stripped naked and tied to her bed.

He never knew what woke her up. He was careful, and he had planned carefully. But as he stepped past her worn sofa, he heard the rustle of sheets in her room. Next came bare feet hitting the floor and the click of metal punching down the hallway, as if she had chambered a round in a gun.

He knew she kept it in her nightstand. He had planned to press it to her temple as he told her about the girl he took last fall. Everyone had heard stories about Tobi Turner, and some had even heard whispers about other girls he had attacked in their beds.

The leaves rustled and branches snapped. He could still rush her. He could still overtake her. She was small, and he was strong. But the risk–reward ratio had now tipped in her favor, and he didn't like battles he didn't know he could win.

He backed silently out the front door, closing it behind him. As he receded deeper into the shadows and the seconds ticked by, his pulse slowed and the jolt of energy that had cut through him eased.

He watched as she slowly lowered her gun and pressed trembling fingers to her temple. She sat on the edge of her bed and replaced the gun in the nightstand. But she didn't shut off her light, as if she felt Death stalking her.

It wasn't that he couldn't wait her out and return. He could. But for reasons even he didn't really understand, he decided to pass her by.

CHAPTER ONE

Monday, November 11, 2019, 10:30 a.m.
Deep Run, Virginia

Dave Sherman was hungover. The days when he could drink any man under the table and then rise and shine the next day were long gone. He was forty-six, so every extra can of beer and shot of bourbon kicked his ass.

Clearing his throat, Sherman winced against the sunlight hitting his face as he looked up at the old red barn. Time and weather had stripped away most of its paint, leaving behind a dark-gray wood that a craftsman in Richmond had already agreed to purchase for a pretty penny.

Most of the reclaimed timbers were destined for a new log cabin in Winchester, and what wasn't spoken for would be soon. This job was going to solve a lot of financial problems. As long as he kept putting one foot in front of the other, dismantled the beams, and loaded his bounty onto the one-hundred-dollars-an-hour flatbed, he would be set.

Sherman drained the last of his coffee. "Let's get moving! Break's over."

The two men rose up off the tailgate, downed the last of their energy drinks, and headed inside the barn. Sunlight seeped through the holes in the tin roof and along the wooden slats dried out by time and weather.

"We're taking down the hay chute next." Nineteenth-century German settlers had crafted the shaft to move feed from the second-story loft to the livestock on the first floor. Protected from the elements, the wood was in near-perfect condition and would make a nice table if he and his men could dismantle it intact.

Sherman ran his hand over the rough grain of the square box, admiring the wooden pegs that had held it together for a couple hundred years. He hated to knock the pegs from their interlocking joints, but a man had to make a living.

The younger of his workers, Nate, a nineteen-year-old kid with scrub for a beard and long blond hair, scurried up a ladder to the loft. Nate moved with the speed and agility Sherman could only reminisce about.

The kid and he operated in concert, working their crowbars back and forth, prying the peg from its hole. However, two-hundred-year-old hewed and crafted wooden dowels did not surrender easily.

"It's not budging," Nate shouted. "Do you want me to force it?"

"You'll crack the wood, and it won't be of any use to me," Sherman growled.

"I think it just needs a few hard blows," the kid insisted.

"Easy, Nate."

Normally, Sherman had patience when it came to this kind of work, but today his pounding head and the young man were getting on his last nerve.

"One solid yank, Mr. Sherman. That'll do it."

Maybe Nate was right for once. "Fine, let's do it."

They both yanked hard, and the joint cracked and looked as if it would break clean until it caught and split right up the center just as he'd feared. Seconds later the wood fell, and he jumped back. The large splinters dropped around him as decades of dust filled the air.

Quick on the heels of the grime, a big object barreled down the partially opened chute and struck him on the shoulder. Flinching as he turned, he prayed his rotator cuff hadn't been retorn. What the hell had hit him?

Sherman wiped the fine coating of muck from his face. "Did you look down the damn chute?"

The kid shrugged. "Didn't think there'd be anything after all this time."

"Dumbass." Sherman glared at what had damn near fractured his shoulder and discovered it was a faded red backpack. As he reached for the pack, his gaze was drawn to the objects that were strewed around. He picked up what looked like a stick and then quickly dropped it. He leaped back and released a string of curses.

Scattered around him was a collection of bones.

CHAPTER TWO

Monday, November 11, 11:30 a.m.

When Mike Nevada ended a fifteen-year career with the FBI, his intention was never to become a small-town sheriff or a gentleman farmer. His strategy had been to take a few weeks off from the Quantico-based profiling team tasked with finding and capturing the most vicious serial killers. He wanted to reflect on some of the choices he'd made and work on the house he had inherited from his grandfather.

And yet, here he stood, the newly elected county sheriff.

Within days of his arrival in Deep Run for what was supposed to have been a vacation, he had received an anonymous tip about untested rape kits. The tip had led to a meeting with the sitting sheriff, but their conversation had quickly degraded into a pissing match. Frustrated, he had left the sheriff's office, resigned from the FBI, and immediately declared his intention to run against the incumbent. The move hadn't been his most logical. But once he started down a trail, he never doubled back.

It was an election nobody, himself included, thought he would win. But he did. And now, two weeks after the votes had been tallied, he was responding to a potential homicide.

Dave Sherman was a good ol' boy who was well liked and had a solid reputation as a contractor in the Deep Run area. When he called 911 a half hour ago with his discovery, Nevada knew it wasn't a prank call or a novice hunter mistaking animal bones for human.

He parked his black Suburban SUV behind the old blue pickup truck, where Sherman's work crew sat on the tailgate. One was smoking. Another was drinking an energy drink. Sherman was on his cell phone, pacing, no doubt counting the dollars he was losing.

The barn was collapsing on the north side, and it looked as though it would tumble upon itself with one good storm. It was located twenty miles outside of the county seat of Deep Run and years ago had been a meeting spot for high school kids looking to party. Finally, law enforcement caught on to the gatherings and started routinely chasing away trespassers. From what Nevada could tell, no one had been out here in years.

Out of his vehicle, Nevada bent the stiff bill of his ball cap a couple of times before settling it on his head. The hat's front panel read SHERIFF in white block letters. Other than the Glock and cuffs holstered on his hip, the hat was his only concession to an official uniform. His plan was to limit the starch and brass to board of supervisor meetings and the occasional parade.

Nevada grabbed his forensic kit from his vehicle. Like all his deputies, he collected basic forensic evidence. Complicated crime scenes were turned over to the state police.

Nevada walked up to Sherman, and the man ended his call immediately. They shook hands. "Hear you found something."

"Thanks for coming so fast, Sheriff Nevada."

Sheriff. Still didn't sound right. "What do you have for me, Mr. Sherman?"

Sherman's sun-etched face testified to decades of working in the open. However, he was clearly pale this morning. "At first I hoped it was an animal carcass. They can sometimes look human if you don't know what you're looking at. But then I saw the skull."

"The barn is owned by the Wyatt family, correct?" Nevada had been gone for twenty-plus years from the valley, but he had grown up here and still knew many of the older families.

"Yeah. They wanted it moved. Apparently, one of the great aunts is thinking about selling the land. I purchased the structure for next to nothing."

"Reclamation. Some money in that, I would imagine."

"Yep. Until a half hour ago, I thought I'd hit a jackpot."

By the look of Sherman's red eyes, he had celebrated the windfall last night. "Show me what you found."

Sherman tucked his cell phone in his pocket, and Nevada and he walked into the dimly lit barn. "Watch your step. There are nails and piles of wood everywhere."

"Appreciate the warning." Fine dust coated his steel-tipped boots as he moved toward the pile of rubble in the corner.

"We were breaking down this section over here," Sherman said, pointing to a long three-sided chute that ran from the ground to the loft. The fourth wall had split and fallen on its side.

Nevada had grown up on his grandfather's farm not far from here and had done his fair share of mucking stalls and pitching hay in a barn that looked very much like this one. Since his return to Deep Run, he'd been immersed in the painful process of strong-arming his pop's homestead into the twenty-first century. The old place was fighting him every step of the way—and winning.

"The backpack was wedged in the chute," Sherman said. "I guess that's what kept the body from falling. The pack was protected from the sun and rain, so it's still in pretty good shape."

Nevada clicked on a flashlight and directed the beam onto the red backpack, which lay on its side. The initials **TET** were embossed on the outside, and there was a yellow yarn pom-pom attached to the zipper. It was old. Clearly long forgotten.

"I've got daughters of my own," Sherman said. "I can't imagine one coming home without her pack. They carry everything in it. Like my wife's purse."

Nevada removed latex gloves from his pocket and tugged them on. "Did you open it?"

"Shit, no. Soon as I spotted that skull, I had my men clear out." Sherman rubbed the back of his neck. "Still makes my skin crawl when I look at it."

Nevada took several pictures of the bag and the bones scattered around it with his phone. He looked up at the chute and tried to imagine how the bag and the body had gotten in there. The pack would have gone in first and then the individual after it. This could be a case of murder or just a damn tragic accident.

He pulled out a roll of yellow crime scene tape and tied it to one post, wound it around another, and knotted the ends to the horse stall gate.

With Sherman standing outside the tape now, Nevada spread out a white cloth and set the backpack on it. The red fabric was heavily stained on the top with a dark substance that smelled faintly of must and death. When the body had decayed, it would have bloated with gas until it burst, secreting its contents onto the pack.

"When's the last time this barn was used, Sherman?" Nevada asked.

"It's been close to thirty years," he said. "When I played ball, we came out here on Thursday nights before the games. Hell of a lot of fun."

"Did you play on the Dream Team?"

"I wish. Those boys came along about five years after me. Took it all the way to the state championship."

"When did the bonfires stop?"

"Sheriff Greene put an end to them shortly afterward."

Nevada bent down and carefully tugged on the zipper. It slid smoothly for several inches, then caught in a crimp. Carefully, he added pressure until the zipper gave way.

Inside were books, along with a pair of girl's jeans, a dark cable-knit sweater, and sneakers. He set the still-folded clothes aside on the cloth and picked up a book for advanced calculus.

Many of the pages were seized together, but after he gently tugged the cover a few times, it opened. On the inside flap was a LEASED TO stamp followed by five lines. The names on the first three rows were crossed out. The last name was written in clear block letters. It read TOBI TURNER.

TET. Tobi Elizabeth Turner.

Anyone who'd lived in Deep Run was familiar with the girl.

In early November 2004, Tobi Turner, a junior at Valley High School, had borrowed her parents' van to attend an evening study session. However, Tobi had never arrived. No one had sounded any alarm bells until she didn't make it home by curfew. The girl's father had called Greene, who made a critical mistake in the investigation: he didn't launch a full-on search until morning.

In a child abduction case, the first hours were crucial. The survival rate plummeted with each passing hour.

Police had located the Turner family van at a truck stop along I-81 late on the second day, but there had been no sign of Tobi. She had simply vanished.

Volunteers had posted flyers of the girl's picture on street corners, in bars, and in grocery stores. The media had broadcast her story for months. Milk cartons and roadside billboards had featured Tobi's likeness. But no credible leads had ever panned out.

She'd disappeared.

Until now.

"Mr. Sherman, it's going to be a while before I can let you back on this site," Nevada said.

Sherman ran his hand over his head. "Shit. Do you really think that's Tobi Turner?"

"Most likely." If this was Tobi, her family was facing more heartache. In his experience, grim discoveries didn't bring closure.

"That poor girl. We searched every corner of this county."

Volunteers from around the state had walked the woods, checked dumpsters, and conducted room-to-room searches in abandoned buildings. "Were you on a search crew?"

"Just about everyone volunteered." Sherman shook his head. "She was here all this time."

Nevada had witnessed enough human carnage to know evil walked among them. Part of the reason he'd tried to take a break in June had been to escape the darkness closing in on him. Now, it seemed, it had found him again.

Nevada called his deputy, who he'd recently promoted to chief of investigations. Deputy Brooke Bennett had been with the sheriff's department for ten years. In her early thirties, she was raising a fourteen-year-old son with the help of her mother. Bennett would likely have his job one day.

"Deputy Bennett." Her tone was crisp and cool.

"It's Nevada. Call the state police. We need their forensic people down here ASAP. I think we've found the Turner girl."

"Tobi Turner?" Shock, sadness, and anger all vibrated around the name.

"Yeah."

Silence stretched over the line for a moment before she offered a terse "Where?"

"The Wyatt barn."

"I'm on it."

"Good." He surveyed the pitched roof and the darkened corners. It was the perfect place for a monster to do his work.

"Sheriff, the timing isn't great, but I received the results on the rape kits."

When Nevada had been elected, he had immediately sent the entire set of rape kits to be tested. He'd also asked Bennett to visit the surrounding jurisdictions and collect untested DNA sexual assault evidence.

"What did you find out?" Nevada asked.

"We only have results on eight from Deep Run. Three samples were badly degraded, and the reports on them were inconclusive. Two matched known felons who are currently incarcerated. And the last three . . ."

Her heavy tone told him there was one more shoe to drop.

"The same perpetrator committed those three rapes," she said.

He stared at the math book lying open on the white cloth. "When did these attacks occur?"

"These three all date back to the summer of 2004."

"Are you sure about that?"

"I pulled the files myself."

Nevada's gaze drifted to the scattered bones. "The same year Tobi Turner vanished."

CHAPTER THREE

Saturday, November 16, 11:45 p.m.

In the early days, he hadn't had the nerve to kill. He'd been afraid. A coward. So he had tracked his targets. And for a time, he had felt a sense of mastery over the weakness that stalked him.

But it hadn't been long before simply watching wasn't enough. He had needed to do more to prove to himself that he could master anything. So he had begun entering women's homes, first when no one was there and then when they were sleeping. He had loomed over them while they had lain tucked in their beds and watched the slow rise and fall of their chests. He had savored the sound of their soft moans and watched as they rolled into different positions as their unconscious minds wrestled with the sensation that something was wrong.

To commemorate his visits, he had stolen personal items as trophies. One earring. A shoe. A scarf. Nothing huge. Small mementos of the time they had shared alone.

The first time he decided to rape a woman, he hadn't really prepared. He'd been watching her in the dark and knew if he left without taking her, that little victory would have been hollow. So he had climbed on top of her. Her strength had surprised him, and he had scrambled to bind her hands and shove himself inside her. It had been a victory, but a narrow one.

He had planned more carefully after that. He had begun leaving behind rope under their beds, knowing the bindings would be waiting for him when he returned.

The next woman had been easier to control. The rope had allowed him to tie her spread eagle to her bed. His body had grown harder when he'd seen the fear in her eyes as he'd shoved her panties into her mouth. He had savored the salty taste of the sweat beading between her breasts as he'd thrust into her. He had loved the *bang, bang, bang* of her racing heart when his hands had wrapped around her neck.

Alone in the room with her, he had realized he was God. He had the power of life and death. Win or lose. It was an intoxicating sensation. With each new conquest, he had taken his partners closer to the brink of death.

When the opportunity to kill had arrived, he had seized upon it. Squeezing the life from her body had provided a greater rush than even he had imagined. It had surpassed any victory or reward the regular world offered. It had put him above everyone. It had been the ultimate win.

And once he had crossed the line, he'd known it wouldn't be long before he was chasing that exquisite high again.

By then the police had been looking for his first murder victim, whose face had appeared daily in the evening news. Her body hadn't been found, but everyone had known something terrible had happened. As the cops had pieced together her last day, he had stitched together an alibi, silenced threats, and kept his head low.

When the storm had passed, relief quickly gave way to a fresh hunger. And soon he had sailed toward fresh hunting grounds.

For fifteen years, he had been very careful. He had moved from town to town, state to state, jurisdiction to jurisdiction. He had selected his subjects with the utmost scrutiny, attacked on nearly moonless nights, and never carried his phone with him or used his own car. No digital trails. He had kept moving. Kept quenching his thirst for death. And now he had a new subject. She'd been on his radar for weeks. He had learned everything about her.

Tonight she would be home alone. After finishing up a double shift, she would slip out of her work clothes, shower, and change into an oversize T-shirt with no panties. He could already taste her.

He approached the side window of her empty house and wedged a screwdriver between the window and casing. He wiggled it back and forth until the cheap vinyl sprang open. He pushed open the window, then hoisted himself up on the sill. His feet still dangling over the garden, he toed off his shoes.

He swung his legs around and lowered himself into the dining room. He moved through the house, double-checking each room. Fifteen years had taught him to never assume anything.

In the kitchen, he spotted a cereal bowl and spoon in the sink. A blue dish towel was crumpled into a heap, so he took a moment to straighten and drape it over the faucet. Porcelain salt and pepper shakers representing Snow White and Prince Charming stood side by side on the windowsill. He plucked up Snow White and slid her into his backpack.

In her room, he walked to the dresser and studied the collection of earrings.

He pocketed a single hoop earring and a diamond stud and then carefully arranged all the jewelry into a neat row.

He removed a skein of red rope from his bag and placed it directly under the bed. Climbing on the bed, he pretended she was under him and struggling and he reached under the bed, making sure he could lay his hands on the rope quickly. He did this several times until he was confident it was perfectly accessible.

He slipped under the covers, drawing the unmade sheets to his nose. He inhaled her scent. His erection pounded.

When he heard a car pull in to the driveway, he hopped off the bed, carefully smoothed the top comforter, and hid in a closet in her roommate's room.

He listened as she turned on music, sang off-key, and puttered around the kitchen. Within twenty minutes, she was in bed, and the blue glow of the television shimmered from atop the dresser.

He imagined her eyes slowly drifting shut as she nestled under the covers. She felt safe. Warm and cozy.

When the television light clicked off, he still lingered inside the closet. He was in no rush.

Another hour passed before he eased open the closet door. Cautiously, he peered into her bedroom and saw her supple form as she lay on her side in the bed. She faced toward the window.

He moved closer. She wasn't wearing her favorite oversize T-shirt, making him wonder if she was still wearing her panties.

She shifted slightly under the covers, and he hesitated before a deep sigh seeped over her lips.

He came up to the bed and stood over her for several seconds. He removed a small flashlight from his pocket, clicked it on, and shined it in her face, knowing it wouldn't take long before the glaring light reached her unconscious mind.

Slowly she stirred, raising her hand to her eyes, and realized the light was real and not going away.

She blinked. "What's going on?"

He didn't speak as he shoved a rag into her mouth. Her body tensed immediately and she struggled, but he was quick with the rope. Her hands and feet were bound before she knew what was happening.

A moaned plea coupled with the panic in her gaze thrilled him. As tempted as he was to take her now, he was disciplined enough to wait. They had time. No need to rush.

He wrapped his hands around her neck and squeezed. She struggled under him, but he kept the pressure steady until she passed out.

When her body went limp, he carried her and her purse out the side door toward her car. He sat her on the ground and then dug her keys out of her purse and opened the trunk. Carefully he dumped her and her purse in the small space and closed the lid with a soft click.

Later he would double back and get his car, which he'd left down the road about a mile, hidden under brush.

In the front seat, he started the car. He turned on the radio, selecting one of her favorite songs.

Humming, he backed out of the small driveway.

Would she beg before it was all over?

Hard to predict how she would react in her moment of truth. But he hoped she would beg.

CHAPTER FOUR

Monday, November 18, 8:00 a.m.
Alexandria, Virginia

Scratch. Scratch. Scratch.

It was the sound of fingers clawing against the dirt, and it had echoed through Special Agent Macy Crow's dreams last night. She was accustomed to nightmares, which had plagued her since she was a small child. But this one had been agonizingly real.

Still unsettled, Macy opened the driver's side door of her four-door Toyota. She tossed a worn black backpack into the passenger seat, slid behind the wheel, and shifted the pressure off her right side and away from the annoying pain. The discomfort had been a daily part of her life since a hit-and-run five months ago in Texas.

The attack had broken her right leg, cracked her skull, and flat-lined her heart for nearly a minute. By rights, she should be dead. She shouldn't have walked again. She shouldn't have returned to work.

But here she was, ignoring not only the lingering discomfort but also the crazy dreams that had followed her back from the other side of the rainbow.

Scratch. Scratch. Scratch.

She started her engine, slid on her sunglasses, and drove out of the apartment building lot onto Seminary Road. She followed side streets to the I-95 south entrance. The morning traffic was already heavy and, like always, pissed her off.

Following a familiar route to the FBI complex, she was more anxious than most days. She juggled jolts of worry and excitement as she visualized her upcoming interview with Special Agent Jerrod Ramsey.

Ramsey headed up a small team that tackled violent crimes. His group had cracked several high-profile cases in the last year. Details about their deeds were scant, but their results made them legendary.

After cutting through the traffic sludge, she took her exit and slowed as she approached the guard station at Quantico. She reached for her badge, flipped the leather case open, and handed it to the marine on duty. "Morning, Corporal."

The marine looked at her picture and then at her, frowning as he'd done almost every day since her return three weeks ago. He handed back her identification and waved her through. She drove to the main FBI building, parked, and presented her badge to the familiar FBI security guard while her backpack was x-rayed.

"Crow, what do you call a pen with no hair?" he asked with a straight face.

Every day it was a new joke about her short hair.

"Shoot me now, Ralph, and just get it over with."

A neurosurgeon had shaved her head minutes before he had cracked open her skull and relieved pressure on her brain. Yes, she currently looked like a cross between Twiggy and a bristle brush. Desperate hunts for hair ties were gone for the near future, but she was aboveground.

"Come on, Special Agent, I bet you know," he gently coaxed with a shit-eating grin.

"What?" She carefully tucked her badge in her jacket breast pocket.

"A bald point."

Despite herself, she laughed. "Jesus, Ralph, you need help."

"Who loves ya?"

Ignoring the Kojak reference, she took the elevator up to the third floor, where Special Agent Jerrod Ramsey worked. She made her way to his corner office and knocked.

"Enter."

She pushed open the door as a leather chair swiveled toward her, offering her her first up close look at Jerrod Ramsey.

Thick brown hair was cut short and swept off a striking face that conjured images of East Coast prep schools, old money, and the Hamptons. He wasn't classically handsome, but the sharp green eyes and olive skin coupled with tailored suits had to be kryptonite to the ladies.

Ramsey rose and adjusted his blue tie before he crossed the room to her.

"Special Agent Macy Crow," she said.

A faint smile hinted of a welcome. "Good to meet you, Agent Crow," he said, extending his hand.

She accepted his strong grip, clasping his hand firmly. "And you as well, sir."

When Macy had declared her intentions to return to the bureau, she had been temporarily assigned to the ViCAP computer section because her former position had been filled. If she wanted back in the field, she would have to apply for another position.

When she had heard Jerrod Ramsey's profiling team had an opening, she had thrown her name into the hat. She had expected a quick no to her request but instead had received what amounted to a "Let's talk."

Either returning from the dead had earned her points, or someone with juice was pulling strings. Whatever the reason, she hadn't looked a gift horse in the mouth and had agreed to the meeting. Last night a courier had delivered a file from Ramsey. He'd instructed her to review the case and be prepared to discuss.

Ramsey offered her one of the two seats in front of his desk. When she sat, he took the remaining one.

"How do you like being back at work? Working with tech in the ViCAP unit must be a change," he said.

"It's been great." In truth, staring at the four walls of a cubicle and a computer screen sucked. But it was the price of readmission.

He allowed the pause to linger, expecting her to fill in the silence with nervous chatter. It was a good trick. And one she used when she interviewed suspects.

When she didn't speak, he said, "I heard you've set a few recovery records."

"Queen of rehab," she said with a smile. No agent wanted a weak partner. "Ready to rumble."

His eyes narrowed. Either he had decided she was too flippant, or he liked her moxie. Or maybe the pointed stare was supposed to make her second-guess and worry while he figured her out.

She again absorbed the silence. What the hell. She was her own person and wouldn't tone herself down for him or anyone else. Near death had a way of cutting through petty worries cluttering everyday life.

He reached across his desk and retrieved a file. Her name was marked on the tab in precise block letters. She imagined he already knew her professional credentials and her Texas origin story. Reading the file now was for show.

"Ten years with the bureau," Ramsey said. "You worked in Denver, Kansas City, Seattle, and Quantico. Human trafficking is your specialty. You led several successful undercover operations."

"Blessed with a slight frame, and in the right light, I pass for a teenager."

He closed the file. "Why not go back to that?"

"The miniskirts and halter tops don't fit as well as they used to," she quipped.

"They'd also showcase your scars."

"Honestly, the scars would have added to my mystique on the streets. But with or without the red racing stripe running up my leg, my days of passing as a teenager are over." Climbing back-alley fences was also no longer in the cards for her. "Time for a new challenge."

"I've heard good things about you," Ramsey said. "Texas Rangers said you cracked a big case for them. ViCAP also likes having you."

"The Rangers solved the case in Texas. I just gave them the crowbar to pry open the cracks."

"Tell me about Texas." Ramsey wasn't going to make her return easy. No slam dunks in this room.

Reciting the story wasn't easy, despite lots of practice. "You have a reputation for being prepared. You must know as much as I do."

"I'm not interested in the facts in a report. I want to hear your version."

She shifted in her seat. "I returned to Texas when my father was murdered. Pop left a message for me. Basically, he said there was a grave in the desert. The grave belonged to my birth mother. Turns out there were three graves. All girls who'd been kidnapped, raped, and murdered after they gave birth."

"Did you know you were adopted?"

"Hard to hide it. When both parents have black hair and brown skin, it's difficult to pass a pale blond kid off as their own." She shrugged. "They were always up front about the adoption. But they left out the part about my birth mother being murdered."

"That must have been a gut punch."

"Learning I'm a child of rape and that I'm half-monster wasn't pleasant. *Gut punch* sums it up."

Her adoptive mother had once whispered that Macy had bad blood. When a girl in her third-grade class had been kidnapped and murdered, the other children had been afraid. Macy hadn't. She had been fascinated by the cops, the cadaver-sniffing dogs, and the blue wave of law enforcement sweeping over their community.

"No one but Macy dare goes near that alley," her mother had whispered to her father. "It's not normal." Her mother hadn't relaxed until the fourteen-year-old murderer had been arrested.

The Texas trip had driven home the true meaning of *bad blood*. Since then, its full weight had rested heavily on Macy's shoulders.

"Violence is forged in my DNA," Macy said. "Maybe it explains why I'm good at hunting monsters." Modesty didn't become her, so she didn't bother with it. "I'm good at what I do, or I wouldn't be here now."

"Do you think you'd have been injured in Texas if you'd had backup?" Ramsey asked.

Macy refused to apologize or backpedal. "I take risks. It's the secret sauce behind my high-profile arrests, and yes, it set me up for the HNR."

"HNR?"

"Sorry, shorthand for hit-and-run. The incident has come up a few times, so I abbreviate it. Federal employees love acronyms."

Ramsey wasn't amused. "Did your injury teach you any lessons?"

"To be more careful. But I can't promise. No agent really knows what they'll encounter in the field or how they'll react."

A muscle pulsed in his jaw. "How are you physically?"

"Solid and better every day." She could lie without blinking, thanks to the undercover work.

If he didn't buy her assessment, he didn't give any hint. "Technically, you're to remain on desk duty for another month."

She decoded the thoughts lurking behind his dark eyes. Instead of wondering, she asked, "Are you saying you want me on your team?"

A smile tugged at the edge of his lips. "Do you want to be on it?"

"Yes, I do."

"Why?"

More silence settled between them as they played an invisible game of chicken. Would she stay silent? Or would she admit that catching monsters was how she justified her existence and eased her crushing sorrow for the brutalized girl who'd died giving birth to her in the desert?

"All I can say is that I love the work," she said.

"Working on my team isn't easy, Agent Crow."

Membership on his team meant long hours and unearthing evidence in horrific cases. Ramsey's agents had a front-row seat to a brand of darkness that most law enforcement officers never saw.

"No one outworks me," she said. "I settled so many cases in Kansas City, Seattle, and Denver because I took risks and didn't give up. I'm here now because I don't give up. I'm the proverbial dog with a bone when I get my hooks into a case."

He didn't speak for a moment. "In the weeks you've been with ViCAP, you've picked up on several patterns in cases around the country."

She wasn't here for a pat on the back. "Are you going to ask me about the case file you sent me? The one I studied last night until one a.m.?"

Intrigued, he sat back in his chair. "Tell me about the case."

She was relieved. They were sailing into the safe waters of murder. "Last week, the skeletal remains of Tobi Turner were discovered in a Shenandoah Valley barn. The teenage girl went missing fifteen years ago. Sheriff Mike Nevada, the new county sheriff and a former member of your team, requested the FBI's assistance after DNA found on the girl's backpack matched the DNA of an unknown serial rapist active in the summer of 2004, three months before Tobi vanished."

Ramsey didn't look impressed. "Continue."

Macy carefully crossed and uncrossed her legs. "Unfortunately, this offender isn't in the CODIS system." CODIS, the Combined DNA Identification System, was a database of DNA collected from prisoners and arrestees. "Tobi Turner and the rape victims all had a similar look. Slender, dark hair, and petite."

"Anything else?"

"I did a data search of the Deep Run area in 2004. There was another girl who also vanished two weeks after Tobi. Her name was Cindy Shaw. She was mentioned in a two-paragraph article. The headline read 'Second Girl Missing?' There were no follow-ups to that article."

He frowned. "Cindy Shaw was not in the file I gave you."

"I always dig deeper than the file."

"Why is Cindy Shaw significant?"

"Ms. Shaw may not be, but she attended Valley High School with Tobi Turner, she had long dark hair, and she vanished. No missing person report was filed on her behalf. Her last known address was a low-income trailer park. I suspect she was an at-risk kid, and when she disappeared, no one cared."

"Not all poor girls who go missing are kidnapped, raped, and murdered."

The reference alluded to her birth mother. And if it was meant to sting, it did. But a little more pain in an overflowing bucket didn't really matter. "Every case surrounding the time period of Tobi Turner's disappearance has to be questioned and examined."

Ramsey looked almost impressed. "What do you suggest I do?"

So there it was. Her shot.

Discipline kept her from scooting to the edge of her seat. "I'd like to go to Deep Run and look into all these cases. I'm a fresh set of eyes, and as you've already suggested, I have a knack for detail and pattern."

Ramsey regarded her for several beats before he said, "I'll send you to Deep Run for five days. I want to see what you come up with."

The green light warranted a fist pump, but she resisted. This was a test. Ramsey didn't care about a personnel manual's BS questions or boxes that needed checking. The field would tell him.

"Should I check in with my superior downstairs?" she asked.

"No. I'll clear it with him," Ramsey said.

"You won't be disappointed," she said.

He raised an index finger. "I'm not looking for a cowgirl who's going to ride into town, shoot it up, or get herself killed. I want you to dig up solid intel, and then you'll debrief the team at Quantico next Monday. I still don't know if you'll make the cut," Ramsey warned.

She hadn't scored, but she had the ball. Time to take her best shot. "Like I said, you won't be disappointed."

"I saw just the slightest limp as you crossed the parking lot. You do a hell of a job hiding it."

She glanced out his window, which overlooked the lot. "I qualified for the mile run time and retained my expert status at the shooting range."

"Both scores have dropped since the attack."

"I can hold my own." She would not apologize or make excuses. She was done talking.

He studied her. "Hell, I can't think of many people who would come back after what happened to you."

"That's ancient history. All that matters now is this case and me proving I belong on your team."

"Glad you feel that way, because I can't cut you any slack. Five days, Special Agent Crow. We'll both know if you make the grade."

She resisted the urge to uncross her legs and relieve the pressure on her nerves. Instead, she grinned. "I'm up to the challenge."

"You'll be working with Sheriff Mike Nevada."

"I assumed as much."

"Didn't you work with Nevada when he was with the bureau?"

"Our paths crossed in Kansas City. He was searching for a serial killer who preyed on prostitutes trafficked along I-35. I was trying to catch the man pimping the girls. Turned out we were hunting the same guy."

Crossing paths with Nevada. It was a nice euphuism for sex between two commitment-phobic agents. They had ended whatever it was they'd had on good terms, but walking away from him had been the only time

28

she'd resented the job. "Nevada was a first-rate FBI agent, and I imagine he's just as good a sheriff."

"I'll let him know you're on your way. Stay in contact," Ramsey said.

She rubbed her hand over her right thigh. "When do I leave?"

"Today. Pack your bag and hit the road."

She checked her watch. "Will do."

Ramsey's smile was polite, but he clearly had his doubts.

***

Nevada stood in the sheriff's office staring at the bare walls marked by the outlines of dozens of pictures that had belonged to the former sheriff. Outside his office, a painter opened a fresh drop cloth, and soon all traces of the last sheriff would be gone. It was now his turn to leave his mark on the community. Moving down to the conference room, he reached for the conference-room phone and dialed Jerrod Ramsey's number.

Ramsey picked up on the first ring. "Agent Crow just left my office."

"Is she coming to Deep Run?"

"She's on her way. Should be there by one."

"And she knows she's working with me?" He never made small talk.

Jerrod paused a moment. "Why wouldn't she want to work with you?"

He selected his words carefully. "We disagreed on investigative methods in Kansas City." They'd also slept together.

"Can you work with her?"

"Yes."

A beat of silence pulsed through the phone.

"That's all that matters," Ramsey said.

"How is she since the accident?" Nevada asked.

"I'm not going to lie, the accident changed her. She's lost weight, and there's a limp."

Heaviness coiled around him. "She's meeting me at the barn where the body was found, correct?"

"Yes," Ramsey said. "I need a team player, Nevada. You know better than anyone that the members of my team are called upon to work as a unit. They need to know each has the other's back."

"Crow's independent as hell."

"So I've gathered. We'll talk next week, and you can tell me if I should hire her or not."

Nevada watched as the paint crew moved into his office. A good word from him would land Macy a spot on Ramsey's team. But he knew better than anyone that the job would take a piece of her soul. "Will do."

CHAPTER FIVE

Monday, November 18, 8:20 a.m.

Macy concentrated on her gait. One step. Two step. Ramsey was watching and no doubt second-guessing his decision to give her a try.

When she pushed through the doors of her building, her shoulders relaxed, and she took a deep breath. She passed through security and walked to her office in the basement.

She hated the windowless space. It was a reminder of her Texas screwup and a glimpse into her future if she didn't crack the case in Deep Run. The possibility of doing real work was exhilarating, and she was anxious to grab what she needed and get the hell out into the field.

"Macy, have a look at this."

Macy turned to the young woman sitting in front of a computer screen. Andrea Jamison, or Andy to the basement dwellers, was a pleasant young woman who never minded hours in front of a computer screen double-checking or inputting data. Slightly round with brown hair and thick-framed glasses, Andy had a wicked sense of humor and, in a showdown of bar shots last weekend, had handily beaten Macy.

"What do you have?" Macy's tone was unusually abrupt.

"Don't we sound testy," Andy said. "Did the boss man on the mountain reject your request to work with his team?"

Andy's cubical was filled with pictures of her mom and dad and three older sisters who were all tall, slim, and married. There was also a collection of Star Trek figurines, which Andy had divided into the Originals, the Next Generation, and whatever nonsense incarnations had followed. Macy ignored Andy's odd obsession with science fiction because she'd turned out to be pretty cool and dedicated to a job she did very well.

"He's sending me to a small town called Deep Run," Macy deadpanned.

Andy's charm bracelet rattled as she swiveled around in her chair and folded her hands primly on her desk. "Do tell."

Macy recapped the case details. "Now all I have to do is crack the case."

"Just in time for the holidays?"

Macy glanced toward a paper turkey someone had pinned on a central bulletin board. "We agreed not to discuss the holidays."

"Turkey time means family, which equals drama." Andy turned toward her screen and typed in "Deep Run." "I don't have anything in my system from their sheriff's department."

"Not surprising, given the DNA wasn't tested until a few weeks ago."

"When you get down there and you've gone through the case files, fill out a ViCAP form and send it to me. I'll have a look around. Serial offenders rarely stop unless they're dead, injured, or imprisoned. And we know your guy isn't in prison."

A year ago, if someone had said she'd be filling out forms to catch bad guys, she'd have laughed. She still had her doubts, but she wouldn't turn her nose up at more help. "Will do."

"I'm serious, Macy. Get me the info. Police work isn't all *Serpico* shit and dark alleys."

"*Serpico*? Have you been streaming old movies again?"

Andy shrugged. "I've got a thing for the seventies right now. But I'm serious, Macy. Send me the stats."

"I really will." Macy turned to her desk and grabbed extra yellow legal pads, pens, and the picture she'd taken with her sisters before she'd left Texas. She hefted the backpack onto her shoulder. "I'll see you next week."

"No cowboy shit. Don't forget your leg stretches. Be safe."

"Roger, Mom."

***

Nevada stood in front of the county board of supervisors panel in his uniform. His starched collar rubbed his skin and fueled his impatience as he stood beside six eager, fresh-faced kids from Valley High School's National Honor Society. As a photographer snapped pictures, he forced a smile and held up the school's newly awarded antilitter certificate.

As the kids smiled, Nevada's thoughts drifted back to his visit to the Turner home yesterday. The purpose of the visit had been to notify Jeb Turner that the medical examiner had identified his daughter's remains.

The instant Turner had opened his front door, his expression had shifted from mild curiosity to pain. The man had understood immediately why Nevada was there.

Tobi Turner hadn't been Nevada's first death notification, but as the old man had wept, he'd felt gutted and angry and prayed he could find the girl's killer.

"Sheriff, can you hold the plaque a little higher?" the student photographer asked.

"Of course." Nevada couldn't remember the last time he'd been around kids who weren't abused, beaten, or dead.

As the kid took a dozen more pictures, Nevada kept smiling. He wanted this dog-and-pony show over.

When the group finally broke up, he grabbed his gear, ready to change and get back to working the Turner case. The board of supervisor's chairman, Sam Roche, cut off his exit. Sam was a retired university professor who'd settled in Deep Run and had been on the board five years.

"Sheriff Nevada, how's your investigation going?" Sam asked.

"It's progressing."

Sam frowned and dropped his voice a notch. "The board is concerned about this case. The optics aren't good. Who's going to send their son or daughter to the local university or relocate a business in Deep Run if we can't promise law and order?"

"Deputy Brooke Bennett and I have been in constant contact with the forensic lab in Roanoke, and I've also reached out to the FBI's profiling team."

"FBI?" Sam asked.

"If you want this case solved quickly, then we can't ignore the truth. We had a serial offender who operated in this area in 2004."

"What're the chances that this person is still here?" Sam asked.

"I have no way of knowing," Nevada replied. "I'm still trying to determine if we've identified all his victims."

Sam held up a hand. "There could be more?"

The naive question would have been amusing if this weren't so damn serious. "Not all women who are raped report the crime. Yes, there could be more."

Sam rubbed a hand over his thinning gray hair. "The media is calling me for a comment. I'm not sure what to say."

"I strongly advise you to not speak to them," Nevada said. "The FBI agent will be here in a few hours, and she and I will coordinate communications to the public."

"What about Greene?"

"What about him?" Nevada was still pissed about Greene's inaction on the DNA kits. If the lazy, dumb son of a bitch had made an attempt to solve the rapes in the summer of '04, he might have saved Tobi Turner's life.

"I don't want the FBI taking over the case," Sam said. "I don't need the world thinking we can't manage our own problems."

"The bureau doesn't take over." He'd never taken credit for the cases he'd solved. Instead, he'd always stood off to the side when local law enforcement had made an announcement to the media. Now Nevada was the local guy and was on the receiving end of the FBI's help.

"Just stay on top of this."

He would swallow every last bit of his pride and accept whatever help was offered to catch this killer. He owed that much to Tobi Turner and the rape victims. "I will."

"You've chased killers like this before?" Sam asked.

"Too many."

"I never thought we'd see something like that here."

"No one does."

Men like Sam ran for the board because they cared about economic development, ribbon cuttings, and policy meetings. They never bargained for high-profile rape and murder cases. "Keep me updated, Sheriff Nevada."

"Will do, Supervisor Roche." He strode out of the office and to his car. He checked his watch. A couple of hours left before Macy would arrive.

Back at the station, he entered through the side door and headed straight to his office. He closed the door and swapped the uniform for jeans, a light-blue collared shirt, and work boots he'd had for over a decade.

With the uniform back on its hanger behind the door, he scooped up the pile of pink message slips on his desk and made his way to Bennett's office.

Brooke Bennett was tall and lean, with an athletic build. Black hair coiled into a bun at the base of her neck highlighted high cheekbones and bright brown eyes. He had heard she had been a track phenom in high school, but all that had gone by the wayside when she had become pregnant with her son. The event could have derailed her life, but she went on to earn her college degree and then had joined the sheriff's department after graduation. She was a dedicated single mom. Her son, Matt, was by all accounts a good kid.

"How is the press release coming?" he asked.

"It's ready." Bennett's gaze lingered on the screen another moment before she hit "Send" and looked up. "It's printing now for you to review."

The printer by her desk hummed and spat out the paper. The headline read GIRL MISSING FOR FIFTEEN YEARS FOUND. He wanted to keep a lid on this case for a couple more days, but the chances of a leak were too great. Dozens of cops had now put their hands on the case, and Turner wouldn't, nor should he, be silent about the discovery of his daughter's remains.

"When will the agent be here?" Bennett asked.

"Couple of hours."

Bennett shifted in her seat. "You reached out to them quickly. And yet we've barely had a crack at the case ourselves."

"You're a solid investigator and a quick learner, but you've never worked a case like this before."

"But you've worked dozens."

"I have. And one of the reasons I asked for Agent Crow is because she's very good with victims of sex crimes."

Her mouth tightened in annoyance. "When the media finds out about the untested kits and links it to Tobi Turner, it's going to be a shit storm."

"Yes, it will." He had never asked who in this department had tipped him and the media off about the kits, but he suspected it had been Bennett. Though he understood the reasoning behind the leak, future disclosures would not be forgiven. "Eventually I'll confirm the connection but not yet."

"They're already saying we blew it."

"Because we did. The heat is only going to get worse. Accept it." He read the release. "Looks good. Issue the press release. Post it on social media. The world needs to know Tobi was found, but not the connection between the rapes and murder. Assume the killer is paying attention to us. He doesn't need to see all our cards."

Her brow furrowed, but she nodded. "Understood."

He checked his watch. "I'm returning to the barn. I want to have a look at the place now that it's quiet."

When Sherman had opened that hay chute, Tobi Turner's bones had scattered in a dozen directions. Every crack and crevice had been scoured by the state forensic team, who had been determined to find every fragment of bone and evidence. It had taken the better part of several hours for the team, working on hands and knees, to sift through the dirt and dust.

"Do you want me to come along?" Bennett asked.

"Not this time."

"I want to learn from her."

"And you will."

Frustration flashed and vanished in the blink of an eye. "Before you go, I received a call about an hour ago from Martha Roberson. She believes her daughter, Debbie, is missing."

He remembered Martha Roberson. She had campaigned against him and had gone so far as to suggest his bid for sheriff was a vendetta against Greene, who had arrested Nevada for trespassing as a teenager. "How old is Debbie Roberson?" he asked.

"Twenty-one."

"Are there any risk factors?"

"No. She broke up with her boyfriend last year, but he is now married and living in Roanoke."

"Is Martha worried about him?"

"No. But Martha insists Debbie is not the type to take off." Bennett tapped a few keys on her keyboard, pulled up Debbie Roberson's DMV picture, and turned the screen toward Nevada. Debbie was pretty with dark hair.

"Drive by Debbie's house and have a look around. Let me know if you see a problem."

"I'll also speak to Debbie's neighbors and see what they know."

"Good."

Nevada left during the lunch hour rush. When he had lived in Northern Virginia, this kind of traffic would have been considered laughable. But five months in Deep Run had lowered his tolerance. He caught himself cursing the four-car backup at the stop sign. "You're losing your edge, Nevada."

He worked his way free of the historic downtown area and drove west. After turning off the main road, he followed smaller country roads until he reached the washed-out gravel driveway to the barn.

He parked and, climbing out of his vehicle, stared up at the barn and a stunning backdrop of endless blue sky, white clouds, and orange leaves.

Places like this were perfect spots for teenagers to party. Greene had arrested Nevada in a setting very similar to this one. He had been fifteen and jacked by a football victory. With liquor stolen from his grandfather's cabinet, he and his football buddies had sat under the full moon by his family's barn and gotten plowed. Greene had come out of nowhere, arrested them, and tossed the lot in jail. His grandfather had waited until morning to bail him out.

When Nevada had become sheriff, he had pulled his case file and for the first time had learned Pop had filed the trespassing complaint with Greene. His grandfather could be a hard-ass, but when Nevada had needed a home, the old man had stepped up.

Nevada clicked on his flashlight and strode into the barn. The crime scene tape strung six days ago had drooped, and gusts of wind had tipped over several evidence tents marking the locations of the bones. He cast his light toward the centuries-old hand-hewed ladder and the hayloft. A year ago, he might have theorized Tobi's death had been an accident. Kids explored a barn and one fell. No one spoke up because they were afraid.

But DNA linked three rapes to Tobi's death. He needed the medical examiner's confirmation, but he would bet a year's salary she was murdered.

How did the killer get Tobi up a wooden ladder? Though it was in good shape, carrying an unconscious or unwilling girl would have been damn near impossible.

Had Tobi's killer forced her at gun- or knifepoint? Or had she gone willingly, never realizing what awaited her? A young, naive girl was ripe for the picking.

Nevada climbed the ladder Dave Sherman had left behind. Sherman was anxious to dismantle the barn, but Nevada refused to release the scene until Macy saw it.

Nevada couldn't straighten to his full height of six foot three inches in the loft and was forced to duck slightly as he moved toward the chute.

The forensic team had swept the loft, searching for any evidence that explained Tobi's death. They had found a knotted strand of red rope among the scattered bones on the first floor but nothing in the loft. Not surprising. Fifteen years erased a lot of evidence.

He stared down the now-three-sided shaft. He theorized the girl had been murdered up here. Best guess, this killing hadn't been planned, had maybe been his first. After the adrenaline had eased, the killer had panicked. He had needed to dispose of Tobi, so he had tossed her pack and small body down the chute to avoid the ladder. Maybe the plan had been to take her somewhere else and bury her.

But the pack had wedged between the wooden walls, and the body hadn't jostled it free. They had both gotten stuck.

Nevada walked toward the small window overlooking the valley behind the barn. This structure was off the beaten path, and he recalled the winter of 2004 had been bitterly cold. Her body wouldn't have decomposed immediately, and anyone searching the barn wouldn't have smelled death. No one had thought to look in the chute.

Had the killer panicked when Tobi's body had jammed up? Had he worried when the volunteers combed the countryside? Had he been grateful for the cold? Had he returned to the barn?

Killing altered a person's behavior. And Nevada hoped someone had noticed.

CHAPTER SIX

Monday, November 18, 1:00 p.m.

Vivid blue sky, white clouds, and golden fall leaves blanketed the Blue Ridge and Allegheny mountains and created a picture-perfect day in the valley. In Macy's book, the beauty was wasted. If she had God's ear, today would have been cold, overcast, and damp. Save the pretty days until she caught this killer.

As she drove south down I-81, Macy mentally replayed her ten minutes of regional research. In the last couple of decades, the Shenandoah Valley's population had ballooned thanks to a growing university, its proximity to Washington, DC, and a thriving tourism trade peddling vineyards, Civil War battlefields, and railroad museums. Filling in the economic gaps were warehouse distribution centers, chain hotels, and strip malls.

The voice of Macy's GPS cut through AC/DC's *Back in Black* blasting from her playlist and instructed her to take the upcoming exit toward Deep Run. As she rolled onto Route 250, a sign for her go-to fast-food eatery gave her an excuse to stretch her legs before driving the remaining ten miles to the crime scene.

After parking, she gingerly rose up out of the car. Her leg bitched and moaned. Stretches weren't optional any more. She grabbed her ankle and pulled until the bunched muscles in her thigh released. After a quick walk around the lot, she made a beeline for the restaurant bathroom.

She glanced into the mirror as she washed her hands. Even after five months, she still didn't recognize the woman with the short hair and thin face.

Nevada was in for a rude awakening.

She wiped her face with a paper towel. "Macy Crow, you're aboveground and headed in the right direction. That's what counts."

At the counter, she ordered a supersize bucket of fries and a large soda. It wasn't that she loved the food—okay, maybe she did love the fries—but the chain restaurant's predictability and sameness were comforting after so many life changes.

A few fries later, she was in her car and backing out of her space when her phone rang. Nevada's number appeared. She cleared her throat and sat a little taller.

"Agent Macy Crow," she said.

"Ramsey tells me you're on your way. Where are you?"

He was direct and rarely charming, and she always knew where she stood with him. "Fifteen minutes from the barn."

"I'm here now."

"See you soon," she said.

Their transition back into a working relationship looked like it was going to be effortless. Whatever they'd had personally was over and done. No hard feelings.

En route on the interstate, she ate her fries and drained her soda. There were no guarantees on when the next meal would be.

The last few miles took her down smaller roads until she spotted the driveway marked by stacked stones. Gravel crunched under her tires as she passed a freshly cleared field. Over the rise of a hill, she saw the old barn, encircled by yellow crime scene tape.

When she had been researching the area, slogans such as "Best Quality of Life" and "Raise Your Family in Deep Run" had popped up on her computer screen. As she had read about the area, she had kept glancing toward the open case file filled with images of Tobi Turner's scattered bones. Recent pictures had captured the barn surrounded by dozens of state and local law enforcement vehicles crammed side by side in the grassy field.

Now as Macy parked, she noted that all the vehicles were gone expect for a lone black SUV. She grabbed her Glock from the glove compartment, holstered it, and stepped out of her car. Her worn hiking boots sloshed in the damp, muddy soil. She tugged on an FBI windbreaker and draped her credentials around her neck. As a stiff breeze blew a lingering chill and autumn scents, she checked her pockets for latex gloves, sunglasses, a small pocketknife, and a pendant light.

Edginess and excitement fused as she strode toward the stretch of yellow tape and searched for Nevada. She ducked under the tape and stepped inside the barn.

Sunlight leaked through the thick rafters, shining down onto the beams, haylofts, and wide-planked floors worn smooth from generations' worth of wear.

During her convalescence, renovation shows had filled so many lost hours. Now she didn't feel they had been so wasted as she studied the barn. A couple of hundred years old, the structure had been constructed of hand-hewed logs and likely had been used for horses or mules. Mumbling to herself, she said, "Now if I could just use what I learned from watching endless 1980s rock band television documentaries, I'll be all set."

A generator started up and spotlights clicked on inside the barn, illuminating the dark corners. Nevada was close.

The light drew her attention to the right corner, which was roped off with red crime scene tape. The forensic tech had designated this area as very sensitive because most of the bones and the backpack had fallen here. Inside the tape, the techs had shifted the dirt as they had searched for the last bits of Tobi Turner.

Macy elbowed aside anger and shifted her attention to the lost girl and her killer. Photos of Tobi's backpack had shown that it had contained simple jeans, a sweater, and tennis shoes, but the fabric remnants and glittering blue cowboy boots found with the body suggested she had changed after she had left her parents' house. Macy suspected Tobi had lied about the study session and had diverted to a party. The killer could have recognized her desire for excitement and used it against her.

A thousand miles away, three Texas graves marked by red rocks told a similar story. Young girls in search of something more had crossed paths with a pure evil who had held them captive and forced each to bear a child for him. Her birth mother had borne Macy and her identical twin sister, Faith. A second girl had borne another sister, and the third a brother. Those graves embodied endless misery and would devastate her if she allowed herself to dwell on them.

"You made it." Nevada's deep voice snapped her back and conjured sweet memories that had no place here.

Macy faced him and saw his shocked expression when he got his first good look at her. He quickly masked the reaction, and his expression became unreadable. Determined to prove the HNR didn't matter, she extended her hand. "Good to see you, Nevada."

In his early forties, Nevada was conspicuously tall. Flint-gray eyes hinted at several lifetimes' worth of hard living. He wore jeans, a dark sweater, a leather jacket, scuffed boots, and a SHERIFF ball cap. Never seeming comfortable in a jacket and tie, Nevada 2.0 looked at home.

"Macy." Nevada restrained his powerful grip as he shook her hand.

Irritated he was already treating her like damaged goods, she quipped, "What happened to you, Nevada? Your grip's a little soft."

He released her hand. "You look . . ."

"Like I was hit by a fucking truck?"

A frown furrowed the lines around his eyes and mouth. "I called the hospital several times, but you never returned my calls."

"Thanks for the effort. Truly. But my focus was dialed into my recovery."

He was caught in a bad spot. They'd slept together a couple of times, liked each other, and split on good terms. Beyond a vague promise to see each other one day, nothing had bound them. What was he supposed to have done after the accident? Drop everything and race to her hospital bed?

"I wanted to help," he said.

When a silence settled between them, she chose to fill it. "There wasn't much you could've done. It was on me."

During rehab, she'd needed to be around people who weren't mourning the old her. God knows she had done enough of that herself. And Nevada seeing her so broken would have been her undoing.

"Did you get my gift?" he asked.

She smiled. He'd sent her a vintage copy of a Twisted Sister album. "'We're Not Gonna Take It' became my anthem."

The quip didn't chase away the intensity in his gaze. "I thought it would make a nice addition to your LP collection."

"It has a proud spot." Right now, she needed to believe whatever was between them was water under the bridge. Her focus remained on getting her life back. "Tell me about the bones. Where are they now?"

"They're in Roanoke at the Regional Forensic Center. Tobi Turner's father wants his daughter's remains released, so we'll want to view them tomorrow."

He wasn't dwelling on the past, but moving forward, and for that she was grateful.

"Understood. What about the girl's mother?" Macy asked.

"She died of early onset Alzheimer's four years ago."

She hoped the disease had erased the woman's worst memories. "Can you give me a recap of what happened here?"

He pointed to the splintered wood of the partially dismantled shaft and recounted the grim discovery. Medical examiners had officially confirmed Tobi Turner's identification with dental records.

"Where's the backpack now?" Macy asked.

"Also with the state's forensic lab in Roanoke. We can see it when we view the remains."

The medical examiner's office and forensic lab were both housed in a newly renovated facility. Good. It maximized her time.

"Has the medical examiner determined the cause of death?" Macy asked.

"He has not issued the final report yet. But if I had to guess, I'd say strangulation."

"Based on?"

"The interviews done with the rape victims."

"I want to read those," Macy said.

"They aren't very detailed."

She tapped her finger against her thigh. "And time of death can't be determined."

"Correct."

"The killer's semen was found on Tobi Turner's backpack."

"Yes."

Wedged in the chute, it would have been protected from the elements. "I want to interview the rape victims. Each reported their abuser held them up to an hour. They might help me piece together what happened to Tobi and identify this bastard."

"My deputy is in her office waiting for us with the case files."

She lingered for a moment, staring at a toppled yellow crime scene tent. Fury whetted her appetite for justice. "Those girls should have been worrying about homecoming and football games and not fighting for their lives."

CHAPTER SEVEN

Monday, November 18, 2:00 p.m.

The town of Deep Run was over two hundred years old and one of the oldest towns in the Shenandoah Valley. Unlike many of its neighbors in the valley, Deep Run hadn't been damaged in the Civil War. Its picturesque buildings were now home to artists and galleries and often served as a backdrop to period movies.

Macy parked behind Nevada in front of the municipal center housing the sheriff's office. A blend of 1930s art deco and 1980s brick storage box, the building was an awkward marriage of quaint and functional.

Out of her car, Macy looked toward Nevada, who remained in his vehicle and on the phone. A small-town sheriff's job was a constant tug-of-war between large and small priorities. Everyone wanted to bend his ear.

Grateful for a moment to herself, she ran her hand over her hair, ignored the case's high stakes, and hoisted her backpack on her shoulder. Through the front door, she crossed a small lobby toward a deputy sitting behind thick glass at a communications console. In his midforties, the deputy had thinning red hair, a round face, and silver-framed glasses. His badge read **SULLIVAN**.

Sullivan glanced up and pressed an intercom button. "You must be Special Agent Macy Crow. Sheriff Nevada said you'd be coming this morning."

"Sheriff's right behind me."

A buzzer sounded, a lock clicked open, and she reached for the door handle. The fresh scent of coffee reached out.

Sullivan got out of his chair and beckoned for Macy to follow him toward a closed door at the end of the hallway, where a woman's voice drifted from the room. He rapped softly on the door.

"Enter."

Sullivan pushed open the door as the deputy ended her call. "Special Agent Crow is here."

Deputy Brooke Bennett rose and moved around a long metal desk, her hand outstretched. She was tall, slim, athletic, and about Macy's age.

The deputy's direct gaze stared unapologetically at Macy as she also sized her up. "Special Agent Crow. I'm glad you found us. I assume you had no trouble finding Sheriff Nevada at the crime scene?"

Macy shook her hand. "No issue. I've found my share of crime scenes in my career."

Behind Bennett's desk were three community service awards and a framed picture of Nevada dressed in full uniform with Bennett, a smiling teenage boy, and an older woman. The boy looked exactly like Bennett, leading Macy to guess he was either a brother or even a son.

Sullivan returned to his desk, saying, "Call if you need anything."

Macy followed Bennett out of her office and into a conference room outfitted with a large whiteboard, an oval-shaped conference table covered in a faux wood grain, and four cushioned chairs. On a credenza by the whiteboard were stacks of files, a couple of dry-erase markers, and a gurgling coffee machine.

Bennett reached for a Styrofoam cup. "How do you take it?" she asked Macy.

"Three sugars and two creams." Macy set her backpack on the table. "While we're waiting on Nevada, I'd like to get background on the missing girls and the rape cases that preceded them."

"Of course."

Macy unzipped her backpack and pulled out her yellow pad, as well as a couple of pens. She was tech savvy, but she preferred writing her notes on pristine yellow paper. Over the course of an investigation, the pad would work overtime, filling up with notes on every line and along the margins.

Bennett laid each file out on the conference table in a precise line, displaying their neatly typed labels. *Oswald, Susan, June 15, 2004. Carter, Ellis, July 15, 2004. Kennedy, Rebecca, August 15, 2004.* The three folders were noticeably thin.

Macy's initial impression was that each attack had occurred in the middle of the month. It was the first hint of a pattern. The dates could be as simple as the rapist's work schedule. He attacked then because he had the time off. Those dates also signaled the new moons of the lunar cycle. The night sky would have been darker. They were also summer dates that spoke of warm weather, time off from school, or a vacation. Whether the rapist understood his pattern or not, she believed the dates weren't coincidental.

Macy flipped open the top folder. *Oswald, Susan.* The first page featured a picture of a pale face splashed with freckles. Susan's lips were drawn tight, and mascara was smudged under watery green eyes. Bruising ringed her neck. The pale-pink flowers of a hospital gown revealed the image was taken during the rape evidence collection. Susan's eyes sparkled not only with tears but also with shame and hints of a broken soul.

Macy curled the fingers of her left hand into a fist, reminding herself why she had been put on this planet. Her sole purpose was finding monsters like this and locking them away.

"Good, you've made yourself at home," Nevada said from the doorway.

Bennett tensed and stood a fraction straighter. "Sheriff Nevada. Coffee?"

Nevada removed his ball cap. A grin softened the hard angles of his face. "When did you start getting me coffee?"

Bennett's expression remained stoic. "I'm putting on a show for the FBI."

He accepted the cup. "Fair enough, but I get you your next cup."

Macy searched for any hint of sexual desire between the two. Not that their sex lives were any of her business. But to her relief, she didn't detect any connection between the two beyond professional respect.

"Sheriff, do you want me to give Agent Crow the rundown?"

"Please," he said.

Bennett gestured toward the chairs. "If you two will have a seat, I will share what we have on these cases."

Macy sipped, noting Bennett had made a credible cup of coffee. She pulled out a chair, and Nevada selected the one directly across from her. When he shrugged off his jacket, the cuff of his sweater rose slightly, revealing a scar that ran up his arm. She remembered the scar and was curious about it. But when they had been an item, both had avoided personal questions.

Bennett opened the first file and taped the victim's picture to the board. She moved through the files, plucking pictures and securing each next to the other until she had completed a chilling lineup of broken, vacant expressions.

Macy's thoughts jumped to the few pictures she'd found of her birth mother. They had all been taken before her captivity, but Macy could easily imagine how the girl must have changed after suffering the trauma of multiple rapes.

Bennett uncapped the black dry-erase marker. "Thanks to Sheriff Nevada, we were able to obtain a federal grant to test backlogged rape kits from Deep Run and the surrounding counties." There were thousands of DNA kits taken from rape victims across the country that weren't tested, often due to rising lab expenses and shrinking municipal budgets. "DNA testing linked together these three rapes, which occurred within a thirty-mile radius of Deep Run."

Bennett tapped Susan's picture. "The first case occurred ten miles from here. Susan Oswald, seventeen at the time of the attack, was living with her parents in a one-story rancher located on an acre of land. Her attacker surprised her while she was sleeping, tied her to her bed, and spent the next hour sexually assaulting her. He left her secured to the bed, and she was not found until the next morning when her mother checked on her."

"Her mother slept through the incident?" Macy asked.

"Her mother had severe health issues. She died the following year."

"There's bruising on her neck," Macy said.

"The rapist wrapped his hands around her neck and squeezed a little, but she assumed that was to restrain her."

"He didn't try to strangle her?" Macy asked.

"No," Bennett said.

"But he wanted to," Macy said. Aware of Nevada's keen attention, she noted the black-and-blue discolorations on each subsequent victim's neck. Each was worse than the last. "He was working up the nerve to kill. The injuries suggest greater aggression with each new crime."

"I believe you're right," Bennett said. "The last victim was strangled until she was unconscious." She pointed to the image of Rebecca Kennedy. "In fact, Ms. Kennedy stated that when she passed out, her attacker revived her. He said it wasn't her time to die yet."

"He was evolving," Macy said. "These all occurred in this county?"

"Correct," Bennett said.

"Greene investigated all these cases but chose not to submit the rape kits?"

"Yes," Bennett said.

"Is he a lousy investigator, or does he have a bias against sexual assault cases?" Macy asked.

Bennett clicked the top of her marker on and off. "For the most part, he was a very effective investigator. He broke up the rural drug labs regularly, his policies cut the drunk driving rate in half, and when Tobi Turner vanished, he was relentless."

"He had one hell of a blind spot in the summer of 2004," Macy said. "Was he undergoing personal issues?"

"His wife was ill at the time," Bennett said. "She died the following year."

Cops were human, and personal lives got in the way of good police work, but a sick wife didn't excuse fifteen years of inaction. "Since you established the DNA connection, have you reached out to surrounding localities?"

"I have," Bennett said. "I sent teletypes to jurisdictions in Virginia, West Virginia, Tennessee, and North Carolina."

"Good. It's important to look beyond your borders," Macy said.

Law enforcement didn't always look beyond the boundaries of their community. The phenomenon was called linkage blindness. This limited view of crime allowed some offenders to operate for years between multiple localities.

Bennett appeared cool, but the steady click, click of the dry-erase marker top suggested this discussion put her on edge. The deputy had worked for the former sheriff for nine years. Based on Bennett's partial defense of Greene, Macy assumed there was some loyalty there.

"I've studied and mapped the attack locations of the rapes, as well as the last known locations of Tobi Turner," Nevada said.

He walked to a large map of Virginia mounted on the wall and ran his finger along I-81, the north-south spine of the Blue Ridge Mountains. "The rapes are comingled into a single area in the west end of the county. The Wyatt barn, where Tobi Turner's remains were found, is on the opposite side of the county."

Investigators used geographic profiling and pinged off of crime scene locations hoping to identify patterns. Nevada was one of the best at this technique and had used it to track many wanted criminals.

"Was the assailant a resident of the area, or was he commuting back and forth to a job?" Macy asked.

"Good question," Nevada said.

Nevada circled his finger around the two target areas. "The houses of the rape victims were off the beaten path, as was the barn. He's familiar with the county."

"Offenders typically don't like to kill too close to home, so I'd say he doesn't live in the two attack zones," Macy said.

"He may not live in Deep Run," Nevada said. "With the interstate, he might not even live in the area. He could be using I-81 as a pipeline to his victims."

"That's a logical conclusion," she said.

"So you're saying he's not a local?" Bennett asked. The pen top clicked again and again.

"We're just throwing out ideas at this point," Macy said. "Have you had any missing persons cases over the last fifteen years?"

"No. We do have a local girl who is currently missing. Her name is Debbie Roberson. Her mother called us and was worried. I went by her house, but there was no sign of her car. I knocked on the door, but no answer."

"What's your assessment?" Macy asked.

"Most likely she's taken a few days off," Bennett said.

"Have you checked with her employer?" Macy asked.

"Next on the list if she doesn't show up in the next hour," Bennett said.

"Do you have a picture?" Macy asked.

The deputy pulled up Roberson's DMV picture on her phone. Macy noted the long dark hair, narrow face, and small stature. "She fits our offender's victim type."

Bennett looked at the picture. "It's been fifteen years since the last known case."

"*Known* being the operative word." Macy shifted in her seat. "The discovery of Tobi Turner's bones would be the kind of stressor that could set him off if he's still around."

Bennett frowned. "The majority of murdered women die at the hands of someone they know."

"Does she have an ex?" Macy asked.

"An ex-husband," Bennett said. "I have a call in to him. However, Debbie's mother stated she didn't believe he was a risk to her daughter."

"So you haven't spoken to him," Macy said.

Bennett folded her arms. "Only to her mother. I'll drive by the assisted living facility where he works this afternoon."

"Does Debbie have a drug problem?" Macy asked.

"None that her mother is aware of, and she doesn't have an arrest warrant."

"People keep all kinds of secrets," Macy said softly, more to herself. "Especially from their parents." She scribbled Debbie's name on the clean yellow notebook pad and circled it. "Let's return to the rape cases. Can any of the rape victims describe the assailant? From what I was reading, he wore a mask."

"In the witness statements, none of the three women saw his face because he always wore a mask," Nevada said.

"So you haven't reinterviewed them yet?" Macy asked.

"We were waiting for you," Nevada said.

"Excellent," Macy said. "I also want you to consider holding a press conference. Announce that the three rape cases were connected. There could be more rape victims out there who never reported their assault to the police. And one of those women might have gotten a better look at this guy."

Bennett unfolded her arms, but her stiff posture radiated stress and strain. "We announced the identification of Tobi's remains this morning."

"But you didn't connect Tobi's murder to the rapes?" Macy asked.

"No."

"Good. Don't. If the perpetrator believes we haven't linked the cases, he might show his hand," Macy said.

"And if the killer is watching the press conference?" Bennett asked.

"I'm planning on it," Macy said. "This guy is organized and careful. We'll rattle his cage and make him realize he's not invincible." Macy drew a solid line under her last notation. "What can you tell me about Tobi Turner?"

Bennett reached for a thick folder and set it in front of Macy. "Tobi was seventeen at the time she vanished. She was an honor roll student, and she played the flute in the band. She attended all the football games, debating events, and dances."

"The kid kept her nose clean," Macy said. "But somewhere along the way, she trusted the wrong person." Her own adoptive mother had infused her with a healthy dose of skepticism that had kept her safe and cynical while growing up.

"Sheriff Hank Greene did quite a bit of work himself on this case, and he worked closely with the state police and FBI," Bennett said carefully. "This file is packed with witness statements, which is the bulk of the information this office had until now."

"Tobi's disappearance received a lot of attention," Macy said. "Makes me think the killer realized he would be captured if he continued."

"Or he simply hunted elsewhere," Nevada said.

"People notice when a girl goes missing," Bennett said. "I searched multiple databases yesterday, and there were no missing persons reports on girls fitting this criteria."

Macy softened her tone, knowing she could sound harsh. "And you may be right, Deputy Bennett. He may have found a coping mechanism. Perhaps he never intended to kill Tobi, and it freaked him out."

"Do you believe that?" Nevada asked.

"No," Macy said.

"Announcing the linked rapes on the heels of our press release about the discovery of Tobi's remains might set him off. The public won't know the cases are linked, but he does. Are we kicking a hornet's nest?" Bennett challenged.

"It's an acceptable risk," Macy said. "If you remain silent, then other women who have a story to tell might not ever come forward and possibly identify him."

"Fifteen years might be enough time for a victim to feel safe enough to open up to the police," Nevada said.

"Fifteen years is also a long time to keep a secret," Bennett said.

"High time to talk about it, then," Macy said.

"You make it sound easy."

"It's never going to be easy."

"Would a press conference expedite this investigation?" Bennett asked.

"It could. Seeing and hearing a sheriff's appeal for more information can make a powerful impression. However, it can trigger a flood of calls that lead nowhere," Macy said.

"That's why they pay me the big bucks, right?" Bennett quipped in a tight voice.

"Set it up," Macy said. "In the meantime, I want to talk to the rape victims and Tobi Turner's father."

"The first rape victim, Susan Oswald, is working today but agreed to speak to you later. The second will be coming by today to talk to you, Agent Crow," Bennett said.

Macy glanced at her notes. "That would be Ellis Carter."

Nevada's jaw clenched and his lips compressed. "That's correct."

"Is there a problem with Ms. Carter I should be aware of?" Macy asked. "You stiffened when I mentioned her name."

"She's my first cousin," Nevada said.

Sullivan knocked on the door and poked his head in the conference room. "Deputy, your son is on line one. He said he needs a permission slip signed, but your mother forgot."

Tugging her ear, Bennett nodded. "I'll get working on that press conference. Excuse me."

As Macy watched Bennett leave, she was struck by the anxiety rippling through the deputy's body. Her demeanor could be explained as a case of nerves. Many local officers mistrusted FBI until they proved their worth. But it was more than that with Bennett. Whatever was chewing on her ran deep.

CHAPTER EIGHT

Monday, November 18, 2:30 p.m.

As Bennett's determined footsteps drifted down the hallway, Macy felt Nevada's scrutiny shift from the case to her. An insect under a microscope would have felt less noticed.

"You've shifted in your seat several times. Are you in pain?" he asked.

"The leg always aches. One of the many odd souvenirs I collected in Texas."

"What other keepsakes did you bring back?" he asked.

"An identical twin sister."

"Seems surreal to know there's another you running around."

Nevada's description didn't begin to encompass the insanity of her life. The only thing that really made sense these days was work. "Tell me about it."

"How are you processing what you discovered in Texas?" he asked.

"You mean, how am I squaring with the fact that I'm half-monster?"

Nevada met her gaze head-on. "I didn't mean it that way."

Bitterness saturated her tone. "Ramsey asked me the same question, but in a different way."

"I know it has to be a lot to process."

Pressure built in her chest as it always did when she discussed Texas. "I won't lie. It's hard to wrap my head around it at times."

"Just for the record, the planet's a better place for having you in it," Nevada said.

That prompted a sour smile. "A girl made a terrible sacrifice so that I could exist. I owe her the scalps of as many of these bastards as I can collect."

"Scalps won't bring her back."

"They'll make me feel better."

Nevada looked skeptical. "Will they?"

"I'll let you know when I catch this one." She resented the sadness tiptoeing around her words. She uncrossed her legs and rubbed her hand over her thigh. "Why are you in Deep Run? I'd have bet a few paychecks you'd never end up here."

He shifted his weight slightly. "I like the slower pace."

She leaned forward, lowering her voice. "I know you. Communing with nature in solitude was never your thing. There's more perking behind those steely eyes."

He tapped a finger on the conference table. "What can I say? Living out of a suitcase got real old."

She wasn't buying it, but she didn't press. They both were better off not knowing. "You said Ellis Carter is a cousin."

"She's my first cousin. Her mother and my mother were sisters. We grew up together. When I found out about the untested kits and launched my bid for sheriff, she confessed she was one of the victims."

"You never knew?"

"She made Greene and her mother keep it a secret."

That piece connected several portions of the puzzle. If anything, Nevada was loyal. "You must have been pissed."

"An understatement. I visited with Sheriff Greene about the kits. He blamed it on a lack of budget. I offered to get federal funding, and he basically blew me off."

"How high did your stack blow?" she asked.

"Through the roof. I left his office and went directly to the court-house and filed my intention to run for office."

Nevada had never been the kind of guy to walk away. "How's Ms. Carter doing?"

"She's doing well. She said counseling helped a lot, and she's moved on with her life."

"But she won't really until this guy is caught."

His hand closed slowly into a fist. "She thinks he called her about five years ago."

She jotted a note on her legal pad. "What did he say?"

"He said, 'I remember you.'"

"And she's sure it's him?"

"She's not positive."

Macy rubbed her hands together. "If he did call her, it tells me he feeds off fear."

"I know." Pain and anger vibrated around him.

"You want this as much as I do."

He dropped his gaze for only a moment, telling her the on-point assessment struck a nerve. "Yes," he said quietly.

Bennett appeared in the doorway. "Ellis Carter is here," she said.

They both rose. Macy tugged the sleeves of her blazer down. Nevada shifted his stance and forced himself to relax his shoulders.

Macy's work with human trafficking victims had driven home many lessons. The first was simple. Time didn't heal all wounds. Counseling certainly helped glue the broken pieces back together, but mended cracks remained vulnerable forever.

However, Ellis Carter appeared to have no weaknesses. At thirty, she was slim and fit with dark hair as black as Nevada's. She wore no makeup to accentuate her clear, tanned skin, but frankly she didn't need it. She made faded jeans, a red pullover sweatshirt, and well-worn hiking boots look fashionable.

Ellis smiled at Nevada and hugged him. "Mike. How goes the renovation?"

Nevada's face warmed in a way that Macy found out of character and attractive. His gaze always possessed an edge when he looked at her. "If I never hold a paintbrush again, it'll be too soon."

"Rumor has it you're dragging your grandfather's place into this century," Ellis said.

"It's fighting me every step of the way, but it's coming around. How's the business?"

"We're wrapping up our fall hikes and winding down for the holiday season. You're still coming to my place for Thanksgiving, right?"

"Wouldn't miss it."

"It'll be a gathering of misfits and should be very fun."

"You know how I love misfits," he said dryly.

Ellis laughed. "Ass. You're going to love this group."

Macy envied their easy banter. When she thought about the holidays, she pictured her Frankenstein family trying to make conversation at the dinner table. *So, your birth mother was held captive when?*

Ellis turned to Macy and extended her hand. "Ellis Carter."

Macy accepted it, offering her best official welcome. "I'm Special Agent Macy Crow. Thank you for coming in today."

All traces of humor vanished. "When I saw Mike, I almost forgot why I was here."

"I didn't mean to ruin the reunion," Macy said.

"No, it's your job. And I'm glad you're here. It does my heart good to know you're all taking a second look at my case."

Bennett pulled out a chair for Ellis but took a seat at the opposite end of the table. Macy retook her seat, and Nevada planted himself right next to his cousin. He wasn't a naturally warm person, but he was fiercely protective.

"Ellie," Nevada said, "as I told you a few months ago, we received a grant so that we could test DNA from a backlog of cases. The samples from your case were among those tested."

Ellis shifted in her seat and pursed her lips into a grim line. "It never occurred to me that it hadn't been tested all those years ago."

"There were budget problems," Nevada said.

"Never figured justice would have a price tag, but I guess everything does," Ellis countered.

Until Macy understood the reasons behind Greene's inaction, she would keep her complaints about his work to herself. "Can I ask you about the night you were attacked?"

Nevada shot Macy a warning as if to say, *Tread real lightly.*

"Don't let my cousin's grim stare put you off," Ellis said. "I'm not made of china."

"I can see that." However, Macy didn't accept the comment at face value. She, too, had mastered the art of projecting confidence even when she was saddled with worry and guilt. "Can you tell me about that night?"

"Where do I start?" Ellis asked.

"The first time you were aware of your assailant," Macy offered.

"I was sleeping in my own bed," she said. "It had taken me hours to fall asleep. My parents were getting a divorce, and I was still dealing with that. Anyway, after several hours I drifted off, but it wasn't a deep sleep. You know how your brain skims under the sleep, ready to pop to the surface?"

"I've had many nights like that," Macy said.

"I guess I never reached REM sleep because I woke up when I heard my bedroom door close. I sat up and saw him standing by the door." She drew in a breath and went silent for a moment.

Bennett rose, grabbed the box of tissues from the credenza. With a slight, almost apologetic smile to Ellis, she placed them on the conference table.

"Thanks. I was hoping I wouldn't need those." Absently, Ellis tugged at a loose thread on her sweater. "I think I startled him because he turned quickly and in a flash was across the room and on top of me. He shoved a rag in my mouth and put a knife to my throat."

"Did you see his face?" Macy asked.

"No. He wore a ski mask. It was black with red trim around the eyes and mouth." Ellis suddenly blinked back tears, plucked a tissue from the box, and dabbed it to her eyes. Nervous laughter bubbled. "You'd think after all this time that I wouldn't tear up."

"It's okay," Macy said. Once Ellis had dried her eyes and appeared a little more in control, Macy added, "Just speak at your own pace."

Nevada was silent, but she sensed he struggled to hide his rage. Most people didn't realize that cases of rape rippled through a family, not only affecting the women but the men as well. A man like Nevada would be blaming himself because he'd not been there to help.

"What color were his eyes?" Macy asked.

Ellis clutched the tissue. "Blue."

"Did he say anything?" Macy asked.

"He whispered to me to be quiet or he would snap my neck like a twig. My heart beat so hard in my chest, and I thought it would explode. Maybe I should have fought him. I'm strong, but I did what he told me to do. I wasn't human to him, and that scared me the most."

"You were a frightened fifteen-year-old," Macy said. "You survived. You had no options."

"Mother was out for the evening on a date. She warned me over and over to keep the back door locked, but after I took the trash out, I must have forgotten. I never forget anymore."

"We all make mistakes."

"Few mistakes are that costly," Ellis replied.

Macy shifted in her chair. "I was working a case in Texas last year. I went out alone to investigate a lead. The interview went fine. I left and I dialed the Texas Rangers to report what I'd found. Only I wasn't really paying attention when a truck came out of nowhere and hit me. The guy was actually trying to kill me and nearly did. I should have seen it coming."

"You would've had no way of knowing he was out there," Ellis offered.

"Sound counsel. Perhaps we should each listen to the other's advice."

Ellis studied her a beat, her brows drawing together. "Fair enough."

"None of this was your fault. None of it."

"There are days that I believe that."

Macy leaned forward, needing Ellis to believe her. "You did nothing wrong."

Ellis's gaze locked on to Macy as she searched for any reason to doubt. "Anyway, he tied me up."

"How did he tie you up?" Macy asked.

The question caused Ellis to pause. "He groped under my bed as if he were searching for something."

"He didn't bring restraints with him?" she asked.

Ellis cocked her head. "He acted frustrated when he pinned my arms above my head with his hands. Finally, he found a coil of red rope." She shook her head. "I'd forgotten that detail until now."

Macy made note of the observation on her pad. "Go on."

"And then he, well, raped me. That part of the whole thing was quick. He didn't seem interested in the sex."

"What interested him?" Macy asked.

"His eyes sharpened when he wrapped his hands around my neck and squeezed. He started counting. One, two, three. And then I gagged, and I think that startled him. He let go of me right away. He sat on the edge of the bed and just stared at me. I thought maybe if I could get him talking, maybe he'd just leave. But I couldn't get the rag out of my mouth. I whimpered, hoping he'd show mercy. But that made him upset."

"How so?"

"He said it wasn't his fault. He said he didn't like being weak. He rose up off the bed and paced back and forth. He got more agitated as he mumbled to himself."

"What did he say?"

"Something like, 'I didn't mean to. I'm sorry.'"

"Sorry for what?" Macy asked.

"I have no idea."

"What happened next?"

"He got back on the bed and wrapped his fingers around my neck a second time and started counting. One, two, three, four, five. I thought he would crush my throat. And then he sprang off the bed and left."

"Did he speak after that?"

"No."

Bennett shifted her stance, reminding Macy she was in the room. "You told the responding officer that your assailant was in your house for about an hour. How can you be sure of the time?"

"I know I didn't fall asleep until after two a.m., and I looked at the clock when he left. It read 3:33 a.m. I remember thinking how appropriate."

"How so?" Macy asked.

"Halfway to hell: 333," Ellis said.

"Nevada tells me you think this guy called you?" Macy asked.

"Yeah. Super creepy."

"Nevada said you operate a hiking business?"

"That's right. I run several expeditions a week."

"Your business is service oriented. How do you know it wasn't a disgruntled client or a guy you might have dated at one time?"

"Clients almost always show up on caller ID, and dates are few and far between for me."

"What did the voice sound like?" Macy asked.

"He whispered, as if he were afraid someone would hear him."

"What did he say?" Macy asked.

"'I'm sorry.'" She shook her head. "Jerk. I hung up and blocked the number."

"Did you try to identify the number?" Macy asked.

"I searched it on the Web and got nothing. I also called it from a public phone a few weeks later. No one answered it."

"Would you be willing to meet with a sketch artist?" Macy asked.

"It's been fifteen years. And I didn't see his face."

"Assailants can be identified with all our senses. Sight is good, but smell, taste, touch, and sound can also create critical impressions. I made calls on my drive over this morning," Macy said. "A talented colleague of mine from Quantico is an excellent forensic artist. She can be here tomorrow, if you'll see her."

"But it's been fifteen years," Ellis repeated.

"You'd be amazed what the mind keeps locked away. She's very adept at exploring the subconscious."

Ellis tapped her finger on the table just as her cousin had. "What time? I have a morning group hike, but I can cancel it if I need to."

"No, don't cancel it. When will you be back off the trail?"

"Noon. It's short."

"Then early afternoon. My friend's name is Zoe Spencer."

"Will you be there?" she asked Macy.

"I'll be just outside the room," Macy said softly.

"I can be there with you," Nevada said.

"No," Macy said. "Ellis and Zoe need to do this work alone. Family, cops, anyone who knows Ellis can alter her responses without even realizing it."

Nevada, never a fan of hearing no, looked annoyed. Even though as a former agent he knew she was right, he still didn't like it.

"I'll be okay, Mike," Ellis said. "I can talk to a forensic artist without melting."

"I know." Emotion deepened his voice.

"We'll see you tomorrow," Macy said.

"Yes." As Ellis was leaving, she paused by the door. "Did they catch the guy who hit you?"

"They did," Macy said.

"And did it make you feel better?" Ellis asked.

"He's never going to hurt anyone else, so that makes me feel better."

"I hear a *but*," Ellis said.

Aware that Nevada was paying close attention, she was tempted to skirt the truth but opted not to. "It changes you. He took a piece of me I'll never get back, and sometimes that pisses me off."

Ellis studied her face for a long moment. "I want you to catch this guy."

"Believe me, it's all I think about," Macy said.

CHAPTER NINE

Monday, November 18, 3:30 p.m.

Macy, Bennett, and Nevada were supposed to interview the third victim, Rebecca Kennedy, but Bennett reported that Rebecca had canceled because of last-minute work deadlines. When pressed for a new time, she would not commit to rescheduling.

"It's disappointing," Macy said to Bennett, "but understandable. If she doesn't make an appointment tomorrow, I'll pay her a visit."

"What would you like to do next?" Bennett asked.

"I'd like to see the homes where these women lived," Macy said. "I find it helps to see what the assailant saw."

"I can take you," Bennett said.

No sooner did she speak than the conference-room phone buzzed. The deputy picked it up, listened for just seconds before her frown deepened. "All right. I'll be right there." She replaced the receiver. "There's a lead on our missing woman. My deputy thinks he might have found her."

"Great. Happy endings are always a welcome change," Macy said. "Give me the victims' addresses. I'll go alone."

"I'll take you," Nevada said. "I know the area, and it'll save you time."

Bennett handed Macy a list of neatly typewritten addresses. She wasn't keen on Nevada looking over her shoulder, but she was on a hard deadline and needed every minute she could get.

She flipped the pages of her legal pad and spotted Cindy Shaw's name absently circled several times. "There was another girl who vanished about the time Tobi Turner did. Cindy Shaw. You ever hear about her?"

Bennett's stoic demeanor softened with recognition. "I knew her from high school."

"What did Greene think about her disappearance?" Macy asked.

"He probably believed what everyone else did. Cindy ran away."

"Why assume that?" Macy asked.

"Cindy had a volatile personality, and I know her homelife wasn't great. Looking back, she displayed all the signs of a runaway."

"Okay." Macy flicked the edge of the paper and then handed it to Nevada.

"The addresses are spread out over thirty miles," Nevada said. "I suggest we begin up north at 213 Galloway Lane. That's where Susan and her mother lived at the time of her attack. It's where she still lives."

"She never left?"

"No."

Macy gathered her belongings and, thanks to too much coffee, excused herself to the restroom before she reappeared to find Nevada waiting by the front door. She nodded to Deputy Sullivan on the way out and followed Nevada to his older black SUV.

She set her backpack on the back seat, dug out her yellow legal pad and a pen, and then slid into the passenger seat. The interior of the car was neat, and his supplies were carefully stored in bins in the back. Unlike in her vehicle, there were no stray french fries or candy bar wrappers on the floor.

Behind the wheel, Nevada slid on sunglasses and started the engine. A glance in his rearview mirror, and he began to back out. He reached for the radio, turning on a country western station. She played music constantly, but her choices tended toward loud, rude rock music.

He turned right and then made a quick left onto the interstate. "The Oswald house exit is ten miles north."

"Did you get back to Deep Run often when you were with the bureau?" she asked.

"I visited when I could, but you know how the job is. I was lucky to get a break once a year."

"Sounds familiar," she said.

"Did you get to see your folks much?"

"After my mother passed, I never returned to Alexandria until the bureau sent me back. Visits to see Pop in Texas were rare."

"I remember your father calling you in Kansas City."

"He called more that last year than he ever had. Must have known the end was close."

"And he never told you about your birth mother?" Nevada asked.

"Only in a message from the grave."

"Why not?"

"My birth father, the monster, was still alive. I think Pop was afraid for me. The man who raped my birth mother had money and power."

"Your father thought this man would retaliate against you?"

"I suppose so."

"He was trying to protect you," Nevada said.

"In his way, yes."

Once they were a couple of miles north of Deep Run, the interstate skimmed through open farmland dotted with billboards. "Do you still have your place in DC?" Macy asked.

"I do," Nevada said. "But I've spent less than a handful of nights in the DC place during the last three years."

They passed a rolling pasture with a herd of cows grazing beside a red barn. Macy had lived in slower-paced communities during her career, but preferred the larger cities so full of much-needed distractions. "And you really like it here?"

"It's growing on me." He shrugged. "I've been sleeping in the same bed for the past five months straight and recognizing everyone I pass on the street."

"And here I am busting my ass to get back in the fray."

"Be careful what you wish for."

"Don't be too quick to judge. I'm still not convinced you'll stay here in Mayberry after this case is solved. You were one of the best."

"I could have worked Ellis's case without leaving the bureau. I left for several reasons. Like an old FBI agent once told me, you got to know when to fold."

She dropped her head back against the headrest. "Jesus, Nevada, now you're quoting country western songs."

He laughed. "I didn't die, Macy. I've shifted gears."

"To what, reverse?"

"To a path that doesn't always lead into darkness."

As they approached the upcoming exit, he slowed and took the westward route along a four-lane road that quickly narrowed to two. They passed more fields dotted with farmhouses, cows, and lots of nothingness. It was too damn far from civilization.

Nevada and Macy had been running in opposite directions since they had met.

"This is Ms. Oswald's house," Nevada said.

"We didn't pass any cameras or gas stations, so it's easy to drive out here at night without being seen," Macy said.

"Around the bend ahead, there's a community with a handful of homes, so there's some traffic coming and going along the road. The people who live there are working class. They're up before the sun and generally home after it sets."

The first victim was attacked in June of 2004. "Do you know who lived in that small community fifteen years ago?"

"No one under the age of seventy."

"Just because a man looks like your sweet grandpa doesn't mean he's not our guy."

"I ran background checks on them all. No one living in the small enclave has ever been arrested or had complaints filed against them."

"Neither has our offender." She drummed her finger on her thigh. "And what about family members who visited grandpa or technicians servicing the properties? There was enough traffic that someone noticed Ms. Oswald."

"Agreed." He parked in front of a one-story brick rancher. The grass was neatly cut, and a flower bed was filled with a thick collection of winter pansies, but there were no tall shrubs or bushes around the house. Beside the house was a small detached garage.

Nevada shut off the engine. His jaw tightened as he surveyed the area. "She was seventeen at the time of the attack and lived here with her mother. They couldn't afford to leave, so they stayed. Susan remained after her mother's death."

"Where does she work?"

"At the hospital. She's a nurse's assistant."

"She should be home from work now."

"Only one way to find out."

They walked up to the front door. He motioned her to the side before he knocked. The sound of deep-throated barking reverberated inside. The curtains to the right of the door fluttered.

"FBI Special Agent Macy Crow." She held up her badge, sensing the person inside was watching closely. "I'm here to talk to Susan Oswald about an unsolved case."

The dog's barking was her only answer, and she was about to repeat her request when several locks on the inside clicked. The door opened to a short pale woman with thick dark hair pulled back in a tight ponytail. She wore no makeup, a bulky sweatshirt, baggy jeans, and clogs. Her face was wide and her eyes a vivid green. She held tightly to a heavy red collar attached to a one-hundred-pound German shepherd. It was in no mood to make friends when its gaze locked on Macy.

"Are you Susan Oswald?" Macy shouted over the dog's barks.

"Yes." Susan made no effort to silence the dog, and when Nevada stepped into view, the dog barked louder and bared its teeth. "I'm Sheriff Mike Nevada. I'm working with Special Agent Crow on the rapes that occurred during the summer of 2004."

"I'm sorry I couldn't come by the sheriff's office. Just got off work."

"It's not a problem."

"I voted for you," she said.

"I appreciate that, ma'am," he said.

"You said you'd shake things up in that police department."

"And I am," Nevada said.

Susan rubbed her hand over the dog's head, whispering words close to his ear that calmed him. "It's been fifteen years since I spoke to Sheriff Greene about my case. Why are you interested? Did you catch the guy?"

"We haven't caught the man yet," Macy said. "We're hoping talking to you and the other women will generate new leads."

"You said there are three others like me?" Susan asked.

"Yes." Macy didn't mention the fourth girl had been murdered.

"What do you need from me?" Susan asked. "I told everything I knew to Sheriff Greene."

"It helps me if I can see the location of the crime," Macy said. "The scene can tell me a lot about the criminal."

"What does my house tell you?" Susan asked.

"It's one story," Macy said. "That makes it easy to get in and out of. Two-story houses have more obstacles. Only one way up and down the main staircase. Were there shrubs planted around your house at the time of the crime?"

"Yes, big, tall ones. There were footprints in the mud outside my window."

The dog appeared to be six or seven years old. "Did you have a dog at that time?"

"No. I got a rescue dog after Mom died. Then after him, I got Zeus here five years ago."

"Why did you stay in the house?"

"Mom and I had nowhere else to live," Susan said as she rubbed the dog's head. "We had to stay, so I got smart. Triple locks on both doors, and all windows are nailed shut."

"Do you mind if we look inside your house?" Macy asked.

Susan pulled Zeus back a few steps and nodded. "You can come inside. I'll show you the room where it happened."

"Thank you," Macy said.

Zeus growled at them both as they passed, still not sure if they were friend or foe.

"Sorry about Zeus. He barks or growls at everything. I love that about him."

Nevada slowly held out the back of his hand for Zeus to sniff for several seconds. Zeus settled onto his hind legs. "He's beautiful."

She rubbed the dog between the ears and eased her hold on his collar. "He's a good boy." With the dog beside her, Susan led them down a hallway. On the right was a narrow avocado-green bathroom with a single sink and toilet, both cluttered with soaps, shampoos, and conditioners. The next door led into a small bedroom furnished with a twin bed, several bookcases crammed with pictures of Susan and an older woman who appeared to be her mother, miniature *Wizard of Oz* figurines, and a white basket filled with red yarn and knitting needles. "This is where I sleep now. I never could bring myself to sleep in that room again."

Susan opened the door at the end of the hallway, stepped back, and allowed Macy and Nevada to enter first. It had been relegated to a catchall storage room. There was a dismantled bed frame with no mattress, a walker, a wheelchair, and sealed brown cardboard boxes.

The one window was on the opposite side of the room, and the thick shades were also drawn.

"According to the files, he came in through your bedroom window?" Macy asked.

Susan crossed her arms over her chest. "That's right. It was June of 2004, and I was sleeping with the window open because it had been so warm that day."

"Do you mind if I open the shades?" Macy asked. "I'd like to look out the window."

Susan dropped her gaze. "Go ahead."

Macy tugged the shade, and when she felt it release, she guided it upward. The window overlooked the bend in the road they'd taken as they'd driven to the house and a thicket of woods. This home was off the beaten path, leading her to wonder if this was a crime of opportunity. The assailant could have been driving around, seen the open window, and taken a chance.

The dog trotted past Macy, sniffing around what was most likely an unfamiliar room to him. "It was just you and your mother then?"

"Yes."

"Would there have been a second car in the driveway?" Nevada asked.

"No. My mother didn't drive. She was forty-nine but suffered from MS. She slept through the whole thing."

Macy studied the ground below the window, which was now neatly cut grass. Not a trace of the bushes once surrounding the house remained.

Susan shifted her stance, as if looking through the window had transported her back in time. "The room I sleep in now was Mom's. For weeks after the attack, I slept on blankets by her bed. When she died the following year, I threw out my bed and mattress and began sleeping in her bed."

"Did you see his face?"

"No. He was wearing a black mask with red trim around the eyes and mouth. The skin around his eyes and mouth was smudged with black shoe polish or something."

"Did your attacker speak to you?" Macy asked.

"He grabbed my neck and said he'd kill my mother if I screamed."

"Did he say anything else about your mother?"

"He made a comment about her wheelchair and how it takes a strong person to care for an ailing family member."

The assailant's comment suggested he knew her and this wasn't just a random crime of opportunity. He could have been stalking her days or weeks before the attack, learning her patterns, habits, and weaknesses.

"How did he sound when he spoke to you?" Macy asked.

"Nervous at first. When he spoke, I told him to get out. I said I wouldn't tell anyone. I said he was being foolish and that he needed to just go."

"How did he react?"

"It made him mad. He said he wasn't weak and he knew what he was doing. He was looking around the room searching for something. He grabbed my pantyhose from the floor. He used it to tie my hands to the headboard. He scooped one of my socks off the floor and shoved it in my mouth. I started crying and he stopped. He stood there studying me like some lab rat."

"What happened next?" Macy asked.

"He climbed on top of me and raped me. It seemed like it took forever, but after he was finished, I looked at the clock for some reason. He'd only been on me for minutes."

"Did he say anything else?" Macy asked.

"He pulled up his pants and looked as if he'd go, but then he climbed on top of me again and wrapped his hands around my neck. He didn't move for several seconds, and then he readjusted his hands a few times."

"He didn't strangle you right away?" Macy asked.

"No. It was like he was figuring out how to do it. But he finally did. Only when I was gasping for air did he get off me. He said he was sorry."

Reliving the event, even after fifteen years, was upsetting Susan. Macy wasn't a patient person by nature unless she was speaking to women who'd been traumatized. In cases like this, she was willing to wait until hell froze over if necessary.

Finally, Susan shook her head. "When I remember that night, there's a lot that really pisses me off, but I think his apology tops the list. Why the hell would he tell me that he's sorry?"

Macy pulled the shade back down. "There could be any number of reasons. You're the first known case we have for this offender."

"Why do you think I'm one of his firsts?"

"He didn't bring restraints. The way he adjusted his hands on your neck. The apology. All these fit the profile of a person trying something new."

"But why was he sorry?" Susan asked.

"Perhaps the violence was also a shock to him as well. He might have fantasized about it, but he'd never tried it. Maybe he truly did feel remorse."

"Did he say he was sorry to any of the others?" Susan asked.

Macy felt Nevada's close scrutiny. He wasn't speaking but he had not missed one word. "None of the victims after you reported that he apologized."

Susan flexed her fingers. "Why is the FBI involved now? It's been fifteen years."

"You can thank Sheriff Nevada," Macy said. "He's pulling out all the stops to solve this case."

Behind the anger darkening Susan's searching gaze, hope flickered. "I'd love it if you could catch him. I want him to feel the anger, fear, and hopelessness he dumped onto me."

Macy wanted him to spend the rest of his life behind bars. "You've been a big help."

"Sure. You come back any time."

"One last question. Did he ever contact you afterward?"

"You mean like a call or something?"

"Yes."

"No, I don't remember any contact."

"Good."

"Should I be worried about him doing something like that?"

"No. I'm glad you have Zeus and have remained strong."

Susan led them out of the room and closed the door behind her before moving to the front door. "I should have thought to offer you a soda or water."

"It's not necessary," Macy said.

Susan glanced back toward her old bedroom. "It'll be nice to sleep again one day, knowing he can't come back."

"I want to give you a heads-up," Nevada said. "I'm going on television in the next day or two and sharing what I know about this criminal. I'm asking the community to call me if they have any leads."

"There could be even more than four victims?" Susan's expression crimped with worry.

"Yes."

"You know how hard it is to talk to the cops about a rape," Macy said. "But not everyone is able. You're making a difference."

"I'm not brave," Susan said. "It's been fifteen years, and I can't even sleep in my own room."

A rape rarely lasted beyond the event for a rapist. But for his victim, the trauma could linger for a lifetime. "If you do receive any strange communication after that press conference, listen but do not engage. And call me right away."

"Sure."

Macy took the woman's hand in her own and squeezed it. A year ago, she'd have avoided physical contact but now felt the need to reassure this woman with more than words. "Don't sell yourself short. You're strong, and it'll take women like you to catch this guy."

Susan held her hand like she was clinging to a life raft. "Could he come back here?"

Macy wouldn't lie to her. Serial offenders were impossible to predict. She knew the guy wasn't in prison, which meant he was dead, too sick to act, or still active. "Anything is possible."

Susan slowly let go of Macy's fingers and drew back. "If he gets past Zeus, I'll be waiting with my cell phone and baseball bat."

"Let's hope it doesn't come to that," Macy said.

As they were leaving, she noticed a high school diploma mounted in a thin black frame from a box store. She'd graduated from Valley High School in 2004. "Did you know Tobi Turner?"

"Not well. But I felt horrible when she vanished. She was just found, I hear."

"Yes."

"Is what happened to her related to me?" Susan asked.

"We're still looking into that," Macy said. "Did you know Cindy Shaw?"

"Everyone knew her. She was wild. I heard she ran away. Why?"

"Just piecing together that year."

Susan opened the front door. "Call me with updates."

"I promise. We're going to look around outside."

"Sure."

When Nevada and Macy stepped outside, the door had barely closed before the inside locks clicked back into place. Down the steps, she walked around the side of the house to the window of Susan's old bedroom.

"He could have parked down the street," Nevada said. "The night she was attacked was a nearly moonless one. If he were wearing black, he'd have been impossible to see. She's about the same age as Ellis, and she lived with my aunt in a one-story house on a country road very similar to this."

"He didn't pick these women at random," she said. "He chose them because they were vulnerable."

***

The knit mask scratched against his face as he walked into his special room. He'd always worn the mask, first as a precaution but now because he knew it amped up the fear factor. He flipped on the lights.

She lay curled in a ball, and for a moment he thought he might have killed her. Strangling her unconscious had been the most effective way to get her quietly into the trunk of her car.

From there, he had driven two miles before he had reached his car. When he had opened the trunk, she had been rousing, but a syringe loaded with sedatives had knocked her out cold.

Transferring her to his car had been easy enough. Then all it had taken was a hard shove to send her car down into a ravine.

"I'm glad we're going to have this time," he said. "With you I can be myself. And it feels so good to be who I really am." At the sound of his voice, she stirred slightly.

Time to play.

After locking the door behind him, he crossed the basement room and knelt beside her. To his relief, her breathing was faint, and when he touched her arm, she moaned softly. He rolled her on her back and jostled her shoulders until her eyes opened. Her expression quickly turned to fear. Good, she was coming around. No fun if she slept through most of his work.

She scrambled out from under him and pressed her back against the wall. "Please."

He was satisfied with his taste in women. He could really pick them. "Please? Please, what?"

"Let me go," she whispered. "I won't tell."

They all made meaningless promises of silence, loyalty, or acquiescence. How many women had begged him for their life and freedom? Their pleas invigorated him and made him feel strong.

Suddenly, he was impatient with the tired script played out so many times. He grabbed a handful of her dark hair and yanked her forward so that her face was inches from his.

Her breath caught, and her pulse thumped in her throat as tears rolled down her cheeks. The fear burning in her gaze offered him some hope that this could still be rewarding.

His erection throbbed, and a sharp rush of adrenaline cut through his body in the most exciting way. "I shouldn't have waited so long to do this again. I forgot how much we both will love it."

"Don't hurt me." Her eyes were wide and watery as the hoarse whisper crept over her lips.

He shoved her hard against the floor and was on top of her before she could scamper away. He wrapped his gloved hands around her slender white neck. She tried to pry his grip free, but she was no match.

He slowly squeezed. "It takes sixty seconds to strangle someone to death. It's all I can do not to climax. One, two, three."

"No," she gasped as he kept counting.

"Eight, nine, ten. We're almost there, sweetheart."

CHAPTER TEN

Monday, November 18, 7:00 p.m.

Nevada called Jeb Turner and asked if he could visit again and also bring Macy. The man agreed, an iron determination humming under his weary sadness.

As he drove east of town, he noted Macy was alert and taking in the scenery as if committing it to memory. He pulled into another small enclave of homes tucked off a back road east of the interstate.

The yard was neatly trimmed and there was a large oak tree in the front yard, its near-naked branches barely clinging to a few orange and gold leaves. Tied to almost every branch was a yellow ribbon. Some were fresh and bright, some slightly worn, while others were so weathered and frayed they were little more than wispy, colorless strands.

The house was a one-story, white-brick rancher that backed up to a new housing development. The land for the development had been cleared six months ago, and at the time of Tobi's disappearance, the property had been thickly wooded.

Out of the car, the two walked to the front door, and Nevada rang the bell. Inside, steady footsteps followed, and curtains covering the large picture window to their right flickered. The door opened to a lean, fit man in his late sixties. His face was deeply lined, but his hair was trimmed and his plaid shirt freshly pressed. Jeans and new athletic shoes completed a crisp appearance.

Recognition flickered in the man's eyes when he saw Nevada. "Mr. Turner, you've had a lot to deal with, sir," Nevada said. "May I introduce Special Agent Macy Crow?"

"I'm Jeb Turner," he said, extending his hand.

"I am truly sorry for the reason behind our visit," Macy said.

His nod was subtle; he was clearly trying to keep the pain in check. "Good thing you called before you came. The reporters have been hounding me for an interview, so I've stopped answering my door."

"I can send a deputy by your house more often, if you think that might help," Nevada said.

"It's not necessary," Turner said. "Reporters don't scare me." He stepped aside and invited them in.

As before when he'd visited, Nevada noticed the home's interior was as neat and well kept as the exterior. The wall facing them displayed a collage of pictures, including a woman wearing a white wedding dress, the same woman holding a baby, and then pictures of Turner, the woman, and the growing girl over the years. A lifetime of moments captured and condensed on one wall.

This part of the investigation was never easy for him. He'd much rather be trading bullets with a suspect than dealing with the emotions of the victims' families.

"That was my wife, Cathy. She died four years ago of Alzheimer's."

"My condolences," Macy said.

"The disease was a blessing. She forgot that Tobi was missing and kept waiting for her to visit. At the assisted living facility, there was a girl on the kitchen staff who looked like Tobi, and Cathy often got them confused. Sara, the girl, was kind enough to play along. Toward the end she was the only one who could give Cathy peace."

Turner indicated for them to sit. Macy perched on the edge of the green couch, and Nevada took the other end.

Turner settled into a well-worn recliner. "How can I be of help?"

Macy wrestled her yellow notepad from her backpack. "When was the last time you saw Tobi?"

"It was a Thursday night, and she was headed back to school for a study session for her history midterm."

"What school was that?" Macy asked.

"Valley High School."

"There's another school nearby, correct?" Macy asked.

"Mountain State High School. That's west of here and a different district, but the kids at the two schools crossed paths enough."

"Tell me about that last day with Tobi," Macy asked.

His demeanor relaxed for just a moment, as if it were fifteen years ago and everything was as it should be. "Tobi almost forgot her backpack, but her mother saw it by the front door and ran it out to her. She was so focused on getting to the study session she almost forgot her books."

"She was a good student?" Macy asked.

"Straight As," he said with pride. "She worked and studied hard. She was on the verge of submitting her college applications. Her grades needed to be top notch so she could get a scholarship."

The man grew silent for a moment as his shoulders stiffened. Reality had chased away the pleasant last moments. Neither Macy nor Nevada spoke. Each knew the man needed to tell his story in his own time.

Turner cleared his throat. "Tobi had only been driving on her own for six months, and we got worried when she drove off by herself." He shook his head. "But there comes a time when you have to let them grow up, right?"

"Tobi never made it to the high school, did she?" Macy asked.

"The cops found our van at a parking lot a mile from the school. Sheriff Greene interviewed all the kids at the study session, but they said Tobi never came into the school."

"Was she dating anyone at the time?" Macy asked.

"She'd gone out a few times with a kid from the debate team, but he'd been in Ohio at a math competition when she went missing. The cops cleared him right away."

"Are you sure there wasn't anyone else?" Macy pressed.

"I've been asked that question a lot. And the answer is always no. Tobi was focused on school, not boys."

Macy knew young girls could and did hide many things from their parents. "When did you know something was wrong?"

"We had given her an eleven p.m. curfew. At half past eleven, I called her friend Jenna Newsome," he said. "They were close that last year."

"And what did Jenna say?"

"She said she didn't know anything," Turner said. "Jenna still lives in town, but I don't know the exact address."

"Was there anyone else close with Tobi?" Macy asked.

"She was friendly with the kids in the band. But she didn't have much time for socializing. Are you going to talk to Jenna?" he asked.

"I am."

"Okay, you speak to Jenna, then what?" Turner demanded. "It's been fifteen years, and the cops came up with nothing. My girl was only found by accident."

Macy sidestepped the comment. "When did you call Mr. Greene?"

"It was past midnight." He shook his head. "I should have called the sheriff five minutes after eleven. It wasn't at all like Tobi to be late, but my wife said to give her a little more time."

"And did the sheriff launch a search?"

"The sheriff didn't sound worried, and I remember I lost my temper. He said he'd look into it."

"And did he?"

"He called me about three a.m. He said he'd heard word there was going to be a bonfire that night and he thought maybe she'd gone there. The football team and cheerleaders held the bonfires to get everyone excited about the game, but basically it was an excuse to get drunk. Tobi was forbidden to go."

"Didn't they hold the bonfires near the Wyatt barn?" Macy asked.

"They were banned from that property. I learned later it was in a field by Talbot's Creek."

Macy scribbled down the location. "What did Mr. Greene learn?"

"He said the few kids who were left hadn't seen Tobi." He shoved out a breath. "I should have driven her to the school that night. But her mother insisted we let her grow up."

Macy absently doodled the name *Cindy Shaw* and found herself drawing small circles around the name. "Did you know Cindy Shaw?"

"I heard the name. She ran away about two weeks after Tobi went missing. I did ask Sheriff Greene about her. The sheriff said not to worry about Cindy."

"Why would she run away?" Nevada asked.

"I have no idea. You'd have to ask her brother, Bruce Shaw. He's a doctor at the assisted living facility. He took care of Cathy before she died. Do you think something happened to Cindy like my Tobi?"

"I have no idea. I'm still just asking lots of questions. Could we see Tobi's room?"

Turner ran his palms over his thighs and stood. "Sure, I'll show it to you."

The three of them walked down the narrow hallway lined with more pictures of Tobi, and he opened the back bedroom door.

Macy was taken aback that the room looked as it must have the day Tobi vanished. It was unsettling to see the lavender bedspread that smelled faintly of laundry soap, the stuffed animals leaning gently against fluffed pillows, and the polished dresser still displaying drugstore makeup and inexpensive silver bracelets. A collection of headbands dangled from the dresser mirror along with a gold medal for debate. She was reminded of just how young Tobi had been when she'd been murdered.

Turner smiled. "She loved that group even though her friends thought it was too baby for a high school girl. But my Tobi liked what she liked and stuck to her guns."

Macy walked to the only window. She carefully pulled back the pink curtains and studied the view of the newly stripped land. "This would have been all woods when Tobi vanished, correct?"

"That's right. It was only cleared this past spring. It's supposed to be a big fancy development. I always wonder who's going to move in to them, but I hear it's selling well."

Nevada studied Macy as she looked out over the land. "Was there a road there at one time?"

"A small dirt road. Almost no one used it," Turner said.

She gently fingered the lock, testing it to see how easy it flipped open. It was tight now, but no telling what it would have been like then. "Was there anything that was missing from her room?"

"Missing? Like what? She had her backpack with her."

"What about jewelry, shoes, a shirt, or a favorite trinket?"

He scratched his head. "One of her slippers was missing," he said finally. "It was weeks after she was gone, and Cathy came in here to clean. She wanted the room just right when Tobi came home. She found the one pink slipper under the bed but not the other one. She looked everywhere, but it didn't turn up."

"Did you keep the one?" Macy asked.

"Sure." He knelt by the bed, fished under the red duster, and pulled out a pink knitted slipper. "Cathy was sure it would turn up like Tobi and kept it. I'm not so different than my wife. I kept it all the same for Tobi, but I suppose I don't need to do that anymore."

"Did you find anything in her room that didn't belong?" Macy asked.

"Nothing that caught my eye, but in the early days I couldn't come in here. Cathy took care of it."

"Was the study session planned?" Macy asked.

"No. It was last minute," he said. "Why would that matter?"

"Again, I'm just asking a lot of questions right now."

He swallowed. "Sheriff Nevada, when can I have my daughter? It's time she joined her mother."

"In a few days," Nevada said. "Agent Crow and I are visiting her in Roanoke tomorrow. Then we'll know better about a release day."

Turner drew in a breath. "Tell my Tobi that her daddy loves her, would you? Tell her."

"I'll tell her," Macy said softly.

***

In his car, Nevada was nearly to the main road when he asked, "Are you fishing when you ask about Cindy Shaw, or do you really think something happened to her?"

"I suppose I'm fishing. One of those loose ends that keeps nagging me." She glanced at her notes. "I want to talk to Jenna Newsome."

"I'm on it."

Nevada located Jenna Newsome easily. She had married a decade ago and her last name now was Montgomery, and she worked in a law office as a paralegal. She told Nevada she was working late and they were welcome to come by. The law office was nestled in a century-old Victorian home that had been gutted and remodeled.

Macy and Nevada climbed the front steps and entered a room decorated in sleek grays that accentuated thick crown molding and a white marble fireplace. A receptionist's desk, made of polished mahogany, offered the only slash of warmth in an otherwise cold room.

The two waited only a moment before a plump redhead clad in a navy-blue dress appeared. She wore pearls, black kitten heels, and a jeweled watch on her left wrist. "May I help you?"

Nevada and Macy each showed their badges, and her smile faded just a bit. "We'd like to speak to Jenna Newsome Montgomery."

"That's me. This is about Tobi, isn't it?"

"It is." Nevada tucked his badge back in the breast pocket of his coat. "Is there somewhere we can talk?"

"Sure. There's a conference room to the left. Let me get someone to watch the phones for me." She ducked into an office before returning and sitting, smoothing her skirt with manicured fingers. "When I read the news she'd been found, I knew it was a matter of time before someone came looking for me."

"You were close friends with Tobi Turner?" Macy asked.

Frown lines deepened. "We were good friends. We were both nerds, liked debate and playing in the band."

"When was the last time you saw her?" Macy asked.

"The day she vanished. I saw her at school."

"And not after?" Macy asked.

"She said something about a study session, but I couldn't go because I was babysitting my little brother."

"The kids at the school said she didn't show for the study session. Do you know where she went?"

"Sheriff Greene asked me the same question. Like I told him, I don't know where she went. It wasn't like her to skip study sessions."

"Was she dating anyone?" Macy asked.

"No. She liked a few guys, but it was always from afar."

"Who did she like?"

"Like all the other girls at school, she was crushing on the guys playing on the Dream Team. They were hot as hell that year. Even slightly cynical geeks like us weren't immune to their aura."

"Dream Team?" Macy asked.

"The local football team made the state finals that year," Nevada explained. "There were four guys that year who were extremely talented. Rafe Younger, Paul Decker, Bruce Shaw, and Kevin Wyatt."

"Wyatt as in the Wyatt barn?" Macy asked.

"Yes, the same family," Nevada said.

"Small town." Macy jotted down all the names. "Did you ever see Tobi hanging out with anyone on the Dream Team?"

Jenna smiled indulgently. "Geeks didn't hang with the guys on the Dream Team."

"Did you see her talking to anyone in particular at the games or during school that fall?" Macy asked.

"I saw her once with Paul Decker. He was hanging around her locker a few days before she vanished."

"Did Tobi ever say what they were talking about?"

"He thought she was cute, or at least that's what she told me later. I was suspicious. Decker was known for chasing the cheerleaders."

"Did you tell Sheriff Greene about Decker talking to Tobi?" Nevada asked.

"The sheriff came by once, and I told him everything I just told you. He took notes, but kept shaking his head as if he doubted what I'd seen. No one ever talked to me about it again."

"Was there anyone else out of the ordinary who hung out with Tobi those last few weeks?" Nevada asked.

"Like Decker? No. Do you think Decker killed Tobi? He was arrested for something, I heard," Jenna asked.

Macy didn't answer the question, instead asking, "Did you know Cindy Shaw?"

"Kind of," Jenna said. "She was an odd duck. She was a hard partier, and she was really into the goth look. Very into the football team that last year and was thrilled that her brother was on the verge of doing really well for himself."

"Did Cindy know Tobi?" Macy asked. "Did she talk to Tobi at all?"

"Not that I know of. Cindy wasn't popular, and she didn't fit with the geeks or the popular kids."

"What happened to Cindy?" Macy asked.

"Everyone knows Cindy ran off. You're FBI. Can't you just track Cindy down and ask her?"

"It's not that simple. But I would like to find her," Macy said. "Any idea where she moved to?"

"I heard Colorado."

"Anybody ever hear from her again?" Nevada asked.

"Not that I know of, but I don't keep up that much. You should talk to Bruce. I'm sure she's talked to her brother at some point."

"I'll be sure to talk to him," Macy said.

"We always thought whoever took Tobi wasn't from around here," Jenna said.

"Why do you say that?" Macy asked.

Jenna shuddered. "Because this isn't the kind of place where killers live. It's a nice, peaceful place."

"Where do you think killers live, Ms. Montgomery?" Macy asked.

"In the big cities."

"Sometimes they do. And sometimes they live in places like this and they look very ordinary."

Jenna shuddered. "That's unsettling."

Macy flipped the pages of her notepad back in place. "Yes, it is."

CHAPTER ELEVEN

Monday, November 18, 8:15 p.m.

When Nevada pulled away from Jenna Montgomery's office, Macy was exhausted and her body ached. Climbing up the tall set of steps to Jenna Montgomery's office had been rough for her. And descending had taken her full concentration.

Macy had remained on point and she had felt sharp during the interview, but now that she was alone with Nevada, she dropped her guard a fraction. The long day was taking its toll, whereas a year ago she'd have blown right through it with energy to spare. Nevada hadn't made a comment, but his frown suggested he was worried about her.

"What did you think about Jenna Montgomery?" he asked.

"I'm not sure. Appeared helpful and all smiles."

"But?"

She ran her hand over her short hair as if it were longer and still draped her shoulders. "At this stage I don't fully trust anyone's account. If Jenna knows something that contributed to Tobi's death, she might be afraid to talk even after fifteen years."

"Or she was shooting straight with us."

"Time will bear it out."

"What's next?" he asked.

"I want to talk to Hank Greene. He was sheriff at the time of these attacks," Macy said. "This is a small town, and word will travel fast. I don't want him overly prepared for when we meet."

"We'll go right now."

"I want to be the one to question him," she said.

"Your reasoning?"

"You just beat him in a contentious race, which I'm sure is still bothering him. And how does he feel about women in law enforcement?"

"He hired Deputy Bennett, and according to her, he was a solid mentor and treated her like all the other deputies."

"Good. At least we won't have to jump that hurdle."

"Want me to call ahead?" he asked.

"No. If he's any good, he'll know we're coming."

Ten minutes later Nevada parked in front of a two-story home that stood at the end of a long gravel driveway. The house was painted a deep gray with white trim and black shutters. An American flag hung from a polished silver pole by the front door, and smoke meandered out from a tall chimney. The upstairs rooms were dark, but the downstairs front room glowed with the light from a large-screen television.

Nevada had nestled the car close to a sidewalk, making it easier for her to exit the vehicle. Though he was trying to slow his pace for her sake, she forced herself to keep up.

Macy rang the bell. They both stood to the side as a matter of course, thanks to so many years in the field.

Heavy footsteps thudded inside, a curtain flickered back, and then the front door opened to Hank Greene.

An outsider might write off Hank Greene the moment they saw his plaid shirt stretching over a big belly, the Sig Sauer holstered to a worn belt holding up crisp jeans and dusty work boots. But to discount the former sheriff would be a mistake. A former marine, Greene had returned to Deep Run in his midthirties and served as a deputy for ten years before running for sheriff, a position he then held for nearly twenty years. He'd planned to serve one more four-year term until Brooke Bennett discovered the untested evidence kits in the storage locker.

Macy still wasn't sure why Greene hadn't sent the kits for testing. Best case was due to budget concerns. Worst case ranged from incompetency to conspiracy.

As Macy raised her identification badge, she said, "Special Agent Macy Crow."

Greene didn't bother to glance at the badge. "I was wondering when you'd find your way out here, Agent Crow. Sheriff Nevada, have you been hired out as her guide and driver?"

Macy and Nevada remained silent, letting the comment pass.

Greene shook his head, making a sucking sound. "Come on inside."

"Are we intruding?" Macy asked.

"You know you are. You'd think losing the election would mean I could watch a television show in peace, not worry about interruptions, but I guess not."

Nevada seemed to accept Greene's bluster, as if sensing Greene liked being in the action and hated the sidelines. She and Nevada were no different, and she'd bet, like her, he didn't want to end up tossed aside.

Inside the house, the spicy scents of coriander and cumin from what must have been a Mexican dinner hung in the air as the sound of a dishwasher came from a now-darkened kitchen.

Greene waved them down a narrow hallway filled with dozens of pictures featuring the former sheriff in his uniform at a variety of local events. There was also a picture of Greene leading the Christmas parade with the cruiser Bennett now drove.

Greene flipped on the kitchen light. "Can I make you some coffee?"

"Yes, please." Macy set her bag on the counter as if she were staking a claim.

She made it a habit to refuse all offers of refreshments from victims. She always insisted she not impose. And as pointed as her questions were, she tried to soften every word and syllable with compassion. However, with Greene, she was willing to show up without calling, accept his hospitality, and drop her belongings on his counter.

As Greene set up the coffee maker, she walked around the room, studying more framed pictures hanging neatly on the walls.

She leaned closer to a picture featuring a fitter Greene from a couple of decades ago. "It's clear you love this town, Mr. Greene."

The coffee maker began to hiss and gurgle. "I'm not ashamed to admit it. I love Deep Run."

"You were sheriff for twenty years?" she asked.

"Twenty-five." He leaned against the counter and folded his arm over his belly as if he were humoring her. "I bet you were in grade school when I got my start."

"You're right," she said. "I was reading Nancy Drew when you were doing the real work."

"Well, I guess we all got to start somewhere." The pot filled and he poured three cups, setting them on the counter. "Milk, sugar?"

"Yes, to both," she said.

Greene dug both out of the refrigerator and set them on the counter, along with a blue spoon.

"Thank you." She ladled two heaping teaspoons into her cup and filled it the rest of the way with milk. Taking a big sip, she closed her eyes. "Delicious." Cradling the cup, she returned to the pictures. "I was up most of the night reading the case files of the three rape cases and Tobi Turner's murder."

"The murder and rapes weren't connected," Greene said.

She watched him closely. "We both know that's not true."

Genuine shock flashed in the old man's eyes as he tapped the handle of his cup with his index finger. "What the hell does that mean?"

Instead of answering, Macy asked, "Why didn't you test the rape kits from 2004? If the budget was that tight, why not seek federal grants?"

"I didn't think it was an option for us," Greene said.

"You applied for other federal grants during your tenure," she said. "One was for a school safety program, and the other one was for body armor for your deputies. Why not DNA testing?"

He sipped his coffee while her eyes sharpened. "What's your point?" he countered. "Why do you care so much about those attacks?"

"When a woman is raped, then has the forethought to save her attacker's DNA and call the cops, it damn well better be tested."

He shook his head. "You make it sound like we didn't try to solve these cases. We talked to dozens of men. We had a couple of suspects that we leaned on hard, especially after Rebecca Kennedy was nearly strangled to death."

"Who were the suspects in her case?"

"Her ex-boyfriend, Paul Decker, for one."

"Paul Decker of the Dream Team?"

"That's right. They were a volatile couple. Fought like cats and dogs when they dated in high school."

"You remember them fighting fifteen years ago?" Macy asked.

"Sure. I worked every Friday night football game. Those two were constantly at each other's throats. I even broke up one fight behind the bleachers, and they both had their share of cuts and bruises. Both swore it was nothing. And they kept on seeing each other. It was crazy."

"Were they seeing each other around the time of her attack?" Macy asked.

"They were," Greene said.

"Paul Decker was arrested five years ago," Nevada said. "His DNA would be in CODIS, and our offender's is not."

Greene shifted his gaze to Nevada. "The DNA test results are back on those cases?" he asked.

"They are," Macy said. "Of the eight cases we sent off, three were committed by the same offender."

"What?" Greene asked.

"That's right. You had a serial rapist in your own backyard."

Greene's brow furrowed. "There was a greenkeeper at the school," he said. "He was picked up. More than a handful said he liked to watch the young girls a little too closely. The man's name was Dave Potter, and he knew two of the three rape victims. But he ended up having an alibi for the first attack."

"Did you do a buccal squab?" Macy asked. *Buccal* meant *mouth* or *cheek*, and the test entailed using a Q-tip to swab the offender's cheek to collect DNA.

"No."

"Where is Mr. Potter now?" Macy pressed.

"He passed away a couple of years ago."

"Does he have family in the area?" Macy asked. "Anyone we could talk to?"

"I can find a name for you."

"Sooner would be best," Macy said.

"You said those rapes were connected to Tobi Turner?" Greene asked. "How?"

"We found DNA on her backpack. That DNA matched our serial rapist."

"What?" Greene's face paled, and some of the swagger left his shoulders.

She didn't speak as she sipped her coffee. She hesitated because she wanted the full weight of her information to sink in. "We've not made that information public yet."

"Sure. I won't say anything," Greene said with a more measured tone.

He appeared thrown off, but she didn't care. "When I was doing background on the murders, I read about another girl who vanished about that time. Cindy Shaw?"

"She didn't vanish," Greene said. "She ran away."

"Where did she go?" Macy asked.

"She said to anyone who would listen she wanted to go to California, but I never knew for sure."

Jenna Montgomery had said Colorado. "Did it ever occur to you that someone killed her?" Macy asked.

"No. That girl could take care of herself just fine." He shrugged, his smile sly. "If you want to know more about Cindy, talk to her brother."

"I'll do that." She held up her cup. "Thank you for the coffee."

Greene looked up, holding her gaze. "I might have made mistakes with those test kits, but I busted my ass looking for the person who hurt those three girls. And we turned this valley upside down looking for Tobi."

Macy had worked enough cases to know when she needed to ease up. She might not like Greene or his methods, but until this case was closed, she might need him. "I'm only in town for five days, Mr. Greene, but you'll be seeing more of me."

"Stop by anytime. I'll help in any way I can."

Neither Nevada nor Macy spoke as they left the house. Only when they were seated in the front seat of his vehicle did he ask, "What's your assessment?"

She clicked her seat belt in place. "Maybe we should test his DNA and compare it to our offender."

"Greene? Jesus, Macy, that's kicking the hornet's nest."

She shrugged. "If he didn't do it, he has a good idea who did. During my research on the town, I saw that the county named the school gymnasium after him. That tells me he did more than show up at the games and keep the peace. And I wouldn't be surprised if he was protecting one of the players."

***

When Nevada dropped Macy off at the police station, it was nearly ten and she was exhausted. Her leg ached as she got into her car, but she was damn careful to make sure Nevada didn't see her discomfort. She drove to the motel close to the highway where she'd reserved a room for five nights. As she pulled up in front of the motel's office, she realized the establishment didn't quite live up to its website.

Macy pushed through the door and approached the front desk. She set her purse on the counter and dug out her wallet and ID. "A room for Crow."

The receptionist studied her and then typed her name into the computer. "Five nights?"

"Correct."

"Sign here," he said.

She filled in the registration card.

"You must be the FBI agent," he said, putting the set of keys on the counter. "You look like a fed."

She scooped up the keys. "Somehow I don't think that's a good thing."

"You here to find Tobi Turner's killer?"

"Not really at liberty to discuss my cases."

She grabbed her purse and left the office. She drove around the side of the two-story building and parked in front of room 107. Grabbing her roller bag, she walked fifteen feet to her room, unlocked the door, and stepped inside. The scent of pine cleaner nearly overpowered the faint aroma of cigarette smoke.

She locked the door behind her, secured the chain, and closed the thick vinyl curtains. She shrugged off her jacket and draped it over a chair by a small round table. Running her hand over her hair, she rolled her neck from side to side as she surveyed the room.

How many places like this had she stayed at while with the bureau? She guessed there was an unused Bible in the nightstand, four white towels in the bathroom, paper-thin toilet paper on the roller, and an ice bucket she doubted had been really washed in years.

She sat on the edge of the bed and with a groan leaned over and unlaced her boots before she kicked them off. She rose and pulled the comforter and sheets back before she lay down. In her early days, she'd carried a blue light that detected the presence of human fluids. Bottom line, she kept her socks on, didn't use the comforter, and carried a fresh supply of wipes in her suitcase for cleaning the channel selector and the phone's receiver.

She removed her gun from its holster and placed it on the pillow next to her right and dominant hand. As she lay back, a sigh escaped her lips. The good thing about being dog-ass tired was she didn't worry about channel selectors, ice buckets, or counting sheep. Her body throbbed as she melted into the soft mattress. Her eyes drifted closed.

The day's events replayed slowly in her mind, but the image that kept returning was Mike Nevada standing at the entrance to the Wyatt barn. Nevada and Ramsey respected each other, and as the new sheriff he needed this case solved. He basically was Ramsey's eyes and ears on this one.

What surprised her was Nevada looking pretty at ease. The Nevada she knew was a hard-charging agent. She always figured him as a lifer being forced out at the mandatory retirement age.

What the hell had changed for him?

The question turned over in her mind slower and slower as her grip on consciousness loosened until finally she tumbled into darkness. She didn't fight it. Sleep would recharge her brain and body, and she'd be sharper in the morning. Just a few hours of sleep and then she'd be up early.

Scratch. Scratch. Scratch.

The sound was distant and easily dismissed at first.

Scratch. Scratch. Scratch.

The sound grew louder. More insistent. Instinct had her fumbling for her weapon as she heard a woman's faint whisper.

"Help me. Find me."

As her fingers groped the cool sheets and then the rough texture of her weapon's grip, a heavy weight pressed on her body, pinning her to the bed. Her heart raced faster.

Scratch. Scratch. Scratch.

"Who are you?" Macy asked.

Scratch. Scratch. Scratch.

Silence settled and the sounds faded.

"Who are you?" An anxious energy rolled over her.

And then, very quietly, *"Please find me."*

"Who the hell are you?"

"Please find me."

Macy sat up in her bed. Her shirt was soaked in sweat, and her heart pounded against her chest like a battering ram. She looked around the room and saw her weapon lying on the pillow where she had left it. The room was bathed in shadows. She was alone. Still, she listened and waited. What the hell?

"I'm losing my damn mind."

CHAPTER TWELVE

Tuesday, November 19, 1:00 a.m.

Under bright stars, Brooke Bennett stood outside the barn where the remains of Tobi Turner had been found last week. She hadn't been to the Wyatt barn since the day in middle school when she and Cindy Shaw had ridden their bikes out here.

Cindy had spotted a large gray circular beehive. A few bees had buzzed, and the core had hummed with movement. Cindy had kicked a few rocks and then had reached for a piece of roughly hewed wood. "I dare you to hit that nest."

"Why would I hit the nest?" Brooke had said.

"You saying you're too scared?"

"I'm not scared."

Cindy had arched a brow. "Then take a swing."

The doubt in Cindy's eye had irritated Brooke. She had been afraid, but she had never backed down from a challenge. "Give me the wood."

Cindy had held back. "You sure?"

Brooke had snatched it away, cocked the wood like a Louisville Slugger, and whacked the gray cylindrical cone hard. The brittle hive had hit the dirt with a dull thud and split open right down the center.

Cindy had run as the bees, fierce and angry, had swarmed. Then, sensing Brooke, they had zeroed in on their intruder.

Brooke had run screaming from the barn, her legs and arms covered with welts. Cindy, a safe distance away, had laughed so hard she had cried.

Brooke had always thought that trouble found some people, while others went looking for it. Cindy had gone looking for trouble. She had been a provocateur, but had always been careful to delegate. To her credit, Cindy had known where the line was drawn.

Brooke clicked on her flashlight and crossed the interior of the barn to the red crime scene tape. As she stared into the partially dismantled chute, she thought about Cindy. By the time Brooke and Cindy had reached high school, they had been running in very different circles. Cindy had been cynical at seventeen. She had drunk hard, and sex had been as automatic as breathing.

But those last few days before Cindy had vanished, she had been stirring up a different kind of trouble. Cindy had been drinking heavily and claimed she knew things. Terrible things.

And when Cindy Shaw had vanished, it should have been a red flag. Tobi Turner had been missing, and the entire town had been searching for her. But no one had cared that the loud troublemaker was finally gone. Brooke knew firsthand how cruel Cindy could be, and she hadn't cared either.

Brooke knelt by the grave and picked up a handful of dirt, letting it trickle through her fingers. She had always believed Cindy really had run off. The girl had threatened to do it often enough. It had been a surprise to no one.

But now Brooke doubted herself. She saw Cindy through an older, wiser lens and forgave the girl. Now she wanted to know what really happened to Cindy Shaw.

Let sleeping dogs lie.

That's what Greene would say if she asked him about Cindy. It's what he had said about the untested rape kits when she found them in the evidence room. When she had pressed Greene a second time about the kits, he had told her to back off. In that moment, something inside of her had changed.

Let sleeping dogs lie.

That advice had rattled in her brain when she had risked a secure future in the sheriff's department and leaked the information about the rape kits to Nevada and then the media. She'd expected the feds to investigate. She hadn't expected him to run against Greene. Or to win.

Brooke crossed the frost-covered ground, following the ring of her flashlight to her car. As she reached for the door handle, the wind rustled in the trees. Her hand slid to her weapon as she searched the darkness. She watched for signs of trouble in the sway of the trees and tall grass. Her skin prickled. She tightened her fingers on the grip of her weapon.

Finally, she pushed aside the unexpected case of nerves and got into her car. As she started the engine, she searched the horizon one last time before she shook off the remnants of worry and drove the five miles to her house.

Mom and Matt would be asleep by now, but at least she would be under the same roof with them for a few hours.

She parked by the house, got out of her vehicle, and moved up the stairs before she quietly unlocked the front door. Stepping lightly, she made her way to the kitchen and opened the refrigerator to find a blue plastic container. Attached to it was a sticky note that read **Brooke**.

"Bless you, Mom." She opened the lid, removed a fried strip of chicken, and bit into it. It was cold, but the flavors were delicious and she was so hungry she was lightheaded. She grabbed a soda and, standing at the kitchen sink, ate her chicken and drained the can.

The clock on the stove read 1:50 a.m. She had three hours to grab some sleep and be back at the office.

Her phone dinged with a text, and she glanced at the screen. It was from Peter Stuart, a reporter based in Roanoke. He was young, midtwenties, and though they'd never met in person, she imagined a newly framed journalism degree from Who Cares University hanging in a small gray cubicle in the center of a newsroom.

DNA results on the rape kits should be back by now.

Leaking to Stuart had been foolish. She should have pushed Greene harder or given Nevada the time to work the case. But she'd been pissed when she'd contacted him. He'd jumped on the story and earned significant airtime. Now he wanted his follow-up. He wanted his next story.

It was likely Nevada knew she'd broken protocol once, and had forgiven her. She doubted he would tolerate a second transgression.

And she honestly did not want to undermine him. He was making headway, and he deserved a fair shot.

Brooke texted back, No comment at this time.

Little gray bubbles rolled in place and then, If not now, when?

She elbowed aside the worry that had been stalking her since her first text to him. No comment.

Let me help you, he texted.

No comment.

I have enough from my sources to post my story.

Did he? Or was he bluffing? She didn't want to snap at the bait he was dangling, but she also didn't want to alienate him. He could be an asset.

Wait and you'll be the first when we have something to say.

I'll give you 24 hours.

Unsettled, she tossed her phone on the counter and reached for a beer in the refrigerator. She popped the top and took a long pull.

A light clicked on in the hallway, and she heard her mother's steady steps. Sandra Bennett appeared in the doorway, wearing a thick pink robe over a long, worn, flannel nightgown. Short gray hair framed a round face, and silver-rimmed glasses caught the overhead light. "I thought that was you."

"Sorry to wake you, Mom. Thanks for the dinner."

She padded across the floor and kissed Brooke lightly on the cheek. "I was getting worried."

"Crazy day."

"Have they found Debbie yet?" her mother asked.

"How did you know she was missing?"

"I paid a call to her mother today, and she told me. With Debbie's father so ill, the church is sending over meals."

"There's still no sign of her."

"I hear she was scheduled for work today, but didn't make it in. That's not the first time Debbie's gotten her schedule confused."

"Is Debbie dating anyone?" Brooke asked. "Has she had any trouble with men?"

"Not that I've noticed."

"Did her mom say if there was trouble at work? Maybe a disgruntled coworker who hated her for ignoring him?"

"Again, no. Her mother says everyone loves Debbie, which is true. She's great with the patients, and she gets along with her neighbors."

Brooke took another pull on the cold beer. "I'm hoping Debbie got a wild hair and went to Richmond or DC for a few days of fun. She's threatened to do it before."

"Everyone needs a break now and then." Her mother reached for a clean mug in the cabinet.

"I know it's been stressful since I was promoted. I'm hoping you, Matt, and I can take a vacation in June after school lets out."

Frowning, her mother moved to the stove, peered inside a cold teakettle before she refilled it with fresh water. She switched on the front burner. "I know you've had a lot on your plate balancing work and Matt."

"Nothing I can't handle," Brooke said.

"Nothing we can't handle," her mother emphasized.

Brooke's mother had been with her every step of the way. She had been her biggest fan when she was a kid, and later when Brooke had found out she was pregnant her senior year of high school, her mother had stayed at her side.

She still remembered that panicked drive to the hospital the night Matt was born. Brooke had been doubled over in the front seat, panting and crying. Her mother had been speeding down a back road when Greene of all people had pulled her mother over. He had clocked her going eighty in a fifty-five. He had realized what was happening, immediately escorted them to the hospital, and hadn't left until Matt came screaming into the world twenty minutes later.

Brooke had spent the next four years commuting to school, taking classes, and then racing home to her baby boy. With her mother's help, she had earned her college degree and landed a job in the sheriff's office as a deputy. She was loyal to Greene and would have had his back if only he had sent those damn kits off for testing.

"You could use a break," her mother said.

The idea of a warm sandy beach was almost too tempting to consider. She took another long pull on the beer and thought about the teenager sleeping upstairs. "I received a call from Matt at school today. He forgot his computer and lunch money. Couldn't get you on the phone."

"I was on the floor with a critical patient and couldn't take the call. I told him to plan better. This is the third time he forgot his lunch money."

"I ran both by the school."

"You do too much for him, Brooke. He has to feel the consequences on the smaller things, so he doesn't fail when it really matters."

"So he doesn't end up like me?"

"I would never wish that boy away. I love him. But you know I wanted a different life for you."

Slightly irritated with her mother and herself, Brooke took another swallow. "Cindy Shaw's name came up today."

"Cindy? Why?"

Brooke dug her fingernail into the label on the side of the bottle. "She vanished the same year as Tobi. The FBI agent thinks there might be a connection."

Worry deepened the lines on her mother's face as she leaned against the counter. "Cindy caused a lot of trouble."

Brooke was more like Tobi Turner, a band geek without a cool bone in her body. When Cindy had paid attention to Brooke in high school, the incident with the bees had been forgotten. And if only for a little while, she had felt cooler. But Cindy had never really cared about Brooke or Tobi or perhaps herself.

"As an adult I look back and recognize Cindy's awful homelife and her substance abuse problems led her to make a lot of poor choices. If I met her today, I'd like to think I'd be a bigger person and show her more compassion."

"I don't know if I could ever have charity for that girl." Her mother dunked a chamomile tea bag into her mug, and when the kettle whistled, she poured hot water into the cup. "You mentioned the FBI. Is that the person who drives the black sedan parked in front of the station?"

"Yes, her name is Special Agent Macy Crow."

"But isn't it your job to investigate the cases now?"

"Sheriff Nevada feels like we need the big guns for this one."

"You're smart enough to figure it out."

Brooke wasn't so sure about that. Her experience ended at the county line. "A fresh set of eyes won't hurt."

Floorboards squeaked upstairs and she realized her son, a light sleeper, was awake. He was smart, clever, and the spitting image of her.

Brooke poured the last of her beer down. "I want to check in on Matt."

As she turned to leave, her mother said, "I'm proud of you."

Brooke closed her eyes, absorbing the words before she kissed her mother lightly on the cheek and then climbed the stairs. She walked down the narrow hallway she'd traveled so many times that a light wasn't necessary. She opened her son's bedroom door. Hints of the fresh coat of blue paint she had rolled on the walls a couple of weeks ago lingered in the air. His clothes were piled on the floor next to a set of size-eleven sneakers she'd given him for his birthday last summer. He was already fourteen and in four years would be off to college himself. When he was born, she'd thought her life was over. Now she wondered what she would do when he was gone.

"Mom."

Brooke sat on the end of his bed and rubbed her son's back. "You should be asleep, baby."

"I'm not a baby, Mom." Matt rolled over and sat up, pushing his thick dark hair out of his eyes.

"You'll always be my baby." Which was one of the reasons she'd brought him the computer today. It felt good to be needed.

"Mom. Stop."

"Got it."

"Are you coming or going?"

"Passing through. I need a quick shower, maybe a little sleep, and a change of clothes before I head back to work." She traced her hand over the star shapes on the coverlet. "Did the front office give you your computer and the lunch money?"

"Yeah. Thanks for bringing it. Where was Grandma?"

"With a patient."

Matt was silent, but she knew the wheels were turning in his head. "Any word how the girl found in the Wyatt barn died?"

"Not yet." Her heart wanted to ache for the man's loss, but she knew grief would only cloud her thoughts and inhibit her from truly helping Turner.

"Are Tyler and the football players having bonfires out there?" she asked.

"I don't know."

"Yes, you do."

"I don't know, Mom. I just know they're obsessed with the place now."

"It's a crime scene."

"I know." He took her hand in his, just like he had when he was little. "It's okay, Mom. I'm not going out there."

"Promise?"

"Promise."

She smiled and kissed her son on his forehead. "You need sleep."

Matt yawned. "So do you."

"I will."

"Did you know the dead girl?" Matt asked.

Brooke was quiet as she smoothed her hand over the light-gray coverlet. "I remember her from school. I remember when she vanished. It was a scary time."

The truth was she barely remembered those weeks. She had been consumed by morning sickness and preoccupied with hiding her pregnancy from her mother.

"You'll solve the case," Matt said. "You're a badass cop."

She squeezed his hand. "I hope so, for the sake of that girl."

"I saw Hank Greene on television today."

"What was he talking about?" Greene wasn't the type to keep his mouth shut.

"He hinted that he's going to challenge Sheriff Nevada during the next election and win his seat back."

"Well, then he's in for a real fight, isn't he? Nevada is no pushover."

Matt drew in a breath. "Whoever killed that girl could still be in town. You need to be careful, Mom."

"I'll be fine. You just make sure you stay away from those bonfires."

"Jeez, Mom. I got it."

Brooke brushed a strand of hair from her son's eyes. If only she could make him understand that monsters were real and they could steal his life if given the chance.

***

Through most of the late evening, Nevada asked around a few of the bars, but it took him an hour before he tracked down Paul Decker at a trailer located in a mobile home park twenty miles west of town. When he pulled up, a light glowed from inside the small residence. Out of the car, he kept his jacket unbuttoned and his weapon accessible. Rock music pulsed out of the trailer, accompanied by the heavy scent of cigarette smoke.

The steady beat of a bass guitar riff stretched on as Nevada waited and listened. He pounded his fist against the trailer's thin metal door before he stepped to the side. "Decker. Sheriff Nevada."

The music stopped, and fleeting silence broke with the steady thud of footsteps approaching the door. Mustard-yellow curtains flickered, and the door opened to Paul Decker. He'd been the wide receiver on the Dream Team, but the lean frame that had earned him the name Lightning now carried an extra twenty pounds of weight, while hunched shoulders, a scraggly beard, and thinning black hair added a decade to his appearance.

Nevada rested his hand on the grip of his weapon. "Decker, I'd like to ask you a few questions. Would you step outside, please?"

Paul raised a cigarette to his lips. "What kind of questions?"

"Step outside. I won't ask again." He smiled, but Nevada knew his smiles tended to look more feral than friendly.

Smoke trailed around Paul's head before he flicked the cigarette to the ground and stepped outside. "Sure."

Nevada looked beyond Paul into the trailer. "Anyone else in the trailer?"

"No, it's just me. What's this about?"

After he'd dropped Macy off, Nevada had pulled Paul's arrest record. Though he knew Paul's DNA did not match the man he was hunting, the former football player might have information about the other members of the Dream Team, as well as about the bonfires Tobi might have attended.

"You were arrested for sexual assault ten years ago," Nevada said.

Paul shook his head. "And I did my time, and now I'm out on parole. I've stayed out of trouble since I came back to Deep Run."

Nevada had reviewed Paul's case file and seen some of the pictures taken of the woman who'd filed the charges against him. Her left eye had been black and blue and swollen. And her right wrist had also been badly sprained. "You hurt her pretty bad."

Paul sniffed as he kicked the dirt with the tip of his booted foot. "My jail time is old news. Why are you here?"

Of all the members of the Dream Team, Paul had shown the most promise and would have had a lot to lose if he were tangled up in the rapes or disappearances of 2004. "Do you remember Tobi Turner?"

"Tobi. Shit. She's the one that went missing."

"She's not missing anymore. Her body was found about a week ago."

"Really? I don't watch the news." He fished a fresh cigarette from his pocket and lit it. Smoke curled around his head.

"When's the last time you saw Tobi?" Nevada asked.

"Dude, it was fifteen years ago. I barely remember yesterday."

"What's your last memory of her?"

"Some geeky kid who liked to hang around and watch football practice. She was cute in a sad kind of way."

"Did she hang around with anyone? Talk to anyone?"

"She was a band girl. Not my style."

"Did Tobi ever come to the bonfires?"

"I don't remember."

Nevada traced the underside of his college class ring with his thumb. "You had a reputation for being even faster with your head than with your feet on the football field."

Pride winked in his pale-gray eyes. "When it came to football, I was the complete package."

"I need you to reboot your brain and give me something about Tobi."

"Man, I told you I don't remember much."

"Tell me about the days before she vanished. You two were seen talking at her locker."

"Really? I don't recall." He took another deep drag on the cigarette.

"I want to be nice," Nevada said. "But you're on parole, and right now, I got no problem calling your probation officer and raining shit down on your dumb ass."

"Shit. Why would you do that? I've been clean since I got out. Working hard, not missing a shift, and staying clear of the bars."

"It's not enough, Paul. I want details about Tobi. What did you two talk about that day?"

Paul's hands trembled slightly as he raised the cigarette and drew in another lungful of air. "I was chatting her up. I saw her looking at me, and I thought I'd have a little fun. She wasn't all that hot, but I was seventeen and would have screwed anything."

"Did you?"

"Screw her? No. That virgin vault was locked up tight."

"A seventeen-year-old would see that as a challenge."

"I didn't. I had plenty of girls then."

"How did Tobi get to the bonfire?"

"I don't know dick about the Turner girl. Last I saw her, Cindy Shaw was making nice with her and acting like they were friends."

"Cindy Shaw?" It wasn't lost on him that Macy had brought the girl's name up multiple times today.

"Yeah."

"Were they friends?"

"Shit, no. Cindy had to be angling for something. My guess is it was money or test answers. Cindy was never nice unless there was a good reason for it."

"Where did you see Cindy talking to Tobi?"

"Next to the new field house, I guess. It was after one of the games. Only reason I remember was because Cindy saw me, smiled, and tugged at her top."

"What do you think happened to Cindy?"

"I heard she was living in Arizona. Someone said she had married a rich guy."

California, Colorado, and now Arizona. No one really knew where Cindy had landed when she'd left Deep Run. "You believe that was true?"

"Shit, who knows? Probably. She was hot and she liked the finer things." Another inhale. "Why do you care about Cindy?"

"Because you just told me she was with Tobi Turner shortly before they both vanished. Anything that relates to Tobi is important to me."

"Cindy was seen with half the school those last couple of weeks. She was all about Bruce and the Dream Team going to the finals. She wanted her big brother to go all the way and take her along with him. Bruce was her ticket out of the trailer park."

The Dream Team had been near gods in the weeks leading up to the championship game. A lot of wrongs, including rape kits, could have easily been swept under the carpet so they could keep playing and winning. "Tell me about the bonfires."

"They were like a good luck ritual." He shrugged. "None of us wanted to do anything to break our winning streak that year."

"Like a lucky rabbit's foot?" Nevada asked.

"Our routine never changed. We liked the big blazes burning in the woods and the shots of Fireball the night before a game. The coach knew about them. He said the bonfires were our chance to incinerate any fears we had. There was no room for doubt on the field."

"That would have been Coach Medina."

"That's right. I heard he died a couple of years ago. Heart attack."

"Medina and Greene were tight, right?"

"Yeah. They played ball together back in the day. Greene liked to stop by practice, and they'd shoot the shit."

"The boys on the team stuck by each other. Kind of like *Band of Brothers*."

"Yeah, we had each other's back on and off the field. That's why we did so well."

"Would you have covered for each other to protect the team?"

Paul ground his cigarette butt into the dirt. "That bond broke a long time ago."

"Why's that?"

He sniffed. "I called around to some of the guys when I was arrested. None of them stepped up."

"That must have stung."

"Sure as shit did. So I'm not protecting anyone."

Nevada wasn't sure he believed Paul. "Good to know you have an open mind. Make your parole officer proud, and keep thinking about those last days with Tobi and Cindy. We'll talk again soon."

CHAPTER THIRTEEN

Tuesday, November 19, 2:45 a.m.

Scratch. Scratch. Scratch.

Macy woke after two hours of sleep. She spent the next thirty minutes rolling around on her back, then to one side and then the next. She punched her pillow. Did deep-breathing exercises. But slumber danced out of reach.

She stared at the shadows crisscrossing the ceiling. The idea of watching 1980s sitcoms while she waited for the sun reminded her of the long nights recovering in the hospital. It was this side of hell.

When the clock on the nightstand clicked over to 2:46 a.m., she cursed and rose. She glanced back at the rumpled bedsheets. Would she ever get a decent night's sleep again? God, how she missed it.

She padded to the bathroom, flipped on the shower, and stripped. When the steam rose up, she stepped under the spray and let the heat work into her stiff muscles. Finally, she unwrapped the small bar of soap and washed.

She thought about the evidence boxes from the rapes and the Turner case. It wouldn't hurt to go through them.

Macy shut off the water and toweled off. Wiping away the condensation from the mirror, she caught her reflection and groaned. She flexed her bicep. Despite a couple of weeks of moderate CrossFit classes, the muscle tone hadn't returned. Her stomach was almost concave and her hips too narrow. She plucked at the awkward spikes of blond hair and eyed the jagged red scar along her leg. The blotchy road rash on her hip and side didn't help either.

"Jesus, Crow," she muttered. "You look like the experiment Frankenstein got wrong." It was either accept her life as it was or cry. And she didn't have time to cry.

Determined not to be vain, she set up the coffee maker, and while it gurgled, she dressed in clean clothes. She ran her fingers through her hair, knowing a real cut had to be in her future. She called the sheriff's office and asked the dispatcher about getting the files, which were housed in a storeroom on site.

Fifteen minutes later, she stepped out into the cool night air, backpack on shoulder, coffee and keys in one hand, the other free. As she always did, she paused and surveyed the parking lot, searching for any sign that something wasn't right. When she was certain she was safe, she pressed her key fob. The lights on her vehicle winked, and the door locks clicked open. After tossing in her bag, she got behind the wheel, doors quickly locked, and started the engine. She cranked the heat.

The drive back to the sheriff's office took her through the quiet streets slightly glistening after a gentle rain. She parked in front of the sheriff's office, sipped the last of her coffee, and pushed through the front door seconds later.

The dispatcher tonight was an African American woman who appeared to be in her midfifties. Slender, she had brushed back her salt-and-pepper hair into a tight bun. Glasses perched on the edge of her nose as she looked up. Unfazed by the sight of Macy, she was clearly accustomed to late-night visitors.

"Can I help you?" Her voice crackled over the intercom.

Macy held up her badge. "Special Agent Macy Crow. I'm working with the sheriff."

"I heard about you. I suppose you're here for the evidence files."

"That's right."

"I'm Deputy Morgan." She pressed the button and the door unlatched.

Macy pushed through.

"Glad to have you." She rose and walked toward the conference room with Macy. "The evidence boxes arrived a few minutes ago. I figured you wouldn't be back until morning."

"I don't sleep well when I'm on the road."

"I like to sleep in my own bed, myself." She flipped on the conference-room light. "No evidence boxes for Tobi. All that was collected at the barn is with the Roanoke lab."

Macy lifted one of the three blue file boxes. It was light. "Can you also see if there was a missing person file for Cindy Shaw?"

"Cindy Shaw?"

"She went to school with Tobi and vanished about the same time."

Deputy Morgan shook her head. "I don't remember the name, but I'll have a look in the system."

"Pull anything you have on Cindy Shaw, would you?" Macy asked.

The phone rang, drawing Deputy Morgan's attention back to her console. Macy dropped her backpack in a chair and opened Susan Oswald's box.

The evidence sticker on the side stated that the materials had been collected on June 15, 2004, by Deputy Marty Shoemaker and collected from Susan Oswald's room. The chain of custody line stated the evidence had been transported from the scene to the locker but had never been checked out again.

There were five plastic evidence bags. The first contained the pantyhose, still coiled into a tight circle. The next bag held two single earrings that did not match. Another held the white fitted sheet from her bed, which had a square cut from the center for DNA collection. There was a bag containing her oversize green Valley High School T-shirt. And finally, a partial plaster mold of a footprint. A paltry collection from an offender who'd left years of pain in his wake.

Macy removed her yellow legal pad and made notes.

The shoe impression taken at the scene next to Susan's window was a right-foot, size-eleven athletic shoe. She listed several shoe companies that could have possibly made it.

As she worked her way through the box, she scribbled more notes.

Collects keepsakes. Doesn't use a condom. Shows remorse?

He was less interested in the sex than the violence. Most likely he craved the girls' fear. He choked each to near unconsciousness and grew increasingly violent. The perpetrator was practicing. Experimenting. Building up skills, courage, or endurance for murder.

Macy picked up the bagged pantyhose and socks in the evidence box. She flipped through her file. According to Greene, "Ms. Oswald says he used the pantyhose to bind her." And then in very bold letters the words: "VERY UPSET."

Ellis Carter's box also contained the cotton sheet that had been on her bed when she had been attacked, a single woman's hiking shoe, and a strand of red rope that had been used to bind her hands behind her back.

Again, Macy searched Greene's case notes. Rebecca Kennedy had also been bound with a red rope, and she had always assumed her attacker had brought the binding with him.

The first time the assailant hadn't been prepared. But in subsequent attacks he came ready with rope. She added red rope to her list.

Macy spent the next few hours going through each box, reading all of Greene's comments, and making more notes. He had interviewed the people who'd lived closest to the victims. One had reported seeing a shadowed figure on the road near Ellis Carter's house, but when the neighbor had gone out to investigate, the person had vanished. He had also interviewed Rebecca's neighbors.

She began to write down questions:

What was his trigger? Were there economic stressors in the area at the time? Was it personal? Did the offender harbor fantasies and finally act upon them?

Once she had inventoried the cases, she pulled up an electronic form for ViCAP and answered as many of the one-hundred-plus questions as she could. At four a.m., she hit "Send" and then followed up with a text to Special Agent Andy Jamison asking her to prioritize the case.

Macy's phone chimed with a response almost immediately. Will do. As she packed away the boxes, her phone chimed with another text. This one was from Nevada. Where are you?

She wasn't surprised he was awake. Insomnia was one of the traits they had discovered they shared in Kansas City. It was a prevalent condition in their line of work. What normal person could sleep after what they saw?

She typed back, Sheriff's office. Evidence analysis.

Nevada responded, Treat you to breakfast. Walt's Diner in fifteen minutes.

Deal. She packed up the boxes and replaced their tops. She shoved her legal pad in her backpack before clicking off the lights and walking out to the dispatcher's desk. "I'll be back in a few hours."

"Sullivan will be on at six," Deputy Morgan said.

"I'm sure I'll be here several more nights," Macy said.

"Well, I'll see you tomorrow evening."

"Where's Walt's Diner?"

"Near the highway in the truck stop. Go out the main road and make a left at the railroad tracks. Follow the signs to the interstate."

"Thanks."

Fifteen minutes later when she pulled up in front of Walt's, Nevada was standing outside the diner, his hands tucked into his coat for warmth. Out of the car with her pack on her shoulder, she locked the door and approached him. "How'd you know I wasn't in my motel room fast asleep?"

"Really? You're on a tight clock. You don't have time to sleep." He opened the diner door and gave her a slight smile. They passed a SEAT YOURSELF sign and found a booth in the back. A waitress delivered coffee and left them with menus.

She opened the menu, and her gaze went straight to the all-American breakfast, complete with eggs, bacon, and pancakes. Decision made, she dumped two sugar packets and cream in her coffee. "You think you know me that well?"

"I also drove by the sheriff's office and saw your car." He sipped his coffee, but didn't bother to look at the menu. "What did you discover in the files?"

"Basically what we already know. He's incredibly careful. He stalks and plans. Nothing was random. He left behind his shoe print three times, red nylon rope three times, and his DNA at each scene. He's not worried about physical evidence."

"He's just a regular Joe."

"He likes to think he is," she said. "But guys like that have moments when they aren't as slick as they think they are. If he's still alive, I would bet he didn't stop with the crimes here in Deep Run." She sipped her coffee.

"Maybe the Turner case spooked him. Greene did a few things right."

"He might have laid low for a while, but I would bet money he found new hunting grounds." She shook her head. "I submitted the case details to ViCAP and asked a colleague to fast-track it."

"If this guy has a pattern, then maybe a cop in another jurisdiction made note of it."

"And filled out his ViCAP form."

When the waitress returned, Macy ordered and Nevada followed with the number six. After she was out of earshot, Nevada said, "I spoke to Paul Decker."

"Where?"

"I tracked him to a trailer outside of town."

"And what did he have to say?" Macy asked.

"Said he remembers seeing Tobi with Cindy Shaw. He said Cindy was always scheming and using other people. Not a glowing referral."

"Did you bring up Cindy?"

"No, he mentioned her without prompting."

"Interesting. What else?"

"Not much really, but I encouraged him to give it some more thought. His parole officer would be so proud of him. If someone on that Dream Team was a part of this, Decker will rat him out to save his own ass." Nevada sipped his coffee. "He's getting called into the probation office tomorrow for a surprise drug test."

Smiling, she folded one of the empty sugar packets in half, sharpening the crease between her thumb and index finger. "Well played, Nevada. Well played."

"I do my best."

She looked around the diner decorated with neon lights and black-and-white photos of the town from the last one hundred years. "Is this your favorite hangout spot?" Macy asked.

"Since I was a teenager. It's open all night. A favorite for truckers, kids after football games, and hunters looking for a predawn hot breakfast."

"I have a few places like that in Alexandria. Bev's on Route 1 is one of my favorites." She savored this easy familiarity between them. "Their number three is my go-to meal."

"You have a thing for pancakes, Crow."

"That's no secret. I have a desperate addiction to sugar." She traced the rim of her cup with her finger. "I actually lived in Alexandria a couple of months before my Texas vacation. I'm amazed we didn't run into each other there."

"I was on the road."

"Not surprising."

"And yet here we are."

She stirred her coffee. "Which begs the question: Why me for this case?"

"You applied to Ramsey's team."

"You could have investigated this case."

"It's nice to have a second set of ears to bounce ideas off of."

"You have Deputy Bennett."

"She's learning fast, but I needed someone who could hit the ground running."

"Figuratively speaking." Her sarcasm didn't coax a smile.

He was silent for a moment and then said, "My last bureau investigation was in Arizona. It was a child abduction case. When we found the little girl, we were too late. You were the first person I called."

"But I was hooked up to a ventilator."

"Yeah."

She tapped her finger on the side of her cup. "What we see can't ever be unseen."

"I forgot about the kid and could only think about you. I didn't sleep until I knew you were out of the woods."

The tender emotion in his voice caught her off guard, and it took her a second before she could speak. "I'm too mean to kill."

He was silent for a moment. "When you reach your limit, and you will, give yourself a break. You don't owe anybody anything."

"I wish it were that simple. I can't quit."

The waitress arrived with their platters, setting down a western omelet with toast in front of him and pancakes, bacon, and eggs in front of her.

He stared at her over the rim of his cup but, instead of pressing, said, "Let's get back to this case."

She poured syrup on her pancakes. "Our offender chose vulnerable victims."

"Including Ellis?" Nevada sounded surprised.

"She was then. Her parents were going through a nasty divorce, and she and her mother were living in a new rental home. Susan had a sick mother, and Rebecca Kennedy was struggling with substance abuse."

"The game's already rigged with this lineup," he said.

Reflecting on him a moment, she poured more syrup on her pancakes and sliced into them. She took several large bites as Nevada also ate. "I'm guessing he's also been moving from jurisdiction to jurisdiction. His plan is to stay just ahead of law enforcement. Maybe he knows not all law enforcement departments communicate with each other."

"I saw it enough when I worked for the bureau," he said. "Maybe your ViCAP application will come through."

She drained the last of her coffee and motioned to the waitress for a refill. "I asked Deputy Morgan to search missing persons and see if there's a file for Cindy Shaw."

"Everyone, including Decker, thinks she just took off. Decker's version has her living happily ever after in Arizona."

Macy picked up a slice of bacon, meeting his questioning gaze. "I don't think Cindy landed in the world of rainbows and Skittles. I've seen too many young runaways get kicked in the head by the streets."

She snapped the piece of bacon in half. "I can't even remember all their names and faces."

"Can't remember—or don't want to?"

"Both."

They ate in silence for several minutes before he spoke. "Deputy Bennett has scheduled a press conference for this afternoon, but before that, we have an appointment with the medical examiner in Roanoke. Tobi Turner's remains are ready for review. Afterward, we can pay a visit to Bruce Shaw and ask him about his sister."

She checked her watch. "It's only five a.m. I better get back to my motel room and sleep for an hour or two."

"I'll pick you up at eight."

"I'll be ready."

***

Nevada sat at the desk in his home office and turned on his computer. As he waited for it to boot up, his thoughts turned to Special Agent Macy Crow. He respected the hell out of her because she was one of the best.

But when he thought about Macy, the most primitive neurons of his limbic system demanded sex. A few times when she hadn't been looking, he had glanced at her breasts, her lips, and the curve of her hips. She'd dropped weight and muscle tone, but as far as he was concerned, she was still hot as hell.

When he had arrived back at his grandfather's farm, he had taken a hot shower and changed into clean jeans, a blue pullover that read **SHERIFF** over the left pocket, and his steel-tipped boots. As the coffee had brewed, he had attached his gun and badge to his belt.

At his computer, he searched the case he'd worked with Macy in Kansas City. A few photos featured the two of them standing side by side in the background as the local police chief spoke at the podium. He remembered that day and the sex they had shared that evening.

Shifting the Internet search to Macy, he pulled up familiar pictures. The first image caught her descending a long set of marble stairs in a Virginia courthouse. She was wearing a poker face, but the wind caught her long blond hair and it gleamed in the light. She wore heeled boots, not the black, thick-soled boots she now favored. That image vibrated with a youthful sense of invincibility.

He typed Cindy Shaw's name into the search engine.

The search didn't grab any hits on Cindy Shaw. Her disappearance was only mentioned once in the media, and that was in conjunction with Tobi Turner.

Assuming she was living in another state, there were no outstanding warrants for Cindy Shaw, and she also didn't have a financial or digital trail. The universe, it seemed, had swallowed her up.

Nevada checked his watch. Realizing time was getting away from him, he finished his coffee and got in his car. At eight a.m., he pulled up in front of Macy's motel room. She came out seconds later and slid into the front seat. They'd worked well together in Kansas City, and he felt they hadn't missed a beat.

"How far is it to Roanoke?" she asked while responding to a text.

"Less than an hour."

"Great. I received a response from the FBI forensic artist. She'll be here tomorrow afternoon."

"Perfect." He pulled out onto the main road. "Did you get any sleep?"

"About an hour."

"Good." He clicked on a local rock station. "The music is tame by your standards."

She smiled. "As long as it's not about horses and broken hearts, I'll survive."

"You must have gotten your fill of country music in Texas."

She rolled her head from side to side, seemingly working stiffness from her neck. "You have no idea."

They drove in silence for most of the trip, each lost in thought as the rolling countryside passed. He took the Salem exit just past Roanoke to where the Western District Office of the Virginia State Medical Examiner was located.

He parked close to the main entrance. He noticed it took her a moment to work the kinks out of her leg after the hour trip, but he said nothing. They made their way inside, showed their badges to the receptionist behind the glass partition, and soon were escorted to the office of Dr. Russell Squibb.

Dr. Squibb was in his midfifties and stood about five foot eight inches. He had a round belly, a balding head, and a firm handshake.

"We appreciate you seeing us," Nevada said.

"I had another call from Tobi Turner's father this morning. That's the hardest part of this job."

"We understand," Macy said. "If you can take us to her."

"Of course."

They followed the doctor down a long nondescript hallway to a large examination room outfitted with several sliding refrigerated drawers where they kept the bodies. Dr. Squibb opened drawer 210 to reveal the sheet-clad remains.

Nevada was good at detaching himself from the horrors of death, but he never wanted to forget the victims were somebody's loved ones. He remembered the girl's pictures hanging on her father's walls. She was bright eyed and smiling as she played soccer and T-ball, sang at her church, and laughed with friends at the beach. He wouldn't wish this on anyone.

Macy shifted, and he saw her left hand curl into a fist. He knew exactly what she was thinking.

The doctor handed them both latex gloves, which they snapped on in seconds. Neither spoke as the doctor removed the sheet to reveal a set of discolored bones laid out in anatomical order.

Dr. Squibb pulled out a pair of glasses from his lab coat pocket, put them on, and proceeded to lift the skull. "We were able to positively identify her through her dental records. The cavities and even the crown on her front tooth to repair a crack were perfect matches."

"How did she fracture her tooth?" Macy asked.

"It happened when she was twelve, according to her father. She was trying to hit a soccer ball with her head, and the ball caught her in the mouth."

With only bones remaining, there was no way to definitively determine what kind of soft-flesh injuries Tobi Turner had suffered. The killer could have raped her before or after death, or he could have masturbated on her backpack. Unless a killer confessed, there was just no way of knowing.

"What was her cause of death?" Macy asked.

"Strangulation. The small hyoid bone in her neck appears to have been crushed."

Those horseshoe-shaped bones were delicate and easily fractured. "Can you tell if he choked her once or multiple times?" Macy asked.

"Sorry," Dr. Squibb said. "Bones can tell us a lot, but they can't always give us the complete picture."

"Your examination results are a big help," Macy said. "This offender has a distinct pattern."

Dr. Squibb rotated the skull sideways. "There's also a circular crack behind her left ear. The fractures radiate out like a spiderweb. He hit her with a blunt object. And given the damage I see here, she was rendered unconscious."

"Would the blow have led to her death?" Macy asked.

"Not likely."

"Any other injuries?" Nevada asked.

"She did have several fractures on the fingers of her right hand," Dr. Squibb said. "They appear to be defensive wounds."

"She fought back," Macy said.

"I would concur." Dr. Squibb lifted up a long flat bone. "This was her sternum."

Macy studied the bone closer. "Is that a hairline fracture?"

"It is," the doctor said.

"What would cause that?" Macy asked.

"It's consistent with a fall, blow to the chest, or even CPR."

"CPR? He tried to save her?" Nevada asked.

"Possibly," Dr. Squibb said. "Perhaps he strangled her and panicked."

"Or maybe he tried to revive her so they could keep playing," Macy said.

"God, I hope you're wrong," Nevada said. "No kid deserves to die like this."

Anger and sadness strengthened Macy's drive to solve this case as she laid her hand on the top of the skull. "Tobi, your dad said he loves you."

As she pulled back her hand, a heavy silence settled in the room. The doctor carefully covered Tobi's bones and then closed the drawer.

***

After Macy and Nevada left the medical examiner's portion of the building, they crossed the lobby to the forensic side. Macy felt a bit like a wimp pushing the elevator button instead of taking the stairs to the third floor. However, she needed to be practical. The less mileage on the leg meant the farther she could go. This wasn't about her proving her stamina. It was about catching a killer. Nevada, to his credit, didn't make a comment.

On the third floor they found their way to the office of a John McDaniel, the forensic expert who'd examined Tobi's backpack. McDaniel was a pudgy man in his late sixties. His graying hair curled over the edges of his collar, and a thick mustache gave him a quirky, almost cartoonlike appearance.

"Mr. McDaniel." Nevada introduced them both, and each showed their badges. "We understand you have Tobi Turner's backpack."

McDaniel stood, shook both their hands with a surprisingly iron grip, and nodded for them to follow. "It's in the other room on the light table."

In the next room, there was a fingerprint chamber, microscopes set up at various stations, and a gun ballistics firing chamber. Resting on a light table was a faded red backpack, unzipped and opened. Beside it was a series of items that they hoped might tell the tale of Tobi Turner's last hours.

"I ran the backpack through a fingerprint chamber to see what I could pull. I did get a partial thumbprint off the strap of the backpack. It's a match to a print lifted from Susan Oswald's windowsill. I've run it through AFIS, but so far no matches."

"What's in the backpack?" Macy asked.

"Have a look. Pair of jeans, a sweater, sneakers, textbook, pencils, lipstick, hand sanitizer, a candy bar, and a condom. There's also a set of keys, including a car key that matches the make and model of the Turner family van."

Macy studied the keys and noted a small piece of plastic that might have once belonged to a key chain.

She shifted her attention to the tarnished condom packet. Macy pulled on a fresh set of latex gloves. "Looks like she never intended to make that study session."

"The clothing fragments found on the body were a gold metallic. The jeans disintegrated, but the metal button and zipper we found are consistent with a designer pair sold in 2003 and 2004. The shoes were heeled boots."

"Maybe she did have a boyfriend." Nevada worked his hand into a glove. "Greene's report says there was nothing unusual spotted at the school the day she went missing."

"Maybe he charmed her," Macy said. "An awkward girl might have been thrilled for a little attention. We know Paul Decker showed some interest."

"Decker referred to her as the 'virgin vault,'" Nevada said.

"Which would have made her a challenge," Macy said.

"Decker also placed Cindy Shaw with Tobi and said Tobi would do almost anything for the team," Nevada said.

"Evil comes in all sizes." Macy all but whispered the last words, and she realized Nevada was staring at her. She cleared her throat. "What else did you find in the pack?"

With gloved hands, McDaniel picked up the textbook. "That leads me to this. I went through it page by page. Have a look at the pages I've marked with a tab."

Macy opened the inside cover. Tobi Turner's name was listed on the third line of **LEASED TO**. The other names had been neatly crossed out. She flipped to the first marked page and saw pencil writing in the margin.

Test on Tuesday. Section Two.

"It appears she liked to doodle and write in the margins," Macy said. "How do you know it's hers?"

"Handwriting matches the signature on the front cover," McDaniel said. "Have a look at the last page in the book."

She flipped to the end and saw another note in bolder pencil.

Bonfire. 8:00 p.m. Thursday.

"Decker called the bonfires their good luck ritual," Nevada said.

"He said ritual?" Macy asked.

"He did. The coach wanted them to burn away all their fears and doubts."

"Odd."

"Why?"

"Ritual can also mean something primitive, like a sacrifice."

CHAPTER FOURTEEN

Tuesday, November 19, 12:30 p.m.

When Macy and Nevada arrived back at the sheriff's office, a collection of news vehicles was waiting for them. She hadn't been expecting the media. "Did you move up the press conference?"

"No. Bennett confirmed it was later this afternoon," Nevada said.

As they crossed the lot, she was grateful she could keep pace with Nevada. The leg felt decent, which was great. She didn't need the distraction.

Inside, they found several reporters with cameras crammed into the lobby. On the other side of the glass, Sullivan spoke into his headset.

The door opened and Bennett appeared, her hat in hand, wearing a stoic expression. "I need to ask everyone to step outside. A representative will be out soon to make a statement. I need you to clear this space."

A rumble of comments rolled over the room as Macy opened the exterior door. Several folks passed without incident, but a young reporter with a thick crop of dark hair paused.

"You're the FBI agent," the reporter said to Macy.

"I'll brief you in a few minutes," Nevada said.

Dark eyes narrowed and the young reporter persisted. "What's the FBI doing here? Are you investigating the murder of Tobi Turner or the rapes?"

"Save your questions for the briefing," Nevada said.

The other reporters hovered close, as if fearful they would miss a morsel of news, and several snapped pictures of her walking alongside the sheriff.

They pushed their way through the crowd, dismissing the reporters' questions. When the door closed behind the reporters, Sullivan waved them behind the secured door. As soon as it latched and they had stepped out of sight of the reception glass, Macy said, "I thought we hadn't agreed on a briefing yet."

"We hadn't," Bennett said. "They called me about a half hour ago. Someone tipped off several reporters about the DNA matches and the FBI presence."

"Who tipped them?" Nevada asked.

"Did you visit with Greene?" Bennett asked.

"We did," Macy said.

Bennett shook her head as her lips flattened into a grim line. "He's your leak. He called a few friends in the media."

"To get back at me," Nevada said.

"Payback," Macy said.

"You're shining a light on his failures, so he might think he has nothing to lose at this point," Bennett said.

"I should have expected pushback," Nevada said.

Frustration, though tempting, wasn't productive. "We have the media's attention a little sooner than we'd planned, but let's make the best of it," Macy said. "I have summarized the case facts so I can answer questions. I assume you can do the same."

"I can," Nevada said.

Bennett adjusted her uniform. "You want to tell the public the rapes are connected to the murder?"

Nevada looked at Macy. He was making this her call. "I do. Better for us to inform the media than Greene."

Bennett didn't look convinced. "Do you really think someone would come forward after all this time?"

"I do," Macy said.

Sullivan leaned back in his chair. "I have Deputy Melvin on the phone. He said he drove by Debbie Roberson's house again, and there's still no sign of her vehicle. He knocked on her door, but no answer."

"And Ms. Roberson's cell?" Bennett asked.

"Not emitting a signal."

"That's a worry," Macy said. "How old is Debbie Roberson?"

"She's twenty-one," Bennett said.

"Unearthing the body of a girl he killed fifteen years ago is a hell of a trigger," Macy said.

"Aren't you getting ahead of yourself?" Bennett asked.

Without taking his gaze off Macy, Nevada said, "Bennett, I want to know the status of Debbie Roberson as soon as you do."

"Understood," Bennett.

"For now, we won't bring up her disappearance to the media," Macy said. "I want the focus on the older cases that we know for a fact are linked."

"Roger." Bennett settled her hat on her head, and Macy set her backpack in the chair.

On reflex, Macy reached for the brush in her backpack, but then, remembering her very short hair didn't need any attention, she followed Nevada and Bennett outside to face a half dozen cameras and twice as many reporters.

Bennett raised her hands over the rumble of conversation. "If I can have your attention," she shouted. "The sheriff would like to say a few words."

When the crowd grew quiet, Nevada stepped up to the podium, moving with a confidence that testified to years of investigations and media interaction. "As you may know, the sheriff's department was awarded a generous grant that allowed us to have the DNA kits in our evidence room tested." In a clear, steady voice, he shared their discovery of a serial rapist operating in the valley, as well as the evidence connecting Tobi Turner's murder to the rapes.

Almost before he had spoken the last syllable, a bevy of questions started firing in his direction. Did the police have a person of interest? How had victims and families reacted to this new development?

Nevada was cool, collected. As he spoke, Macy's gaze skimmed over the gaggle of reporters and then beyond to anyone else who might have been standing on the sidelines watching. Several cars driving by the sheriff's office on the main road slowed, but none stopped.

"Why is the FBI involved?" a reporter asked.

"This is a serial offender case," Nevada said. "And the FBI has access to resources we do not. I feel we'll be more effective solving this case with their participation."

Nevada introduced Macy and offered her a spot beside him at the podium. Macy moved forward, comfortable in a role she'd filled before. Since last June she had triumphed with a series of small victories, but this one made her feel more like her old self than any other.

"As the sheriff said, local law enforcement and the FBI are looking for a serial offender. Based on eyewitness testimony, he wore dark clothing and always had a ski mask covering his face. His fascination with strangulation steadily grew more violent until it escalated to murder. We are now reaching out to the community and asking everyone if they saw or heard something around the dates of the attacks that might be of help." She turned to Bennett. "Is there anything you'd like to add, Deputy?"

The deputy looked slightly taken aback for a split second, and then she stepped up to the podium. "If there are any persons out there who believe they were a victim of this man, please contact us. We want to help." She repeated the office's phone number and waited for the questions to fire in her direction.

The set of questions was almost identical to what had been thrown at Nevada. She simply repeated his answers verbatim. They were a united front.

After fifteen minutes of back-and-forth, Nevada replaced her at the microphone, thanked everyone for coming, and followed Macy and Bennett back into the building. When they stepped behind the locked doors, the sound of ringing phones greeted them.

Sullivan looked up from his console. "Deputy Bennett, one of our guys found Debbie Roberson's car."

"Where?" she asked.

"At the entrance to the state park."

"Are there signs of a struggle?" she asked.

"The car is unlocked, and her purse is tucked under the front seat. He popped the trunk and found red rope." The ringing phones forced Sullivan back to his console to answer the barrage of incoming calls.

Macy stepped forward. "Ask the deputy to string crime scene tape around the car and stay with it until we arrive."

"I'll drive out and have a look at the car," Bennett said. "I'll call you as soon as I appraise the situation."

"She worked at the Deep Run assisted living facility, correct?" Macy asked.

"Yes," Bennett said.

"Bruce Shaw works there, so I can kill two birds with one stone and ask him about her," Macy said.

"I'm coming with you," Nevada said.

***

Nevada was a pace behind Macy as they strode through the front door of the Deep Run assisted living facility thirty minutes later. At the front desk of the new Adele Jenner Wyatt wing of the facility, he asked to speak to Dr. Bruce Shaw. After procuring a promise to page him, Nevada and Macy waited in a small conference room off the main lobby.

He caught her staring at a stack of magazines featuring articles on the latest diets, fashion, and desserts. She thumbed through one. She didn't appear curious about the text but seemed distant and sad.

He remembered the call from Dr. Faith McIntyre, medical examiner in Austin, Texas. Faith had said that she was scrolling through contacts on Macy Crow's phone, and he was listed under favorites. And then she had told him how badly Macy had been hurt.

He'd immediately called a contact in the Texas Rangers and learned the details of the attempt on her life, as well as the case she'd been investigating when she'd been attacked.

After closing the magazine abruptly, Macy dropped it to the table and moved to a pamphlet rack. She inspected the brochures absently, but he noted her hand trembled slightly.

"You look agitated," he said.

She carefully replaced a pamphlet on long-term care. She faced him and with a shrug said, "I spent weeks in one of these. I worked my ass off because I knew if I didn't, I was screwed in terms of my career and my personal life."

"And you did a hell of a job. There's nothing to be nervous about now."

She ran her hand over her short hair. He was sorry he'd respected her wishes to tackle physical therapy alone. He should have been at her side. "And here you are, back in the game."

The door opened, and a man dressed in a white lab coat entered. In his midthirties, he had short dark hair brushed off his narrow, angled face. Bruce Shaw had been the quarterback for the Dream Team, and he'd had more girls chasing him than any teenage boy could imagine. He had maintained a lean, fit body.

Nevada rose. "Dr. Shaw, thank you for seeing us."

Shaw shook his hand. "Anything to help, Sheriff. I just caught your press conference on the television. Hell of a thing. No one ever thinks that kind of thing could happen in a town like Deep Run."

"No, sir," Nevada said. "I'd like to also introduce you to FBI Special Agent Macy Crow. She is working the case with my department."

Shaw shook her hand. "Pleasure, Agent Crow."

The three sat around a small, round conference table. Macy pulled out her yellow legal pad and flipped to a clean page. "Dr. Shaw, our visit has two purposes. The first is to ask about an employee, Debbie Roberson. Her mother hasn't spoken to her in days, and she's worried."

His eyes widened, and he reached for his phone. "Let me check the schedule." He scrolled for several seconds, frowned, and then said, "She's supposed to be on duty."

"Could she have switched shifts with another employee?" Macy asked.

Shaw shook his head as he typed a text. "It's policy that she inform her manager. I've just asked Mrs. Bland, her supervisor, to check."

"Has she missed work before?" Nevada asked.

"She has," he said. "In fact, she's on the verge of receiving a letter of reprimand for the last time she switched shifts and didn't properly communicate it."

Macy scribbled a note on her yellow pad. "Has anyone been giving her trouble? Have you noticed any signs of abuse or harassment directed toward her?"

"No. Debbie is young and somewhat immature. However, the patients like her, and she's very popular with the families, which is why Mrs. Bland keeps her on. Is Debbie really in jeopardy?"

"We don't know yet," Nevada said. "Just covering all the bases."

"You said you were here for two reasons," Shaw said.

Macy looked up from her pad. Her face was relaxed, but Nevada sensed she was anything but. "Can you tell us about your sister?"

"Cindy?" He shook his head. "That's random."

"One of the primary reasons I'm here is to investigate the death of Tobi Turner. Several people we spoke to said Cindy was seen with Tobi close to the time she vanished."

"How much do you know about my sister?" he asked carefully.

"That's exactly my question for you, Doctor," Macy said.

He rubbed the underside of a gold college ring. "We grew up under challenging circumstances. Our mother was addicted to meth and was more worried about her next hit than Cindy and me. Football was my outlet. The team became my family. Unfortunately, Cindy's outlet was the bottle, and then she started smoking meth shortly before she vanished."

"The people we spoke to say she ran away," Macy said.

"She did. When I heard she'd left, I drove to the bus station and tried to talk her into staying. But she was determined to leave Deep Run. She was convinced a better life was waiting for her."

"When was this?" Macy asked.

"Early November."

"After Tobi vanished?"

"Yes," he said.

"Did you ever hear from her again?" Macy asked.

"No. But I also didn't try to find her. I was drowning at the time, too. I tried in my own way to save her, but she wouldn't let me. In the end, I had to let her go."

"She never contacted you once?" Macy asked.

"I received a postcard from Dallas about a year after she left. She mailed it to the trailer, and it was forwarded to me at college. I called the number she'd written in her note, but no one answered." He leaned back, as if distancing himself from a memory. "You're both in law enforcement, and you must know the odds for a seventeen-year-old runaway aren't good."

"I've seen the odds beaten before," Macy said.

"Then why wouldn't my sister contact me?" Bruce said.

"I don't know," she said. Macy studied him silently. "Why would Cindy befriend a band kid, a math geek like Tobi? Seems like apples and oranges."

"Cindy was good at working the angles. She needed money for the drugs. She was probably using the girl."

"Did Cindy ever mention Tobi?" Macy asked.

"Not to me."

"Did Cindy go to the bonfires?" Nevada asked.

"Yes. She loved being around the team," Bruce said. "The football team adopted me, and I guess she hoped they would adopt her as a mascot."

"Did they?" Macy asked.

He dropped his gaze, plucking a thread from his pant leg. "Not really."

Macy tapped her index finger against her notebook. Nevada had seen that look before. The wheels were turning, which they would do constantly until she cracked this case.

"Thank you for your time," Macy said as she handed him a card. "If you think of anything, no matter how inconsequential, call me."

Bruce locked gazes with Macy. "You said you've seen the odds beaten before. Do you think my sister is still alive?"

"Do you?"

"I hope so." Bruce looked sincere, but that didn't mean much. Nevada had seen stone-cold killers convince a judge and jury of their innocence.

"Call the number after you've given our conversation some thought."

***

Macy shifted in her seat, ignoring the discomfort in her leg as Nevada drove by Debbie Roberson's house. It was a small one-story brick structure that backed up to woods. "Just the kind of place our boy likes," she said.

Nevada parked and the two got out. She walked up to the mailbox and opened the door, finding a couple of days' worth of mail inside. They followed a gravel path to the front door.

She rang the bell, and both waited for a sign that someone was inside. There was nothing.

"Have a look around back?" he asked.

"I also want to look in the bedrooms by the side windows."

"Sure."

Around the side of the house, she pushed through a tall thicket of shrubs to a window. She studied the ground but saw no signs of a footprint. Still careful not to step directly in front of the window, she rose up on tiptoes and peered into the window.

"It's a bedroom." The bed was unmade, and there was a collection of clothes on the floor. It was messy, but there didn't appear to be any signs of trouble. It could have been her room after several days of working a case.

They walked around the back toward a small patio. Nevada went first, watching the path closely as they approached the brick deck. He held up his fist, indicating for her to stop.

"What is it?" she asked.

He squatted and studied the imprint of an athletic shoe. "Looks to be about a size ten to twelve."

Macy stepped around him and tried the back door. "It's locked." She peered through the window to see a chrome dinette set covered with craft supplies, including paints, a glue gun, and sparkles. "No signs of trouble. Debbie could have blown off work and gone on a trip."

"I've got basic forensic equipment in the car. I can make a plaster cast of the shoe impression. It might be overkill, but better safe than sorry, especially if the weather turns bad."

"After you make the cast, let's head over to the park and see if anything new has developed. I'd also like to track down her roommate, who might have a better idea of what Debbie's been doing."

***

The sun overhead was bright when Macy followed Nevada in her own vehicle to the park where Debbie Roberson's car had been found. They had opted to take separate cars, knowing the investigation at this stage could take them in different directions.

Neither was sure where this development would lead, or if it were even connected at all to their investigation. But the red rope found in the trunk was a significant warning flag that couldn't be ignored.

They had at least three hours of daylight remaining today, which would be a big help if a preliminary search of the park's surrounding woods needed to be conducted.

Nevada's SUV pulled into the park's entrance next to a muddied red SUV with a gray magnetic sign on the side reading **WILDERNESS EXPERIENCE**. The back tailgate was open, and it was loaded with survival gear.

Macy grabbed her FBI windbreaker from the back of her car. On the other side of the lot, Bennett was talking to two young hikers.

By the time Macy crossed the lot, Ellis Carter was out of her vehicle and talking to Nevada. The two appeared to be discussing the trail and Roberson's vehicle.

Macy walked up and offered her hand to Ellis. "What brings you here?"

"I texted her," Nevada said. "She works with the search and rescue teams. Whenever we have a lost hiker, Ellis goes out."

"Are you sure that's wise, given her connection to the case?" Macy asked.

"She's the expert. If anyone can be found in those woods, it's her."

"And doing something makes me feel less like a victim," Ellis said.

Macy understood that sentiment all too well. "Nevada, do you really think it's as simple as Debbie getting lost on a hike?"

Nevada looked at his cousin. "Ellis is the expert on the trail."

"The last few days have been near perfect and would attract hikers." Ellis glanced up at the mountains behind them. "That trail starts off easy and can lure you into thinking it's a piece of cake. She could have gone up it, been fooled, and found herself in trouble."

"Fall into one of the hollows up there and you won't get any cell service," Nevada said. "A hike gone wrong would explain a lot."

"What's there to explain?" Ellis asked.

Nevada didn't hesitate to add, "Macy believes Debbie Roberson is the type of woman our offender would take."

Ellis stilled for a beat. "The man who came after me?"

"Yes," Nevada said.

Ellis rolled her head from side to side and glanced off at a distant mountain before she nodded. "Oh, hell yeah, I'll search this trail for you. Nothing would give me more pleasure than to help catch this guy." She checked her watch. "I can be back in a few hours."

"I'll go with you." Nevada wasn't a man to let his cousin make that hike alone and unarmed.

"It makes sense that you search the trail and eliminate that possibility," Macy said, looking at the car and the mountain. "I'll text my forensic artist, Special Agent Spencer, and tell her to expect you tomorrow morning instead of this afternoon." She was typing before Ellis could answer.

"Good," Nevada said.

Agent Spencer texted Macy back almost immediately with a curt, Understood.

"I'll change," Nevada said. "I have gear in my car."

"Burning daylight, cuz," Ellis said.

The crow's feet etched near the corners of his eyes deepened when he smiled at Ellis. "I hope I can still keep up with you."

"Bet you can't," she said.

As he walked away, Macy asked Ellis, "Tell me about the search and rescue crew."

"We're based in Harrisonburg and serve the central valley area. When the sheriff's office has a lost person, they call us, and then I put out a call for certified search volunteers."

"And you've worked with Nevada before?"

"A few times when we needed an extra hand. He used to be part of the search crew when he was in college. Last week Mike helped me find an elderly dementia patient who'd walked out the back door of the Deep Run assisted living facility. It was cold as hell, but Nevada stayed with me until we found the man sitting on a fallen tree two miles away without a stitch of clothing on."

"Did the facility say how the man got out?"

"They're investigating."

Nevada returned still wearing his ball cap, but he'd pulled on a lightweight sweatshirt and changed into a pair of well-worn hiking boots. He hefted a small backpack of survival gear.

"Did anyone suggest that Debbie could be suicidal?" Macy asked Nevada.

"I don't know," he said.

"How cold has it been here the last few nights?" Macy asked.

"Midthirties," Ellis said. "Cold enough to freeze to death without the right gear."

The trio crossed the lot toward Debbie's vehicle, a blue 2008 Chevrolet sedan. She searched around the vehicle for footprints or signs of a struggle. There were footprints, but none appeared to be a man's athletic shoe. She snapped pictures with her phone.

"There are tire prints by Roberson's vehicle," Nevada said. "Looks like someone parked right next to her."

"I can take casts while you two are on the trail." Macy worked her fingers into latex gloves and eased open the trunk, which the deputy had opened earlier. Lying in the center of the trunk was a coil of red rope. "We might end up with a random collection of impressions, but maybe in this case we are on to something."

Ellis stared at the rope and absently rubbed her fingers over her wrist. The color drained from her face.

"Don't look at it," Macy said. "Focus on the mountain. You can hike that mountain and right now, I can't. I'll take care of this."

"It shouldn't upset me," Ellis said.

"We've got to get moving, Ellis," Nevada said.

Ellis turned away from the trunk.

"Good luck on the trail," Macy said.

Nevada glanced up toward the sun. "I'll keep you posted."

As Nevada and Ellis walked toward the trail, Macy snapped more pictures of the car and the area around it. The car appeared to be decently maintained. No dents or scratches and no signs that anyone had tried to break inside.

Occasionally, she paused to make notes on her legal pad, knowing it could be months at least before she would present these pictures and the contextual detail to a judge or jury.

After the photos, she was back at her vehicle and opening a gray plastic tub she kept in the trunk. Two days ago, in anticipation of this trip, she had freshly stocked it with forensic supplies she could use during the investigation.

She grabbed a plaster kit designed to capture the tire track and carefully mixed up the powder with water. She moved quickly to the only really defined strip of tire treads and poured the mixture into the imprint, waiting the fifteen minutes for it to set. She collected and bagged it.

As she rose, pain shot up her leg. She paused, curling her fingers into a fist, as she waited for it to subside.

"Damn it," she muttered.

Macy had the chops to do the work. But she worried that the pain coupled with diminished stamina, not to mention the damn sleeplessness, would be her undoing.

CHAPTER FIFTEEN

Tuesday, November 19, 4:15 p.m.

As Bennett crossed the park's parking lot toward Macy, the officer's mirrored sunglasses tossed back Macy's reflection. Macy figured she and Bennett were about the same age, but in so many respects their lives were worlds apart. When Macy had been juggling high school graduation and college, Bennett was already a mother. Macy had lived at a dozen addresses in the last decade, while the deputy still lived in the house she grew up in.

"Do you find it odd that Ms. Roberson didn't lock her car?" Macy asked.

"Not everyone around here locks their front doors or cars. I know it must be different in the big city."

"Do you lock your front door on your house?" Macy asked.

"Damn straight." The deputy slid her long hand into a latex glove. "I can't sleep with an unlocked door, Mayberry or not."

"Working in law enforcement does challenge your faith in your fellow man."

Bennett pulled on the second glove. "I have a son and a mother to protect. I trust no one when it comes to them." The deputy eyed Macy with a long stare and then lifted her shades. "Let's have a look inside the car."

As Macy gloved up, Sullivan arrived, and Bennett instructed him to monitor the perimeter.

Macy opened the front door of the car and studied the interior. The bucket seats were made of black faux leather with cracks on the driver's seat. The steering wheel was worn in spots, and two of the radio buttons were missing. The glove box was crammed full of extra fast-food napkins, a tire gauge, and a worn owner's manual still in its original plastic sleeve. Coins filled the drink holder, and on the floorboard of the car was a plastic grocery bag containing a jar of peanut butter and a loaf of white bread. The receipt inside the bag read LUCKY'S, 11/16/19, 9:07 P.M.

"Lucky's?" Macy asked.

"It's a convenience store close to the highway near your motel room."

"Hopefully, they have surveillance tape."

"I'll call now and tell them to hold whatever they have."

While Bennett made her call, Macy patted her hand under the passenger seat but found nothing. A search under the driver's seat revealed Debbie's purse, as had been reported. It was tucked out of sight.

It was never smart to leave a purse in a locked vehicle, let alone in an unsecured one. Women did it all the time thinking thieves never looked under seats or beneath coats or blankets on the seat. Most didn't realize there was always someone watching parking places. As soon as the driver walked away, thieves gained entrance using a rock or hammer and snatched the valuables so carefully tucked away.

The worn purse was outfitted with a half dozen zippered pockets. The largest compartment held Debbie's wallet, which contained no cash but all her credit cards.

The bag had been chosen for functionality and not fashion. It was stuffed with a dozen mundane items, including a ring of keys, tampons, rumpled receipts, gum wrappers, condoms, and a small bag of pot.

Macy wasn't going to prejudge the woman on its contents. A twenty-one-year-old virgin who hadn't tried weed was as rare as a unicorn.

There was no sign of Debbie's cell phone. The phone's absence explained why Bennett hadn't been able to track the woman to this location. Someone had either shut the phone off entirely and removed the battery or destroyed the device.

Macy returned to the vehicle, searching for anything unusual. The windows were intact, and there were no pry marks on the doors. She also found no blood or hair fibers on the seat, steering wheel, or door handles.

Bennett tucked her phone back in a pouch on her belt. "I spoke to the store manager. He's holding the tapes for us."

Thinking out loud, Macy said, "Ms. Roberson finishes a three-day shift, and then she stops for groceries, knowing there're no groceries at home."

"She buys only the essentials," Bennett said. "Payday isn't for five more days."

"And she puts it on the card."

"And then she comes face to face with someone who knocks her out and dumps her in the trunk of her car," Bennett said. "He drives here, and transfers her to another vehicle."

"Then why is her purse under the seat?" Macy asked.

"That doesn't strike me as something an assailant would do, but women do it all the time."

"Could she have been meeting someone here? She then crosses paths with a bad guy?"

"Or she knew her attacker." Macy glanced around at the tall trees and mountains. Nevada would be up there for a while. "Let's go to Lucky's and follow up on the video."

"I'll have Sullivan remain on site and keep the area secure."

"Perfect."

"We're lucky," Bennett said. "The manager only keeps the footage for three days and then erases it. He's never had a robbery, and the last time anyone needed to see a recording was when the Pollard boy got drunk after a football game and knocked over a display."

"Good. We don't want to waste time, then." Macy's phone rang. She glanced at the display and recognized her sister's number. Stifling a groan, she stepped away from the car and pulled off her gloves before clearing her voice. "Faith."

Faith McIntyre was her twin sister, a fact she still had trouble wrapping her brain around. She'd always known she was adopted and thought maybe biological siblings might come into her life, but a twin? Really?

"Where are you?" Faith asked. "The reception isn't good."

"I'm at the entrance to a national park in the Shenandoah Valley."

Faith dropped her tone a notch. "I know you want your life back, but are you rushing things?"

Hearing her own doubts echoed back annoyed her. "I'm handling it. You only know the broken and battered me. The real me loves this kind of work."

"You sound tired. How are you feeling?"

Bennett, as if sensing this was a personal call, walked back to her cruiser. "Other than the need for some coffee, I'm fine."

"I don't believe you," Faith said. "The doctor told you not to rush things."

Since Macy's accident, Faith had been there for her. She'd been at the hospital after Macy's emergency surgery and had spoken to the doctors who couldn't say if she would live or die. Her newfound twin had been there when Macy had woken up confused and frightened. She had stuck around during rehab and cried with Macy at the funeral of the young teen mother who had died giving birth to them.

Faith was never too motherly. It was Macy who chafed at being accountable. From her latchkey kid days to her work at the bureau, Macy had always been on her own. This new hovering thing just didn't fit her well. "I'm not rushing anything. For the first time in months, I feel like myself."

A long silence, and then, "I'm calling you again tomorrow."

Macy tipped her head back and pinched the bridge of her nose, reminding herself that Faith wanted to help. She truly cared. "Sure. Call away. But you'll be wasting your time. I'm fine."

"It's my time to waste."

A smile tugged at her lips. "Thanks for checking."

"Anytime."

Macy pocketed the phone, shifted her weight to her right side, and walked toward Bennett. "Let's have a look at the security footage."

"Stay on my tail. I don't want to lose you," Bennett said.

Hearing the challenge, she fired back, "I might not walk fast, but I drive just fine."

In her vehicle, Macy relaxed back into the seat and waited for the discomfort to ease. The docs said the leg just needed time. Unfortunately, that was one thing she didn't have.

She turned on the ignition and followed the deputy's brown-and-white vehicle out of the park toward town, where the small convenience store was located.

She fished three ibuprofen from her backpack, chewing them up for quicker action. With no water to wash down the bitterness, she kept driving. Ten minutes later she felt decent as she pulled into the convenience store parking lot behind the cruiser. She followed Bennett through the door and toward the clerk.

The store was a good size and featured a diner and a small grocery. The clerk behind the counter was a thin man in his early thirties with a thick crop of dark hair that was cut short on the sides but long along the middle. The company's blue smock draped over a white short-sleeved T-shirt. Multicolored tattoos stretched from his wrist past his elbow. A small diamond earring winked in his right ear. His name tag read Bobby.

The clerk smiled when he saw Bennett. "Deputy. I got that footage for you. You're going to be interested to see it."

Bobby sized up Macy, branding her an outsider. "You can see it in the back office if that will help."

"Thanks, Bobby. And this is Special Agent Macy Crow. She's with the FBI."

"FBI? I saw you on the television today during that announcement you made. Get any good tips on the hotline yet?"

"Not yet, but it's early," Macy said.

"So what are we looking for?" Bobby asked.

"I'm looking for Debbie Roberson," Macy said. "She's still missing."

"You think this killer has her?" Bobby asked.

"Hard to tell," Bennett said. "But folks like you helping will make all the difference."

Bobby came out from behind the counter, and they followed him past the snack and chip aisle and beyond the beer coolers to a small office. The neat space featured a desk, a chair, a bulletin board with the month's work schedule, a personalized coffee mug, and four sharpened pencils lined up in a neat row. Front and center was a dated computer running four feeds from the store's security cameras.

Bobby clicked on the upper right image, which showed the front of the store. He backed up the imaging forty-seven hours and hit "Play."

"I didn't realize she was missing until you called. I remember seeing her a couple of days ago, but she looked fine and there was no sign of any trouble."

"What day was she here, Bobby?" Bennett asked.

"Saturday evening. She said she was grabbing a few groceries to get her through the next couple of days until payday. She said her extra money had gone to fixing a flat tire. I offered to float her a few days, but she said she didn't mind peanut butter and jelly sandwiches."

"Did she say how she got the flat?" Macy asked.

Bobby shrugged. "Picked up a nail."

"Was she alone when she came in the store?" Macy asked.

"She was."

"And she didn't appear nervous or upset? Hurt? Sick? Depressed?"

"No, normal Debbie," Bobby said.

"Do you remember where she parked in your lot?" Macy asked, hoping small-town life meant people paid closer attention to details like that.

"As a matter of fact, I do remember. She parked off to the side."

"Any idea why?" Macy asked.

"Because the kids from the high school were here. They take over the parking lot and store when they come through. It was after the postseason football party."

"How did the team do this year?" Macy asked.

Bobby shook his head. "Not well. Ended with a five-and-four season."

"Not like the Dream Team days, right?" Macy prompted.

Bobby grinned. "That season will go down in history," he said.

"Shame about Tobi," Macy said.

"Yeah."

"Did you know her? I mean, seems everyone in Deep Run knows everyone."

"I knew her," Bobby said. "She was nice."

"Did Debbie say if anyone else was in her car?" Bennett asked.

"If there were, she never mentioned it," Bobby said.

Macy sensed Bennett's impatience as Bobby fast-forwarded the video. She leaned in as the footage skimmed back in time to Saturday evening.

Bobby hit "Stop" at the 9:05 p.m. time stamp and then hit "Play." The camera caught a collection of teenagers bustling through the front door. They were laughing, and two were kissing. "That was about the time a few kids tried to buy beer, but I carded them all. I'm not going to lose my liquor license over a couple of kids. I don't care if they are on the football team."

Macy imagined that comment was for the deputy's benefit. Both women kept their gazes on the black-and-white feed and watched as Debbie, dressed in pastel scrubs, entered the store. They watched her grab peanut butter and bread and head directly to the register. She spoke to the clerk briefly and then exited the store.

"That's Debbie Roberson," Bennett said.

Macy studied the woman's face, looking for signs of stress, worry, or even happiness, as if she were glad to see someone. Just as Debbie moved offscreen, her expression seemed to change. "Can you back that up?" Macy asked.

"Sure."

"Play it in slow motion." As the scene unfolded again, Macy watched as Debbie exited the store and her eyes shifted from casual to alert. She had seen something or someone. "Do you have a camera that covers this area?" Macy pointed to the top right corner of the screen.

"Not totally, but camera three records from a different angle." He clicked on camera three, and the trio watched it catch the edge of a blue four-door Ford Focus. A man rose up out of the car, but his head was downcast, making it impossible to see his face.

"Do you know who that is?" Macy asked Bennett.

"No."

"What about you, Bobby? Did you see the guy?"

"No. I was trying to make sure the teenagers didn't walk out with half the store."

"Would any of those kids have been out in the parking lot about that time?" Macy asked.

"Sure. There were at least a dozen."

"Do you have names, Bobby?" Bennett asked.

"Well, there was the Wyatt boy. And the Piper brothers and the Donovan kid."

"Tyler. Tyler Wyatt was out there?" Bennett asked.

"Yeah, with his girlfriend, Amy Meadow."

Macy wrote down the names. "Anyone else you remember?"

"No, but talk to Tyler or Amy. They're the king and queen of the high school and know everyone."

"Wasn't there a Wyatt on the Dream Team?" Macy asked.

"That would be Kevin. Tyler's older brother."

"Older brother? That's a big age gap."

"I guess it happens."

"How long have you worked here, Bobby?" Macy asked.

"Sixteen years. My dad owns the place."

"So you've seen a lot of kids come and go."

"Sure."

"Remember Cindy Shaw?"

He nodded. "Haven't heard that name in a long time."

"I hear she was friends with Tobi," Macy prompted.

"I don't know if I'd say they were friends, but they hung out sometimes."

"Can we get a copy of all the footage you have?" Bennett asked. "I want to review everything."

He dug a thumb drive from his pocket. "I thought you might ask, so here you go."

"Thanks, Bobby." Macy offered the thumb drive to Bennett, but the deputy held up her hand, deferring to Macy. She pocketed the thumb drive. "I'll double back if I have more questions."

"Sure. I'm here just about all the time."

Outside the store, Bennett said, "I thought we were here to talk about Debbie."

"We are, but I can't lose sight of the fact I'm here for Tobi and the rape victims. Don't underestimate a guy like Bobby and what he notices. How do we get to the Wyatts' house?"

"Follow me. Amy Meadow's family lives one street over, so we have a chance of seeing them both."

"Lead the way."

Macy followed the deputy's marked vehicle across the small town and around the university toward the western edge. The farther west they drove, the sparser the developments became. She then saw brick pillars marking the entrance to a fairly recent community.

They wove through the neighborhood, and the deputy parked in front of a two-story brick home set back from the road on an acre lot.

Macy opened the back of her vehicle and removed a buccal DNA test kit. She tucked the sealed glass vial containing a swab in her jacket pocket before joining Bennett by the mailbox. Streetlights, sensing the approaching dusk, had begun to flicker on.

"This has to be one of the most affluent sections of town," Macy said.

"It's where the new money lives. Old money is a little farther out west toward the mountains, where you find the large horse farms."

"And this is the home of Tyler Wyatt?"

"It is. His older brother, Kevin, also lives here part time. He is an attorney who splits his time between here and Washington, DC."

"Kevin Wyatt has a long commute," Macy said.

"Kevin has stayed close to home since his dad died. He thinks it's important for his little brother that he's present."

"What about the boys' mother?" Macy asked.

"She's always traveled a lot. Not home much." Bennett shifted her stance. "His family and the Shaws can probably trace their roots back to the beginning of this town."

"The Shaws and Wyatts are related?"

"Cousins of some kind."

"Given their economic differences, I'm assuming they weren't close."

"The families were not, but Bruce and Kevin got pretty tight when they played ball."

"And now?"

"I don't know," Bennett said.

"You know a lot about this family."

"I grew up in the area. And Tyler Wyatt is no stranger to the sheriff's department. He received a new car for his sixteenth birthday and was clocked going over one hundred miles an hour two days later. He also was caught drunk at one of the football games. In both cases, his brother hired an attorney."

"What was his brother like in high school?"

"Much the same."

"Well, let's hope Tyler was paying attention at the convenience store on Saturday night."

"He's very intelligent. Just bored and spoiled."

Macy did not grow up in a world where high-dollar attorneys rode to the rescue. Lower-middle-class and poor kids did jail time on lesser charges. Feeling an old chip on her shoulder, she pushed the emotion aside and rang the bell.

Steady, even footsteps echoed in the house, and seconds later the door opened to a tall man dressed in a charcoal-gray suit, a white monogramed dress shirt, and a loosened red tie. His prematurely gray hair was brushed back away from a round face.

"Deputy Bennett," Kevin said. "This is a surprise."

"Mr. Wyatt, is Tyler home?"

"What's he done?" Kevin asked.

"Nothing. He happened to be in Lucky's convenience store on Saturday night, and we think he and Amy might have seen something."

"Seen what?"

"That's what we're trying to find out," Macy said as she pulled her FBI badge from her breast pocket and introduced herself. "He might be a big help to us."

Kevin gripped the doorknob before stepping aside and inviting them into the foyer. "Can you tell me what this is about?"

"A woman is missing," Bennett said. "We know from surveillance footage that your brother and Debbie Roberson were in the parking lot at the same time. We're hoping Tyler saw something."

Kevin's jaw worked at the joints as if he were weighing the pros and cons. Finally, the pros appeared to win. "Tyler, come downstairs." A door opened, and the faint bass beat of music grew louder.

"Coming," Tyler said.

"Are you Tyler's legal guardian?" Macy asked.

"Our mother travels a great deal, and I step in when she's gone. I have full legal authority, then, when it comes to Tyler."

"What does your mother do for a living?" Macy asked.

"She travels. For pleasure," Kevin said.

"Sounds like fun," Macy said.

"It is, for her."

Meaning it wasn't for Tyler and Kevin. "How often do you commute in from DC?"

"A few times a week."

"That's rough," Macy said. "Traffic never lets up."

"Yes, indeed."

"Does your family own the Wyatt barn?" she asked.

"No. My father sold it almost thirty years ago, but the name has stuck."

"You heard about the recent discovery at the barn?"

"I did."

"Did you know Tobi?" Macy asked.

"Knew of her, but we never spoke."

"Band geek versus Dream Team kind of thing?"

"High school kids can be very judgmental. I wish I'd been kinder to her."

"You weren't nice to her?" Macy asked.

"Most of the football players, including me that year, were too stuck up for their own good."

Heavier footsteps thudded across the upstairs floor before Tyler appeared at the top of the stairs. Tall like his brother, he was wiry and strong. Likely the same build his older brother had enjoyed at that age before long hours at the office and stress had caught up.

When Tyler saw Bennett, his face flushed a faint pink as if he were mentally ticking through what he had done recently that would warrant a visit from the law.

"What's up, Kevin?" Tyler asked.

"You're not in trouble," Kevin said. "The police have questions about a missing woman."

"Tyler," Bennett said. "You and Amy were at Lucky's on Saturday night."

"Yeah. Everyone was there, even Matt," Tyler said.

"Matt?" Macy asked.

Bennett's frown deepened. "Matt is my son. He's fourteen."

Macy sensed the deputy's frustration over this new bit of information about a curfew-breaking son. "Continue, Tyler."

"We were all getting food after the rally at the high school."

"Tyler, did you see Debbie Roberson?" Macy asked.

"Yeah."

"How did you know her?" Macy asked.

"She worked at the assisted living place where my grandmother lived until she died. Grandma liked her. She was nice."

"Did you two speak?" Macy asked.

"Yeah. I said hi and so did she. She was wearing her scrubs and looked like she just got off work."

"Did anyone else speak to her?" Macy asked.

"Yeah. A guy. He used to work at the old folks' home, too. I think his name is Rafe."

Bennett shifted her stance as she reached for her phone and typed in a name. When an image came up, she showed it to the boy. "This him?"

Tyler studied the picture. "Yeah. That's him."

"Rafe Younger," Bennett said.

"Did Younger say anything to Debbie?" Macy asked.

"I wasn't really paying attention. But she laughed when he spoke to her. She got in her car and left."

"What did Younger do?"

"Drove off, I guess," Tyler said. "I don't know. I didn't sense anything odd."

"Did you see anyone else around Ms. Roberson?" Macy asked.

"No. But I wasn't paying attention. Matt had just—" He glanced toward the deputy and stopped.

"Matt just what?" Bennett asked calmly. "I'm not mad, seriously."

"Nothing," the boy said.

Bennett looked as if she wanted to press the matter, but let it go. "Okay."

"Is that all the questions you have?" Kevin asked.

Macy thanked both Kevin and Tyler Wyatt, but as she turned, she asked Kevin, almost as an aside, "What about Cindy Shaw? You must have known her. A cousin, right?"

"The two families never mixed, but yes, she was a cousin."

"Why didn't the families mix?"

"My aunt was a meth addict. And Cindy was following the same path as her mother," Kevin said.

"And Bruce?"

"He tried to be a good brother to Cindy, but his life was football. She finally realized that and took off."

"And Bruce stayed."

"His future was here. He moved in with my family the second half of senior year."

"I hear Cindy was really into the bonfires," Macy said.

"The bonfires?"

Macy smiled. "You know, the big pregame events that were a good luck ritual for the Dream Team. Seems to me if you mix teenagers, booze, and hormones, it's a recipe for something to happen."

"I don't understand your meaning," he said carefully.

"Did anyone ever get hurt at those shindigs?"

He glanced quickly at the deputy but then shook his head. "Not that I remember."

Macy reached in her breast pocket and pulled out the cylinder holding a buccal swab. "Would you allow me to swab the inside of your cheek? I'm gathering samples from every male who might have been in contact with Tobi those last days. It's really just to eliminate you so I can move on to the real suspects."

He hesitated. "How will DNA help you find Tobi's killer?"

"I'm not sure it will, but we're being proactive with the DNA testing given the recent news about the untested rape kits. It's more of a PR thing."

"I still don't see how I figure into the equation."

"Exactly. And the sooner I don't have to look in your direction, the better for us both. It'll only take a second. I promise." He was an attorney and knew he could say no, and if she wanted to press, she'd have to get a court order.

"I'll check with my attorney. If he gives the go ahead, I'd be glad to."

"Why not just do it now?" Macy asked.

Kevin smiled. "I never deal directly with the cops even if I have a speeding ticket."

Macy reminded herself that even innocent men were cautious. "Next time I see you, I'll ask."

"I'm sure he'll be fine with it. What's going on with Debbie Roberson?" Kevin asked.

"Hopefully it's all a false alarm, and she'll show up just fine," Macy offered. "Thank you for your time."

Bennett rattled her keys as they moved toward their cars. "You believe Tobi's killer is wrapped up in the Dream Team?"

When they reached Macy's car, she drew a line under her notes and then jotted Kevin Wyatt's name down. "I have no idea. But I have three unsolved rape cases and a murder from the year this Dream Team went all the way."

Bennett's brow knotted. "The team received a lot of exposure, which in turn brought to town a lot of people who weren't normally here."

"How can I find Rafe Younger?" Macy asked.

"I'll see if I can track him down."

"I'd like to speak to Debbie's mother, too," Macy said.

"Special Agent Crow, you're here to investigate the rapes and murder, not this case."

"Deputy, have you ever had one of those moments when a word you wish to recall is on the tip of your tongue, but for the life of you it remains out of reach?"

"Sure."

"When I get that feeling with a case, I don't ignore it. In fact, I run with it until that funny feeling goes away."

"What are you saying?"

"I've got that feeling now."

"You think Debbie's case is related to Tobi's?"

"It makes no logical sense, but I can't shake the feeling."

"What if you're wrong?"

She thought for a moment and lightly touched the side of her nose. "I rarely am."

CHAPTER SIXTEEN

Tuesday, November 19, 5:00 p.m.

As Bennett parked her cruiser behind Macy's car in front of the Roberson's small brick rancher, Macy finished checking her emails and tucked her phone away. She looked up at the Roberson's two-story house. It was painted in white and was chipped in several spots. The lawn was neatly raked with several mature trees still clinging to a few orange and gold leaves. A row of boxwoods ran along the front of the house in a freshly mulched bed.

Out of her car, Bennett settled her hat on her head and drew in a breath. "I don't want to make a death notification to this woman."

Macy had made a few death notifications, and each had left an indelible image in its own way. "I can never decide which reaction is worse. The stony silence of an elderly woman who's lost her forty-year-old son or the hysterical tears of a man who's learned his runaway daughter has been murdered."

"How do you handle it?"

"Tuck the feelings away in a small box. Later, when you have time, you can deal with them." Macy rang the bell. "Don't even think about death notifications right now. Mrs. Roberson will sense it. As far as we know, Debbie is alive and well."

"Do you really believe that?"

Instead of answering, Macy notched back her shoulders. "Let me ask the questions."

"Sure."

When no one came to the door, Macy rang again. This time a dog's bark echoed in the house. Bennett's gun belt creaked several times as she shifted her stance.

Footsteps echoed in the house, along with a soft command for the dog to be quiet. The door snapped open to a tall, thin woman wearing worn jeans, a football sweatshirt, and her hair pulled into a ponytail.

"Deputy Bennett," the woman said.

"Mrs. Roberson. Is your husband here?"

"Yes, he's in the TV room. You'll have to go in there if you want to speak to him."

"Mr. Roberson has ALS," Bennett explained to Macy. "Mrs. Roberson, this is Special Agent Macy Crow from the FBI."

"FBI." Her brow knotted as if she knew a federal presence meant the scope of the case had grown. "Tell me that you've found my Debbie," Martha said.

"We have not," Macy said. "But we'd like to talk to you and your husband."

"Nothing? That's good news, right?"

"I don't know what it means, ma'am," Macy said gently. "May we come inside?"

"Of course." The woman stepped aside and led them down a small hallway to a room outfitted with a hospital bed and a large nightstand crammed with medicines. Across from the bed, a large television playing a game show sat on an old dresser.

In the bed lay a man propped up on pillows with a thick quilt tucked up almost to his chin. Long and broad shouldered, he had been a big man before the disease had chewed away his nerve endings, had robbed him of movement and left him with a thin, withered frame.

Behind the hollowed features were alert, dark eyes that regarded Macy with keen interest. He moved his lips, but only a garbled sound could be slightly heard.

"Ronnie," Martha said, "you remember Deputy Bennett. With her today is Special Agent Macy Crow with the FBI."

His gaze narrowed as he searched Macy's face.

"Good to meet you, sir." Macy took his cool hand and shook it. After the HNR, most of the hospital staff had been great, but there were a few doctors and a physical therapist who had treated her like a potted plant. It was a life lesson that would forever change how she treated the injured. They were crippled, but damn sure not pathetic.

Mr. Roberson's fingers flickered as he tried to squeeze her hand in response.

"Sheriff Nevada requested an FBI agent to investigate a different matter. I happened to be along with Deputy Bennett when we received your call."

The fingers twitched.

Macy directed her question to the Robersons. "When did you last see Debbie?"

"It's been a week," Martha said. "She's good about coming by, but sometimes all this here gets to be too much. She and her dad are very close and it's hard. Last week she was upset, so I told her to take a break and not visit for a couple of weeks. She didn't like the idea of that, but I insisted." Martha looked to her husband. "She was supposed to call every day, but I haven't spoken to her since Friday night."

"No second-guessing, Mrs. Roberson," Macy said. "That's only going to chew you up inside."

The older woman dug a tissue from her pocket and dabbed the corners of her eyes. "You're right."

"Was there anyone in her life who was a problem for her? Threats, unwanted gifts, visits that felt more like stalking?"

"I've been thinking about that all night. And I remember her saying she thought she saw a man outside her house one night a few weeks ago."

"Did she recognize who it was?" Macy asked.

"No. She said he was wearing a dark hoodie and his face was shadowed. He had what looked like a notebook in his hand."

Some killers stalked their victims before they committed their crimes. In some cases they spent weeks or even months gathering information about habits, patterns, and schedules. "Did she ever see him again?"

"If she did, she didn't tell me."

Bennett shifted her stance. "She never called in a report to my office."

Maybe the man on the street corner was no one. And if it had been the man who took her, he might have been spooked after being spotted. Or maybe he was more careful with his reconnaissance.

"Debbie was also dating a new guy. She wouldn't tell me his name so I wouldn't make a big thing of it. She's been through a lot with her divorce. Ronnie and me just want her to be happy."

"That's normal for a parent to want the best for their child, Mr. and Mrs. Roberson," Macy said. "When did she go on this date?"

"A few weeks ago, I guess."

"Did she know Rafe Younger?" Macy asked.

Martha frowned. "Rafe and she were a passing thing. I think the two were both on the rebound and lonely. She moved on from Rafe, and I'm glad."

"Why?"

"He can't hold a job. And he likes to drink. Not a good combination."

"What do you know about Rafe?" Macy asked.

"He worked with Debbie at the assisted living place."

"And he lives nearby?" Macy asked.

"Last I heard, he was living in a tiny place just west of here. Do you think Rafe took Debbie?"

"He was seen at Lucky's on Saturday the same time Debbie was, but so far that's all I have. They simply could have bumped into each other. What about handymen? Cable guy? Delivery man?"

"Nothing that she told me about." Martha squeezed her husband's hand. "And we've racked our brains for any kind of clue."

"Mrs. Roberson, do you have Rafe's phone number?" Macy asked. "Or an address?"

"No. Debbie said his phone was disconnected and he moved around a lot."

Mr. Roberson's face twisted in a mixture of frustration, sadness, and futility. He tried to speak, but again it was garbled. His wife patted him on the hand. "Ronnie, I'm going to show these ladies some pictures of Debbie. We'll be right back."

His eyes cut to his wife. He knew she was shielding him from this stress. Finally, he nodded, and Martha led them down the hallway toward the front door.

"There are no pictures," she whispered. "But I can't bear to have any stressful conversation in front of him. It upsets him and he only ends up getting sicker."

"Is that why you asked Debbie to take a little time off?" Macy asked.

"Debbie wanted to put her father in the Deep Run assisted living facility. I didn't agree, and we argued. I'm not sending my husband away from the only home he's had. He grew up in this house. He needs me."

"And your daughter saw it differently?" Macy asked.

"She did. She works at the facility and thought she could negotiate the price down. Even with a discount, I couldn't afford it. Not that I would even if I could."

"Mrs. Roberson," Bennett said, "we did find your daughter's car at the state park entrance. We found her purse and keys, but there was no sign of her. What would she have been doing there?"

"Hiking. She loves those woods. She likes being outside. Is it good or bad that you found her car?"

"It's a starting point," Bennett said. "She was last seen at the convenience store, and now we have her car."

Martha took Bennett's hand in hers. "Find my daughter. I know Ronnie and I weren't kind to you when you pulled him over a few years ago. I know we even made it worse for you when we filed a complaint, but please help us."

"I swore to do my job, Mrs. Roberson, and that is exactly what I'm going to do," Bennett said.

Tears glistened in the woman's eyes as she nodded and released the deputy's hand.

As Bennett stepped outside, Macy handed her business card to Martha. "If you think of anything, no matter how small, call me."

"What if I can't?"

"Don't give up," Macy said.

Macy followed Bennett outside and toward their cars. "What happened with Mr. Roberson?"

"I arrested him for drunk driving four years ago. He became belligerent and tried to hit me. I defended myself and he filed charges. Dashcam footage backed up my story. The judge sentenced him to thirty days in jail."

"Does he have a history of violence?"

"He'd never been arrested before."

"What did he do before he got sick?"

"He taught history at Valley High School for twenty-five years."

"While Tobi Turner was there?"

"Yes."

***

The mask rubbed against the stubble on his face as he caressed the soft skin of her neck. He loved the way her bruises matured from faint red marks to deep purple. Soon they would grow angrier and band around her slender neck like a collar.

Now that he was alone with her, a sense of power raced through his body, and the pressures of the world didn't feel so overwhelming.

Her eyes fluttered open. It took several moments for her gaze to focus on him and register where she was. When she did, she flinched and tried to scurry away. A swift knee placed adeptly on her abdomen stopped her retreat and held her firmly in place.

She knew she was trapped. She knew she was going to die, and she was terrified.

"You shouldn't be afraid now," he said. "You know what's coming next. This is our special time together."

"Please." Her voice was raspy, like rough sandpaper.

He'd done his share of begging, pleading, and borrowing from those who mattered most of his life, and it felt so damn good to be on the receiving end. "Please what?" he asked.

"Please, let me go. I won't tell. *Please.*"

He rubbed his index finger over her lips. "I love it when you beg."

CHAPTER SEVENTEEN

Tuesday, November 19, 6:00 p.m.

The sun had just set and the temperature was dropping on the trail, but Nevada and Ellis were moving at a good clip. They'd discovered signs of bears and deer but nothing suggesting that Debbie Roberson had hiked this way. Nevada was an expert at tracking people, and he could tell this trail had been well traveled in the last few days. If Debbie Roberson or anyone else had trekked this path coerced, there was no way of knowing if any of the shoe depressions in the moist soil, bent leaves, possible signs of a struggle, or other clues had been left by Debbie.

With each passing minute, Nevada believed more strongly that she had never entered the park. "A shelter is up ahead. Let's take a break and regroup."

"The trail is wet and the climbing is harder. Do you really think she made it this far?" Ellis asked.

"No. I don't." He glanced up through the thinning canopy of brown, yellow, and red leaves toward the bright light of the half moon. "But let's finish it."

"Will do."

As they approached the open shelter, he shrugged his backpack off and set it down. Without a word, he and Ellis sat, both glad to be off their feet, if only for a few minutes. He reached in the side pocket of his pack and pulled out a water bottle and a PowerBar. Ellis did the same, and for several minutes they ate in silence.

Finally, he pulled out the map of the park and a flashlight and studied the primary trail snaking up and around the mountain. If Debbie had stayed the course, she could conceivably have looped around to the other side and tried to reach her car a different way. There was still a slim chance she'd fallen or was injured. "If we keep going, we could finish the trail in an hour."

"If Ms. Roberson is truly lost, she could've taken any number of the side trails and followed them."

"Or she could be moving between the trails and going in circles."

Nevada drained his water bottle and closed his eyes, trying to picture where she could have gone. He did the same when he tracked fugitives. Mentally, he ran pathways, escape routes, and the proverbial trapdoors that his prey might use. Debbie wasn't his prey, of course, but he hunted her just the same.

"I still can't believe you gave up the bureau for this kind of work. It's important, but, Nevada, you were making a difference."

"It was time for a change. And I'm still making a difference."

"I'll grant that you're good for Deep Run. But what prompted this?"

"I like the solitude."

"You can take the boy out of the country, but not the country out of the boy? Is that what you're saying?"

"Something like that."

"That's bullshit." She rubbed a callus on her palm. "And please tell me you didn't give it all up for me."

"Sorry, it's not about you, Ellis."

"Are you sure? I'll never forget the look in your eyes last summer when I told you about what happened to me." They'd gone out for dinner and drinks, and she'd had too much wine. If she hadn't been more than a little drunk, he doubted she'd ever have told him. "I've never seen such anger."

He cracked the knuckles on his right hand. "I'm going to find this guy, Ellie."

"And then what? You're going to strap on that starched uniform for the next twenty years?"

"One hurdle at a time, Ellie."

"Is this about Macy Crow?" she asked.

"What do you mean?"

"Please. When she's close, you all but vibrate with energy. Are you two an item?"

"No."

She laughed, wagging her finger at him. She knew instantly she'd caught him in a lie. "You were and still want to be. Is this case your way of sending her flowers?"

The truth irritated him. "You're being a pain in my ass, Ellie."

She punched him in the shoulder just like she had when she was a kid. "For what it's worth, I like her. And I hope it works out."

He didn't respond, unwilling to acknowledge a hope that was more a pipe dream than a possibility.

"I guess if you and Macy do hook up, you'll definitely leave Deep Run."

He appreciated the peace of this place. It was far from the chaos of Washington, DC, which never stopped moving. Out here he had no immediate neighbors and could take a piss off his back porch anytime he liked. And at night the sky was full of breathtaking stars that couldn't be seen from a city filled with lights. But Ellie was right. Once he caught this guy and Macy left, it would be hard to stay put.

"I'm committed to a two-year term," he said.

"Okay, and then you'll leave." She shook her head. "I'd like to see Macy stay. Maybe when she's done proving to herself whatever it is she needs to prove, she might settle down. That girl is carrying a wagonload of baggage."

Again, the assessment was dead on. Nevada was beginning to believe his cousin would have made a better detective than he ever could be.

The crunch of footsteps on the trail had them both standing. Nevada unholstered his Glock. As isolated as the woods appeared, it was more crowded than most realized.

He stepped out of the shelter to see a young couple making their way down the trail. They both wore mud-splattered clothes and boots. When they spotted him, they stopped, and the female took a step back behind the male.

"We're search and rescue," Nevada said. He removed Debbie's picture from his pocket. "Have you seen her?"

The male approached slowly and studied the image. "We haven't seen anyone on the trail."

The female approached, looked at the picture, and shook her head. "No, sorry."

"How long have you been on the trail?"

"Since early yesterday," the woman said. "We camped out on the top of the mountain and are making our way down the front side."

"How did you enter the trail?" Nevada asked.

"The north side. We wanted to hike the entire loop."

They had entered the park from the opposite direction. "And no signs of anyone?" he asked.

"Not in the last couple of hours. It's been real quiet, which is unusual. It's busy up here in the fall."

"What about earlier? Did you see anything in the woods that caught your attention? Clothing? A discarded shoe? Trash that didn't look right?"

"Nothing out of the ordinary," the man said.

"What about sounds? Anything that seemed off?"

"No, unless you count the bear we ran into. Thankfully, it was a young one and not interested in us." Dark eyes narrowed. "Are you a cop? You sound like a cop."

"I'm the sheriff of Deep Run. But I'm a search and rescue guy right now, trying to do a job."

"We didn't see anything," the woman repeated. "But if we do, can we call your offices?"

"Yes, please."

He believed the couple hadn't seen Debbie, but neither had they been *looking* for her. An untrained eye out here could easily miss signs of her presence. After he collected their contact information, he said, "When you get to the base of the hill, there will be one of my deputies. If you see anything, report it to him."

"Sure, no problem," the male said.

"Thanks," he said.

The couple continued down the trail.

"We're heading up the mountain, aren't we?" Ellis asked.

"I am."

"Which means I am," Ellis said. "Where you go, I go."

"There's a ninety percent chance that Debbie Roberson never set foot in this park," Nevada said.

***

Macy and Bennett arrived at the Shady Grove Real Estate offices minutes after seven to interview the third rape victim, Rebecca Kennedy. An early wake-up call that morning coupled with the nonstop investigation was taking a toll.

Macy had no time to be tired, so she would suck it up. She would get her old life back even if it killed her.

The Shady Grove Real Estate facility was a one-story building with a small front porch and a couple of inviting rockers beside a sign that read **WE DON'T JUST SELL HOUSES; WE CREATE HOMES.** The windows were large and inviting, and the place still had a new-building look that would surely fade soon.

They knew Rebecca worked late hours but hadn't called ahead to announce their visit. Macy didn't want to give Rebecca time to fabricate a reason to avoid an interview.

Bennett strode to the front desk, catching the eye of the woman behind the counter closing up for the day. "Jenny, remember me from the self-defense speech I gave at Rotary a few months ago?"

"I do," Jenny said, smiling. "Good memory for names."

"Can you ring Ms. Kennedy and have her come out here? I have a few questions."

"I think she might be finishing up with a client."

"Well, ask her to get to a stopping place and come out front. It's important." Though Bennett rarely raised her voice, her clear, direct tone gave no room for argument. Jenny nodded and quickly ducked around a corner.

"Ms. Kennedy owns this business?" Macy asked.

"Yes, she opened it after she graduated college. She's done very well for herself."

Five minutes later a petite, slim woman came around the corner. Her dark hair was pulled back into a ponytail, and she wore a navy-blue dress and flats. Sadly, she fit the perpetrator's target profile of a pretty young woman. And her small stature would make her easier to subdue.

Macy reached into her jacket pocket and pulled out her badge. "Ms. Kennedy, I'm Special Agent Macy Crow with the FBI. I'd like to ask you a couple of questions."

The woman looked at Bennett and then back at Macy. "Now's not the best time."

"I know it's not ideal, but I'm going to need to hear your story," Macy said.

"I gave a statement to Sheriff Greene when it happened."

"I may be able to get you to recall a detail that can help apprehend the man who assaulted you."

"I'm sorry I didn't come by the offices yesterday. I just couldn't bring myself to face that place."

"We understand," Macy said.

Rebecca crossed her arms. "I saw you on the news this morning, and then I hear Debbie Roberson is missing. What the hell is going on in this town?"

"Is there somewhere private we can talk?"

"It'll have to be quick. I have a client arriving soon. There's a lounge over here." Rebecca led them across the lobby to a small alcove furnished with a small round table and several chairs around it. A large box of tissues sat in the center.

Macy eased into her seat and shifted her weight until she found what might pass for comfortable before removing her legal pad from her backpack. She flipped to a clean page. "Ms. Kennedy, take me back to the night you were attacked. Do you remember what the weather was like?"

"The weather?" Absently, Rebecca fingered the edge of her turtleneck. "It was hot. Really humid."

"It was August, correct?"

"Yes. August 15. I worked a late night at my dad's real estate firm. I was an intern in his office in those days. My parents had separated, and it was my chance to spend time with him." She brushed imaginary lint off her very clean sleeve. "I stopped by the grocery story to pick up a soda and a frozen pizza. I was excited about putting my feet up and watching a movie. I had my mother's house to myself that night, and I was glad for the solitude."

"Where did you buy your soda and pizza?"

"Lucky's market." The same place Debbie had last been seen.

"And did you see anyone in the parking lot or in the store that made you nervous?"

"No."

"Was there anyone else in the store?"

"Just the clerk and me."

"Bobby?" Macy asked.

"Yeah. There was also a couple of the high school kids in the parking lot." A faint smile tugged her lips. "They were comparing fake IDs. Stupid because in those days everyone basically knew who was or wasn't underage."

Macy smiled, hoping it didn't look as strategic as it felt. "I tried to pass off my share of fake IDs as a teenager. Never had any luck."

"Me neither. I still occasionally get carded. It's flattering now." She smiled.

"So where did you go after Lucky's?"

"I drove home and stepped out of the car. I was juggling my bags and keys and trying to get the back door unlocked. I remember feeling really creeped out, like someone was watching me."

"Did you see anyone?"

"No. I even scanned the woods, thinking I'd see someone, but there was no one. I shrugged it off and went inside."

Rebecca grew more somber. "I put the pizza in the oven, took a shower, and when I got out, I ate a slice in front of the television in my room."

"Where was your room?"

"First floor in the back of the house."

Everything she'd said so far fit the pattern of this offender. "I went to bed and fell asleep with the television still on. I startled awake to a hand over my mouth and a man wearing a mask standing over me." She closed her eyes and shuddered.

"I know it's not easy, but help us catch this guy, Ms. Kennedy."

She nodded. "At first I was so stunned I froze, but then I guess the adrenaline kicked in. I tried to bite and kick him. God, he was powerful. The more I fought, the more he seemed to enjoy it. Then he pulled this rope out of nowhere and tied me up."

Macy leaned forward. "The rope wasn't in his hands when you first saw him?"

"I don't think so."

"Close your eyes."

"Why?"

"It might help you remember."

Rebecca closed her eyes.

"You were lying in your bed. Was there air-conditioning?"

"Yes. I could hear it humming."

"Good. The sheets are soft. And then you feel a man on top of you? Did you get a sense of his size?"

"He felt huge." Her brow knotted. "His feet extended over the edge of the bed."

"You said he was wearing a ski mask."

"Yes. It was black with a tight weave. I could only see his eyes and a little bit of his mouth. The openings were trimmed in red."

"What color was the skin you saw around the eyes and mouth? Was he a Caucasian? African American?"

"He was a white guy." Her lip quivered. "This is going to sound weird, but he smelled nice."

"How did he smell?"

"It was a spicy cologne. I smelled it once on a guy years later and nearly freaked out. But I got up the nerve to ask him the brand."

"And?"

"He said it was called Beacon. I even went to the local mall and found a bottle of it. I smelled the tester at the counter and started crying. The woman must have thought I was nuts."

Macy noted both details in her pad. "Go on."

"He yanked up my nightgown and was quickly inside me. He kept staring at me but had a weird look in his eyes."

"What color were his eyes?" Macy asked.

"Blue."

"Why did they look weird?"

"Honestly, he looked sad." She shook her head. "Anyway, he finished pretty quick and then he tugged up his pants. I thought he was finished and was going to leave. But he wrapped his hands around my neck. He tightened his grip, and I started gasping for air."

"How did his hands feel? Were they rough or smooth?"

"Rough."

"Did you see hair on his arms?"

"Yes. It was dark."

"Did he have a tattoo or scar?"

She closed her eyes and drew in a breath. "There was a scar on his abdomen. I remember seeing it when his shirt rode up while he was raping me."

"Where was the scar?"

"Straight across his gut. And it didn't look like it was from surgery but from an injury. It was jagged and ugly."

"You're doing very well, Ms. Kennedy. Tell me what happened next?"

Rebecca raised her fingertips to her neck. "He tightened his hands around my neck. His eyes changed. They didn't look sad anymore but excited. He liked doing that better than the other thing."

"Did you pass out?"

"No."

"Did he speak?"

"It was garbled, almost like he was talking to himself."

"Was his voice deep or high pitched?" Macy asked.

"It was barely a whisper. He sounded hoarse. Young. I don't think he was much older than I was at the time."

Macy noted Bennett's keen attention, but she seemed willing to let Macy run this interview. "Did he say anything else?"

"No. But he paused at my dresser and took one earring from a set that had been my favorite. I wore those earrings all the time."

"Do you still have the remaining one?" Macy asked.

"No. But it was a gold knot with a pearl in the center."

"And then?" Macy asked.

"He left. I didn't hear him leave the house, and for a long time I thought he was still there."

"Was he?"

"Yes," she whispered. "He came back in the room, and it was like he couldn't hold himself back. He crossed the room and began softly touching my neck. In a split second his caress turned to a chokehold more vicious than before. My vision blurred and I passed out."

Rebecca drew in several deep breaths, as if reminding herself that she was not in that room with him and able to breathe.

"What happened next?"

Rebecca balled up the tissue in her clenched fist. "When I came to, he was sitting there staring at me. I was terrified the moment I realized where I was. I could tell under the mask he was really enjoying this."

"What happened then?"

"He strangled me again."

"How many times did he do this?"

"Five, maybe six times. I lost count, but the last was the worst. I felt like I was floating, and the world seemed to be slipping away."

In the ambulance, after the hit-and-run, Macy had coded. No bright lights or the voice of God to guide her, but she did hear her pop's voice. He told her to stay right the hell where she was.

"My neck was so sore that it hurt to even touch it myself," Rebecca continued. "I remember looking up that last time into his eyes and knowing I wasn't going to come back. I didn't want to die, but I couldn't stay in that room and keep being tortured like that. So I gave in to it. I stopped fighting, stopped trying to breathe, and just let go."

"And?"

"I passed out. When I woke, he was rubbing his hands as if they were tired. He finally got up, but instead of coming back for me, he left. I didn't move for the rest of the night. I was so afraid he would be there to hurt me again. Finally, my mother came home and checked on me."

"Where was she?"

"At her boyfriend's house. She told me not to shower and then took me directly to the hospital."

"Was there any sign of him when your mother arrived?" Macy asked.

"No. She didn't see anyone." Rebecca hesitated as her eyes now glistened. She tipped her head back and again touched the edge of her turtleneck.

"I know this is hard," Bennett said. "But you're doing a good job."

"I don't want to remember," Rebecca said. "I've always made it a habit to leave the past buried."

"But the past has a way of sneaking up on us," Macy said.

"True." Rebecca drew in a breath. "I voted for Nevada because I needed this guy caught more than I wanted to forget."

"Has this guy ever contacted you since the attack?"

"I did get a weird call last year," Rebecca said.

"From whom?"

"I don't know. I picked up the phone and said hello, and there was silence on the other end. And then some man whispered, 'I will always remember you.' He hung up and never called again."

"You think it was him?" Macy asked.

"I'm certain of it. I told Sheriff Greene. He wrote it all down, like it mattered, but I don't think he did anything."

The note hadn't been in Rebecca Kennedy's file. Macy was silent while Bennett pulled a couple of tissues from the box on the table and handed them to Rebecca, and the woman dabbed the corners of her eyes.

Rebecca inhaled. "You know, I don't swim anymore because I hate the idea of holding my breath. That is such a stupid little thing, but it irritates me. I used to love to swim."

Trauma of this kind left lasting marks on the victims. "Would you be willing to meet with a forensic artist?"

Rebecca blinked. "But I didn't see his face."

"You never know what you'll remember. Her name is Zoe Spencer. Very talented and effective at what she does. Give her the chance to help you."

"Do those sketches really work?" Rebecca asked. "I mean, I've seen them on television, but it seems like such a long shot."

"They do work, and some studies show they've been more effective than collecting fingerprints. If you're willing, I'll set this up for tomorrow. Agent Spencer will be talking to another woman in town about the same thing."

"Yeah, sure, I guess. If you think it'll help."

Macy sensed the woman's reticence and attributed it to fear. "If you heard his voice again, would you recognize it?" Macy asked.

"I don't know." Rebecca glanced toward the window. "He's still out there, isn't he?"

"I think so," Macy said.

"He could come after me again. I mean, he called me that time. Why would he do that?"

"To scare you and to show you he still has control over your life. It isn't about the sex; it's about control and domination."

"Well, he's done a damn good job."

"Time to turn the tables, Ms. Kennedy."

"Okay."

"Where are you living these days?"

"In town. I live in the third-floor attic room of an apartment building. My room has no windows. Crazy, right?"

"Not at all," Macy said.

"I haven't done anything." Her eyes glistened with unshed tears.

"You've survived." Macy paused while Rebecca collected herself. "Do you live alone?"

"Oddly, I live with my mother. I've come full circle. Can you imagine being our age and living with your mother?"

Macy had loved her mother and mourned her death deeply, but they had not been the best of roommates. She had always assumed their issues had grown out of their personalities. Nonstop-action Macy versus television-game-shows Mom. Computers versus magazines. A thirst for adventure versus a fear of the unknown. She realized now that what had stood between them hadn't been temperament, but the secrets surrounding her birth mother.

"No." She softened the abrupt answer with a smile. "One last question. Ms. Kennedy, did you know Cindy Shaw?"

Her eyes blinked. Twice. "Yeah, I knew her. Everyone knew everyone back then. It was small-town living, not like it is here today."

"Do you have any idea what might have happened to Cindy Shaw?" Macy asked.

"I was pretty messed up that fall, and she was the least of my worries. Why are you asking about her?" Rebecca asked.

Macy was beginning to wonder herself. "Because no one knows what happened to her."

Rebecca wiped away a tear. "Cindy had a pretty shitty life, and she wasn't getting along with her brother. It was probably just too much for her."

"She ever contact anyone after she left?" Macy asked.

"I never heard her name again."

Macy wrote the initials *CS* on her notepad and circled it a few times before she asked, "Were you dating anyone around the time of your attack?"

"Paul Decker and I went out a few times in the weeks before it happened, but I kind of stopped calling him back."

"You broke up with him?"

"Yeah, I suppose I did."

"Do you think he was your attacker?"

"Paul? No. He didn't attack me," Rebecca said.

"Why do you say that? You didn't see the guy's face."

"I would know if it were Paul. I mean, we were *together* if you know what I mean."

"Sex?" Macy asked.

Rebecca blushed and glanced toward Bennett. "Yeah. Sex."

"And he wasn't angry with you for breaking it off?" Macy prompted.

"It was really a mutual thing," Rebecca said.

What might have been mutual in her mind might not have been in his. "Did he also date Cindy?" Macy countered.

"Paul dated around and probably still does. Any smart girl knows he's never going to be in it for the long haul. But sometimes fun and sex are all a girl needs."

Fun and sex. Both concepts were far from Macy's life right now. "Ms. Kennedy, thank you for your time."

"Look, I know I said I don't like talking about this, but if talking will help find Tobi's killer, I'll talk to your friend."

"Agent Spencer will be in town tomorrow. Will you see her then?"

Her body tensed, but she nodded. "Absolutely."

Rebecca walked Macy and Bennett out the door. After Macy gave her a business card, they moved out to the parking lot. The half moon was bright. She checked her watch. Seven thirty.

"I think Tobi's killer was practicing with the rape victims and he came close to murdering Ms. Kennedy," Macy said. "He figured it out with Tobi."

"Yes, he did." Bennett looked almost resigned. "We have to solve this case."

"I know." She studied the deputy. "We both have a lot riding on this."

Bennett nodded. "We're in this together."

"You say that like it's a bad thing," Macy said.

Bennett shoved out a breath, shaking her head.

The quip was intended to breach the strain always humming between them. But judging by Bennett's deepening frown, it was going to take a blowtorch to thaw out the deputy's icy layers.

***

He was thirstier than he thought and grabbed another beer, drinking until it was drained. Another rim shot and a miss. He scooped up the empty beer can and slammed it into the trash.

"You're a disappointment," he said to the semiconscious woman in the corner. "I expected more of a challenge from you. The best wins are earned."

Air hissed over her lips as he threaded his fingers together and cracked his knuckles.

"Look at me."

Her eyes twitched, and that was enough for him to know she was still in there. They still had at least one more moment to share.

He squeezed, and her body's primitive reflexes sent a warning to her muscles, which tensed. He held steady pressure. His erection pulsed. His heartbeat quickened.

Five, six, seven, eight.

Older and wiser, he didn't want death to come in a quick, heady rush. No more spiking adrenaline to ruin his rhythm.

Nine, ten, eleven.

Her pulse slowed, and a faint gurgling sound rumbled in the back of her throat. Her eyes were barely open. This wasn't their first dance. And now he completely dominated her. She no longer fought. Cried. Or begged. And oddly, he was as disappointed as he might be after a fine meal ended or a fine glass of good scotch was emptied.

Her mouth opened wide, sucking in air, and reminded him of a beached fish. Slowly her eyes closed completely.

"Open your eyes." His ripe, breathless excitement sounded adolescent. "I want to see your eyes."

A tear trickled from the corner of her right eye, but she didn't look at him. She didn't respond and her muscles slackened. His fingers ached and his muscles cramped.

Twenty, twenty-one. Beyond forty-five seconds, the brain started to die and drift to a space past fear and terror.

He didn't want her to cross into the unknown just yet. He wanted to savor his victory. Sweat beaded on his forehead as he rubbed the cramps and sore joints of his hand, trying to remember a time when his body didn't ache.

He grabbed her upper right arm, savoring the feel of her flesh in his hand. Unable to resist, he sank his teeth into her flesh. He bit hard, tasted her blood in his mouth, but he felt no reaction from her.

"I've won, sweetheart. I wanted to keep the game going. I liked the way you cried when you were scared. Sexy as hell."

As he traced the purple bruises along the column of her white neck, he kissed her still, full, soft lips. "I am a winner."

Finally, he slowly pulled off his mask. The air felt cool again against his sweaty skin.

The mask had been a necessity in the early days when he hadn't worked up the courage to kill. But even after he had no longer been afraid to kill, he'd kept the mask because it incited fear.

He walked to a small refrigerator, grabbed a beer, popped the top, and took a long swig. It didn't quench the bone-deep thirst that had plagued him for as long as he could remember. It was a craving. A need to prove he was a winner.

This death should have taken the edge off his thirst, but it didn't come close to chasing away the restlessness. A few days ago, he had been ready to explode with the need to prove himself. And he had. He had demonstrated yet again he was on top of the heap.

Yes, he felt more control now, but the calm would not last. It never did. The hunger would soon return, and it would consume him until he was forced to find another woman.

CHAPTER EIGHTEEN

Tuesday, November 19, 8:15 p.m.

En route to the police station, Macy searched the Internet for the cologne Beacon and discovered it was widely accessible online as well as at the local mall in Roanoke. She ordered a travel size and asked that it be shipped to the sheriff's office. Smells could trigger memories, and she was prepared to have all the former victims smell the scent to see if helped them recall details.

When Macy and Bennett pulled into the station's parking lot, a news van from Channel 9 was parked and waiting. Macy swallowed a curse and kept her gaze forward, wondering if reporters had a secret power drawing them to cops when the timing was at its absolute worst.

"He's from Roanoke," Bennett said. "His name is Peter Stuart, and he covered Tobi Turner's disappearance multiple times over the years. A couple of his stories went national. He's not had national coverage for several years, and I know he sees this as his ticket back to the top."

"That kind of ambition is dangerous. I've seen guys like him broadcast information before it's verified."

Bennett frowned but kept her thoughts to herself.

Macy's attention was drawn to Stuart's fit frame, which stretched over six feet tall. A dark suit coupled with trimmed black hair framed an angled face that TV loved and she found uninspiring.

"Deputy Bennett!" Stuart shouted as he jogged across the parking lot, his microphone outstretched like a fishing pole ready to yank up whatever nibbled on its line. "Can I ask you a few questions?"

The deputy squared her shoulders, stopped, and turned. This was an active investigation, but like it or not, they were on display. Macy paused, and neither made a comment as he reached them. Behind him was a man with a camera perched on his shoulder.

"We understand search and rescue has returned, and they have not found Debbie Roberson," Stuart said.

This was news to them both, but neither gave a hint.

"What do you think happened to Debbie Roberson?" Stuart asked. "Has she been murdered?"

"We're still investigating the case and do not have a statement at this time," Bennett said.

"You've got to give me something. Search and rescue said nothing," Stuart said.

Nevada wasn't the chatty type, so Stuart must have been at the park when Nevada and Ellis exited the trail empty handed.

"As soon as I have information, I will brief you," she said.

"Tobi Turner has a similar look to Debbie Roberson."

"What's your point?"

"Just saying you have females with similar looks. One is dead and the other is missing."

Bennett stiffened, the faint hint of color rising in her cheeks as she shook her head. "No comment at this time."

"Are you sure about that, Deputy?" he challenged.

Macy immediately spotted the deputy's protective posturing. What was it about the reporter that put the deputy on edge?

"What is your name, Special Agent?" Stuart asked.

Normally the FBI stayed in the background on these local investigations. But to turn away from the reporter and the rolling camera would send a bad message to the public. "Special Agent Macy Crow."

"Do you have a comment?" Stuart asked as he watched Bennett turn and walk toward the station.

"No, sir. When we have an update, we will call a press conference." Macy caught up to Bennett. Both were silent, each knowing the less said publicly to the media, the better. Whoever was out there was likely watching and taking in everything they were saying.

Once inside the station house, Macy asked, "You know him?"

"Of course I do," she said. "He's a local reporter."

"It's more than that."

Bennett faced her. "What are you suggesting?"

"Are you two dating? Do you have any kind of relationship?"

"No."

Macy noted the faint rush of color in the deputy's face suggesting there was something between the deputy and the reporter. "Then that leaves a professional relationship. You were the one who told him about the rape kits."

Bennett stared at Macy with an icy, unreadable expression, which Macy realized now was a defense tactic. The deputy wasn't trying to be a badass. She was scared.

"News of the untested rape kits made it to Nevada and to the media. How did that happen?"

"I have no idea."

Though Macy could force the issue now, she didn't. There was more Bennett wasn't saying. She could theorize all day about what the deputy was holding back but opted to wait and watch her more closely. Most people eventually tipped their hand in some way.

Bennett typed in the access code, and the door opened. Nevada was waiting for them on the other side. He held a half-empty water bottle and was still dressed in hiking gear that was now muddied and sweat stained.

"Looks like you managed to slip by Mr. Stuart," Bennett said.

"It's a gift," Nevada said.

"Stuart tells us you didn't find anything," Macy said.

He shifted his gaze from Bennett to her. "The reporter was waiting for us at the north entrance. He's surmising that we discovered nothing."

"You traveled the entire route?" Bennett asked.

"We did."

"Did you find anything on the trail?" Macy asked.

"We did not, Special Agent. And we spoke to two sets of hikers who haven't seen anything either."

"Did you get their names?" Macy asked.

Nevada slid long fingers into a pocket on the side of his leg and handed Macy a crisply folded piece of paper. "Names and telephone numbers of both sets."

Bennett glanced at the list Macy was holding. "Do you think she was ever on that mountain?"

"I don't. If she was taken from the parking lot, she likely was transferred to another vehicle. I would bet money that neither she nor her attacker stepped foot on the trail."

Macy pocketed the list. "We spoke to Rebecca Kennedy, and she's willing to work with a forensic artist."

"Good. Ellis is ready and willing as well," Nevada said. "She said she'd be here first thing in the morning."

Bennett placed a call to Ellis Carter and confirmed her morning appointment with the sketch artist. Her call to Rebecca Kennedy went to voicemail, so she left her name and number and requested a callback.

"There's not much else we can do tonight," Nevada said. "Bennett, go home and get some rest."

"I'll be back early in the morning," Bennett said.

Nevada nodded, and when she left, he said to Macy, "I'm parked out back. I'll drive you to your motel and pick you up in the morning."

His help was convenient, but he was also too easy to rely upon. It wouldn't help her bid to regain independence. "No, thanks. I prefer to have my own transportation. See you in the morning."

Nevada didn't press, and she left the sheriff's office and walked to her car. Settled behind the wheel, she locked the doors before starting the engine.

As she drove, she kept the radio off, needing the silence to process the day. Her mind kept circling back to Tobi Turner's textbook, with the girl's handwriting scrawled in the margin. "You were a smart girl, Tobi. What did he say to you that was so charming?"

She parked at the motel and, grabbing her backpack, walked by the lobby on her way to her room. The evening clerk at the motel front desk shot her a couple of curious glances, but the guy had the sense not to pry.

In her room, she locked her door, dropped her pack on a small chair, and eased onto the bed. She popped two ibuprofen and then carefully lay back.

Promising herself she would not yet fall asleep, she let her eyes drift shut as she replayed the evidence she'd collected that day. Three rapes and a murder connected by DNA. Debbie Roberson and Cindy Shaw remained missing. Was she trying to force puzzle pieces that weren't meant to fit together?

She heard a horn honk as a vehicle drove by the motel; someone down the hallway was digging ice out of the ice machine. As the footsteps moved closer to her door, her hand went to her gun as she listened. The footsteps came and then passed by her door. The heater in her room kicked on.

Her grip on her gun eased and the sounds outside faded. She felt herself drifting. Once, her eyes snapped open, but then they quickly drifted closed. Just five minutes. Five minutes to rest her eyes and give the ibuprofen a chance to work.

In the distance a young girl called out to her. She didn't recognize the voice.

"Who is it?" she asked.

Silence.

Her fingers brushed the grip of her weapon. "Who is it?" This time she was on guard and in no mood to play guessing games.

"I need your help."

The voice was a soft whisper but loud enough now for her to make out the words.

"I need your help. I'm lost."

"Who are you?" Macy asked.

"It's dark and black and I'm afraid."

"I can't help you if you don't tell me who you are." Macy's training kicked in, and she began ticking through her list of priorities. Identify subject. Ascertain danger.

"Help me."

Ahead, Macy saw the outline of a woman. Long hair brushed the edges of broad shoulders. Macy moved toward the woman, but no matter how many steps she took, she couldn't seem to reach her.

"Identify yourself," Macy said.

The thump of Macy's heart filled the silence, and she was about to repeat her request when the woman whispered, *"I used to be Cindy Shaw."*

In the distance a ringing yanked Macy out of the haze.

Her eyes popped open and she sat up, her hand on her weapon as she looked around the room. The chain on the lock was in place. The phone rang as traffic rumbled by the motel outside.

She sat still, and her heart rate settled as she glanced toward the red digital letters of the bedside clock: 9:01 p.m. She had been asleep for only twenty minutes.

"You know what, Cindy? If you want my damn help, you're going to have to do better than screwing with my sleep."

She fished her phone from her pocket. "Special Agent Macy Crow."

"It's Nevada. We found Debbie Roberson."

Macy rubbed her forehead, trying to clear her head. In her other dreams, she'd had conversations with her father, brother, and one with her adoptive mother. They'd all been people she'd known, and each could be explained away by old memories being rechanneled in a brain that was still rewiring itself. But whatever she'd just experienced had been different.

She cleared her throat. "Is she dead?"

"According to Deputy Bennett, she's alive and well and at the station right now. Want a ride?"

She'd been wrong about Debbie. Was she also wrong about Cindy Shaw? Jesus. Her thoughts used to be so linear. She never had crazy dreams. She followed hard evidence and not feelings. "I'll be out front in fifteen minutes."

***

Ninth graders didn't mix with senior football players, but Matt had his chance to run with the big dogs. He sat in the back seat of Tyler Wyatt's new red truck, sandwiched between the meaty shoulders of Doug and Benny Piper. Deke Donovan rode shotgun in the front seat next to Tyler.

The headlights of Tyler's truck cut across the Wyatt barn's aged wood and the yellow crime scene tape floating in a breeze. Excitement glowed from Tyler's eyes when he glanced into the rearview mirror and caught Matt's expression. "You sure you want to do this?"

Matt puffed his chest, trying to forget the promise he'd made to his mother. "Sure, why not?"

"Aren't you afraid of what your mommy will say if you get caught?"

Matt wasn't stupid. He knew Tyler and the boys saw him as their Get Out of Jail Free card. If they got caught trespassing at the Wyatt barn and nosing around a crime scene, they were counting on his mom going easy on them.

"I'm not afraid." That was a lie. He was nervous. But he wanted to prove to the guys they didn't need to keep him at arm's distance because of his mother.

"Then let's go inside," Tyler said.

A cold wind chilled his skin when he got out of the truck. The lights of the truck shining behind them, the five boys walked toward the barn. Tyler ripped off the crime scene tape, balled it into a loose knot, and tossed it aside.

Inside the barn, the headlights illuminated the dismantled shaft. For a moment none of the boys spoke as they took in the scene. "I popped Amy Meadow's cherry here," Tyler said. "And to think Tobi was watching us the whole time. Maybe I should tell Amy. Be fun to see her expression."

As the other boys laughed, Matt chuckled, too, but he felt no joy. Being here didn't feel right.

Tyler picked up a loose board and whacked it hard against the shaft. The brittle wood split up the center, and a large section fell to the dirt floor. He handed the board to Matt. "Now it's your turn."

Matt took the stick and cocked it like a baseball batter.

"Go on, hit it," Tyler said.

"It feels kind of wrong," Matt said.

"Wrong? What's wrong about it?" Tyler asked.

"I don't know. A girl died here."

"It's not like you're hurting her, unless maybe you're afraid her ghost is going to get you."

The other boys goaded Matt until finally he swung and hit the shaft. Another large section of wood splintered and fell into the dust.

The boys cheered, and Tyler clamped his hand on Matt's shoulder. "Breaking stuff makes you feel like a winner, right?"

Part of him did enjoy the destruction. It felt good to release some of the anger that was always chewing on his gut.

Tyler leaned closer and in a voice loud enough for them all to hear said, "Amy isn't the only one who lost her cherry here. Know who else did?"

The boys laughed and egged him on to tell.

Tyler wagged his finger. "Matt, do you know the answer?"

Matt's smile melted as the energy suddenly shifted. The boys now looked at him as if they were a pack and he was prey. "I hear your mother could fuck like nobody's business."

The other boys' laughter rang around Matt.

"I wonder if your mama moaned like Amy did when I was grinding into her."

Matt's fingers tightened around the stick. "Don't talk about my mother."

"Why? You said yourself she's an uptight pain in the ass," Doug said.

Matt would never say for sure exactly what happened next. But when Benny punched him in the arm, he snapped. He and his mother practiced self-defense moves, and she always said to come out swinging. Make the first shot count. No such thing as a fair fight in the streets. He cracked the stick against Benny's head. Adrenaline surged through his body. The other boys stared in stunned silence before they raced toward him. They were bigger. But he was faster. And it turned out, a whole lot meaner.

***

Nevada picked up Macy fifteen minutes later, and the moment she climbed into his vehicle, he was glad he'd bought strong coffee for her.

She looked like she'd slept some but oddly looked less rested than she had when she'd left the sheriff's office.

The scent of the coffee pulled her gaze to the cup holder. "For me?" she asked.

"Three sugars and two creams."

She tore back the cup's tab and sipped. "Bless you."

As they pulled out onto the road that led to town, he asked, "You look like you've caught some sleep?"

"If you can call it that."

"The leg?"

"For once the leg feels pretty good."

"Really?"

"Yeah. It's all good."

"The Macy I used to know could sleep through anything."

She sipped more coffee. "The new Macy has dreams."

"What kind of dreams?" He kept his tone low and nonjudgmental.

Instantly, she seemed to regret the confession, as if deciding nothing good came from being too forthcoming. "The kind of dreams I get when I've had too much coffee. Weird, odd, and in the light of day, they mean nothing."

"Coffee never bothered you before."

"Sadly, it does now. Getting tagged by a three-thousand-pound pickup changes a lot of things."

"The limp will improve and the hair will grow back. What else has changed?"

"I now have a weird fascination for country western music."

"I'm serious, Macy."

"So am I. I found myself tapping my foot to banjo music the other day. Frightening."

Nevada said nothing, but he could almost hear the wheels grinding in her head. Instead of telling him what was really on her mind, she shifted the conversation back to the case.

"So where has Debbie Roberson been for the last three days?" she asked.

"Holed up with an old boyfriend, Rafe Younger."

Macy groaned. "Such an obvious explanation. If I had followed up with Rafe sooner, I'd have known that. Did Debbie blow off her job for him?"

"She said she notified her boss that her roommate agreed to swap shifts."

"That's not what Dr. Shaw said."

"A simple miscommunication? Work schedules get mixed up all the time. Everything pointed to Debbie being in trouble."

"But she wasn't."

"It was a false alarm."

Macy sat back, staring out the window. "I have three days remaining to make headway in this case, and I've wasted precious time today running down a rabbit hole. *Stupid.*"

Nevada parked in front of the station and they both went inside. The deputy on duty buzzed them in, and they found their way to the conference room, where Bennett sat with an annoyed-looking young woman.

Dark hair framed the young woman's face, drawing attention to smudged mascara and full, pouty lips. Looking freshly fucked and irritated, Debbie tapped her foot.

Beside her sat a lean man, sandy-brown hair, tanned skin. He was a good decade older, but unlike his partner, he didn't appear concerned.

"Ms. Roberson and Mr. Younger, I'm Special Agent Macy Crow, and you must know Sheriff Mike Nevada."

Both nodded, but it was Debbie who spoke. "I called my mother and she melted down over the phone. She said everyone thought I was dead."

"We're glad you are safe," Macy said.

"I can't believe you thought I was dead," Debbie said.

Rafe leaned forward, hands clasped. "We didn't mean to screw things up for you."

Macy sat across from them but Nevada remained standing, leaning against the wall off to her right, his arms crossed. When he and Macy had worked together in Kansas City, he had let her do most of the talking while he played the role of the proverbial silent, brooding bad cop. By default, she was good cop, but if Debbie didn't lose the attitude, he was fairly sure it was going to be a case of bad cop/bad cop.

"Where have you been?" Macy asked.

"We just took off," Debbie said.

"You left your purse in your car at the park with the doors unlocked."

"That was stupid, I know," she said. "We got caught up in the moment, and I forgot about my stuff. I thought I'd locked my car, but I guess I forgot."

"Where were you?" Nevada asked.

"An inn about twenty miles west of here. The Warm Springs Inn. I didn't tell Mom because I didn't think it would matter. I'm twenty-one, and we don't always talk every day."

"She's also not crazy about Rafe," Macy said.

Debbie shrugged her shoulders. "She's uptight."

Macy scribbled down the name of the inn. "Your cell phone was not transmitting a signal."

"It got messed up at work," Debbie said.

"What do you mean?" Macy asked.

"I don't know. I pulled it out of my purse, and it wasn't working. I didn't have time to get it looked at."

It was a perfect storm of incidents that had led to the wrong conclusion. It wasn't anyone's fault, but knowing Macy as he did, this mistake would make her question her own judgment. "While I've got you here, Mr. Younger, let's talk a little about Tobi Turner. Did you know her in high school?"

Rafe looked startled by the question and then quickly shook his head. "I was playing ball then. That was my focus, and I had about five friends that I remember."

"Who's Tobi?" Debbie asked Rafe.

"She was murdered, Ms. Roberson," Macy said. "She went to school with your boyfriend."

"Oh."

"Mr. Younger?" Macy prompted.

"Sure, I knew her. We all knew each other. And when she vanished, everyone was a little freaked out."

"Did you think I'd been killed like her?" Debbie asked.

"The thought did cross our minds, Ms. Roberson," Macy said.

"Why? It was fifteen years ago."

"The killer has not been caught, and frankly, you look a lot like Tobi. It was a coincidence I couldn't ignore," Macy said. "What about Cindy Shaw, Mr. Younger? You know her?"

"Sure." Rafe folded his arms. "Do you think she was also murdered?"

The smart-ass tone clearly set Macy's teeth on edge. "I don't know, Mr. Younger. I sincerely hope not."

"She wasn't the kind to stick around here. She saw her ticket to freedom and she took it."

"What was her freedom ticket?"

"She said she was coming into money. I guess it came, and she took off."

"Where does a girl who lived in a trailer on the outside of town get enough money to quit school and move across the country?"

"She didn't confide in me. We weren't that close."

"Who would she have confided in?" Macy asked.

"I don't know. I really didn't care about Cindy Shaw. No one got that upset when she left."

"Keep talking," Macy said.

"Cindy had a vested interest in Bruce making it to the big time. She thought once a scout picked him up, it was a matter of time before the NFL money rolled in. Cindy would have done anything to help her brother."

"Such as?"

"I caught her going down on one of the scouts behind the field house."

"Is that your idea of *anything*?" Macy asked.

"Whatever her brother wanted, she got for him." Rafe was silent and then sighed. "I saw her arrive at the bonfire with Tobi Turner."

For a moment the detail seemed to simmer with Macy. They both knew that Tobi had driven to school, changed clothes, and then ridden to the bonfire with Cindy. "That's also not a crime."

"Cindy gave her a glass of grain alcohol," Rafe said. "Stuff tasted like lemonade, but it kicked like a mule."

"What's the point?" Macy asked.

"Tobi drank it straight down and Cindy served her another. I think the point was to loosen her up for one of the guys on the Dream Team."

"Do you remember who ended up with Tobi?"

"No. I wasn't paying attention at that point. I only thought about it later after the girl vanished."

"Did you tell Greene?" Macy asked.

"No."

"Why not?"

"What happened between the guys at the bonfires stayed between the guys."

She threaded her fingers together and clasped her hands tightly before she released them. "Which of the four guys was most likely to assault a girl?"

"We were pretty intense. We were trained to be savages on the field. That mind-set made us champions."

"Town heroes with perks," Macy said.

"It wasn't like that," Rafe said. "All the girls wanted to be with us. They were the best years of my life."

"So basically Cindy drugged girls and gave them to the team?" Macy asked.

Rafe shook his head. "You're making it sound terrible. It wasn't."

"Tell that to Tobi."

Nevada heard the bitterness and anger in her voice and knew then it was time to pivot. "We found a red rope in the trunk of your car, Ms. Roberson. Did you put it there?"

"I found it in the bushes by my bedroom window. I wasn't sure where it came from, so I tossed it in the trunk and forgot about it."

"Finding a new length of rope in the garden seem a little odd to you?" Macy asked.

"I figured my roommate dropped it."

"Who is your roommate?"

"Beth Watson."

"When we knocked on your door yesterday, there was no answer," Nevada said. "And I drove by last night and didn't see any signs that anyone was home. Where is Beth?"

"That's weird," Debbie said. "Beth said she'd be home. I should go by the house and check."

"We'll send a deputy by," Nevada said.

"You thought something bad happened to me, and it didn't. Don't you think you're getting a little weird about nothing?"

"Do you have somewhere else to stay tonight?" Macy asked.

"Why? I want to go home." Debbie's voice amped up a notch.

"I'll send a deputy with you," Nevada said. "If he gives the all clear, we'll consider this case closed."

Debbie rolled her eyes. "Fine."

"And remain available," Macy said. "I might have more questions." She stepped into the hallway, dragged a shaking hand through her very short hair as Nevada followed behind her.

"Are you all right?" he asked.

In a lower voice she said, "Her no-big-deal attitude just pisses me off."

"Join the club."

"No matter what she thinks, finding that rope by her window is a red flag."

"Deputy Rogers should be here any moment to accompany her home."

Macy blew out a breath. "I want to get buccal swabs from all the members of the Dream Team. We know Decker isn't a match, and I still need samples from Younger and Shaw."

"There were a lot of guys on that team," Nevada said.

"We'll start with the stars."

"Sounds good."

"Younger next."

"I'll get a kit," Nevada said. He returned minutes later with a sealed vial that contained a cotton swab. "Remember, you get more flies with honey."

Macy grinned. "I can be very sweet."

"I'm not touching that one."

They both entered the room, and when Debbie looked up and saw Macy's expression, she realized how angry Macy was. Good.

"Mr. Younger, I'm hoping you can do me a favor," Macy said.

Younger shifted in his seat. "Sure, if I can."

"Would you allow me to test your DNA?" Macy asked.

He sat a little straighter. "Why?"

"So we can confirm you weren't involved in what happened all those years ago." She made a point not to mention the rapes or murders.

"You strike me as a good guy, and when I speak to the media, I can say right up front that you weren't involved once I have the test results."

He glanced toward Debbie, who shrugged. "Sure. I'll do it."

"Excellent." Macy pulled on gloves, opened the vial, and when Paul opened his mouth, she swabbed the inside of his cheek before resealing the swab in the glass tube.

"That's it?" Younger asked.

"That's it. I'll send this off to the lab, and you can just get on with your life."

"Can we go now?" Debbie asked.

"Sure," Macy said.

The two rose and left without comment.

Macy held up the vial to the light. "I've seen offenders rise to a DNA challenge only to run as soon as they leave the station house. We'll need to get this analyzed as quickly as possible just in case."

"I'll have a deputy drive it down to the lab in Roanoke," Nevada said.

"I'd also like a swab from Bruce Shaw," Macy said.

Nevada looked taken aback for only a moment. Bruce might be a respected doctor in town, but they both knew that didn't mean much right now.

***

He drove down the quiet country road that he'd traveled a dozen times in the last couple of months. He had not had a body in his trunk when he'd done his recon work, but he had fantasized about it. How many times had he measured the inside of his trunk? How many times had he loaded bags of sand into his trunk to see how his car handled with the extra weight? And when he had realized he had to kill, he had carefully lined the interior with plastic.

He slowed as he pulled to the side in a small turnaround that most folks used when they realized they'd made a wrong turn. The road saw enough traffic to ensure she'd be found soon.

He put the car in park and got out. He could bury her in a grave, and that would buy him years. It had taken the cops fifteen years to find Tobi, and that had been dumb luck. But he wanted this one found. He wanted to see the media swarm, to hear the faint whispers of fear, and to watch the Keystone Cops chase their own tails in circles. He was smarter than all of them put together. He was throwing down the gauntlet.

The plastic crinkled when he hefted the corpse out of the trunk and cradled her cold body close. He had forgotten how unwieldy dead weight could be.

After laying her on the ground, he removed the plastic and then shoved it in a large garbage bag, which he stowed in his trunk. Kneeling, he brushed the hair from her eyes and smoothed his fingertips over her pale cheeks.

He took care to straighten her large T-shirt and made sure its hem covered her private parts. No need to be crass, and he certainly didn't want the world to think he was a pervert.

He removed a disposable phone from his pocket and dialed a familiar number. It rang three times before he heard a gruff "Hello."

"It's me."

A long pause followed, and then, "What do you want?"

"An alibi."

More silence. "I did that once before."

"And you were generously rewarded."

"The stakes are higher now."

Rising, he stared up at the bright half moon. "The stakes are always high. That's what makes it interesting."

He wouldn't make threats. They both knew that one word to the cops would bring their house of cards tumbling down.

"What do you want?"

Smiling, he drew in a deep breath and relayed exactly what he needed said if anyone should come asking about him. When he ended the call, he stared up at the bright sky and thought about the next woman.

He had his eye on several, but there was one that rose to the top of his list. Already he imagined his fingers around her slender neck and the final moments they would share.

CHAPTER NINETEEN

Tuesday, November 19, 10:00 p.m.

When everyone left the conference room, Macy sat in silence and dropped her face into her hands. Since she had rolled into town, she had learned precious little. And at the rate she was going, she would drive back to Quantico empty handed and out of a job.

Nevada pushed through the door. "Let's take a break."

"I don't need a break. I need to solve this case."

"Two hours won't make a difference, and getting away from the station might help clear your head."

"I've barely gotten started on this investigation."

He picked up her backpack. "Break. Food."

Knowing her mind was running in circles, she realized an hour or two might be what she needed. Macy followed him out the back door of the station and got into his car. He started driving, and she didn't pay close attention to the passing buildings until he took a road leading out of town.

"Where are we going?" she asked.

"To my house. I'll make us a meal, and then we can get back to it in a few hours."

"To your house. I'm not sure that's smart."

"Afraid you can't keep your hands off of me?" he challenged.

She studied his amused profile and realized how much she'd missed his sense of humor. "Your honor is safe with me, Sheriff."

He laughed and turned down more roads, following a series of smaller and smaller side streets until he took a hard right onto a freshly paved blacktop driveway. It snaked up the side of the mountain, winding around a switchback curve, and then pushed up to the final stretch.

The house waiting for them was not what she had expected when she had heard *farmhouse*. It was large and at least a five-thousand-square-foot extravagance of stone, tall glass windows, and a wide covered porch that wrapped around the entire front of the house.

"Wow, Grandpa rolled large," she said.

"He built roads for a living."

"And made a small fortune."

He hit a button on his visor and a garage door on the side opened, allowing him to pull in. He shut off the engine. "I'll give you the grand tour."

"Why not?"

A combination lock opened the door leading from the garage into the kitchen. She paused to study the neat display of mountain bikes, hiking gear, and ski equipment precisely arranged along the walls.

"How long did he live here?" she asked.

"Forty years."

"This gentleman was also Ellis's grandfather?"

"No. I'm related to Ellis on my mother's side. George, my grandfather who built this house, was my dad's father."

"You were close to George?" She'd slept with the guy, but neither had really talked about their pasts.

"My grandfather raised me from age fifteen onward after my parents died."

"You never told me that. How did your parents die?"

"Car accident. Hit head-on by a drunk driver."

"I'm sorry about your parents."

"It was a long time ago." He waved her in before he disappeared inside.

She traced her finger over the handlebar of a mountain bike, realizing she wanted to know more about Nevada. Curiosity served her well on the job, but it wouldn't in this case. She liked the guy a lot, but the less she knew about him, the better. Regardless of their pasts, their futures were headed in opposite directions. If she went inside Nevada's house, the odds of her sleeping with him were high. God knows she wanted it. But when the case ended and she returned to Quantico, she would again endure the one-two punch of loss and longing.

"Since when did fear stop you?" she muttered.

Shouldering her backpack, she followed him inside. Nevada shrugged off his boots and hung his coat on a peg in the entryway. Her gaze was drawn to the vaulted ceiling cutting high into an A-frame and a wall of windows that overlooked another deck and the rolling mountains behind the house.

She toed off her shoes and crossed in sock feet to the window. "You have the high ground. Expecting an invasion?"

"As Grandpa used to say, no one ever expects one." He selected a glass from open shelving and filled it with water before handing it to her.

"Thank you."

He opened the double-door, subzero refrigerator and pulled out several precooked meals. He set the temperature on a convection oven and unwrapped the meals. "Do you eat meat?"

"Don't I strike you as a carnivore?"

He laughed. "No comment."

She set her bag down and got out a bottle of ibuprofen. She popped two and drained the glass of water.

"How's the leg?"

"Surprisingly good."

"Would you tell me if it weren't?"

"Probably not."

While the oven came to temp, he removed cheese and bread from the refrigerator and sliced pieces of both. He placed them on a plate in the center of the island.

The oven now ready, he popped the two meals in. "Grab a piece of cheese, and I'll show you around while dinner cooks."

"This is not what I expected."

"What did you expect?"

"Let's say I shouldn't assume anymore."

He moved into another room and flipped on lights. This room was smaller with a lower ceiling and painted in a dark-navy color. In the center was a tall stone fireplace, its firebox blackened by decades of use. Beside it was a neat stack of wood. Across the room was a large mahogany desk covered in more piles of papers. "Now that it's getting cooler, I'm gravitating toward this room."

"Snow on the trees and a crackling fire. You're on the verge of being a holiday greeting card."

Again he smiled as he showed her several more rooms on the first floor, including a room with a pool table and another with gun cases displaying shotguns that ranged from modern era to antique.

"Very nice, Nevada."

"It's a work in progress." He walked down the hallway back into the kitchen and flipped on more lights.

She settled on a barstool around the large kitchen island made of reclaimed barnwood. Industrial pendant lights hung above. The place smelled faintly of fresh paint. "If you'd told me in Kansas City we'd be sitting here now, I'd have laughed."

"You and me both." He glanced at the timer on the convection oven, which had five minutes remaining. He removed two plates from the cabinet and set them on the table.

Whatever he was cooking smelled delicious. "So what are we eating?"

"Steak and potatoes."

"My two favorite food groups." As he set out silverware and two cloth napkins, she said, "Did you ask Ramsey for me on this case?"

He stood still for an instant as he placed a fork on a gray napkin. "I called him when the DNA results came back. He told me he'd received your application. He also told me in the few weeks you'd been at ViCAP you'd connected the dots linking six stabbing cases in five different cities to one offender."

"It wasn't all me. If local law enforcement hadn't entered the case data, we wouldn't have had anything to analyze."

"That offender liked to use a serrated knife."

So he had done more homework than she'd imagined. "He stabbed his victims in the lower left portion of their backs." There was little correlation between the victims other than a method of death that was very specific.

When the timer dinged, he grabbed a set of hot mitts and removed the steaming food packages. Removing the top seal filled the room with the scents of beef, butter, and fresh herbs.

"I know my frozen foods, Nevada, and this is a cut above."

"I special order it." He set one on each plate and placed one before her. "The killer made knives for a living."

"His blades have a national reputation with his customers."

"What brought your attention to the case?"

"Two stabbings occurred in Raleigh, North Carolina, in a ten-hour period. Local law enforcement sensed he'd done this before and filed a report with ViCAP. My colleague Andy and I pulled up all stabbing deaths and then narrowed our search from there. Once we identified ten possibly related cases, we sent the case to a forensic pathologist to look at the images taken of the wounds and then created a likely weapon profile from there."

"How did you trace it to him?"

"I visited several knife experts in the area. Our boy has a fan following in the world of handcrafted weapons. I checked out his website and then cross-checked dates of the murders with the trade shows on his events page. He was picked up in Tennessee five days ago."

"You're smart as hell, Macy."

"If I were so smart, I wouldn't have connected Debbie Roberson's romantic getaway to the serial offender we're hunting."

"Better you sounded the alarm and she ended up fine than the other way around."

"Nice of you to say, but I still feel foolish."

"You are nobody's fool, Macy."

She ate in silence and realized she was hungrier than she had thought. When she finished off the last slice of steak and drained her soda, Nevada looked pleased.

"Once again, you've fed me when I didn't realize I needed to eat."

"Here to serve."

"Let me clean."

"No, I have this."

As he took the plates away, Macy walked to the large windows that overlooked the sloping yard below. Moonlight bathed what looked like a work shed and beyond that a stone firepit with adirondack chairs around it. She could imagine him sitting out there with the fire blazing, drinking a beer under the stars.

When she heard him approach, her gut tightened with longing. He stopped several inches away from her, but she could feel the snap of energy radiating from his body. Delicious sensations flooded her.

She didn't want to think about cases or bad guys or weird dreams, at least for a little while. "I'm wondering if you could help me out with something."

"What's that?" His voice sounded deep and rich.

She worried he might not want her anymore. Scrub brush hair, thin arms and legs, and scars conjured images of a scarecrow, not a seductress. Instead of wondering too much, she kicked caution to the wind as she faced him.

"I haven't had sex since Kansas City."

He didn't touch her but his attention intensified. "That so?"

"I've missed it. I've missed you."

Nevada reached out and cupped her face. "I'm glad to hear you say that. I've been wanting to do this since I first saw you."

He tilted his head and pressed his lips to hers. She leaned into his touch, savoring a skin-to-skin connection that was purely sensual. In the last five months, she had equated touch either with a physical therapist's painful bends and twists or a sister's hug. Both had their place, but, lord, how she missed feeling wanted and desired by Nevada.

She closed her eyes and, gingerly rising up, wrapped her arms around his neck and deepened the kiss. His hand slid down her back and cupped her buttocks. He squeezed and pressed her against his erection.

He kissed her shoulder. "You're tense."

"My body has changed."

"It feels good to me."

"I have scars. I'm so thin." Insecurity and worry were new additions to her repertoire. "Figured I better put that out on the table."

He smoothed the short strands of hair away from her face. "It's okay."

Unwanted tears burned her eyes. "I don't want you to hate my body."

"Your naked body is all I've thought about since I saw you arrive."

"You haven't seen it." Moonlight filtered through the trees.

"Show me. Now."

"Strip?"

"Yes. Take your clothes off, Macy."

It was an order she could refuse, but as much as she feared his reaction, a perverse part of her wanted to see how he handled himself.

She reached for the button between her breasts and unfastened it. She reached for the next and then the next until she shrugged off her shirt and let it puddle around her ankles.

He traced the line of her white, very practical bra. His eyes looked bluer, more intense, but his expression remained unchanged. The first time they had slept together, he'd appeared just as aloof and withdrawn. Her job brought her into contact with so many emotionally damaged and needy people that she found his detachment oddly calming.

He traced the faint pink tracheotomy scar at the hollow of her neck. "You're a warrior." His voice was husky, full of desire. "A survivor. That puts you in a different league. That makes you even more beautiful now."

He slid her bra straps off her shoulders and smoothed his hands over her arms. He kissed the creamy white flesh of her breast as he reached behind and deftly unhooked her bra. Her breasts were high, her nipples hard as he fingered one and kissed her on the lips.

A dry moan escaped her lips as she struggled to keep her thoughts from tumbling out of control. She fumbled for his belt buckle and unfastened it, sliding her fingers under his waistband. It was one thing to survive, but it was another to feel alive.

"If you don't take me to your bedroom right now, I'm taking you on the countertop," she said.

A chuckle rumbled in his chest, but he took her by the hand and guided her through the house to a large room on the first floor. Another span of windows overlooked the wooded valley bathed in moonlight before he pressed a button by the door and privacy screens dropped.

She removed her weapon, cuffs, and Mace and set them on the nightstand before tugging off her socks.

Nevada watched her with fascination as she shrugged off her pants and let them fall to the hardwood floor.

"Keep going."

Her gaze locked on his, and she slid off her panties.

He walked up to her and caressed her body, tracing his index finger over the long scar that snaked up her leg. Then he smoothed his hand over the road rash scars, which she hated the most. The rosy blotches spread up her side and over her shoulder.

She closed her eyes, focusing on his touch and refusing to shrink away. He kissed her shoulder, her neck, and the top of her breast.

He took her by the hand and led her to the bed and, as she sat down on the firm mattress, he undressed. His erection made her wet. She scooted to the middle of the bed and opened herself to him, feeling drunk now with sensual desire.

He lay on top of her and kissed her fully on the lips. She arched her hips, and he placed his erection at her moist center.

"Let me know if I hurt you," he said.

She nodded, not sure how her body would react, and slowly he slid into her. She held her breath for a moment, accepting him and praying her body didn't betray her now. Instead of pain, she felt pure pleasure.

"How does it feel?" he asked.

"Really damn good." She traced her hands over his buttocks. "Amazing."

He began to move inside of her, slowly at first, waiting for her body to fully relax. As she grew accustomed to him, she began to move her body against his and whispered, "More," in his ear. He moved faster and harder.

His touch sent heat coursing through her body. She cupped her breasts and arched toward him, and when he pressed his fingers to her center and rubbed small circles, it was akin to tossing a match onto gasoline. Passion exploded through her and built so quickly she couldn't temper it.

"Let it go," he said.

Macy wanted to wait for him, but the orgasm exploded in her, crashing through every nerve and muscle in her body.

When the sensation eased and she looked up at him, he seemed pleased with himself.

His eyes were dark with desire. He thrust faster inside her, and this time she pressed her body to his and touched him in the places she remembered he liked. He groaned her name and ground hard into her as his own release cut through him.

When he was spent, he lay on top of her. Both were covered in perspiration, and his racing heart matched the pace of her own.

"You're still the best. Just as I remember," he whispered against her ear.

"Out of practice," she said, a little breathless.

He kissed her lightly on the lips. "Maybe we can work on that."

"Maybe."

***

Scratch. Scratch. Scratch.

Macy dreamed of Cindy Shaw calling her name, begging for help. The young girl's cries were so vivid they startled her out of a sound sleep. She sat up in the bed, her heart racing and sweat beading between her naked breasts. She searched the unfamiliar room and had no idea where she'd been sleeping.

A strong hand rubbed her lower back, up her spine, and cupped the back of her shoulders. She turned quickly, ready to bolt, before she realized it was Nevada. He stared at her with keen, alert eyes as his fingers massaged some of the tightness away.

He sat up and looked into her eyes. "You were dreaming. Was it the hit-and-run?"

His hand slid down her back, the soft and steady pressure of his callused palm against her bare skin easing the fight-or-flight response.

"I never dream about the accident anymore," she said.

"But something was bothering you."

She pulled her fingers through her hair. "It's nothing."

"You were screaming, Macy."

"It wasn't that bad."

"Ever known me to exaggerate?"

Telling him about the dream would blow her credibility. He might be able to deal with the physical scars, but to learn she could be off her nut was another matter.

"Macy, you can tell me," he said.

A sad smile curved her lips. "You know, people always say that until they hear the truth."

"I mean it." His hand felt like a steady, constant support.

She sat in silence, weighing the pros and cons. The cons were shouting at her to keep her mouth shut. "I really don't understand the dreams myself."

He didn't speak, letting silence coax out more of her secrets. The trick hadn't worked when Ramsey had tried it on her, but with Nevada, she knew she could trust him. "The dreams always start with a scratching sound."

"Explain."

"Like someone is digging in dirt."

"Digging a hole."

"This is where it gets weird. I'll be honest. You'll be supercool about it, and then in the light of day, you'll wonder who the hell I am."

"Spill it." He sharpened his tone like a fine blade.

"Whoever is making the scratching sound isn't digging into the ground but out of it. I can't explain it other than it's like a buried-alive vibe and whoever is trapped is trying to escape."

His silence wedged between them.

"I know. I *know*. Insane. Or worse, some kind of weird brain damage." She tried to scoot away.

He gently held her by the wrist. "I didn't say that."

When she finally found the courage to look at him, she saw a curiosity in his gaze that reminded her of him when he was piecing together a case. That gave her some courage to say, "I don't understand it."

"When did it start?"

"I thought I heard sounds when I was still in the hospital in Texas. I chalked that up to the pain meds. But it persisted through rehab, and whatever it was followed me back to Virginia."

"It?"

"I know. I talk about *it* like it's something other than me, but it must be coming from my brain. All I can think is that my hardwiring has changed."

"Who's doing the scratching?" And when she only looked at him, he cocked a brow. "You know, don't you?"

She closed her eyes. Weird. And weirder. "I've been dreaming about Cindy Shaw. She's been asking me for my help."

"How long has Cindy been communicating with you?"

"The scratching sounds became more persistent the day Tobi Turner's body was found. Cindy's name finally came up Sunday night while I was researching the Turner case. Once I read her name, it's like a floodgate opened and my brain wouldn't let her go."

"That's why you've been asking around about her."

"Yes. I keep hoping I'll hear that she's fine and good and that my brain just has a crazy way of processing information."

"Okay."

"Okay? What does that mean?"

"Every time you dream, I want to know about it."

"Why?"

"So I can help you figure this out. Who knows? Your subconscious might be on to something."

She scratched the side of her head. "I feel like I'm on the bus to crazy town."

A smile tugged at the edge of his lips. "We all have shit, Macy."

For whatever reason, that made her laugh, something she'd not done for a long time. "Jesus, Nevada. I don't get you."

"I'm pretty simple. You have an issue that's troubling you, and I want to help."

"Why would you want to get messed up with my semideranged self?"

He brushed his finger along her jawline. "I have no idea."

Again she laughed. "No, seriously. Why?"

"Because I don't think you're crazy. You suffered a brain injury, and because you're so damn tough, you came back from it. Maybe your neurons do process differently now, but that doesn't mean they're not effective."

"You make it sound reasonable."

He tugged her forward and kissed her on the lips. She felt herself melting. This time when they made love, it was a slower and steadier pace. She allowed him to explore her body more, and she rediscovered his.

She felt at peace, almost floating, when she lay curled in his arms, and she hoped the outside world would let her be for just a little while longer.

Nevada's phone rang.

He groaned and, turning toward his nightstand, reached for the cell. "Sheriff Nevada."

As a muffled voice on the other end of the line spoke, his expression hardened. Both knew their reprieve was over. She moved to get out of the bed and dress, but he sat straighter and wrapped long, rough fingers around her wrist.

"Yes, I'll notify Agent Crow, and we'll be right there," he said.

When he ended the call, she asked, "What?"

"A dead body was found on the side of Route 12. The woman has been strangled."

She thought about the house where Debbie lived. One-story house. Located off the beaten path. Items missing from her house.

It fit the profile of the rapist who'd crossed over into murder. Debbie had been located but not her roommate. "Send Bennett over to Debbie's house to find out where her roommate is now."

CHAPTER TWENTY

Wednesday, November 20, 6:30 a.m.

When Macy and Nevada rolled up on the scene, emergency lights from local and state cop cars lit up the night sky. Bands of morning sun nudged against the darkness as they slowly warmed the frigid air.

Macy burrowed her hands in her coat pockets, hoping forensic arrived soon to cover the body with a tent and protect it from the heat and any possible news helicopters filming from above.

She focused on the flap of the crime scene tape encircling the body of a woman who lay a couple of feet from a turnaround. The victim, wearing only an oversize T-shirt, was left on her back with legs and arms bound by red ropes. Her long dark hair splayed out behind her as if it were staged.

After removing latex gloves from her backpack, Macy slowly worked her fingers into them as she moved toward the victim. She'd never gotten used to moments like this.

She crossed the graveled road to the tape, ducked under it, and gingerly knelt by the body. Her leg moaned in protest, but she used her discomfort as a reminder that she was alive.

Nevada came up beside her, his ball cap hiding his expression as he, too, cataloged the scene's details.

Macy keyed in on the woman's neck, ringed in black-and-blue bruises in various stages of healing and discoloration. The killer had used his hands to strangle the victim multiple times, over what Macy estimated were several days.

The victim's wrists and ankles were discolored with bruises, likely caused by restraints during the assault.

Scratch. Scratch. Scratch.

Choking someone to death was a very personal form of murder. Using a gun or even a motor vehicle were both profoundly effective forms of killing, but neither required the touch and eye contact of strangulation.

Macy leaned forward, studying the body's position. The manner of death, a body's final positioning, also said something about the killer. Killers in a rushed panic left remains in a dumpster or field, a shallow grave, or even a hay chute.

More methodical killers took the time to display their bodies. In the case she'd worked in Denver, the murdered sex workers had been left naked and spread eagle with their right breast removed. The killer had wanted to humiliate them.

"What do you think?" Nevada asked.

As tempting as it was to link this case to Tobi's, she paused. "Locked-in thinking has sidelined too many investigations."

"I want your assessment."

At the risk of repeating last night's mistake, she stuck with her gut. "It's the guy we're looking for." A quiet breeze fluttered through the ends of the victim's long hair.

"Why leave her body out here?" Nevada asked. "He hid Tobi's body."

"Best guess, Tobi was his first kill. Tobi was intoxicated, he lured her to the hayloft, and something went wrong. Maybe she was inebriated. He wasn't getting the jolt of fear he hoped from his rape victims, so he graduated to strangulation. God knows how long it went on."

Nevada studied the woman's pale features. "She looks like Tobi."

"I know. Any word from Bennett on the roommate?"

"Not yet." His gaze skimmed the area around them. "Why leave her out for us? There's enough open land around here to ensure a body wouldn't be found for weeks, months, or even years."

"You know the answer to that," she said. "He saw the press conference, and he wants you to know he's here and still a force to be reckoned with."

Macy rose, wincing a little as her right knee groaned. She walked around the body, searching for something that would make her better understand this killer. "How he is perceived matters to him. He values his reputation."

"I see a monster," Nevada said.

"No argument here. But the nuances matter to him," Macy said. "If it's the same killer, he's matured in the last fifteen years. He's craving a greater challenge. When stalking didn't satisfy him, he raped. And when that wasn't enough, he killed. I'll bet money he's killed in other jurisdictions."

"In the moments when he has his victim all to himself, he's everything to her," he said, almost to himself.

"And when he takes life, he sees himself as a winner. And when he gets away with a crime, he wins yet again."

"Leaving this body here is going to make it easier for us to catch him."

"He's upped the stakes of the game," Macy said. "He keeps raising the stakes. I'm almost certain he's gotten away with other rapes or murders. And now he craves a greater challenge to prove he deserves the win." She shook her head as the insects buzzed around her.

Boots crunched on the gravel behind her as Bennett walked up. She stared at the body, unable to take her eyes off of it.

"What is it?" Macy asked.

"I went by to check on Debbie Roberson. She was packing to spend the night at her parents' house. But her roommate, Beth Watson, was still not at home, so I asked Debbie for a picture. I snapped copies with my phone." She turned her phone around to reveal the stern, unsmiling face of a young woman in her late teens. Macy glanced at the body.

It matched the image on the deputy's phone.

"He wasn't watching Debbie, but Beth," Nevada said.

"He could have been stalking them both, but Debbie went out of town unexpectedly," Macy said.

"Leaving Beth behind," Bennett said.

As they studied the body and the area immediately around it, the sun rose just as the state's forensic van crested the road and parked in front of the sheriff's vehicle. Two technicians exited. Both were dressed in dark-blue slacks and gray shirts with the Commonwealth of Virginia emblem over the right breast pocket.

Nevada ducked back under the yellow tape and strode toward them. He introduced himself, and the three spoke briefly before the technicians began to unload their equipment.

Bennett stared at the body, her face an ashen color.

"You've worked death investigations before, correct?" Macy asked.

"Car accidents, a meth lab explosion, and a convenience store robbery. Nothing as evil as this."

Macy stared at the rolling hills around them, covered in a fresh carpet of fall leaves. "Easy to think it can't come to a remote and beautiful place like this. But it's always here. In fact, it never left."

"Do you think he's gotten wiser regarding DNA?" Bennett asked.

"DNA is what tied his rape cases to Tobi Turner's murder. It's his signature. If it truly is the same guy, and he left Beth Watson out here to be found, he's left DNA on the body to be found. He wants us to know it's him."

A rumble of noise washed over the growing crowd, and Bennett turned and immediately muttered a curse only Macy could hear. "Greene is here."

"It's the biggest case this part of the state has seen in years. You should have expected it."

Greene wore khakis, a white shirt, a windbreaker, and a white Stetson. He could have passed for law enforcement, and she guessed that was exactly the kind of look he wanted to project.

"Has he always worn the hat?" Macy asked.

"Nope. That's a new look," Bennett said.

"Riding in to the rescue?" Macy asked.

Bennett glowered. "I'm sure he sees it that way."

Macy had juggled her share of local politics. The actors might vary, but the basic dynamics were the same. Everyone thought their way was the best. Everyone wanted to look their best. Including the perpetrators.

And honestly, Macy wasn't so different than the former sheriff. She wanted to solve this case herself. She *wanted* the win in her column.

Bennett glared at Greene. "There was a time I really believed in that guy. I still want to. But when I think about those kits under the carpet, I question everything I knew about him."

"And he lost because of what he did. But for now, don't alienate Greene," Macy said. "He knows this county better than anyone. One day soon he might come in handy."

Hank Greene approached Nevada. The old sheriff was grinning as he extended his hand. Nevada gripped the old man's hand, but didn't smile as Greene leaned in slightly and spoke. Nevada released his hold and shook his head.

"Nevada has dealt with dozens of men like Greene before," Macy said. "If Greene thinks he's going to do an end run around Nevada, he's sadly mistaken."

The news crew moved toward Nevada, who made a brief statement before excusing himself. As he strode back toward them, Greene tugged off his white Stetson and held it over his chest, like a humble public servant. The boom light snapped on, a reporter's microphone was thrust in his direction, and the questions started flying.

Greene was at ease and serious all at once. He turned toward the crime scene, seemingly explaining his take on the scene. His views might or might not have been right, but that didn't really matter if the sound bites for the morning news were good. Perception was everything.

"Why didn't you talk longer to the press, Sheriff?" Bennett asked.

"Talking to the reporters feeds into this killer's ego. It's news blackout until we have DNA. We control the narrative."

"They'll want a statement," the deputy persisted.

"Let the reporters, the public, and the killer wait."

Nevada surveyed the crowd and then brought his focus back around to Macy. "Do you think he's watching?"

"Killers often return to the scene of their crimes to witness the carnage."

"Agreed," Nevada said. "Deputy Bennett, pick two deputies and make sure their dashcam and vest cameras are on and rolling. I want film of who's here."

"Will do," she said.

Hank Greene approached the crime scene tape and, out of habit or arrogance, appeared ready to duck under it. Nevada stopped him.

Greene frowned briefly and then recovered with a smile. "Special Agent Crow, good to see you again."

Macy nodded. "Couldn't stay away, I see."

He grinned. "I've been sheriff of this county for almost thirty years. You know if you don't get hard leads in the first forty-eight hours, the investigation can drag on for months or years."

"Like the Turner case?" Macy asked.

His smile dimmed, but before he could answer, a helicopter's blades cut through the air above them. She looked up to see a television station logo. The story would be statewide, possibly national, by midmorning, putting her successes or failures on a bigger stage.

***

Energy tingled through him as he watched the telecast of the gathering crowd along the street where he'd dropped Beth's body.

He'd left clues at other murder scenes, expecting the cops to pick up on him. But so far, no one had linked his crimes. However, it seemed Macy Crow was sharper than most, and she was fitting together some of the pieces.

He smiled as he replayed the broadcast. He'd expected attention, but this kind of notoriety was more than he had ever dared to hope for. This crime wouldn't be forgotten anytime soon.

He should have relaxed and bathed in the prickle of excitement, but already he wondered how he would up the stakes. Go big or go home.

As he'd watched Macy and Brooke, he'd known killing one of them would bring down heaven and earth on this town. Each was strong and would put up one hell of a fight. Taking one of them might be his undoing, but the challenge was too tempting to resist.

The only question was, which one?

CHAPTER
TWENTY-ONE

Wednesday, November 20, noon

Not everyone stayed to watch the crime scene being processed, but Macy did. Most onlookers left, and news crews returned to their television stations to file their reports. Greene sat in his warm vehicle enjoying hot coffee while Nevada remained leaning against his vehicle watching. Always watching.

The evidence-collection process wasn't like it was on television. It wasn't quick. It wasn't exciting. It was a tedious, slow process, and it took weeks—if not months—to analyze it all. Smoking guns were rare.

Plaster of paris was poured into several footprints and tire tracks found near the body. Later, the technicians would begin the monotonous process of eliminating the footprints left by law enforcement and analyzing the ones that possibly belonged to the killer.

The victim's hands were covered in paper bags to protect any DNA that might have been trapped under her fingernails. Her temperature was taken, and her bruises and cuts were documented on a sketch pad and with a digital camera.

As the technicians gathered their bits of information, Macy took meticulous notes on all the evidence found, having faith that the random pieces she collected would join together into the composition of a killer.

Her phone chimed with a text and she glanced down. It was from Special Agent Zoe Spencer. The agent indicated she was at the station house, and Ellis Carter had arrived. Rebecca Kennedy had never shown, and despite repeated calls, they'd not made contact.

I'll have a sketch in a couple of hours, Spencer texted.

Perfect, Macy texted back. **See you then.**

It was close to one when the ambulance arrived to take the body to the medical examiner's office in Roanoke. Hank Greene climbed out of his vehicle, and the news reporters slid on their jackets and checked their appearance as the cameramen turned their lights on.

Cameras rolled as attendants lifted the body into a bag, laid it on a gurney that was wheeled to the waiting van. At least the woman no longer lay on the side of the cold, exposed road.

Bennett approached Macy. "Nevada has asked me to follow the van to the medical examiner's office. With all this attention, he wants me to personally make sure there is no problem with the chain of custody. Autopsy likely won't be until tomorrow afternoon."

"Understood. When you get back to town, I would like to meet with Bruce Shaw again. I want to talk to him about Beth Watson and also get that buccal swab."

"I can take care of both."

"Good. I'll talk to you when you get back to the station."

As the van and Bennett's car pulled out, the other vehicles followed in a procession down the narrow road out toward the main highway.

Nevada moved toward Macy as she walked to his car. Each step hurt, and she was anxious to pop a few ibuprofen.

Her phone dinged with a text from Spencer. **We're finished.**

On my way, she texted back before saying to Nevada, "Agent Spencer and Ellis are finished. I'd like to talk to them both while the sketch is still fresh in both their minds."

"Let's go."

Without a word, the two rode back to the station. He parked in the back, and they entered through the rear.

"Seeing as you're her cousin and clearly worried about her, let me go first?" Macy asked.

His expression was a blend of annoyance and gratitude. "Take good care of her."

"Of course."

She stopped by the break room, downed a couple of ibuprofen, and chased them with water. She knocked on the door.

"Enter," Spencer said.

Macy pushed open the door and found Ellis clutching a handful of tissues. She had red-rimmed eyes and was slightly pale.

"Are you all right?" Macy asked.

"I'm fine," she said with a faltering smile. "For some reason, I just got emotional. I haven't in years, but when I saw the sketch, I lost it."

"That's good progress." Or so she'd been told.

"Cathartic," Ellis said.

Macy turned to the tall, slim woman making the final touches on a sketch. Zoe Spencer was in her late twenties and had joined the FBI after graduate school. She was not only one of the best sketch artists but was also a leading expert on art forgery. She wore simple, fitted black pants, a gray V-neck sweater, and a silk scarf around her neck; her auburn hair was coiled into a neat bun. Her flawless skin required only red lipstick and mascara.

"Agent Crow." Spencer rose. "It's good to see you again."

They'd crossed paths on a case last year, and Macy had found Spencer to be highly effective. "Thanks for coming."

"Thank Agent Ramsey. He's the one who authorized the visit. He said this case now takes the highest priority on his docket."

"Did you make any progress with the sketch?" Macy asked.

Spencer's stoic expression softened when she looked toward Ellis. "Ms. Carter did an excellent job. She has wonderful recall."

"It didn't do that much good," Ellis said. "I only saw a guy in a mask."

Spencer turned the sketch toward Macy. The pencil sketch, drawn with exacting detail, gave them all the first glimpse of Ellis's attacker. The man had a long, lean face, a thick neck, and vibrant blue eyes that stared back with an unsettling sharpness. His lips were full, and his jaw appeared more pointed than square.

"It's not a full likeness," Spencer concluded. "But it's a start."

"I can't believe I remembered that much," Ellis said.

"As I said, you have a sharp mind," Spencer said. "The final print is ready to be released to the press as you see fit."

Macy stared at the eyes that jumped off the page at her. The door opened and Nevada stepped in. He took one look at Ellis and his expression hardened.

"Are you all right?" Nevada demanded.

"I'm fine, Mike," Ellis said firmly.

"As I just told Agent Crow, she did well," Spencer said.

Nevada exhaled a breath, and Macy sensed he was trying to dissipate the pent-up anger. "Thanks, Agent Spencer."

"Anytime." She turned and poured a cup of coffee, which she handed to Ellis before making one for herself. "Ellis did remember her attacker had a distinct smell of sweat and body odor."

"Like he'd just worked out or was working manual labor." Ellis crushed the tissues in her hand. "And his front tooth was slightly chipped. I can't believe I never remembered it before. But when I saw the eyes, it came flooding back."

"You said he also said something to you," Spencer said.

"He said, 'You'll never forget me.' The asshole was right."

"A memory doesn't have to have power over you," Spencer said. "Focus on where you are now."

Ellis sipped her coffee and set it down. "Speaking of which, my coworkers are meeting me in town. We're headed to the closest bar." She extended her hand to Spencer. "Thank you for the coffee, but I need something stronger."

"I don't blame you," Spencer said. "Again, excellent work."

Ellis scooped up her backpack, hugged Nevada, and left. Spencer began to pack up her pencils, erasers, and drawing pad. "And now I must drive to the Roanoke airport and catch a flight to Nashville."

"What's there?" Nevada asked.

"A case." She raised her gaze to him. "I still don't picture you here, Special Agent Nevada."

"It's *Sheriff*, and it's home. I belong here."

"My home is where I set up my easel, preferably far away from where I grew up." Spencer snapped her art case closed.

Macy couldn't throw stones at Nevada for moving back home. She lived a mile from the same apartment complex she'd grown up in as a kid. When the shrink she was forced to see after her assault asked why she'd returned to the area, she really hadn't known. It just felt right.

Spencer took one last sip of coffee. "I believe the sketch will help. I'm disappointed we couldn't connect with Ms. Kennedy, but I have to go now. If you need me again, it might be a few days." The tap, tap of Spencer's heels echoed down the hallway.

Macy sat in a chair, laid the sketch in front of her, studied it for a long moment, and then took several pictures of it with her phone. Sharp eyes. A narrow face. Trim body. All that could have changed. With age, men filled out and grew more muscular or fatter.

"Can we get a copy of the high school yearbook from the 2004 to 2005 year? I'm looking for a boy with a chipped tooth."

"I'll get one sent to the office," Nevada said.

Who the hell are you?

"Where is Debbie Roberson?" Macy asked.

"She's at her mother's house," Nevada said.

"Does she know about Beth?"

"She does. And we have a deputy driving by the house hourly."

Pointing toward the sketch, she said, "Good, because this guy is not finished with Deep Run yet."

***

It was past six and pitch dark by the time Brooke had driven to Roanoke and watched as Beth Watson's body was rolled in on a gurney and put in cold storage. As she headed back north to Deep Run, she called Matt.

"Mom." A video game bleeped and buzzed in the background.

"Just checking in, kiddo."

"Where are you?"

"On the road headed back to town. It's going to be another long night."

"What else is new?"

"Speaking of new, Tyler Wyatt said you were hanging out with him."

Silence. "Just for a few minutes."

"What were you doing at Lucky's?" An eighteen-wheeler blasted by her car as it built up speed for climbing the next hill with a full load.

"Just hanging out. No big deal."

"If I find out you're drinking, pal, that video game I hear in the background is going in the trash."

"God, Mom, you don't have to be so uptight. Weren't you a kid once?"

"I was. And I made big mistakes that I don't want you to repeat."

"I'm a guy. I can't get pregnant."

The barb hit her hard in the heart, and she counted to ten. "I'm talking about trusting the wrong people."

"Sorry, Mom. Low blow."

"Kids like Tyler Wyatt use money to get out of trouble. You and I don't have that luxury."

"I get it. I really do."

"I hope so." She loosened her grip on the steering wheel. "Is Grandma home?"

"She said she'd be here in a few minutes."

"Good. I'll see you later. I love you."

"You, too, Mom."

She hung up, dropping the cell phone in her lap. The days of her protecting Matt from all the ugly truths in the world were quickly coming to a close.

A half hour later, she pulled into the parking lot of the assisted living facility. The parking lot, illuminated by large lamps, was half-full of cars. There was a woman juggling a flower arrangement as she headed inside and also a man pushing a much older man in a wheelchair along the sidewalk.

Out of her vehicle, she walked inside to the front desk. "I'm Deputy Bennett. I'm here to see Dr. Bruce Shaw."

"He left about an hour ago," the receptionist said.

"Do you have a number for him?" she asked.

"Sure." The receptionist wrote down the doctor's number on a sticky note.

Brooke thanked the woman, and back outside, she called Bruce. He picked up on the third ring.

"Dr. Shaw." His voice was deep and unsettlingly breathless.

Brooke reintroduced herself. "I'm hoping we can meet. I have a few questions for you about one of your employees."

"Didn't you hear? Debbie is safe and sound."

"Yes, I know that. My questions concern someone else."

"Who?"

"I'd rather not get into this on the phone." In the background she heard cheering. "Where are you? I can come to you."

"I'm at a soccer game. I'm the coach, so now is not the best time." More cheers in the background, and Bruce shouted, "Good job."

She thought about the buccal swab in her car. "So when?"

"How about I meet you back at my office in two hours. I'll be finished up here and can swing back by."

"I'll see you here at seven."

She hung up and walked toward her car, and the streetlights hummed around her as a cold gust of air washed over her. As she reached for her car door handle, a shiver rattled up her spine and an uneasy feeling knotted in the pit of her stomach.

Brooke's hand went to her sidearm, and she surveyed the parking lot. The man who was pushing the wheelchair was now heading inside. The lights snapped and hissed. But there was no one else in the lot.

She slowly got in her car. Behind the wheel she waited and watched—for what, she didn't know.

A sudden need to see her son overtook her. If life had taught her anything, it was to listen to her instincts.

CHAPTER TWENTY-TWO

Wednesday, November 20, 8:00 p.m.

Nevada and Macy arrived at the house Debbie Roberson had shared with Beth Watson. The state forensic van was on scene, and per Nevada's orders, everyone was treating this house as part of the crime scene.

Debbie Roberson stood outside her house, her arms folded over her chest as she spoke to the deputy securing the scene.

"I thought Ms. Roberson was at her mother's house," Macy said.

"Apparently not," Nevada replied.

"She doesn't look happy."

"She's damn lucky to be alive," Nevada growled.

As they strode up to the woman, Macy said, "Ms. Roberson."

Debbie turned from the deputy, her face a mixture of anger and fear. "They won't let me inside to get my things."

"The house is a crime scene," Macy said. "They can't let you in right now."

"How could it be a crime scene? Beth wasn't found here."

"But this is likely where the crime originated," Macy explained. "The crime scene encompasses all the places the killer and victim interacted during the abduction and murder."

"Her car isn't here. Does that mean you're going to do all this to her car?"

"As soon as we find it, yes," Nevada said. "It's very likely he transported her or her remains at some point in that car."

Debbie shook her head. "I'm still trying to wrap my head around the fact that Beth is dead."

"Yes, ma'am," Nevada said. "What can you tell us about her?"

"Before she moved in with me, she'd lived in town for about six months," Debbie said. "She was a friend of a friend who needed a place to live. We became good friends. She's from a small town in southwest Virginia. Her dream was to be accepted into the university's CNA program. She wanted to be a nursing assistant."

"What about family?" Macy asked.

As police personnel came and went from her house, Debbie shook her head. "She has a brother. His name is Mark, but I've never met him."

"Mark Watson?" Nevada asked.

"Yes. I believe he's serving in the navy and is deployed now. He may be difficult to get ahold of. From what she told me, he was her only sibling."

"Is the brother older or younger?" Macy asked.

"I believe he's older."

"Are their parents in the picture?" Macy asked.

"Father wasn't a figure in her life, and her mother died a couple of years ago. She's made her own way."

"Was she dating anyone?" Nevada asked.

"Not really. I mean, she went out a few months ago, but she's kind of a homebody."

From Debbie, they learned that Beth worked sixty to seventy hours a week and she was well liked. There was no unwanted attention from staff or strangers. No red flags. There was nothing that made anyone nervous or fearful for Beth's safety.

"Did you tell anyone you were switching schedules with Beth?" Macy asked.

"Beth said she took care of it."

"Are you still staying with your parents?" Macy asked.

"It's a little crazy at home." A sad smile curled her lips. "My mom is pretty freaked out and is hovering."

"What about your boyfriend?" Nevada asked.

"Rafe's not really my boyfriend, and he was pretty weirded out by the attention at the police station. He's not answered any of my texts or calls."

"Do you have any other friends?"

"Yeah. I'll make some calls. I really need to get my scrubs and pack a bag."

"That's going to have to wait," Macy said.

"This sucks," Debbie muttered.

"Yes, it does," Macy replied.

Nevada walked Debbie to her car, his head tilted toward the woman as she continued to talk and point back at her house. Finally, shaking her head, Debbie got into her car and drove off.

As Nevada strode back toward Macy, his phone chimed with a text. "It's from the medical examiner. Dr. Squibb is making Beth Watson's examination a priority."

"I know Bennett was planning to talk to Bruce Shaw, but I'd like to talk to him myself." Macy dialed the doctor's office number.

"Questions about Cindy?"

"Yes. And also about Beth and the schedule switch with Debbie. I still think there is something there, but I won't know it until I see it."

Macy dialed Bruce Shaw's number. The phone rang once and went to voicemail. *"This is Dr. Bruce Shaw. I'm not available. Leave a message. And if this is a medical emergency, call 911."*

"Dr. Shaw, this is Special Agent Macy Crow. Call me. I have a few questions for you."

They each donned latex gloves and paper booties and entered a house that could easily pass for the homes of the other victims. "Once we search the property, we can view the autopsy," Nevada said.

"Is Deputy Bennett joining us?"

"She texted me. She's touching base with her son and then coming by."

Bruce Shaw had lived in several cities as he had earned his medical degree and then fulfilled his internship and residency. Had there been an uptick in crimes when he'd moved to a new town? "Guys like this just don't give up the best gig of their sorry lives."

Macy dialed Andy's number. Andy picked up on the third ring. "Tell me you have a ViCAP hit."

"And good evening to you, Agent Crow." Andy chuckled, clearly used to Macy's abrupt approach. "As a matter of fact, I have two possible hits. In Baltimore in 2007 a masked man raped two women. He used red rope to secure their hands. A woman was strangled to death six months after the rapes. Again, red rope was used. In Atlanta, 2012, there were two deaths. Both women had been strangled repeatedly and their hands bound with red rope. Oh, and all the victims lived in one-story homes. I've asked for the DNA taken at all the crime scenes to be sent to Quantico, along with their case files."

"Nice job."

"It is, if I do say so myself," Andy said.

"Baltimore and Atlanta are within driving distance of Deep Run," Macy said.

"I'll keep searching," Andy said. "There could be more cases. I'll call you when I have more information on the Baltimore and Atlanta cases."

"Maybe we'll get lucky."

"Macy, it's not luck. It's communication and computers."

As an afterthought, Macy added, "See what you can find out about Cindy Shaw. She was a high school senior who vanished about the same time as my murder victim."

"I'll see what I can find."

"Andy, I take back everything I said about computer people." Macy hung up to Andy laughing. "Did you get most of that, Nevada?"

"Yep."

The front door opened to the small living room she'd seen through the window yesterday. Now inside, she could see the blue couch was worn, but at one time had been top of the line. A couple of green upholstered chairs also looked older, but expensive. The same could be said for all of the furnishings she observed.

In the hallway, they both stared at the stacks of unopened paint cans, rollers and brushes, piles of newspapers, and plastic tarps.

"I think my aunt Susan had a couch similar to that one. Same color, but not as expensive," Macy said. "Only she covered hers in plastic, and whenever I sat on it in shorts, my skin on the back of my legs stuck as I tried to stand up." She ran her fingers over an end table, tracing a line of dust. "Looks like the folks at the retirement center or their families handed down furniture to Debbie. She must be popular."

Nevada's gun belt creaked as he shifted his weight. "Several families requested her, and she was able to work a great deal of overtime."

"Leaving Watson here alone often?"

"Adding more to my theory that Watson's death feels planned, not impulsive."

"Agreed."

Most murders were unplanned. In those cases the amateur killers accidentally left something behind that more often than not led to their capture. Called Locard's exchange principle, it meant that no one entered a scene or left it without leaving some trace such as DNA, hair fibers, fingerprints, trash, or a footprint.

Macy entered the kitchen. The table was a throwback to the eighties with a set of six matching chairs. Debbie or Beth had placed two square green place mats out, as if she expected to share her breakfast with someone.

"Our rapist took one item from each victim's home," Macy said. "He liked to break up sets." She walked up to the counter and keyed in on a prince figurine. She picked it up and shook a dash of salt on the palm of her hand. "Where's his princess?"

Nevada looked around the room. "I don't see it."

She noted the back door handle had been dusted for prints. It was ajar. She made a note to check with the investigative crew to determine if they had found the door this way.

The refrigerator was stocked with a dozen cans of beer, a nearly empty jar of peanut butter, a jar of kosher pickles, a bowl full of butter packets, and various other condiments.

Macy checked the cabinets, revealing more hand-me-down dishes, cups, and glasses. "Reminds me of Mom and her crazy collection."

"She passed away when you were in college, correct?"

She was surprised he remembered the detail. "Yes."

"Did she ever talk to you about your adoption?"

Macy didn't look anything like her adoptive parents and had become accustomed to answering queries about adoption from an early age. "Not much. When I asked her years ago about my birth mother, she said she didn't have any details about her."

"Do you think she knew the truth?"

"I'd like to believe Mom and Pop didn't know the worst of it, but I'll never know. My mother was an expert at ignoring some things. Pop knew my birth mother had died in childbirth, but he never reported her death."

"Your father was afraid of what would happen to you, his wife, and him if he did."

It didn't surprise her that Nevada had dug into the details of the case. "I suppose so."

Macy glanced at a wall calendar dangling under a couple of frog magnets. Both Debbie and Beth had penciled in their work schedules. Debbie had crossed out the dates from Sunday to Tuesday and added Beth's name.

They walked down the hallway toward the bedroom and found two technicians in the back bedroom on the left. One was shooting pictures of the room, and one was dusting for prints by the open window.

The sheets on the bed were rumpled and the remote sat on the nightstand, along with a bag of chips. He could picture Beth sitting here watching television.

"Beth was a strong woman," Nevada said. "Physically. If a big patient needed help with mobility, they called Beth."

"There weren't defensive wounds on her hands," Macy said as she walked to the window and peered out. "He surprised her. Maybe she dozed off while she was watching television."

In the adjoining bathroom, gray pajama pants and a football T-shirt were discarded on the floor. An uncapped tube of toothpaste squeezed in the middle sat alongside her toothbrush, which lay on its side. In the shower there was a collection of shampoos, a razor, and a sliver of white soap.

"Her last evening had been normal until she dozed off and awoke to him standing over her." She turned toward a secondhand dresser with eight drawers and faded brass oval pulls. On top of the dresser were six earrings scattered around. At first glance the chaos was another casualty of an overworked medical assistant ready to kick back after a long shift.

"The earrings were arranged in a neat row. Side by side. A collection of singles, something anyone who has earrings has. But the singles get tossed in a drawer or jewelry box because you're still holding on to the hope that the mate will be found. I've never laid mine out on a dresser like this."

She reached in her back pocket and removed her phone, snapping several pictures of the collection.

"The intruder collected one of each earring for a trophy or souvenir," Nevada said.

She glanced to the nightstand holding a picture of Beth. Her smile was genuine and brilliant as the sun captured the green in her eyes. "Beth's wearing a delicate set of hoop earrings with small gemstones."

Nevada found the lone moon-shaped earring with the sparkle gem on the dresser. "Whoever killed Beth was watching her for a while."

"I agree." Macy turned to the technician. "Any idea how he came into the house?"

The tech lowered her camera. "The back door was open."

"Are there shoe prints leading up to it?" Nevada asked.

"I might have a partial footprint," the tech offered. "I've marked the print with red flags and have made molds."

"Could you identify what kind of shoe it was?" Nevada asked.

"I'd say a man's athletic shoe, size ten or eleven based on the print found near the gate."

"We'll have a look."

Macy followed Nevada out the back door of the house. He clicked on a flashlight, illuminating the path as they moved toward the back fence. The light caught the red flags and white remnants of the cast. He pointed the light over the fence. "This is rough terrain and a hard area to search at night. We can double back tomorrow."

"I can keep up. Let's go."

"Suit yourself."

Macy followed Nevada as he studied the area around the back door and then along a narrow footpath that led to the gate. He opened the gate and they stepped through it, moving toward the dense stand of woods.

As he approached, he moved carefully and deliberately toward a thicker swath of muck and then another. He knelt and studied a drying mud puddle under the glare of his flashlight. Stamped in the middle was an arching shoe impression common in many sports shoes.

Macy knelt down, cringing a little. With her phone she snapped pictures. "Did it rain here recently?"

"Saturday night."

"Beth and Debbie look alike. Maybe he didn't care which one he took. Both were his type, and killing either one would have given him the thrill he needed."

"The forensic technician needs to make a cast of this footprint."

Macy rose a little too quickly and her leg cramped in protest. Pain jolted her and she stumbled slightly. She caught herself by grabbing Nevada's arm.

His hand wrapped around her forearm, steadying her. "Are you all right?"

"I'm fine." She shrugged out of his grasp. "I'm good."

"We can take a moment, Macy."

Macy curled her fingers into a fist, resisting the urge to massage her leg. "Pain reminds me I'm alive. It reminds me of my purpose."

Nevada studied her a long moment, then shook his head and cursed. "Ramsey sent you to me knowing you weren't ready for this. You need more time to heal."

"You make it sound like Ramsey sent the B team."

"I didn't mean that. Ramsey put the case before your health, Macy."

Macy possessed a fair number of foul words in her arsenal, and she swallowed a mouthful. "When this case is solved, everyone will see how effective I still am."

***

Brooke Bennett received several texts from Bruce Shaw, informing her he was running late. First time it was the game, which had gone into overtime. The second time, it was a call from his neighbor about a busted pipe.

By the time they met up in the assisted living facility's parking lot, it was after ten. He pulled up in no particular rush and rose out of his car as if he had all the time in the world. He was wearing sweats and a sweatshirt. He moved with the step of a much younger man.

She rose out of her car. "Dr. Shaw."

He turned and smiled, moving toward her with purpose. "Deputy Bennett. What can I do for you?"

"I want to see the work schedules for the last month for the facility."

"That's going to take some time," he said. "I'll have to get with personnel, and they don't open until nine a.m." He grinned. "Banker's hours."

"I want to ask you about Beth Watson."

He folded his arms. "What about her?"

"She was found murdered this evening."

He stilled, drawing in a slow, even breath. "That's terrible. Jesus. What happened?"

"I can't give the specifics right now. Can you tell me if she had any trouble with anyone at work?"

"No. Hell, she was a nice kid. Tough homelife. I felt for her. She reminded me of where I came from."

"Was there anyone or any incident that struck you as odd lately?"

"We did have a break-in a few months ago. We had money stolen from petty cash and liquor taken from the café."

"I don't remember that."

"I spoke to Sheriff Greene about it."

"You called him directly?"

"He and I go way back. He was a big supporter of the team."

She removed the cheek swab from her pocket. "Speaking of the team, that brings me to the second reason for my visit. Special Agent Crow has asked me to collect cheek swabs of all the football players from the 2004 season."

He arched a brow. "Does she think one of us did it?"

"She's covering all her bases. Do you consent?"

"Sure, go ahead."

"Would you rather it be somewhere more private?"

"I have nothing to hide."

She quickly pulled on gloves and removed the swab from its container. He opened his mouth wide.

As she leaned in toward him, she caught the scent of sweat from what must have been a strenuous workout. The muscles in her back tightened, and a tremor shot down her arm. Her heart beat faster.

"You okay, Deputy?" he asked. "You look a little pale."

"I'm fine." Pursing her lips, she wiped the inside of his cheek and quickly replaced the swab in the vial.

Shaw was studying her closely. "Is that it?"

"That's it."

"I'm here to help, Deputy Bennett. Call me anytime."

With a wave, he turned. As he crossed the lot, his cell rang. He stopped, and a sudden shimmer of tension rippled through his body. He spoke in hushed, clipped tones she couldn't make out as he started walking quickly away from her. His expression was angry when he vanished through the facility's front door.

What the hell was that about?

She rubbed the back of her neck and got into her vehicle. She dialed her mother's number and the call went to voicemail. "Mom, call me. I've got a few questions for you about Bruce Shaw."

***

It was eleven when Nevada dropped Macy off at her motel room. "Thanks for the ride."

"You can still stay with me."

"I won't get any sleep," she said.

"Is that a bad thing?"

She smiled, leaned forward, and kissed him on the lips. "See you in the morning, Nevada."

"The last time I dropped you off was at the airport. Next thing I know, I'm getting a call and hear you're in a coma."

She searched his face. "I'm a big girl, Nevada."

"Who likes to take risks."

"Like I told Ramsey, it's who I am."

He frowned, shaking his head, and she knew there were more thoughts swirling in his head. "I'll wait until you get inside."

She grabbed her pack, got out of the car, and crossed toward her motel door. She slid her key through the lock and pushed open the door, doing a quick search of the room. She glanced back at Nevada's car and raised her hand to give him the all clear. He blinked his headlights, and he waited until she closed and locked the door.

Macy then pushed a heavy chair in front of the door. She removed her weapon, set it on the small vanity by the bathroom, and kicked off her boots. She turned on the hot spray of the shower and stripped. She stepped under the hot water and nearly whimpered with relief as the water pelted down on her skin.

She lingered until she'd chased the chill from her bones and then, out of the shower, toweled off. She slid on an FBI T-shirt, set her gun, phone, and charger on the nightstand, and grabbed her pack before scooting under the covers.

The next half hour was spent on the laptop writing up case notes and compiling a list of witnesses to interview tomorrow. Email came next. There was a message from Andy. The subject line read "Cindy Shaw."

Andy had accessed the motor vehicles records and found a driver's license issued to Cindy Shaw in 2004. The color photograph showed a young girl with long dark hair, a wide smile, and a sprinkle of freckles that didn't soften the wariness in her brown eyes. Macy had seen countless runaways with the same look.

Cindy looked like Tobi, Beth, and the rape victims. "Jesus, kid. What happened to you?"

Macy scrolled down the email and saw Andy's notation that there were no other records either criminal or public on Cindy.

She closed her laptop and pinched the bridge of her nose. She laid her head back against the headboard and closed her eyes.

Scratch. Scratch. Scratch.

The sound was faint at first, but it persisted. It was the sound of fingernails clawing into dirt. Someone was trying to dig out of a grave.

"I'm still here," Cindy said. *"Don't leave me behind like everyone else."*

"What do you want?" Macy asked.

"Find me like you did the others. I want to come home."

"What others?"

"Find me."

"Where the hell are you?"

A slamming car door outside her room woke Macy up, and she bolted upright in her bed. Heart pounding, she searched the room expecting the worst. She grabbed her gun and swung her legs over the side of the bed. The chair remained in front of the locked door.

"Of all the dead people I'd like to have a conversation with, you're not it, Cindy Shaw." She ran her hand over her hair. "How about you, Pop? Why don't you chime in? You owe me a few good conversations. And Mom? Could use a good word or two."

She sat on the edge of the bed, set her gun down beside her, and buried her head in her hands. "And now I'm inviting my dead parents to speak to me. I have officially lost my mind."

There was a logical reason for all this. She'd bet an MRI and a good neurologist could explain it. Even a shrink might be welcome at this point. Anyone who could explain why her brain was now processing facts in the voice of a dead girl she'd never met.

Gingerly, she lay back against the pillows, and for several minutes, maybe even a half hour, she stared at the white popcorn ceiling. Slowly, her racing heart shifted down a notch, and the unnatural buzzing energy seeped from her body. Her eyes closed. Finally, she drifted off to sleep.

Scratch. Scratch. Scratch.

CHAPTER
TWENTY-THREE

Wednesday, November 20, 11:10 p.m.

Brooke drove down the long drive that led to her house. Every muscle in her back ached. Her stomach growled with hunger. She expected to see the glow of the television in her mother's room, but the house was dark.

She climbed the front steps and let herself in the front door. A nightlight glowing nearby was supposed to make Brooke's late-night arrivals easier and prevent her from tripping over whatever size-eleven shoes Matt left lying around.

The house was peacefully quiet, and she was glad. She walked back down the center hallway to the kitchen and opened the refrigerator. There was a plate of chicken, rice, and broccoli wrapped in plastic with a sticky note attached that read **EAT!**

Brooke smiled as she grabbed the plate and popped it in a small microwave. She plugged in two minutes and hit "Start." While the machine hummed and the plate turned, she opened the fridge and pulled out a soda. She twisted off the top and took a long pull before holding the cold bottle to her head.

Footsteps had her turning to find Matt standing there. He was wearing gym pants, a basketball T-shirt, and his dark hair stuck up at the crown of his head.

"I wasn't sure you'd make it home," Matt said.

"I had to take a break. Is Grandma upstairs asleep?"

"No." Matt yawned. "She got called in to work. She knows I can take care of myself."

Of course her son could take care of himself. But having come from the scene of her first homicide, she didn't like the idea of him being alone. "Did Grandma say when she'd be back?"

"She said she would drive me to school in the morning."

Brooke stepped closer and hugged her son. His muscles tensed and he tried to pull away, but she held tight. Not only to him but to the memory of when he'd been a little baby and wanted nothing more than to cuddle. Finally, he relaxed into her embrace. There was still some of the little boy in her young man.

Brooke kissed him on the cheek. "Thanks for letting your mom give you a hug."

He wiggled out of her arms. "I hear there was a murder."

His statement brought the outside world crashing back. "There was. A girl not much older than you."

"How did she die?"

Brooke walked to the stove, checked the lid of a copper kettle, and then turned the burner on. "I can't say. When I can, we'll talk about it."

"Seems weird that would happen in Deep Run."

"It happens everywhere, son," she said. "There's no such thing as really safe in the world. It's an illusion, which is why I need for you to be very careful."

"I'm not a baby, Mom."

She looked over at her son, this young man, and knew he was right. "Point taken."

When he ran his fingers through his thick dark hair, she saw the scrapes on his knuckles. "What happened to your hand?"

"Nothing."

"Something happened." She crossed immediately, taking his hand in hers. He tried to pull away, but she held tight. "Were you in a fight?"

He shrugged in a way that reminded her so much of herself at that age. She had had all the answers and then some. "It wasn't a big deal."

"Was it Tyler?"

"He's got it in for me, but I can take care of him."

"Fights are a big deal, Matthew. They can get you kicked out of school."

"It was just a scuffle with the guys. It's not a big deal."

The kettle whistled, screaming and hissing until Brooke lifted it from the burner. She didn't bother to reach for a teacup, her mind now distracted. "Matt, you better get to bed. I'll stick around tonight and get you to school in the morning."

"Grandma said she'd do it."

"I'll do it." She kissed him on the forehead and forced a smile. "Go on."

"Okay, Mom."

When she heard his bedroom door close, she climbed the stairs to her bedroom and stared at the neatly made bed. Instead of turning in, she sat on the edge. She turned to a picture of Matt and her taken months after he was born. Her long dark hair flowing around her face, she was a kid herself. Her mother, her pastor, and her friends had all told her to put the child up for adoption. And she honestly had considered it. To this day, it pained her to think of it. She hadn't wanted to see him when he was born. She had been exhausted, terrified, and humiliated to be a seventeen-year-old unwed mother.

It was Sheriff Greene who had come to see her in the hospital and told her she owed it to herself to hold her son at least once. And when she still had hesitated, he had asked the nurse to bring the baby to her.

Sheriff Greene had laid Matt in her arms. Her boy had been a squawking, fussy bundle with a red face and dark hair that already looked like it needed to be cut. He wasn't much to look at. And she had fallen head over heels in love with him.

Brooke was still pissed at Greene for his mishandling of the DNA, but no matter what, she could never hate the man.

She set the picture back on the nightstand. The shutters outside rattled in the wind. She rose up and went into her son's room, sat on the edge of his bed, and rubbed his back until he sat up.

He yawned. "What's going on, Mom?"

She pulled another cheek swab from her pocket. "Open wide, sport. Need a quick swab."

He complied, and as she sealed the swab back in the case, he asked, "What's that for?"

"Just a crazy ancestry project, buddy. No worries. Go back to sleep."

When he rolled over and went back to sleep, she hurried down the front stairs and out the front door. She stood in the fresh air for a moment and drew in deep breaths. Jesus. Was this a hornet's nest she really wanted to kick?

Footsteps pounded the ground behind her, and in an instant the seconds slowed. Her hand reached for her weapon. Her body braced for an attack. A flicker of movement caught her peripheral vision. A ski mask appeared right before a right cross connected with her jaw. Pain radiated through her skull and her brain short-circuited. She staggered and then dropped to her knees. She fumbled for the stock of her weapon, but the assailant grabbed it from her.

He then yanked her back, slamming her body into a tree. The pain rocketed through her body. She fell to the ground and instantly he was on top, pinning her midsection. He shoved a damp cloth against her nose and mouth.

She held her breath, still flailing her legs. She could hear his steady, even breathing as her own heart raced and her lungs burned for air.

"Breathe," he ordered. When she didn't comply, he lifted his weight and then slammed it against her midsection, knocking the air out of her. Agony rocked her body.

"Let it go," he sang softly in her ear. "Let it go. Don't want to wake up Matt, do you?"

He had been watching her. He knew about Matt. Knowing her son could be in danger lit twin flames of fear and anger.

"Give in to me," he ordered. "Give me this win, and I'll let Matt live."

But he wouldn't kill her right away. He would take his time with her. Her submission now could not only buy her son his life but could also give her time later to find a way to escape.

Memories of garish purple bruises around Beth Watson's neck sent chills down her spine. She didn't want to die at all, especially like that. There was so much in her life she had to do.

But she inhaled and took the chemicals into her bloodstream. She felt lightheaded, and the seductive wave of the drugs washed through her body, dulling the sharp pain burning in the side of her head.

As her muscles gave way, she heard him chuckling.

The pain receded, and what little light there had been from the moon faded to total blackness.

CHAPTER
TWENTY-FOUR

Thursday, November 21, 7:30 a.m.

When Macy and Nevada arrived in Roanoke at the Western District Office of the Virginia State Medical Examiner, neither spoke as they showed identification and donned paper gowns and latex gloves before they entered the large autopsy room containing the remains of Beth Watson. Classical music played on the overhead speaker.

Dr. Squibb was gowned up and inspecting his instruments as a technician wheeled in a gurney and placed it against the stainless steel sink attached to his workstation. The tech locked the gurney wheels and then positioned the instrument table closer to the doctor.

"Thanks for working us in, Dr. Squibb," Macy said.

"Of course," Dr. Squibb said. "If you don't mind, we need to get started. We've got a full caseload this morning."

"Whenever you're ready," she said.

The technician clicked on an overhead light that glistened on the sharp instruments. Dr. Squibb pressed a button with his foot, which activated the overhead microphone.

The doctor stated his name, as well as Nevada's, the tech's, and hers. "These are the remains of Elizabeth Jean Watson, born June 3, 1999. Today is November 21, 2019, and it is 8:02 a.m."

The technician carefully removed the sheet to reveal the pale body of Beth Watson.

Macy's chest tightened as she thought about her own near-death experience. How close she had come to being dissected on a medical examiner's table just like this one.

Dr. Squibb cleared his throat. "The subject today is female. She appears to have been a healthy weight and fit."

The doctor moved to the top of the gurney and rotated the patient's neck to the right and displayed the black-and-blue bruises that ringed her neck. The doctor inspected the markings more closely. In several spots, the bruises mirrored large fingers.

"Can we see the x-ray images?"

The technician clicked on a computer screen, and the victim's neck appeared. The doctor studied it. "The hyoid bone is broken." This delicate bone often snapped during strangulation. "However, the bruising on her neck shows different states of healing, meaning she wasn't just strangled once but multiple times over several days." The confirmation was no surprise, but it was necessary.

"Can you determine how many times she was strangled?" Macy asked.

The doctor rotated the neck several times and then asked to see the x-ray image of the sternum. "Three, maybe four times." No one spoke for several beats before the doctor continued. "Note there are hairline cracks in her sternum. He performed CPR on her."

"Just like Tobi Turner," Nevada said.

"The bone evidence of both victims is almost identical," Dr. Squibb said.

Macy tapped her fingers against her thigh, drawing in a breath as if she were somehow breathing for them both.

Dr. Squibb held up the victim's right hand. The edges of the nails were jagged.

"Where did he keep her?" Macy asked, more to herself.

Scratch. Scratch. Scratch.

The remnants of the dreams clawed out from the shadows, sending rippling chills through her body. "Has the dirt on the bottom of her feet been analyzed?" she asked.

"We sent a sample over to the lab," Dr. Squibb said. "It's a priority." But that still meant it could take months. Television had conditioned the public to believe that lab results happened in a matter of hours, days at most. In reality, the state labs were swamped with DNA and blood samples from an endless number of cases. It was common for test results to linger for months in the lab queue.

The doctor began with the external examination, noting that Beth Watson weighed one hundred and sixty pounds and was five foot nine inches tall. There was minor bruising on her ribs, knees, and shins, and restraint marks ringed her wrists and ankles.

"You've sent her blood off for testing?" Based on the condition of Beth's bedroom, which showed no signs of a struggle, Macy suspected Beth had been unconscious when the killer had taken her from the house.

"We're running the standard toxicology screen analysis," Dr. Squibb said.

Dr. Squibb noted there were no signs of drug use, nor were there scars from old injuries or surgeries. She had four tattoos, the most prominent being the image of a galloping horse on her right shoulder.

As the doctor lifted her right arm, he found two arching marks that resembled upper and lower teeth.

"Did he bite her?" Macy asked.

"Appears so."

"Can you tell if a front tooth was chipped?"

"They don't appear to be."

"He may also have gotten it repaired," Macy said.

The technician photographed the marks and made a notation on a printed diagram representing a human body.

Macy squashed down a jolt of anger. "Did you recover any hair, fluid, or fiber samples from her body?"

"We collected semen samples and three hair strands."

The doctor reached for the scalpel and drew it across the right side of her chest just above her breast, and then over the left side of her breast, joining the two incisions in a V shape. The blade tip then continued down her chest and over her abdomen, creating the classic Y incision. It was a savage but necessary final act.

For the next hour Macy and Nevada watched in silence as the doctor sliced through the thin layer of fat separating skin from bone. Bone cutters snipped through the ribs on both sides of her chest, allowing him to remove the breastplate and set it aside. The heart, lungs, and internal organs were now exposed. Over the next three hours he examined and weighed her internal organs. In the end, he determined she'd been perfectly healthy.

By the time Macy and Nevada left the autopsy room, a weight had settled on her shoulders, reminding her it was her job to eradicate the perpetrators.

"I want this guy so bad I can taste it," Macy said.

"You'll have to get in line behind me."

When she and Nevada got into his vehicle, she checked her messages and found one from Andy. She dialed her number. "Andy, what do you have?"

"You have two more hits. A woman matching the description you gave me was strangled to death in 2015, and another in 2017."

"Where?"

"The 2015 murder occurred in Charleston, West Virginia, and the 2017 murder occurred in Bluefield, Virginia, which is less than sixty miles from Deep Run."

"Was there DNA?" Macy asked.

"There was, but it was badly degraded in both cases," she said. "The bodies of both women weren't found for months after they vanished."

Her heart raced faster. "Were their remains buried?"

"No, they were both dumped on the side of the road. In that part of the world, the side of the road isn't always a neat shoulder. It can be a drop off the side of a mountain."

"What about red rope?"

"Discovered bound to the hands of the 2017 victim."

"Who's the local law enforcement contact?"

"Sheriff Wade Tanner," Andy said.

"Do you have a phone number?"

Andy rattled it off. "I also have a possible hit in western Maryland, but I'll know later today. The locality's application was incomplete."

"Andy, in any of the cases you mentioned, were there teeth marks on the victims?"

Papers shuffled and then she spoke. "In Atlanta, the victim had a significant bite mark on her upper right arm. Should I add that to the list?"

"Yes. And thank you, Andy. I appreciate it." She glanced toward Nevada, feeling the first easing of the pressure that had been building in her since she'd walked out of Ramsey's office. "Did you hear?"

"I did."

She looked up Bluefield on her phone. "Mercer County borders Virginia. We can be there in less than two hours."

"I know Sheriff Wade Tanner. I worked a bureau case in his jurisdiction seven or eight years ago. Let me call him."

He dialed Tanner's number, but she could hear the sheriff's clipped, deep voice on his recorded message. Nevada left a message.

Macy was making progress, but would she nail him before he killed again?

***

Brooke's head pounded when her eyes fluttered open. She tried to sit up, but pain shot through her body, sending her backward to the stained carpet. She lay for a moment, her heart beating fast as she tried to collect herself.

Where was she?

Drawing in a breath, she pushed up to a sitting position and rested her back against the concrete. Her throat also hurt, and when she raised her hand to her neck, the flesh felt tender and bruised.

She reached for her weapon and discovered her gun belt had been stripped away, as had her shoes and socks. The pins securing her hair had been removed, leaving her long dark hair to fall past her shoulders.

As she looked around the small room, she was now more pissed than afraid. How could she have been so stupid? She'd heard his footsteps come up behind her, but she'd not reacted fast enough.

Her mind went to Matt sleeping in his bed. Worry and fear swirled around her anger. It was one thing for her to pay the price for not being on guard, but not her kid. Tears burned her eyes before she stopped her thoughts midstream. She was no use to Matt sitting in here crying like a child. This prick wouldn't have it easy with her.

Gritting her teeth, she pushed to a standing position and felt along the walls until her fingertips brushed over a doorknob. Hope came and went just as quickly as she rattled the knob and realized it was locked.

She considered shouting and pounding, but knew this was what he wanted from her. Fear. And she'd be damned if she'd give it to him.

Drawing in a deep breath, she ran her fingers again over her neck. He'd strangled her while she'd been unconscious. Not very sporting, even for him. Out cold, she'd not shown him the fear he craved, so he'd left her alive. For now.

If she was sure of anything, it was that he would return and strangle her again.

One way or another, she had to get ready for him.

CHAPTER
TWENTY-FIVE

Thursday, November 21, 1:30 p.m.

Nevada and Macy had arrived in Deep Run when Sheriff Tanner called. After a brief exchange, the two agreed to continue the discussion on a closed circuit connection in the conference room.

Sullivan poked his head into the room. "Received a text from Deputy Bennett. She says her boy is real sick. She'll be here as soon as she can."

"Is there anything we can do?" Nevada asked.

"Probably, but the deputy never asks for help and likely would be embarrassed by it."

"I'll follow up with her in the next hour," Nevada said.

"And this package arrived for Agent Crow."

Macy opened the package and pulled out the small sample of Beacon cologne. She removed the top and sprayed a light mist on her wrist. She inhaled, hoping she'd smelled this before. She had not.

She handed the bottle to Nevada. "It's not familiar to me. I think our guy might have changed his scent."

He sniffed and then recapped it. "It's not familiar to me either, but I'll pass it around the office. Someone might recognize it."

"You never know."

Fifteen minutes later, the two were sitting at the conference-room table looking at the telecast of a leather-bound chair and the Mercer County seal mounted on the wall behind. Seconds later a man in his sixties settled in front of the camera. He had a white mustache, a cleanly shaved head, and he wore a khaki shirt with the sheriff's star pinned over his heart.

"Sheriff Tanner," Nevada said. "Appreciate you talking with us."

"Glad to help. Apologize for not being around when you called, but as you'll learn, this job will take you to every corner of the county. How's it up there in the valley?" he asked.

"Fall came and went fast. It'll be a long winter."

"I hear that."

"I'm joined today by Special Agent Macy Crow," Nevada said. "She's working a series of rapes and a murder all connected by the same DNA."

"Afternoon, Agent Crow."

"I appreciate the time," she said.

"Of course." He rustled through papers. "I pulled the case files you referenced in your message, Sheriff Nevada. I didn't think anything would come of that ViCAP application I submitted."

"New details have been entered in the system," Macy said.

"We found a body in Deep Run." Nevada opened a tablet and then an email from Tanner. "Agent Crow thinks we have a serial offender who remained active after he left our area."

Tanner flipped open his file. "Guys like this don't stop until they're caught."

"Who's your victim?" Macy watched as Nevada opened an attachment. The motor vehicles picture of a young brunette came onscreen.

"Her name was Becky Taylor. I sent you her picture and several crime scene photos about ten minutes ago."

"I have them right here," Nevada said. He viewed the image of a woman curled on her side. She was dressed and her hands and feet bound with red rope.

"The medical examiner figured she was exposed to the elements for about five months when found in late April," Tanner said.

"And the cause of death was strangulation?" Macy asked.

"It was."

"What about a bite mark?" Nevada asked.

"Upper right thigh," Tanner said.

The older sheriff glanced at the file, shaking his head. "Becky was nineteen when she was murdered. She was arrested for prostitution and drug charges several times. I did some asking around the trailer park where she grew up. They tell me the deck was stacked against her from the get-go. No daddy and a drug-addicted mom. She was pretty much on her own as soon as she could walk."

She sounded like Cindy Shaw. "Known associates?" Macy asked.

"They knew her at the truck stops where she did most of her work. Everybody knew of her, but no one could say for sure when she vanished or who she was last seen with."

The world swallowed up girls like Becky Taylor who turned to the sex trade for so many reasons, including money, acceptance, and even affection. "According to the ViCAP report, the DNA was degraded."

"That was 2017, so unless you folks at Quantico got more fancy ways of testing DNA, there's not much to be done."

"Can you send the DNA to Quantico?" Macy asked. "It wouldn't hurt to run it through our labs."

"You give me the address, and I'll get it there."

"Thank you." Macy tapped her pen against her yellow legal pad. "Were there any other girls like Becky who vanished?"

He ran his fingers over the length of his mustache. "Girls go missing all the time."

"Any report of johns who tried to strangle sex workers?" Macy asked.

"I can do a search and see if any of the girls filed complaints. It's going to take some time."

"That would be great. We've got his DNA, and we think he had a chipped front tooth."

When the conference call ended, Macy went up to a whiteboard and taped up the pictures of Tobi Turner, Cindy Shaw, Becky Taylor, and Beth Watson. All the women had long dark hair and were in their late teens or early twenties.

"Where did Cindy Shaw live?" Macy asked.

"In a small mobile home park."

"Like Becky."

"Yes."

"I'd like to visit the park where Cindy lived. There might be someone there who remembers her."

"Let's go."

"You don't think I'm chasing a ghost?"

"I don't know what you're chasing, but looking at that board, I see a direct link between Cindy and the other three victims. It makes sense to determine if anyone remembers her."

"Maybe I've been processing logical evidence stored away in her brain." Even as she spoke the words she really wanted to believe, they didn't quite ring true.

They drove to the small Stafford Estates, located twenty minutes from the center of town. Truck tires painted white and cut in half, along with handfuls of winter pansies, marked the entrance and the gravel road that fed into the park between the rows of about two dozen mobile homes.

Nevada pulled into the park, and they drove down the center past several units before they reached a white one trimmed in black. There were a couple of lawn chairs outside, and it reminded Macy of her pop's place.

Macy climbed out of the vehicle and walked up to the trailer door. She knocked and stood to the side as Nevada, hand on his weapon, waited just to the right.

The door opened to a young woman who appeared to be six or seven months pregnant. Brown hair was pulled back in a ponytail, and she wore a blue uniform with her name badge pinned above her right breast pocket.

Macy held up her badge. "My name is Special Agent Macy Crow, and I'm here with Sheriff Nevada looking for the family that used to live in this trailer. Do you remember hearing about the Shaw family? They would have lived here about fifteen years ago."

"My husband and I have only been here three years. But if you knock on the door across the street from me, Ms. Beverly might remember. She's been here at least twenty years. Knows everyone."

"Thank you."

"Knock loud," the woman said. "She's hard of hearing."

"Thanks for the tip." Macy crossed to a smaller trailer surrounded by a garden bed bordered with white rocks.

Macy knocked on the door and could hear the blare of a television. When she didn't hear any movement, she pounded on the door with her fist. Finally, the television grew silent. She knocked again.

Inside the trailer, footsteps moved toward the door before the curtains fluttered and an old woman peered out. She then opened the door. She appeared to be in her seventies. She was a small woman with gray hair tied tight with a hair tie. She wore an oversize T-shirt, jeans, and slippers.

"Ms. Beverly?" Macy asked.

"That's right."

She introduced herself and Nevada again. "I was wondering if you remember a family that lived across the street. They were the Shaws. The daughter was Cindy."

"Sure, I remember them. The mama was Eunice, the boy was Bruce, and the girl, Cindy. The mama died fourteen or fifteen years ago, and the girl moved away about that time. The boy is still here in town. He's a doctor and done real well for himself."

"How did the mother die?" Macy asked.

"Drugs. Eunice was always hooked on them."

"What can you tell me about Cindy?" Macy asked.

Ms. Beverly shook her head. "Bless her heart. She had a rough go of it. She'd been fending for herself since she was in second or third grade. Eunice was always off with a man, and when she was home, she was always fighting with one man or another. I used to feed Cindy and Bruce peanut butter and jelly sandwiches when they got home from school. Lord, but those children could eat. When they got into high school, Bruce found out he had a real talent for football. Once the team got ahold of him, we didn't see him much anymore."

"Can you tell me who Cindy hung out with before she moved away?" Macy asked.

"There were some of the boys from the high school. There were a few older ones as well. She was a pretty little thing and was hungry for attention. I told her she was going after the wrong kind, but she would only laugh at me and tell me to stop worrying."

"Do you have any names?"

"No. I saw cars come and go, but I never was formally introduced."

"Did she ever say if any of the men were violent with her?" Macy asked.

"There was one," the woman said. "Cindy tried to hide it from me, but I saw the bruises on her neck."

"Bruises?" Macy asked.

Ms. Beverly raised her wrinkled hand to her neck. "I asked her about it, but she said it was nothing she couldn't take care of herself. She said she had figured out a way to get rich, and when she did, she'd come for me. That was sweet of her, but I've seen too many girls like her. Think they can smile their way to a better place. But it never works."

"Do you think she moved away?"

Ms. Beverly pressed arthritic fingers to her lips as she shook her head. "No. She would have told me if she was leaving. She wouldn't have just left without a word."

"You ever talk to Sheriff Greene about Cindy?" Nevada asked.

"I called him a couple of times and finally he came by. I got the sense he wasn't real serious about finding her."

"Why do you say that?" Nevada asked.

"I told him she wouldn't just leave, and he scratched out a few words in a notebook, but wasn't paying me no mind. Of course, the case never went anywhere."

"Was Bruce worried about his sister?"

"After she vanished, he came by the trailer and cleared out his things. I asked if he'd heard from her, but he told me not to worry. He'd seen her get on a bus."

"Did you believe him?"

Ms. Beverly shook her head. "No. I could always tell when that boy was fibbing."

An old woman's intuition wouldn't stand up as evidence in court, but Macy believed her. "Where did Bruce move to?"

"He moved in with Kevin Wyatt. Those two are cousins and were always close. Thick as thieves during high school. I couldn't blame Bruce for hanging out with the Wyatts. It was a normal home, and the only time Eunice paid any attention to Cindy and Bruce was when she was between men and scared."

"Scared of what?"

"Being alone, I suppose." She held up a hand. "I have a picture of Cindy still tacked to my refrigerator. Want to see it?"

"I do."

The woman vanished into the kitchen and returned with the picture. The colors were faded and the edges curled. "It was taken right out front of my home."

Macy studied the picture of the smiling girl, who appeared to be about fifteen. She wore tight jeans, a V-neck sweater, and what looked like an arrowhead necklace. "When was this taken?"

"About a year before she vanished. Bruce had just given her that necklace, and she was so proud. She wanted me to take a picture of her wearing it."

"How did Cindy feel about her brother spending so much time on the football field and with the Wyatts?"

"She was angry. Felt abandoned."

The girl's brother, her only lifeline, had left her behind. "Do you mind if I snap a picture of it?" Macy asked.

"No, go right ahead."

Macy took several pictures of the photo and then collected Ms. Beverly's contact information. She thanked her for her help.

Macy and Nevada got into his car. "She said Kevin and Bruce were thick as thieves."

"Think one might have helped the other kill Tobi?"

"I don't know. But I want to talk to them both again." Macy dialed Kevin Wyatt's number. It went to voicemail. "This is Agent Crow. I'm still looking for that buccal swab, Mr. Wyatt. Call me."

"Wyatt likes to drag his feet. When Tyler gets in trouble, he always lawyers up."

"Eventually, he'll have to give in."

Nevada tapped his finger on the steering wheel. "Until then I'm going to follow up with Greene."

"I want to come."

"Not this time. He's never been a fan of outsiders, and he might be more inclined to talk to me if I'm alone."

She didn't like being left out but trusted Nevada enough to ask the right questions. As he started his vehicle, his phone rang. It was Sullivan.

"Sullivan," Nevada said.

"I received a call from Sandra Bennett. She says she can't find Brooke."

"I thought she was home with her son," Nevada said.

"It doesn't look like that was correct."

"Where is Sandra now?" Nevada asked.

"Her house."

"I'm on my way."

***

When Nevada pulled up in front of Brooke Bennett's house, Sandra was standing on the front porch talking to Sullivan. Sandra's face was tight with worry.

"This doesn't look good," Macy said.

"No."

They walked up to the front steps. "What's going on here?"

Sandra stepped toward Nevada. "Have you heard from Brooke?"

"No, she hasn't reported in for her shift," Nevada said. "What happened?"

"I don't know," Sandra said. "I was working late, and when I got home, her car was parked out back, but there was no sign of her. Matt said she was home late last night, but he didn't see her when he awoke this morning for school."

"The boy wasn't sick?" Nevada asked.

"No. He was fine. Why would you ask that?"

"Your daughter texted me and told me her son was sick and she'd be late."

As a precaution, Nevada and his deputies all carried a phone with GPS tracking when they were on duty. He checked and searched Bennett's location. "It says that she's here."

"She's not," Sandra insisted. "I've looked everywhere."

"The phone is here." Nevada turned his attention to the grounds surrounding the house as he called Bennett's number. A faint ring echoed from behind a stand of bushes. He slipped on latex gloves and then rooted around in the shrubs until his fingers brushed the phone.

The phone's display had a record of Bennett's text to Nevada as well as several texts from Bruce Shaw. She'd also placed a call to her mother around ten last night. "Why did she call you?"

"She said she had questions about Bruce Shaw," Sandra said.

"What kind of questions?" Nevada asked.

"I have no idea. We never spoke."

"Deputy Bennett said she would get a cheek swab from Shaw," Macy said.

Nevada called dispatch on his radio and advised them that Deputy Brooke Bennett was missing. He wanted all deputies searching for her immediately.

"I'd like to speak to Matt," Nevada said.

Sandra hesitated and then nodded. "He's in the kitchen. He's upset, so go easy on him."

"Of course I will," Nevada said.

Nevada and Macy followed Sandra into the house and back toward the kitchen to where a young man who looked like his mother sat staring at his phone.

"Matt," Nevada said.

The boy stood. "I've been waiting for Mom to call."

"We're trying to find her now, Matt. When did you last see her?" Nevada asked.

"It was about midnight. I heard her come in."

"Where were you, Sandra?" Nevada asked.

"I was called back in to work."

"Where's that?"

"The Deep Run assisted living facility. I'm an on-call nurse there. I wasn't scheduled, but the boss said several staff members didn't show."

"You must know Debbie Roberson and Beth Watson," Macy said.

"Sure. It's terrible what happened to Beth."

"Who called you in to work?" Macy asked.

"Dr. Shaw."

Macy and Nevada exchanged glances, but neither spoke in front of the boy. "Matt, what did your mother say to you?" Nevada asked.

"Just said she'd be here to drive me to school." He glanced at his grandmother and then, dropping his gaze, said, "She was annoyed Grandma wasn't here."

Sandra shook her head. "I'm so sorry, pal."

"What happened next?" Macy asked carefully.

"She came back upstairs and kissed me good night." He shook his head. "I barely remember her. I was so tired."

It was quiet for a moment as they all processed the situation.

"What if someone hurt her?" Matt asked.

"No one has hurt your mom," Sandra said.

Nevada glanced toward Matt's scraped knuckles. "Your mom is a smart deputy. What happened to your hands?"

The boy put his hands into his pockets. "It was a fight."

"With whom?"

"Tyler Wyatt. He said some bad things about my mom."

Nevada laid his hand on the boy's shoulder. "What kind of things?"

His face flushed red. "Like how her cherry got popped at the Wyatt barn."

"How would he know that?"

"I guess his brother told him. I don't know for sure." Matt lifted his gaze to Nevada's. "I thought he and the other guys invited me to the barn because they liked me. But they just wanted to screw with me."

"You don't look so bad. What kind of shape is Tyler in?"

"I don't know. But I got in a few good licks before he and the others ran off. Are you going to arrest me?"

Nevada patted his hand on the boy's arm. "No. Let me talk to your grandmother. Mind waiting for us a few more minutes?"

"Sure. Whatever you say."

Nevada and Macy walked into the living room with Sandra. "What can you tell us about Dr. Shaw?"

"He's always been nice to me. The patients love him."

"How does he get along with the staff?" Macy asked.

"Fine. He's done a lot for the facility. Because of him, the new addition got built."

"That's the Adele Jenner Wyatt wing."

"Yes, it's state of the art. It's been great."

"I assume the money came from Kevin Wyatt."

"Yes, he's a big benefactor of the facility since his grandmother stayed with us."

"You ever see Dr. Shaw with Beth Watson?" Macy asked.

"No more than usual."

"Did he seem to show any special interest in her or any other woman?"

"Not that I noticed. Are you suggesting Dr. Shaw would hurt a woman?"

"I'm not suggesting anything," Macy said.

Nevada dialed Bruce's number. The call went to voicemail. He left his name and number and asked for a callback. "Sandra, is there somewhere else you and Matt can stay?"

"I don't want to leave," Sandra said. "What if Brooke comes back?"

"I'll keep a deputy posted here. But it'll help me to know you and Matt are safe."

"Matt and I can go to Mr. Greene's." She looked up at Nevada, almost apologetic. "He's always looked out for Brooke, Matt, and me."

"That's a great idea," Nevada said. "Mr. Greene will be the first person I call when I find Brooke."

Matt appeared at the doorway. "I don't want to go."

"We'll find your mom faster if we're not worried about you," Macy said.

"Get your things, Matt," Nevada said. "I'll have Deputy Sullivan drive you and your grandmother there."

When the boy vanished into the house, Nevada asked Sandra, "Are there any security cameras on the property?"

"We talked about installing them but have never gotten around to it. They're expensive," she said.

"Has anyone made threats against your daughter?" Macy asked.

"There was a guy a couple of weeks ago. He called the house a few times, but she hung up on him."

"Who was it?"

"She tried to brush it off and say it was a telemarketer. But I didn't believe her. But when I pressed, she refused to answer."

"Do you have the number?" Nevada asked.

"It's on her cell, I suppose."

Nevada scrolled through the numbers. There had to be over one hundred calls. He checked the texts. He spotted the ones from Stuart. "Was your daughter talking to the media?"

Sandra nodded. "Last summer. She was so mad about those untested DNA kits. Mr. Greene wouldn't listen to reason no matter how much she pleaded with him."

"So she leaked it to the press?" Nevada asked.

"But she's not given them anything since," Sandra said. "She just wanted those kits tested."

"Was your daughter raped in high school?" Macy asked.

Nevada's jaw tightened as he looked at Macy. The question caught him off guard. In all his dealings with Bennett, she'd never once let on that she had been raped.

"Why would you ask a question like that?" Sandra asked.

"That's not an answer to my question." And then in a softer tone, Macy said, "I'm on Brooke's side. I'm trying to help her."

Sandra's face crumpled with sadness. "Yes."

"Is that when she became pregnant?" Macy asked.

"Yes. But she hid it from me for months. She was nearly six months pregnant when I found out."

Nevada calculated back to when Bennett would have gotten pregnant with Matt. Could Matt's biological father be the rapist they were chasing? "Does she know who assaulted her?"

"No. She was unconscious for most of it," Sandra said.

Nevada was irritated with himself for not picking up on the signs Macy had seen. He was also frustrated with Bennett because she'd not confided in him.

Matt came out the front door with his backpack slung over his shoulder. As Sullivan stepped forward, Macy asked Nevada, "Do you mind if I drive them?"

Nevada studied her a moment and then handed his keys to her. "Sure."

She smiled at the boy. "Matt, I'm Agent Crow. I'll run you and your grandmother over to Mr. Greene's."

He tightened his grip on the strap of his pack and walked toward her. Nevada patted him on the back and told him it would all be fine. Sandra grabbed her purse, and she and Matt climbed into Nevada's vehicle.

***

Macy slid behind the wheel, adjusted the seat and mirrors. "Nevada's a tad taller than me," she said, trying to put him at ease.

Matt hooked his seat belt. "You don't look like FBI."

"I've heard that a few times lately." She started the engine and pulled away from the scene.

"Do you really think my mom is going to be okay?" Matt asked.

"As long as Nevada and I have a say in it, Matt."

He tightened his grip on the armrest and stared ahead. His lips were tight and he blinked back tears. "She loves her job."

"I know she does." She handed him her phone so he could read out directions. "Which way to Mr. Greene's?"

"Get on I-81 south," Matt said.

"I can do that."

The silence was broken only by more directions from the boy, which had them arriving at Mr. Greene's house a half hour later. She parked, and he got out with his grandmother.

"My daughter is worried that she's not good enough for the new work promotion," Sandra said.

"She said that?" Macy asked.

"To me," Sandra said.

"She's very good, but I've worked these kinds of cases longer." She looked at them both. "I'm not the bad guy here. I want to help."

"We know that." Sandra laid her hand on her grandson's shoulder.

"Matt, think back to when your mom was in your room. What did she say?"

"I don't remember."

"Close your eyes. Tell me what you remember."

"That's weird," he said.

"Humor me. You saw your mom downstairs and then got into bed. Did you fall asleep quickly?"

The boy closed his eyes. "Yeah. I was beat. But I could hear her pacing downstairs."

"And then she came to your room?"

"Yeah."

The boy closed his eyes again. "I was in bed asleep. The clock in the hallway was ticking."

"Your mom must have said something to you? Or did she kiss you on the cheek maybe?"

He opened his eyes. "She said something about ancestry."

"Ancestry?"

"She rubbed the inside of my cheek."

"With a cotton swab?"

"Yeah. I guess that's what it was."

Macy exchanged glances with Sandra and then said, "Wait right here." She opened the back of the vehicle, rummaged through Nevada's very neat boxes, and found what she was looking for. She held up a buccal swab. "Did it look like this?"

"I guess."

Macy pulled on gloves and unfastened the sealed top. "Did she ask you to open wide?"

"Yeah. Why?"

"Can I take a swab?" Macy asked.

Sandra frowned. "Why?"

Both Bennett and Sandra were afraid that a monster had fathered the child they loved so now. "It could help find Brooke."

Sandra nodded and Matt opened his mouth. Macy quickly ran the cotton tip along the inside of his cheek and secured it back in the vial.

"What's that all about?" Matt asked.

"It's something I need to check on for your mom."

Mr. Greene stepped out on his porch, and Matt ran to him and hugged him close. The former sheriff whispered something in his ear, and the boy nodded and then buried his face in the man's chest. Finally, the boy pulled back and wiped a tear away with his hand.

Sandra hugged Greene. "Thank you for taking us in."

"Of course. I've got fresh bagels inside. Go on in, and I'll be right behind you."

Sandra glanced back at Macy. "Find Brooke."

"I will."

When the front door closed behind the Bennetts, all traces of softness left Greene's face. "What the hell is going on?"

"I don't know. Is there something about Brooke Bennett that I need to know?"

"What do you mean?" Greene asked.

"She's been tense through this entire investigation."

"She's a professional," he countered.

"I didn't say she wasn't," Macy said. "But she was very controlled and stoic when we spoke to the rape victims. It was almost as if she were trying to hold back on her own feelings. Her own experience. And then Tyler Wyatt makes a crack to Matt about his mother having her first sexual experience in the Wyatt barn."

Greene's jaw tightened. "You don't know what you're talking about."

She dropped her voice a notch and asked, "Who is Matt's father?"

He raised his chin. "She never said and I never asked."

"Brooke was seventeen when Matt was born."

"She made a mistake as a teenager. She wasn't the first, and she won't be the last."

"My point is that she got pregnant about the time of the rapes. But then you suspected that, didn't you?"

Greene shook his head. "You're stirring things up with wild accusations."

"I have Matt's DNA. It'll take a quick test to find out if he's our offender's offspring."

"A boy doesn't need that kind of burden. You should leave well enough alone."

"That's what you told Bennett, wasn't it? You feared she'd confirm Matt's paternity."

"This is insane. Matt's a good boy. A good kid. A monster like that couldn't possibly be his father."

Macy let the comment pass. "If you have any suspects, you need to tell me now. I think this guy took Bennett."

Greene frowned. "If Brooke knew, she wouldn't hide it."

"I think she honestly doesn't know who did this to her. But she's trying to figure it out now. I need more information if I'm going to find her."

"I can't help you."

"Why didn't you run the DNA rape kits fifteen years ago? And don't tell me you didn't understand DNA. You have a solid record and were a good cop. I'd bet a paycheck you thought you might be protecting someone close to you."

He shoved out a breath and his shoulders slumped a fraction. "My wife was sick that summer. It was consuming me, and I let a lot fall through the cracks. My plan was always to go back and catch up. When Tobi vanished, I honestly didn't connect her case to the others. And then Sandra Bennett told me Brooke was pregnant. She also told me about what happened to her daughter."

"Did you talk to Bennett?"

"Sandra begged me not to." He ran a hand over his head. "I caught up to her at school. She didn't want to talk to me at first, but finally admitted she was attacked at the bonfire. She swore she only had one drink and she didn't remember what happened."

"What did she say?" Macy asked.

"When she woke, she was in the woods, no clothes, with scratches on her body."

"And you didn't connect what happened to Bennett to the other girls?"

"I thought one of the guys at the bonfire did it."

"Did you talk to any of them? The Dream Team members were regulars at the bonfires."

"Those boys brought life and pride to this town. I knew they could be rowdy, but I never figured any one of them would hurt a young girl. And Brooke wanted to be at the bonfire, and she did drink."

Macy shoved down her anger, doing her best to remain calm. The goal was to get information, not to argue about his methods right now. "Neither of those implies sexual consent."

"I figured she'd agreed to go into the woods with a boy and it got a little rough."

"You didn't talk to any of them, did you?" And when he didn't respond, she shifted tactics. "Did Cindy Shaw report a problem to you?"

He shook his head. "That girl had all kinds of problems. She was always getting into scraps. I must have picked her up a dozen times for all kinds of infractions."

"Meaning she did come to you?"

"Yes, but she didn't make sense. She kept talking about her brother and how he was leaving her behind. She said she could bury him and his friends, if she wanted to."

"Bury how?" Macy asked.

"She never would tell me."

"And by the time you did know about Bennett's situation, Cindy was gone."

"Yes."

"Did you tell Bruce Shaw that Cindy came to see you?"

"Yeah, I told Bruce." As he stared at her, his trademark confidence faltered.

"What do you think happened to Cindy?" Macy demanded.

"Bruce told me he drove her to the bus station. He told me Cindy wanted to leave town."

"Cindy was last seen with Bruce?"

Greene shook his head. "Bruce didn't hurt his sister."

"How do you know that?" Macy asked.

"He's a stand-up guy."

"If you know something about Bruce, you have to tell me. Bennett's life might depend on it."

"I only talked to Bruce," he said, more to himself.

Matt called out to Greene, but the old man held his ground. "Be right there, buddy. Just talking to the agent."

When the front door closed, Macy asked, "Did any of those guys on the football team have a chipped tooth?" Macy asked.

"A what?"

"A chipped tooth."

"A few did. Football is a rough sport, and boys aren't always smart about their safety equipment." Greene was silent for a long moment. "You think a member of that team committed the rapes and killed Cindy."

"I do. And if you had put aside your love of that team, you might have realized it, too."

He frowned and folded his arms over his chest. "This is a small town. If I started questioning someone about murder and rape, the rumors would have spread like wildfire. I could have ruined a few very bright careers."

"You also could have saved the lives of other women."

He dropped his gaze, shaking his head. "You don't know that."

"The hell I don't."

***

He flexed his fingers as he thought about the rough calluses of his hands wrapping around the smooth, taut skin of Brooke Bennett's neck. Exhilarating did not begin to describe the rush.

Brooke was a challenge he could not resist. She was a fighter now just as she had been back in the day. He'd been on the verge of killing her all those years ago, but the blare of a honking horn at the bonfire had distracted him. Nervous he could be caught, he'd run.

He should run now. Better to leave town and find new hunting grounds. Moving around had kept him safe for over fifteen years. But if he left now, he would have to leave Brooke behind or kill her quickly. And he wasn't interested in either option.

This was just getting fun.

CHAPTER
TWENTY-SIX

Thursday, November 21, 4:00 p.m.

Macy and Nevada rolled up at the assisted living facility. She was anxious, like she often was when she was close to solving a case. She wanted to hit Shaw with dozens of questions, but knew she had to keep her cool.

Once inside, Nevada asked to see Dr. Shaw. The receptionist informed them he'd called in sick.

"I want to see his office," Nevada said.

"He keeps it locked."

"Someone has a key," Nevada said.

The receptionist looked taken aback. "I can call maintenance."

"Do it now," he said.

"You can meet Oscar down the hall by the third door on the right."

Macy and Nevada approached his office. Nevada checked the door and confirmed it was locked. Minutes later an older man appeared with a ring of keys and tried several before he opened the door.

"Thank you," Nevada said. He switched on the light.

The office was furnished with a large desk, two chairs in front of it, and a small conference table.

Macy was drawn to the wall behind his desk and the framed diplomas hanging on the wall. "He did his undergraduate work in Maryland. Graduated medical school in Georgia, and he interned in Charleston, West Virginia. It all matches up with the murders Andy pulled from ViCAP."

Nevada stared at a framed picture of the Dream Team. Bruce was front and center. Rafe Younger, Paul Decker, and Kevin Wyatt stood around him. "Cindy goes to Greene and tells him that she's the one who took Tobi to the bonfire. As devoted as the girl had been to the team, it was taking her brother away from her. Greene all but confirmed that no matter what she'd done to ingratiate herself to him, the team and Kevin had their hooks in him."

"She knew who'd lured Tobi away from the bonfire."

"And Tobi's disappearance genuinely bothered her, so she tells Greene what she knows. Greene, instead of investigating, goes to Cindy's brother, who is the only stable force in her life."

"Bruce convinces Greene that his sister is overreacting," Macy said.

"And then Bruce kills his sister?" Nevada asks.

"Or he shares what she's done with a teammate, like Kevin, and he kills her. They were thick as thieves."

Nevada shifted his gaze to a black-and-white photo taken of an old farmhouse. "Judging by the terrain, the property is in the area, but I can't quite pinpoint the location." He snapped a picture of the image.

"DNA will identify Matt's biological father and perhaps the killer. But none of this puts us closer to finding Bennett," Macy said.

"Kevin still hasn't given his DNA."

She dialed his phone, and again her call went to voicemail. "And it looks like he's now dodging me."

***

Everyone left a digital footprint these days. Carry a cell, drive a car less than ten years old, or browse the Internet—someone was watching. This digital connection made it easier for guys like Nevada to find people. Give him a laptop and a few basic details, and he could find anyone.

Nevada sent Sullivan by Kevin's house, and he discovered the residence was empty and locked up tight. Next Sullivan went to Bruce's house, but there was no sign of him either, or of his car. Neither man's cell phone was transmitting, and neither had used credit cards in days. Bruce's car was finally tracked to a parking lot on the university campus, but a search of the vehicle revealed no sign of him. Kevin remained unaccounted for.

Rafe Younger wasn't so clever about covering his tracks. He'd used his credit card to buy gas in Deep Run, beer in Staunton, and then to rent a room in a small motel an hour southwest of Lexington, Virginia.

Nevada and Macy parked in the motel lot where Rafe Younger was currently living. The motel was one story and consisted of fifteen rooms. Nevada got Rafe's room number from the clerk, and he and Macy knocked on room 106. Each stood to the side with weapons drawn.

Inside the room a television switched off. "It's Sheriff Nevada. Mr. Younger, you have five seconds to open the door."

For a moment there was silence, and then footsteps moved toward the door and a chain scraped free of its lock. The door opened to Rafe Younger. A cigarette dangled from his long fingers.

"What is this all about?" Rafe asked. "Something happen to Debbie again? She's not here."

"She's with her parents," Nevada said. "I have questions about Bruce Shaw."

"Bruce?" He took a long drag on his cigarette. "What about Bruce?"

Nevada and Macy swept the room to make sure Rafe was alone. Lying on the rumpled sheets of the unmade bed was a half bottle of Fireball, a pizza box, and an ashtray filled with cigarette butts.

Macy sat Rafe in a chair.

"What's going on?" Rafe asked.

"I want to know about the night Tobi showed up at the bonfire. I want to know what happened."

Rafe took another drag, still confused. "Nothing happened."

"That's not what Cindy Shaw said."

"Cindy. Jesus. She was always messed up. Drank more than even me."

"Earlier you said Cindy got Tobi drunk. Who took Tobi into the woods?"

"I don't know about that. I told you I was drunk."

"You know," Nevada said, "you and your teammates were legendary when it came to sticking together. Your loyalty is going to earn you an accomplice to murder charge in about two minutes."

"Murder? I didn't kill anyone."

"You're protecting one of your boys."

"Look, Tobi did get drunk, and maybe one of the guys popped her cherry, but no one hurt her."

"Come on, you four boys didn't have to chase girls because they came to you. You were rock stars. You also didn't like any girl to tell you no. Which one of you four got carried away with Tobi?"

Nevada moved to within inches of Rafe, using his height to intimidate. Macy moved to the door and put the chain back on it.

Rafe shifted, dropping his gaze. "I don't want any trouble."

"Then answer the question," Nevada said.

"We bent the rules," Rafe said. "But I never was into hurting anybody."

"What about Bruce Shaw?" Macy asked. "He preferred a type of girl, didn't he? Young, with long dark hair. Remind you of anybody?"

"We all had types. Shit, I'll do a blonde with big tits anytime. But that don't mean I'm going to kill one." He ground his spent cigarette into a nearby ashtray.

"Fair enough." Nevada leaned in closer. "Let's talk about Bruce."

"Bruce was always there for the team. He was there for me. I couldn't have asked for a better friend. Sometimes he blew off steam, but it was never anything extreme. Sex, booze, most of the usual stuff an eighteen-year-old would do."

"Most? When did he start stalking girls?" Macy asked.

Rafe closed his eyes. "He didn't stalk girls." He shook his head. "And I didn't have anything to do with those murders," he rushed to say.

"There's another woman missing. You'll go down for her murder if I can't save her."

Rafe looked up at Nevada. "I saw a notebook once in the locker room. It was in Bruce's gym bag."

"What kind of notebook?" Nevada asked.

"Like a diary. I picked it up because I was curious. I thought I'd tease him about writing poetry or about his feelings. Then I realized he was keeping notes on girls."

"Did you see a name?" Nevada asked.

"Yeah."

Nevada reached for his cuffs.

"Ellis. And Brooke."

"Brooke Bennett?"

"Yeah. She was smoking hot before she became a cop and forgot how to smile."

"What else did you see?" Nevada asked.

"Nothing. Bruce came up and he saw me reading it. I gave it back, but when he looked at it, he got real quiet. He swore it wasn't his, and he told me to keep my mouth shut."

"Did anyone else see it?" Macy asked.

"Kevin Wyatt saw it. He was standing right there. He didn't look shocked. It was like he knew what it was."

"Was there anyone else there?" Nevada asked.

"Sully also heard us talking."

"Sully?" Macy asked. "Deputy Sullivan?"

"Yeah."

"He wasn't on the team," Nevada said.

"But he helped out a lot. He loved it all."

Sullivan had never mentioned the diary. "Are Kevin, Bruce, and Sully close friends?"

"Kevin and Bruce were always tight. Sully came along for the ride sometimes."

Sully was in the system because he was a cop. Kevin still hadn't given a DNA sample. And Bruce was in the wind.

Nevada pulled up the image of the black-and-white photo in Bruce's office. "Have you ever seen this place?"

Rafe studied the picture. "I'm not sure."

"Focus, damn it!" Nevada ordered.

Rafe leaned in. "I think we all went there once when we were playing ball."

"Who's we?" Macy asked.

"You know, the guys on the football team." Rafe shook his head. "We did so much partying then. It's hard to remember."

"Let's go," Nevada said.

Macy heard the frustration in Nevada's voice. But the life of Bennett was at stake, and saving her was the only option they could entertain right now.

"Where?" Rafe stammered.

"To the station," Nevada said. "You and I are going to be looking at aerial maps until you figure it out."

CHAPTER
TWENTY-SEVEN

Thursday, November 21, 8:00 p.m.

When Macy and Nevada arrived at the sheriff's office with Rafe in tow, Sullivan greeted them. Macy had questions for the deputy, but before she could ask one, he reported that Ms. Rhonda Burns was waiting for them in the conference room.

Nevada escorted Rafe to a holding cell. "Stay put."

"Am I under arrest?"

"Do you want to be? I'll be right back." He closed the cell door.

"Sure seems like an arrest."

Nevada strode back to his deputy. "Sullivan, we need to talk."

"Sure, boss. What's up?" Nevada pulled Sullivan and Macy into his office.

"What did you do with the football team during the 2004 season?"

"Not much. I was in school and needed a part-time job. The coach hired me to take care of the equipment."

"Rafe said you were around when he spotted a notebook in Bruce's gym bag. Kevin was also there."

"They might have seen it, but I didn't. I wasn't in their club. I was staff as far as they were concerned."

"What was the deal with Kevin and Bruce?" Macy asked.

"Tight. They covered for each other."

"Did you go to any of the bonfires?" Macy asked.

"Hell no. I stayed away from that."

"Why?"

"I wasn't welcome." The phone started ringing. "Do you want me to take a DNA test?"

"Yes," Macy said.

"Fine. Get one right now." The phone continued to ring. "You want me to get that, or am I relieved of my duties?"

"Get back to your station, Sullivan," Nevada said. "I'll have one of the other deputies swab your cheek right now so this is settled."

"Sure thing, Sheriff."

After he left, Nevada looked at her. "What do you think?"

"Sullivan seems legit. He's not afraid to take the test. But I'm annoyed he didn't mention he knew these guys."

"The Dream Team was tight. And it makes sense they'd not have trusted a staff member with their secrets."

Macy ran her hand through her hair. Her frustration was growing as an invisible clock ticked away the remaining time on Bennett's life.

"Let's talk to Ms. Burns," Nevada offered. "She might have something to add."

"After all this time, the chances feel slim she has good information, but a small chance is better than none."

They entered the interview room and found a platinum blonde sitting at the table. They made the usual introductions. "What can we do for you?"

She shifted, tucking a curl behind her ear. "I heard your press conference and wanted to share a story."

Macy laid her yellow pad on the table and flipped over a dozen or so pages before she reached a fresh one. "What can you tell us?"

"I used to live in a one-story rancher ten miles west of here. I was out there a couple of years and never had any trouble until a night in June of 2006."

"2006?" Macy noted this was a new date in their timeline.

"That's right."

"What happened?" Nevada asked.

"I never had any trouble sleeping out in the country. That's where I grew up. But I can still remember being awakened in the middle of the night. I could have sworn I heard someone in or just outside the house. But when I racked a round, whoever it was took off running."

"And?" Nevada asked.

"Not much. But two days later when I was cleaning, I found a strand of red rope under my bed. I'm a bit of a clean freak, and I know for sure that rope wasn't there when I'd vacuumed three days earlier. It freaked me out, but eventually I talked myself out of it. When you announced Tobi had been found, it just got me to thinking about it."

"And you're sure the rope was under the bed?" Macy's mind turned with possibilities.

"Absolutely."

"Did you save the rope?" Macy asked.

"No, it gave me the creeps, so I threw it out. Do you think this guy was stalking me?"

Nevada shook his head. "I don't know. But if it is our guy, it tells us he was still in the area a year after the crimes we're investigating."

"I found something else outside my bedroom. I didn't save it either and had forgotten about it until now," Rhonda said.

"What was it?" Nevada asked.

"It was a key chain with the Spice Girls on it."

"Spice Girls?" Tobi Turner had loved the pop band. "You're sure about that?"

"I'm positive," Rhonda said. "Does that even make sense?"

This killer took trophies from his victims, and he'd taken Tobi Turner's key chain. "This has been really helpful," Macy said. "Thank you for coming in."

After Ms. Burns left, Nevada brought Rafe into the conference room by the large county map. "Show me where that house is."

Rafe studied the map for almost a minute as he ran his finger along the interstate and then guided it down back roads farther and farther west. "I think it was here," Rafe said.

"Whose place was it?" Nevada asked.

"It was an old cinder block house owned by the Miller family, I think. We used to go out there and party. Bruce loved it."

"There's nothing around the house." Much like the hub of a wheel, it was dead center in relation to the rapes, the Wyatt barn, and the drop location of Beth Watson's body.

"A good place to keep an abducted woman," Macy said.

"You and I will drive out there while Mr. Younger stays here," Nevada said.

"Are you arresting me?" Rafe asked.

"You're free to go, but it would be in your best interest to work with me now."

Rafe met Nevada's fierce glare and nodded. "Happy to help."

"Good man. Sullivan will fix you up with coffee and a sandwich if you're hungry."

When Macy stepped outside, she barely had a moment to breathe a full lungful of air before the reporter, Peter Stuart, approached carrying a small handheld camera and a microphone. "What's the status of Deputy Bennett?"

***

The clink of keys outside Brooke's prison door woke her from a half sleep that had seeped into her bones despite her best efforts to stay awake.

Brooke kept her eyes closed but curled her fingers into a fist. She'd sworn she'd never be a victim again. And yet here she was, a cop, trussed up and ready for the slaughter.

The last time, she'd been sixteen—she'd gotten drunk and had been clueless about danger. She allowed her memory to drift back to high school and that football season she'd spent years trying to forget.

***

It was the bonfire, and everyone from school was celebrating the last game of the regular football season. Excitement rippled over the crowd, because everyone knew if the team won on Friday, they were going to state finals in two weeks.

The liquor warmed her body and chased away the night chill. She felt so mature. So cool. The world was a pleasant, swirling blur, until it wasn't.

The drinks hit her with the force of a baseball bat. Brooke stumbled, but she righted herself as a wave of nausea washed over her. Music and laughter pulsed behind her. She stumbled toward the woods, dropped to her knees, and then threw up.

Finished, she looked back toward the bonfire through watery eyes. The dance of the flames was mesmerizing, and she missed the warmth on her skin that cool night. As she pushed to her feet, leaves crunched behind her.

A strong hand gripped her forearm and she felt grateful. Help had arrived. "Please," she whispered. "Help me."

"I'll help you."

They turned and walked away from the fire deeper into the woods. "Not this way," she said, confused.

"Do you want them to see you like this?"

"No." She was so turned around. Lost.

He handed her a flask. "It'll make you feel better."

Desperate to feel like herself again, she drank. But whatever relief she expected didn't come. Her head spun and her knees buckled.

***

Brooke had woken up at dawn. Her blouse had been ripped, and her bra torn open. Her pants had been stripped off and laid beside her. Humiliated, she'd dressed and walked home. To this day, she only had vague memories of rough hands on her body as someone penetrated her with such force she'd cried out.

Now, just outside the doorway, a man stood. He made no sound, but she could feel his gaze roaming over her body.

Adrenaline jacked up her heart rate, and staying still was difficult. If this was the man they were hunting, she knew what he wanted. The women Macy Crow had interviewed had all said the same thing. He wanted to see fear. She might die, but she could deny him what he wanted most.

"I know you're awake," he said.

She stayed still.

Maybe if he got pissed, he'd make a mistake, and she might have a chance to save herself. Help didn't even seem like an option.

"You're as tough as you ever were," he said. "I like that."

The raspy voice was familiar. They *had* met before. She barely remembered the night of her rape, but since the lab had confirmed the same assailant committed all the assaults, she'd tried unsuccessfully to remember. Matt's DNA would have proven if her case was connected to the others, but there was no telling what had happened to that sample.

He rolled her on her back, straddled her midsection, and pressed his full weight onto her abdomen. He slapped her face hard. "Wake up."

Her head rattling with pain, she looked up into the masked face of her captor. Carefully, he removed his gloves, tugging each finger free. He set the gloves aside and carefully traced the hollow of her neck with his index finger. She flinched. Memories of lying on her back in a cold field and struggling to breathe came back to her.

"Are you afraid?" he asked.

Think like a cop. Focus on the facts. One day I will be a witness to this. I will survive.

Eyes, blue. Skin, Caucasian. Midthirties, maybe older. Fit. One hundred ninety to two hundred pounds. His nails were clean, neatly trimmed, and his hands free of calluses.

She inhaled, noting the perspiration scent of a man.

He wrapped his hands slowly around her neck, rubbing the underside of her jaw with his thumb. Slowly, he tightened his grip, twisting his hands. "One, two, three."

Black jeans. Dark hoodie. Athletic shoes.

As his count grew higher, she struggled to pull air into her lungs as she tightened the muscles in her neck. This must have been what drowning felt like. Her brain fogged, and her gaze grew hazy as she gasped for air.

"I like a challenge. So brave, little Brooke. Just like the last time."

The reference to the past was not lost on her, even though she was desperate to breathe. A gurgling sound rose up in her chest, and her lungs burned. Panic rushed her. She did not want to die. She still had so much left to do. She had a son to raise.

She stared at him until her gaze completely dimmed and she felt herself falling into the blackness. Her heartbeat thundered, slowed, and then stopped altogether.

Suddenly, the panic was gone. Her mind floated upward above her body and his reach.

Her next sensation was crushing pain in her chest. She drew in a deep, painful breath and awoke to find his face hovering inches above hers.

He'd brought her back from death.

"Not yet, Brooke," he said softly. "Don't leave me just yet. You're a strong one. We can do this again and again."

CHAPTER
TWENTY-EIGHT

Thursday, November 21, 9:00 p.m.

"No cowboy shit."

Andy's words replayed in Macy's head as she stared into the reporter's camera and microphone.

Macy reminded herself that Bennett had been missing fifteen hours, and if she were still alive, her life expectancy wouldn't be long.

When Sullivan beckoned Nevada back to the office, she made her decision to act. She knew this was the kind of move that would not win her a place on the profiler's team in Quantico. This move was going to find her permanently chained to an FBI department housed in a basement somewhere in Podunk, America. Of course, all this was assuming she still had a job.

"Special Agent Crow, do you have an update?" Stuart asked.

"Can you broadcast live if I have an announcement?" Macy asked.

"I can."

"Perfect. Let me know when you're ready."

He raised his phone and turned on a social media live application. He nodded and then introduced her.

"Deputy Brooke Bennett was taken from her home last night. I believe her abduction is directly linked to Tobi Turner's murder, the three rapes that occurred in Deep Run in the summer of 2004, and the disappearance of Cindy Shaw that same year." She held up the sketch Spencer had made. "We are currently searching for a white male in his midthirties. He uses red rope to bind his victims, and when he is capable, he resorts to sexual assault. Though he is wearing a mask, there might be something familiar about the man's eyes. One woman just came forward after hearing our last news conference, and I'm hoping there are more individuals out there who may know something about this man. If you have a neighbor or colleague who fits this description and you've noticed unusual behavior, contact the Deep Run sheriff's office immediately." She paused and focused on the camera. "I've done a profile of this individual. He thinks of himself as weak and inferior to other males and has a desperate need to prove he can win. He is most likely impotent and uses violence to compensate for his shortcomings."

"Agent Crow, do you have any leads on his identity?"

"Several," she said. "And we're receiving more by the hour."

Challenging this killer openly was the kind of action that would get his attention. With luck, he'd shift his focus from Bennett to her.

She answered several more questions and then turned back toward the station. Nevada was standing outside the door.

And he looked pissed.

***

He saw Macy Crow's interview minutes after it aired. At first he was amused. Who did she think she was? Years had passed, and he'd never been caught. Did she think she'd show up in town and just catch him?

But there was something in her voice that grated on his nerves and forced him to watch it again. And again. The more he watched the replay, the angrier he got.

"Shit, she is just baiting you," he said to himself. "Don't fall for it. All the cops have is a lame sketch."

"He thinks of himself as weak and inferior."

Macy's words echoed in his head.

He was not inferior. He could beat her anytime, anywhere.

"Dumb bitch." She thought she was going to catch him. She thought she was in control. But he was in control.

He had the power!

"He thinks of himself as weak and inferior."

Again her words stoked his fury.

That pompous bitch! He reached for his phone and dialed a familiar number. When he heard a gruff greeting, he said, "I need you now."

"This is bullshit. I told you I can't keep doing this."

He gripped the phone, clinging to the reins of his temper. "One more time."

"You've said that before."

"I mean it this time."

***

Sucking in a breath, Brooke suddenly awoke. Her hands and feet were bound, making it awkward for her to push into a sitting position. She searched the darkness broken only by a light filtering under the cracks of a now-closed door.

She raised her bound hands to her throat and swallowed. The insides of her chest and throat burned as if they had been scraped raw. She tilted her head back against the wall to open her airway. She drew in deep breaths until she could think clearly.

She reached for the button on her waistband, decided whoever this guy was, he'd not raped her. Yet.

He'd taken her shoes, belt, and all the decorative pins she could have used as a weapon.

Her eyes adjusted to the dim light, and she could make out that she was in the same small room. The last time, she had barely had time to study it before he had arrived, but now she had a chance to assess.

It was not a basement, but a room. She searched the perimeter for a window, a grate, or a sharp edge to cut her bindings. When she found nothing that appeared to be of help, she reached for the bindings around her ankles and pulled hard, but the knots were locked down tight. She kept wedging her fingers into the bindings and pulling until a small section of rope gave way and she was able to unknot her ankles. Her heart pounding, she bit into the bindings around her wrists, trying to loosen them. She lost track of the time as she pulled at the knots and worked her hands back and forth until they came free.

When the red rope fell to the floor, she rubbed her raw wrists and wiggled her numb fingers until some of the circulation returned.

Outside, approaching footsteps stopped her cold. She closed her eyes and lay very still. All she needed was to place one strike to his knee or midsection. She had a chance of disabling him. Maybe then she could punch his throat or nose. She wanted to inflict the maximum damage. All this was assuming that her aim was true. If she missed, she'd just piss him off, and when he played his strangulation game, he could take it too far and kill her.

Holding her breath, she readied to kick. Floorboards shifted. But he never entered the room. Her heart beat in her throat as she waited for him. But the footsteps retreated.

Brooke quietly stood, her fists raised and body poised to fight. The muffled sounds of angry male voices reached the room. She strained to hear what the men were saying, but couldn't make out the words. Hoping her jailer was distracted, she unclenched her fingers and twisted the doorknob. To her surprise, it turned, and the door opened. Her heart pulsed in her throat as she thought about the possibility of getting free. Then she hesitated. This was a trap. It had to be. What was he luring her toward?

However, she made the decision to go, knowing that staying assured her death. She opened the door and peered down the hallway. Slowly she moved, one careful step at a time, and made her way into a small living room. She looked around, ready to see him watching or lunging toward her. But she was alone in the room that was now bathed in shadows. She heard only silence. Flexing her fingers, waiting for an attack, she hurried toward the front door.

Outside she heard two men arguing.

"What the fuck have you done?" She recognized the voice. It was Bruce Shaw.

Whoever he was talking to spoke in low, deep tones, and it was impossible to hear his response or to identify him. Who was here with him? God help her if there were two.

"You're talking about killing a cop this time. Her disappearance is all over the news. It's a matter of time before the cops figure all this out."

For a beat, there was only silence. And then a gunshot fired and she flinched. She stepped back from the door, searching the simple living room for something she could use as a weapon. Her heart pounded in her chest. *Think, Brooke, think!*

Outside, she heard one of the men mumble a curse. She peered out the window and saw a dark figure dragging another man, but in the darkness she couldn't tell who was who. She waited, listened until the figures vanished around the side of the house.

If she could get out the door and make it to the woods, she had a chance. Gritting her teeth, she stepped out onto the front stoop. Her toes curled.

The half moon hung over her, and cold air whipped through the trees. Ahead were woods. And somewhere in the distance she heard running water.

But as she took a step, a shadow lunged from the darkness and grabbed her by the back of the neck. He slammed her hard against the house.

"Crow thinks I'm inferior. Do you?"

Fury, not fear, rolled inside her. She should try to calm him. She should find a way to talk him down. Instead, she simply said, "Yes."

Her head hit the siding, and she was so stunned she could barely stand. He dragged her back into the house, forcing her to stumble forward into the living room. He slammed the front door and then dragged her back to her prison room. He was on top of her again, squeezing her throat.

"I am in control," he said. "Me. Not you. Not him. Not her. *Me!*"

CHAPTER
TWENTY-NINE

Thursday, November 21, 11:00 p.m.

The air in the car was thick with frustration and anger as Macy and Nevada drove down the back road furrowed with potholes. Nevada's jaw was clenched, and when he rounded a final bend, he said, "Speaking to the press like that was stupid. You've now made yourself a target."

"Maybe if I make him mad enough, it will take his mind off Bennett."

"We've already excluded Younger's DNA. We have Shaw's DNA, but no results yet. And I will get a sample from Kevin Wyatt."

"Wyatt is still not answering his phone."

"You should not have baited this killer." He pressed the accelerator. The engine roared and the tires spun faster. "The house Younger mentioned should be around the next turn."

"Let's park here and walk in so no one hears us coming."

He pulled to the side and shut off the engine. Macy got out of the car, quietly closing the door before checking her weapon. They moved side by side for the last few hundred yards. Her leg and hip were tightening up the entire way, but she pushed through, knowing Bennett was running out of time.

As the small gray house came into view, she thought about the house in Texas where she'd found the unmarked graves. On the heels of that memory was the sound of a revving truck engine seconds before it plowed into her body. She flinched but shoved the surge of fear aside.

She put one foot in front of the other. She needed to focus and provide cover for Nevada.

As they approached the small house, they detected activity. There were fresh tire treads and footprints. The prints appeared to have been made by a man's athletic shoe.

Nevada raised his finger to his lips as he moved past her. As much as she wanted to be the one to take this guy down, she had to be practical. They would be most effective if she provided cover while he took point.

He tried the front door and discovered it was locked. She always carried a lockpick set in her kit. Not wasting a moment, she identified the lock as a pin tumbler. After pulling out a wrench and pick, she worked the pair into the lock until all the pins were set and the lock clicked open.

Nevada arched an amused brow before saying, "Stay behind me."

She nodded, and the two moved into the central living room of the house. Her gaze swept the room, searching each of the closed doors that fed into it. A padlock noticeably secured one door.

While she watched the door, Nevada swept the one-story house for signs of anyone else. When he gave the all clear sign, she moved to the padlock, holstered her weapon, and picked it faster than the first lock. She quickly removed it, flipped open the latch, and pushed open the door.

The room was dark, and the cold air was heavy with the scent of sweat. Her heart slammed against her ribs, and she tightened her hold on the grip of her weapon. She listened for the sound of breathing or movement, but couldn't hear over her own quick breath.

Nevada cast his light into the room until it rested on Bennett's body. "Shit."

Macy holstered her weapon, ran toward her, and knelt beside her. Carefully, she rolled her on her back and pressed her fingertips to the black-and-blue skin of her neck. For a moment, there was only stillness, so she repositioned her fingers and prayed. And then she felt the faint pulse. Tears burned in her eyes.

"She's alive," she said.

Nevada was already dialing for assistance.

***

Macy rode to the hospital with Bennett in the back of the ambulance. The wail of the siren and the rocking rhythm of the ride reminded Macy of her own ordeal as paramedics shouted Brooke's name and tried to get her to open her eyes. Macy knew Bennett would have a long road ahead of her if she survived this.

They rolled into the university hospital's parking lot, and personnel were on hand to admit Bennett. As staff quickly pushed the gurney toward the emergency room, the paramedics recited Bennett's vital signs to the doctors.

Macy hustled behind, following as far as the swinging doors. A nurse dressed in scrubs blocked Macy and informed her she would have to wait in the lobby.

"I need to know who did this to her." Macy hadn't been able to stop shaking since they'd found Bennett.

"And I need to save her," the nurse retorted before she vanished.

Running her hand over her head, Macy turned to a lobby crowded with people filling out forms, reading magazines, and watching televisions mounted on the walls. She replayed her actions since she'd arrived in town. Why hadn't she been more aggressive with Kevin about the swabs? Could she have pushed Greene even harder?

Unable to sit, she paced, and when her phone rang, she reached for it, thinking it was Nevada. She was surprised to see Faith's name on the display.

She walked to the window overlooking the parking lot and faced away from the people in the lobby. "How did you know something was wrong? Is this some kind of twin symbiotic thing?"

"Damn right, sis."

That coaxed a small smile as she watched an ambulance drive off. "I'm standing in the emergency room. Another cop was injured."

A door clicked closed in the background. "Who?"

"She's one of the deputies in the county. She was attacked by a guy we're chasing." She pressed her fingers to her closed eyes, willing tears to stay in check. "I'm trying, but it might be too little, too late."

"You're a good cop, Macy."

"But was I good enough? If it were another agent in my shoes, would they have gotten to Deputy Bennett sooner? I was so hell bent on getting back to work I didn't stop to really consider if I should. Maybe I don't belong in this job."

"That's bullshit," Faith said. "You're one of the best."

Images of the bruises ringing Bennett's pale neck rose to the front of her thoughts. "Jesus, Faith, this guy strangled her multiple times."

"She's a cop, Macy. She accepted the risks of the job. It could just as easily have been you."

"She's a deputy in a small town. She's never seen a case like this."

"Do you think she'd appreciate the fact that you're underestimating her? Do you think she'd like hearing she's just Barney Fife from Mayberry?"

Macy pictured Bennett's stoic expression. "She'd probably kick my ass."

"Would she want you blaming yourself or going after this guy?"

Macy drew in a breath. "She'd want me to nail him to the wall."

"Then why are you still on the phone yammering with me? Go kick somebody's ass and be quick about it. Call me when it's done."

Click.

She stared at the phone in disbelief. No goodbye, no good luck. Faith understood her better than she realized. Nevada strode in. The tightly woven coil inside her eased a fraction.

"How is she?" Nevada asked.

"She's still unconscious."

"All right," he said. "We'll wait for a little bit."

"I hate waiting."

"Macy, it sucks being on the outside, but sometimes that's all you have," Nevada said.

"Who are we talking about now?" she asked.

"Me, after your accident." He laid his hand on hers. "I never want to go through that again."

She had been focused on herself after the accident. All she had wanted to do was get better. She had thought about him. Several times she had felt so alone it was all she could do not to call him, but she had been afraid of showing any kind of weakness. "I didn't want you to see me that way."

"I could have dealt with it," he said. "You didn't have to fight your way back alone."

A doctor dressed in green scrubs approached them. "You're FBI?"

They both stood and she said, "Yes. We brought in Brooke Bennett. Is she awake?"

"Not yet."

***

Once Nevada and Macy had spoken to the doctor and learned Bennett wouldn't likely wake until morning, they returned to the house where they'd found her. Surrounding the house were state and federal officers who were sweeping the structure and grounds for evidence.

Sullivan met them outside. "We were able to locate the clerk from the county land records office. He was not happy to be pulled away from his evening show until I told him about Deputy Bennett."

"And?" Nevada demanded.

"The clerk ran right into the office and started digging. The land passed through three hands in the last twenty years. It had a reputation for being a party site for the kids at one point. Long story short, a limited partnership called Pocket Inc. purchased the house. I called the attorney of record, and he told me his client was Bruce Shaw."

"What's the status of the crime scene?" Nevada asked.

"The technicians are going over the room where they found Deputy Bennett. It's mostly hair and fiber samples in that room, but in the other bedroom there are journals," he said.

"What kind of journals?" Nevada asked.

"Apparently this guy liked to make sketches and notes of the women he stalked. There're notes on hundreds of women from up and down the East Coast."

"What about Baltimore, Atlanta, and Bluefield, West Virginia?" Macy asked.

"I haven't been in the room to see," he said.

"Good work," Nevada said. "We'll take it from here."

"How is Deputy Bennett?" Sullivan asked.

"She's going to recover with time," Macy said.

"Thank God for that."

"Agent Crow, about that Beacon cologne," Sullivan said. "It's been bugging me all day."

"What about it?" she asked.

"Wyatt wore it."

"You are sure? Rebecca Kennedy said her attacker wore Beacon cologne."

"Yeah. The guys used to tease Wyatt about it. They were always taking the bottle and tossing it in the trash. They said it made him smell like a pretty boy. I saw the bottle more than a few times."

Kevin had not given DNA, and now she had a witness who said he wore the rapist's scent. "Wyatt would have been under a lot of pressure during the Dream Team years."

"He's always had a lot on his shoulders," Sullivan said. "Father wasn't around much, and his mother isn't wrapped real tight."

"Deputy Sullivan, go by Wyatt's house again," Nevada said. "If he's there, bring him in."

"Yes, sir."

Macy and Nevada each donned latex gloves and booties, gave their names to the officer standing watch at the crime scene tape, and then entered.

Now that she really had time to look at the room, Macy could see it was freshly painted and the floors had been refinished in the last couple of years. There was a stone fireplace, with freshly stacked wood on the grate.

The furniture was new, though nothing fancy, and the flat-screen television wasn't connected to cable. Beside it was a DVD player and a stack of movies. Macy perused the titles, which featured older heroes who were former athletic stars and were trying to make a comeback. Blackout curtains were installed over all the windows.

"Sheriff Nevada."

They both turned to see a man in his fifties wearing a state police forensic jacket. His hair was neatly trimmed, and he had a clean-cut look that was reminiscent of a Boy Scout. "I'm David Holland from Roanoke. I was called in to run this crime scene."

Nevada shook hands with him. "Appreciate you coming in. This is Special Agent Macy Crow. What do you have?"

"I'd like to show you the journals we found in the second bedroom," Holland said.

The three entered the small bedroom, which was equipped with floor-to-ceiling shelves on the far wall. The shelves were filled with hundreds of black-and-white marble composition notebooks. Along the thin spine of each were dates: June 2004. September 2007. November 2019.

"How far do the journals date back?" Macy asked.

"Sixteen years. The first, from what we can tell, was written in April of 2003. The author of the books was making notes on Cindy Shaw."

"What does he say about her?" Macy asked.

"Rather intimate details of her daily routine. He's also drawn sketches of her, and in many of the pictures she appears to be dead."

Macy moved to one shelf with an array of small trinkets lined up in a neat row. Many were single earrings, necklaces, panties, and single high heels. She spotted the princess pepper shaker missing from Beth Watson's home.

"Are there journals from Baltimore or Atlanta?"

"It appears so. And several other cities."

Nevada drew in a breath. "Are names listed?"

"Yes. He not only lists his target's name, address, and phone number, but also a detailed description of likes, dislikes, schedules, and pictures."

"Any containing Deputy Bennett?"

Holland lowered his voice. "Yes. And some of it dates back to when she was a teenager."

Eventually, the evidence of Bennett's rape would come out. "She's going to need time to heal," she said. "Give her a chance to regain some of her strength before she has to publicly deal with this. Keep a tight lid on what you can."

"Bennett's one of our own, and we'll protect her in any way we can. Every man and woman here is prepared to stay on the scene until this guy is found."

"Did he write anything about himself in the journals?" Macy asked.

"Surprisingly, no. But with all this collection, there have to be fingerprints and DNA linking Shaw or whomever is responsible."

Lights flashed from the other room, drawing Macy and Nevada into the space where Bennett had been held. The walls in the windowless room were padded with an extra barrier for soundproofing. There was a foul scent in the room, and the carpeting was stained in multiple places.

"He's got to be feeling out of control," Holland said. "His world was turned upside down, and we have a direct link to every crime he's committed."

"And that's going to make him extremely dangerous," Nevada said. "He's got absolutely nothing to lose now."

***

Rage was too tame a word to describe what he was feeling. He coiled the red rope around his hands while he watched the images from the camera he'd mounted on the tree outside of his special house. They'd found it, Brooke, and all the journals he'd worked so hard to create over the years.

He looked down at his hands. He'd cut off the blood supply, and the skin not only was pale but also tingled. If he kept this up much longer, he'd do some real damage.

Macy Crow was not going to make him look like a fool. She'd destroyed what he had worked so hard to build, and she would pay dearly for it.

The house she'd invaded had sentimental value to him. It was a safe place to hide when he needed it. It had been the place where he'd become a man for the first time. It had offered him sanctuary when the world just got too loud.

And now it had been desecrated.

He glanced at the revolver in his hand. Carefully, he opened the chamber and counted six bullets. It wasn't his preferred method, but it was effective. "Macy, if you wanted me to come after you, then you shall get your wish."

***

By the time Macy and Nevada left the crime scene, it was nearly midnight. Instead of feeling fatigued, her body was still in high gear, but she knew that wouldn't last forever.

They drove to the Wyatt house, where a collection of county and state vehicles was parked. Their lights flashed, illuminating the darkness, and several neighbors had gathered outside their homes.

Nevada strode up to Sullivan. "Any sign of Wyatt?"

"No," Sullivan said. "The house is empty."

"What about Tyler?" Macy asked.

"I called his cell and he answered. He says he's in Texas with family. He said his brother put him in a hired car and sent him down to Roanoke to catch a plane earlier today."

"When is the last time the boy was in contact with his brother?" Macy asked.

"They haven't spoken since Wyatt put him in the car."

"Did the boy say if his brother appeared off?" Macy asked.

"Tyler said his brother was calm and cool like he always is. The kid has no idea what's going on," Sullivan said.

"And Wyatt's mother?" Nevada asked.

"I left her a voicemail message. No call back." Sullivan flipped through his notes. "I called his family dentist. He did have his front tooth repaired in July of 2004. He'd chipped it during a football practice, but he had it repaired within a week."

"So Ellis was right," Macy said.

"Appears so."

All the arrows pointed to Kevin. "But that doesn't change the fact that Wyatt's in the wind."

"We'll find him," Nevada said. "It's a matter of time."

Thick clouds covered the sky, blocking out the stars and the moon. After they spoke to several other state officers, the two got back in Nevada's car. The energy she'd felt less than a half hour ago was waning fast.

"I've got to get a couple of hours' sleep," Macy said.

Nevada backed out of the long drive until he reached the road, where he cut his wheels hard. "You can sleep at my place. I don't want you in that motel room alone."

She laid her head against the headrest. Though she now suspected that Kevin was the primary offender, Bruce was involved in some capacity. "The whole point is for me to be alone so that Wyatt or Shaw will come for me."

"You're not up to catching anyone tonight. We need to sleep, regroup, and figure out our plan of attack in the morning."

She saw the wisdom of Nevada's logic. "But Wyatt and Shaw are out there and may have another woman."

"There's a statewide BOLO out for either man's arrest," Nevada said.

"Both are too smart to trip a BOLO."

"In the morning. I promise," Nevada said.

She relented and they drove to his house. By the time they arrived, the adrenaline had abated and she was more tired than she had realized. She struggled to hide her stiff gait as the pair approached the house.

"Take a hot shower," he said. "Want a drink?"

"Beer."

"Corona, right?"

"Good memory."

He locked the front door behind them, and she walked into his bedroom and turned on the hot water in the shower. As the steam began to rise in the stall, she stripped out of her clothes, laying them on the bed before stepping under the hot spray. She turned her back to the shower and leaned against the cool tile. The water's heat felt wonderful and seeped into her aching bones.

The door to the shower opened, and Nevada stepped in behind her, resting both hands on her hips. She straightened and leaned back until she felt his chest rub against her skin.

He lathered his hands and began to rub the tense muscles along her lower back and right hip. A soft moan rumbled in her throat at the pure pleasure.

"You're an angel," she said.

"Not hardly." He kept rubbing her back and hip.

Finally, when she felt the tightness release and some of her stamina return, she turned and wrapped her arms around his neck, kissing him. Her breasts rubbed against his chest as he leaned into the kiss.

He cupped her buttocks with his hands and in one move lifted her and pressed her back against the tiled wall. Carefully, he eased into her, and she dropped her head back, savoring the sensation of having him inside her. She gripped his shoulders and tightened her legs around his waist, moaning softly as he pushed deeper into her.

Neither of them spoke as they gave in to the sensations and let themselves just simply enjoy. When she tipped over the edge, he came inside her.

For a moment, neither moved as the heat of the shower beat down on them. Finally, he kissed her softly on the lips and pulled out of her. He shut off the water and grabbed two towels from the rack.

They dried off, and she reached for the beer he'd left on the counter. She took a long pull and, for the first time in a long time, felt like herself.

She slid under the covers of his bed, savoring the soft sheets. She curled on her side, and he nestled behind her. "We only have a few hours to sleep," she said.

"I know. Let's enjoy it."

***

Scratch. Scratch. Scratch.

The sound woke Macy before dawn, and when she sat up, she had the sense that Cindy was close. She couldn't logically explain the feeling, only that the girl was nearby.

Macy looked toward Nevada's spot, but discovered he was gone. She glanced at the clock and realized that she'd been asleep for two hours.

She got out of bed, gathered her clothes, and slipped into the bathroom. When she emerged fifteen minutes later, she was dressed and following the scent of what smelled like freshly brewed coffee.

She found Nevada in the kitchen, dressed in his customary jeans and sweater. She slid up to him and traced her hand slowly over his back. He relaxed into her touch as he poured her a cup of coffee into a travel mug, doctored it with milk and sugar, and handed it to her.

She kissed him and accepted it. "Thank you."

"The mug is not a hint. You can stay as long as you like."

"I want to have a look at those journals," she said. She searched around for her purse and, once she found it, dug her phone out. "Ah, I didn't charge it."

He opened a drawer and handed her a charger. "A gift."

She plugged it into her phone and then the wall. There was no call from the hospital, but that would be her first stop anyway this morning. "I hope to hell Bennett is awake. I need to talk to her. And then I need to examine the journals. We need to figure out where both men are hiding."

He finished his coffee. "The sooner we get this guy, the easier I'll sleep."

***

They arrived at the hospital thirty minutes later, and after Macy showed her badge at the front desk, they rode the elevator to the third floor and found the nurses' station. She showed her badge again. "I'm here about Deputy Bennett. How's she doing?"

The nurse glanced at her computer screen. "She woke up about fifteen minutes ago and is asking for you, Agent Crow. Her throat is badly swollen and she can barely talk, so we're watching her closely. But if she keeps progressing, she'll be out of here in a day or two."

"Has her son seen her?" Macy asked.

"He and his grandmother will be here shortly. We just wanted to make sure Deputy Bennett was stabilized before we allowed visitors. She has to remain calm."

Macy and Nevada entered Bennett's room. The lights were dim in the small room. She lay in her bed, her dark hair splayed on her pillow. Her neck was ringed in bands of black-and-blue bruises. A half-full IV bag hung beside her bed and trailed down to her bruised arm. A heart monitor beeped.

Macy's skin still crawled whenever she entered a hospital. *Jesus.* While Nevada stood at the foot of the bed, she pulled up a chair. The deputy's hands were scratched and the fingernails scuffed.

"Brooke," she said as she took her hand. When she didn't respond, Macy said louder, "Deputy Bennett."

Bennett's eyes snapped open, and she looked around wild eyed before she realized she was safe. With a wince, she sat up and spoke in a raspy whisper. "Agent Crow."

It was a hard thing to think you were completely in charge of your life and then have your feet swept out from under you. "We are kindred spirits now. I think we can be on a first-name basis," Macy said.

"Macy. I feel like I was kicked by a mule."

Macy removed her notepad and pen from her backpack and flipped to a clean sheet. "You've been through a lot."

Bennett swallowed and drew in a breath. "I'm starting to remember. Where's Matt?"

"He's with your mother and Mr. Greene. They'll be here soon."

Bennett nodded. "Thank God he's safe."

"You know the drill, Brooke. I have some questions to ask."

Her lips flattened with grim determination. "Sure, don't hold back."

"Did you see his face? Do you know who did this to you?"

Bennett glanced toward Nevada, and then closed her eyes as she shook her head. "I didn't see his face. I was so focused on staying alive."

"He never took his mask off?" Nevada asked.

"No." She paused and swallowed. "He likes the fear."

Macy picked up a cup from the side table and filled it with water from a pitcher. She grabbed a straw and placed it in the cup, holding it up to Bennett's mouth.

Bennett drank, but immediately cringed as the cool liquid skimmed over her bruised throat. She took a second sip and then nodded her thanks. "Did they get any DNA from under my fingernails?"

"They were scraped and sent in for testing along with collected skin cells," Macy said.

She shook her head. "Macy, I thought he was going to kill me that second time. He was so angry. I'm not sure what set him off."

"I set him off." Macy stared at the woman's battered body, and the weight of her actions rested heavily on her. "I gave an impromptu news conference and called him out. I'm so sorry. I thought I could smoke him out and get him to come after me. But I almost got you killed."

"No, that was well played," Bennett said. "It was a matter of time before he was going to kill me."

"Maybe I could have spared you more pain if I'd just been more patient."

"After he strangled me the first time, I was out for a while. When I woke up, I heard him outside my door, but he didn't come into the room. I tried the doorknob and was shocked to discover it wasn't locked any longer. He must have forgotten to lock it because he had a visitor. I heard two men arguing. One I know was Bruce Shaw, but I couldn't identify the second man."

"The second voice wasn't familiar to you?" She needed Bennett's testimony to unfold without any prompting.

"No. It was muffled and it was all I could do to stand. Then I heard a gunshot."

"Gunshot?" Macy asked.

"Yes. I'm certain of that. Then I heard what sounded like a body being dragged. But I was more focused on getting to the woods."

"But you didn't make it."

"No. He grabbed me from behind and dragged me back into the house."

"Did you see his face this time?"

"No. He wore his mask." She rubbed her breastbone. "And he was so enraged and he wanted me dead. You might have made him angry, but I also egged him on toward the end. I knew he was angry, but I didn't care. I wasn't going to die without telling him what I thought about him. I should have been thinking about Matt, but I wanted that monster to know I thought he was weak."

"But I set him off."

"Don't play the blame game. There are no winners."

Macy laid her hand on Bennett's. She shared an odd bond with the woman, who, like her, had nearly been murdered.

Bennett gripped the sheets, pushed herself up a little, and tried to swing her legs over the side of the bed. "Don't tell Matt about what happened to me."

"I'm not saying a word," Macy said. "That's for you if you want to discuss later."

"I took a cheek swab from my son," Bennett said, almost in a whisper.

"Matt told me. I also did the same. His DNA has been sent off for testing."

Tears glistened in Bennett's eyes. "I did my best to forget about the rape. What little I remembered, I tried to block out."

"You lived and thrived."

She swallowed, winced, and turned her face toward Nevada. "If I had spoken up, maybe Tobi would be alive."

"A wise woman just told me the blame game has no winners." Macy gripped Bennett's fingers.

"He can't get away." Bennett's gaze was tired, but determined.

"He won't."

"Where did you find me?"

"A property owned by Bruce Shaw," Macy said.

"Shaw gave me his DNA."

"We didn't find it," Macy said.

"Mom!"

They turned to see Matt and his grandmother standing in the door. The boy stood back for a moment, terrified at the sight of his mother's bruised neck and face.

"It's okay, Matt." Smiling, Bennett pushed the button on her bed, allowing her to sit up more. She held out her hands.

Matt stepped toward her, hesitating as if he were still afraid to touch her. "Mom, what happened?"

Bennett took his hand in hers and pulled him toward her. She wrapped her arms around him, and he relaxed against her, sobbing softly. "Just a few scrapes and bruises, baby."

The boy tightened his hug, causing Bennett to wince.

Matt drew back. "Did I hurt you?"

"Nope," she said as she smoothed his hair out of his eyes. "It's just what I needed."

***

He stood outside the back entrance to the hospital, a cigarette in hand. He had showered in a cheap motel room that only required cash and no identification and had changed into scrubs that he had stolen from the assisted living facility. Anyone who saw him now would think he was staff taking a smoke break. All he had to do was wait for the back entrance to open and slip inside.

He knew Macy and Nevada were there with Brooke. It wouldn't be easy to grab Macy, but he had the element of surprise. People let down their guards in hospitals, assuming with all the nurses and doctors that they were perfectly safe.

The side door swung open, and he tossed down his cigarette and sauntered up to the door, holding it for a maintenance worker pushing out a trash can.

"Thanks, man," the worker said.

"No problem."

Stepping inside, he let the door close behind him. He moved to the staircase, where there would be less risk.

It had been less than twelve hours since they'd brought Bennett here, so she was likely still on the third floor. All he had to do was lure Macy near the stairwell or an empty room. He wasn't interested in playing this time. This time, he had one simple goal.

To kill Macy Crow.

CHAPTER THIRTY

Friday, November 22, 9:00 a.m.

As Macy and Nevada walked toward the front doors of the hospital, she was anxious to leave. To be out in the fresh air and away from the buzz of fluorescent lights, the rattle of wheelchairs, and the hurt and sickness.

Just as the automatic doors swung out and Nevada stepped through, Macy's phone rang. She stopped and glanced at the unknown number. "Agent Macy Crow."

"This is Dr. Myers," he said. "I'm one of Brooke Bennett's doctors. She asked if she could speak to you alone for a moment."

"Alone?" Macy asked, glancing at Nevada. "She was with her son."

"He's about to leave, and she would like to see you about something that she remembered."

"Sure, I'll be right back in." She glanced toward Nevada and smiled. "Let me see what this is about, and I'll join you out front in a few minutes."

Nevada frowned. "What's going on?"

"Brooke might have recalled something. She wants to talk to me."

"I'll come with you."

She held up her hand, pressing gently against his chest. "She said she wanted to see me alone. I'll see what it's about and text you."

He looked past her toward the lobby, scanning for any threat. "See you in a few."

She took the elevator back up to the third floor. As she stepped off, she walked past the nurses' station toward Bennett's room. In the distance, she spotted Matt stepping into the hallway. He looked up at her, his expression troubled as he rubbed his eyes. Even from this distance, she could see he had been crying.

Her attention on the boy, she didn't notice the man in scrubs who quickly came up beside her. In one instant, he bodychecked her into an empty room.

She stumbled and quickly righted herself as she reached for her weapon. But a man's right hook connected squarely with her jaw and dropped her to her knees.

Pain exploded in her head. When her injured knee hit the tiled floor, more agony rocketed through her body and took her breath away. Rough hands jerked her weapon from its holster and sent it sliding under a bed and out of her reach.

Macy struggled to take several short, quick breaths and draw air into her lungs. He flipped her on her back and buried his knee into her chest. Only then did he wrap his hands around her throat and begin to choke her.

Her attacker wasn't hiding behind a mask this time. She was looking into Kevin Wyatt's eyes.

Pure hate exuded from him. He didn't even look human. "You think you are so smart. You think you are better than me."

Macy dug her fingers into his hands as he tightened his hold around her neck.

"Who's the weak one now?" His breath hissed warm against her cheek.

She clawed at his fingers and tried to pry them open. Adrenaline jolted her heart, and it raced faster, burning through the oxygen reserves in her lungs.

"One, two, three . . ."

His eyes darkened with a savage lust as her efforts to break his hold failed. She arched her back and kicked her feet, hoping the noise might catch someone's attention.

"Six, seven, eight," he whispered.

There was no breath left to pull into her burning lungs. Her heart rammed into her chest and her head spun out of control. It felt like it had in the ambulance in Texas just before she coded.

She blinked, felt her eyes strain, and imagined capillaries bursting. She'd always feared dying in a hospital but never thought it would be like this. She fought to stay conscious.

The room's door opened. She shifted her gaze to the sight of worn athletic shoes. Her pulse thumped in her throat. She struggled to scream.

"Nine, ten, eleven," he said.

A boy's cry for help echoed in the room as the athletic shoes raced toward her. Someone jumped on Kevin's back.

"Get off of her! Get off!" For a moment, Kevin's grip loosened, and she pulled in a breath. She realized her rescuer was Matt.

Kevin knocked the boy off his back with such force he crashed hard against the wall. The boy blinked as he tried to stagger to his feet but then fell backward.

Kevin refocused on Macy and retightened his grip. "You're going to die now, bitch."

***

When Nevada had dropped Macy off at the Kansas City airport last spring, Macy had smiled. She'd looked cocky and self-assured as she had passed through security and vanished around a corner. He'd had a bad feeling that day, but had brushed it off. Weeks later she'd nearly been killed in Texas.

When she had disappeared into the hospital moments ago, the same feeling had tightened in the pit of his stomach.

He had ignored the sensation once, but he wouldn't do it twice. He jogged toward the elevator and caught it right before the door shut. He checked his watch as the elevator opened at the second floor and a doctor stepped into the car. He was less than two minutes behind her. He punched the third-floor button several times until the doors closed. "Come on. Come on."

Macy had wanted to prove she was still the agent she'd been. She had never liked receiving help from anyone. He understood that drive. And when Ramsey had called with the idea of sending her to Deep Run, he'd jumped at the chance to give her this case. She was smart and savvy. This case had her written all over it. He also knew the cases she would have to chase would keep her away from him fifty weeks out of the year.

Screw it. He had her back whether she liked it or not.

As the elevator doors opened to the third floor, he heard a young boy's scream. Drawing his weapon, he moved down the hallway, looking in the open rooms for signs of trouble. When the boy yelled for help a second time, he identified the room and pushed through the door. He barely registered seeing Matt struggling to get up. His focus was on the man strangling an unconscious Macy.

As much as Nevada wanted to shoot him, he knew the bullet could easily pass through and hit Macy. He holstered his weapon and in one fluid movement, slid his arm around the killer's neck. Nevada placed his other hand behind the man's head and squeezed until the carotid artery closed. The man fought him, trying to reach back and hit him, but Nevada held steady. The man's thrashing slowed and then stopped.

Nevada saw Matt's bloody lip and Macy's swollen face and bruised neck. "Matt," he said. "Get a doctor."

The boy blinked and rose. "Okay."

Nevada loosened his hold as he reached for his cuffs but as he did, Kevin's eyes opened and his body tensed. Kevin reached back for

Nevada's gun. Nevada reacted instantly, retightening his grip, compressing with maximum pressure. The sounds of alarms in the hallway and nurses calling for supplies drifted in the distance as Kevin strained to get his gun until, finally, his fingers dropped to his side. Nevada reached for his cuffs, secured Kevin's now-limp arms behind his back.

He shifted his attention to Macy, who lay curled on the floor. Her face was pale and her lips blue.

"Macy!" he shouted as he rolled her on her back.

She didn't respond. He pressed fingertips to her red and scratched throat. There was no pulse, and she wasn't breathing.

"Hold on for me, Macy," he said. He could not lose her again. He would not.

As two nurses and a doctor burst into the room, Nevada tipped Macy's head back, cleared her airway, pressed his mouth over hers, and breathed.

***

Macy was floating in the pool she had swum in with her father when she was five years old. On that clear day, she had ignored her father's warning to wait, and she had jumped into the ice-cold water. The instant her head had slipped below the surface, she had kicked her legs, but instead of rising to the surface, she had sunk. She had realized then she'd made a terrible mistake. Sunlight had glistened on the water's surface above her, and all she could do was watch it slip farther away as she had sunk.

Like then, her body was weightless now. The rigidity had dissipated from her muscles. Her knee didn't ache. She wasn't worried about being an agent. She felt good. At peace.

She'd been here before.

And just like before, she knew she didn't belong here, no matter how serene it felt. She wanted to be back in the sunlight. She wanted to feel the sun on her face, the challenges of life's struggles, and love.

A hand reached into the water, and if she wanted to live, she would have to fight hard to reach it. She thrashed her legs and arms, determined to rise on her own. As she wrestled her limbs upward, the distant sounds of alarms blaring and Nevada shouting her name greeted her.

Nevada. She wanted life. And she wanted Nevada in that life.

"Clear!"

A jolt of electricity rocketed through her body, snapping through sinew and bone and propelling her upward. She kicked harder and felt her fingers skim the edge of the water. Her heart faltered. Beat once. And then stopped.

"Clear!"

Another shock rocketed through her heart. It beat once. Then twice. And then a steady, calm rhythm. A hand gripped her fingers and pulled her hard, yanking her into the light and the warm sun.

Macy sucked in a breath. Over and over she sucked air into her lungs, until she realized there were no more fingers wrapped around her throat. Her jaw ached and her ribs throbbed, but she was alive.

Nevada gripped her hand as he called her name again. "Macy! Look at me. Look at me."

Bossy. He sounded so damn bossy.

The defibrillator's high-pitched sound ramped up again, and she felt someone hovering beside her.

She pried open her eyes and was greeted by the blur of faces hovering over her. Her entire body ached, but she was so happy to be back. She angled her face toward Nevada. When she saw all the worry and relief colliding in his dark eyes, tears burned in her own.

The doctors prodded and poked her. A cold stethoscope pressed against her chest, and someone was thumping the vein in her right arm to start an IV line.

"Macy!"

"I'm back." Her throat was raw and it hurt to talk. "Where's Matt?"

"He's fine. The doctors are with him."

"He saved me," she said.

"I know. The kid is amazing," Nevada said.

The nurse again pressed a stethoscope to her chest and listened to the strong beat of her heart. "Do you know your name?"

"Macy Crow." Her voice sounded rough and gritty.

"How many fingers am I holding up?" the nurse asked.

She squinted at the fingers inches from her face. "Three."

A needle pricked her arm, and she felt the cool saline solution roll through the tube and into her vein.

"Let's get her up," a doctor shouted.

As she was hefted onto the padded gurney, her blouse lay open, her body exposed to everyone around her. There was nothing like coming back from the dead and then making an entrance.

Nevada shrugged off his jacket and covered her chest. She smiled up at him. As far as she was concerned, she could be in Grand Central Station with a parade of marines marching past.

She was alive.

And that was all that mattered.

EPILOGUE

Macy stood in the living room of the house where Nevada and she had found Bennett. Forensic teams had collected hair, blood and fiber samples, and preliminary evidence that proved Beth Watson had been murdered here.

Crews were also searching the land outside the house. Kevin had coded at the hospital, and though the staff had tried to revive him, he'd died. His death left law enforcement with the task of piecing together his violent spree.

Bruce Shaw's body had been the first to be discovered. Dumped in a ditch, it had been hastily covered with sticks and brush. The medical examiner had found a single gunshot wound to the head, which had matched Bennett's testimony detailing the argument between Bruce Shaw and her attacker, as well as the sound of a gunshot.

Kevin and Bruce, as Ms. Beverly had said, were thick as thieves during their high school, college, and graduate school years. Kevin had saved Bruce from the trailer park, and from then on Bruce had been so grateful he'd have done anything for Kevin.

The casts of the tire impressions found at the park matched Kevin's vehicle, and fingerprint evidence and handwriting analysis proved that Kevin Wyatt was the author of all the notebooks found in the house. Based on the meticulous notes in the journals, police suspected Kevin had stalked nearly one hundred women. The journals provided extensive details on each woman, including work patterns, recreational activities, friends, and lovers. Kevin's financial records and old credit card receipts proved he had purchased gas in Baltimore and Atlanta on the same days women had disappeared there. Macy suspected he had murdered the women while visiting Bruce, and Bruce had helped him transport some of the bodies out to the country, where they could be buried in secret near the house.

The forensic teams had excavated the front section of the field and made several disturbing discoveries, including the remains of six women. The bodies, all in varying stages of decay, were transported to the medical center in Roanoke. The medical examiner's office had matched three sets of remains to missing persons cases in Montgomery County, Maryland.

Currently, law enforcement was trying to match the trinkets displayed in Kevin's trophy room to the women he had stalked. Why some women were left alone, others raped, and still others killed remained a mystery.

So far, there'd been no sign of Cindy Shaw or any evidence indicating what had happened to her.

Macy now believed Kevin had seen her broadcast, had become enraged, and had summoned Bruce, who had been the one person who knew his dark secret. Kevin had had one more body that needed burying, but as Bennett had testified, they'd argued. Bruce hadn't wanted any part of killing a cop. Kevin had decided Bruce's days of being useful were over and had shot and killed him.

Macy was able to piece together the motivation behind Kevin's need to kill. Apparently, Kevin had struggled to maintain his control and cool not only on the football field but also in school and in the corporate world. Whenever he suffered a setback or felt powerless, he stalked, raped, and then finally murdered.

According to the journals, days before Tobi had vanished, Kevin had suffered a knee injury. The Dream Team's last and most important game had been days away, and there had been so much at stake. Not only had the pride of the town rested on Kevin's shoulders, but his teammates had also needed the professional scouts at the game to see them all play well and win. He had been incredibly stressed about letting his team down.

Cindy, still trying to gain Kevin's favor, had delivered Tobi to him. Kevin had taken Tobi to the barn. He had not intended to kill her but had noted in his journal that the asphyxiation game he'd enjoyed so much had unexpectedly turned to murder.

Panicked, Kevin had dropped Tobi's backpack and body down the chute. His plan had been to bury both in this field. But they had gotten stuck, and he had lost his nerve. Police suspected he had called Bruce and told him what had happened. It had been Bruce who had told him to leave the body where it was.

The following week, when the entire town had been looking for Tobi, both boys had joined the search crew, and both had been conveniently assigned to the Wyatt barn so that they could report back they'd found nothing.

However, Tobi's disappearance had scared Cindy, and she had gone to Greene to tell him about Tobi and Kevin. Greene had thought the girl's drug use had addled her brain, so he had called Bruce and told him to get control of his sister. Bruce had confided in Kevin, and when Kevin had realized his accomplice was now a problem, he'd followed Bruce and Cindy to the bus station. After Bruce had left his sister at the station, Kevin had lured her away and killed her.

Nevada had interviewed Kevin Wyatt's mother, Vivian, and she had appeared shocked and stunned as she listened to the details of her son's crimes. Vivian had known nothing about the Deep Run country house or the graves. She had lawyered up quickly, agreed to be available at their request, but had packed up Tyler and left for Richmond.

When Macy and Nevada went to talk to Greene again, he'd not answered his front door, though his car had been in the driveway. Nevada had gone around back and found the former lawman sitting with his back to an old oak tree. He'd shot himself in the head. In his hand was a note that read, simply, "I'm sorry."

Evidence suggested Greene had protected the Dream Team from both rape and murder, and once his cover-up had been discovered, the prospect of going to prison had been untenable to him. Brooke and Matt Bennett were standing their ground and staying in Deep Run. DNA had confirmed that Kevin Wyatt was Matt's biological father. Bennett had always worked hard to shield her son from the truth, but now that it was out, she was trying to help him deal with it.

It was one thing to learn a hard truth like that in your thirties but quite another as a teenager. Macy had shared her own story with Matt and Bennett and had offered to talk anytime either needed it.

Macy's phone rang. "Agent Crow."

"You're now up to forty-one cases. Congratulations," Ramsey said.

Macy had remained in Deep Run the last week coordinating the case details, but had supplied Ramsey with daily updates. "Thanks."

"I send you down to crack one case, and you come back with a bushel of them."

"I had a lot of help."

His laughter rumbled through the line. "I'm going to need you back here by Monday. We need to do another face-to-face debrief with the team."

The team. "Does that mean I'm officially a part of the team?"

"Do you still want it?" Ramsey asked.

Getting back into the game had been all she'd wanted. But dying a second time had shifted priorities. She had been living at Nevada's house this past week and had discovered she didn't crave the big-city hustle or need to chase criminals. Some of her most peaceful and beautiful moments had been spent alone with him.

But could she live out here full time and walk away from the game? Could she turn down her ticket to the big leagues? She wasn't so sure.

"The answer would have been a slam dunk two weeks ago," she said.

"And now?"

"We'll get into the details when I return to Quantico."

"Fair enough." His chair squeaked, and she imagined him staring out the window in his office. "Hell of a job, Crow."

It was high praise from a man notorious for giving out few compliments.

As much as she wanted to revel in Ramsey's praise, she couldn't quite call this a victory until she knew what had happened to Cindy Shaw.

The rumble of tires drew her attention outside. Nevada parked, and as she stepped outside, he spotted her and strode toward her with a determined gait that still made her heart beat a little faster.

Because they were on the job, he didn't wrap his arm around her, but stood close enough so she could feel his heat and energy. "They're going to start excavating the back field today."

"Hopefully, Cindy's there," she said.

"She was nobody's angel, Macy."

"I can't excuse what she did," Macy said. "She caused a hell of a lot of pain, but the deck was stacked against her from the beginning."

Several agents and deputies fanned out onto the field, each carrying shovels. Macy and Nevada followed them and watched as they moved past the overturned soil in the top field toward the untouched lower section.

"They've pledged to dig up the entire field," Nevada said.

"Good," Macy said. When the Texas graves had been excavated, she'd been in the hospital fighting for her life. This time, however, she was here to bear witness.

Shovels cut into dirt at the far end of the field, which remained undisturbed. Each man with a shovel dumped his soil into a single pile beside the orange flag that the forensic team would sift through later.

Shovels continued to dig in the rich black dirt. This went on for another hour before one of the men in the field yelled out, "I have something."

Cold autumn wind cut across the field as Macy and Nevada strode through the knee-high scrub toward the group of men huddled around. The site was eighteen inches deep.

Exposed was a human skull. Its right orbital glared upward. As Macy looked at the remains, she scanned the bone structure. The skull had a low forehead, a narrow nasal passage, and a high cheekbone.

Tests would have to be run, but Macy had worked with enough pathologists to know this victim had likely been a female Caucasian.

For a moment all the agents and deputies stood silent. A tarp was brought over and laid beside the grave as a technician got down on hands and knees and began to work the skull free with a small trowel.

Macy had no proof of the woman's identity, but she had an overwhelming feeling it was Cindy.

The excavation of the grave went on for several hours, and it wasn't until techs were sifting through the dirt that they found the small arrowhead necklace Bruce had given Cindy.

Macy leaned closer to Nevada, savoring his scent and looking forward to going home with him.

"I couldn't have done this without you," he said.

"It was a team effort. We work pretty well together," she said.

"Yes, we do." He looked down at her, his smile softening his hardened features.

She loved looking at his face, and the idea of not being with him again worried her. "If I have more of those crazy dreams, I'll understand if my craziness is too much for you."

He shook his head. "You're going to have to try harder than that to scare me away. I'm in this for the long haul."

"I sure hope so." There was no guarantee the dreams would stop, or that their jobs wouldn't take them in different directions. But in this moment, she didn't want to worry about any of that. Grinning, she said, "One thing is for sure. It's never going to be dull for us, Nevada."

ABOUT THE AUTHOR

Photo © 2015 Studio FBJ

New York Times and *USA Today* bestselling novelist Mary Burton is the popular author of thirty-five romance and suspense novels, as well as five novellas. She currently lives in Virginia with her husband and three miniature dachshunds. Visit her at www.maryburton.com.